CHALLENGE THE
WIDOW-MAKER
and other stories of people in peril

CLARK HOWARD
(Photograph by Cheryl Cole)

CHALLENGE THE
WIDOW-MAKER

and other stories of people in peril

Clark Howard

Crippen & Landru Publishers
Norfolk, Virginia
2000

Cover design by Victoria Russell

Crippen & Landru logo by Eric D. Greene

ISBN (limited edition): 1-885941-39-0
ISBN (trade edition): 1-885941-40-4

FIRST EDITION

10 9 8 7 6 5 4 3 2 1

Crippen & Landru Publishers
P. O. Box 9315
Norfolk, VA 23505

Email: CrippenL@Pilot.Infi.Net
Web: www.crippenlandru.com

Dedicated
with love
to my granddaughter

AMANDA LAUREN HOWARD

TABLE OF CONTENTS

INTRODUCTION

I have never been comfortable writing about my own work. Or talking about it, even informally. Maybe it's because I feel that one's work, especially one's short stories, should simply stand on their own, without further attention from their author.

On the other hand, I have always been greatly appreciative, frequently surprised, occasionally even quite touched, when *others* wrote or talked about that same work. I am inordinately proud that my short stories have been praised by numerous people whom I myself admire and respect — among them, writers such as Ed Gorman, Edward D. Hoch, the late Fred Dannay ("Ellery Queen"), and Stanley Ellin; the critic Marvin Lachman; the late editor Eleanor Sullivan; *Ellery Queen's Mystery Magazine* editor Janet Hutchings; and Douglas Greene, short story connoisseur and publisher of this collection.

It has also been very gratifying to have my work receive awards over the years — an Edgar Allan Poe Award (plus seven other nominations) from the Mystery Writers of America; five Ellery Queen Readers Awards from the *Ellery Queen's Mystery Magazine*; and nominations for awards from the Western Writers of America and the Private Eye Writers of America. Inclusion of my work in numerous anthologies of stories by many of my peers whose own writing I admire (and even envy) has been another ongoing compliment much appreciated during my career.

Being asked to write this introduction has required me to revisit the twelve stories in this collection, and in doing so I was surprised to find a certain thread that links them together, an underlying characteristic that I seem to subconsciously have woven into their fabric as a group. That characteristic is the quality of pride that often surfaces in the people who populate these stories — be those people ex-convicts, professional boxers, gang members, prostitutes, waitresses, bootleggers, oil field workers, the very old and the very young, the good, the evil, and the ordinary. Sometimes it is the pride of hardheaded Southerners or stoic Native Americans; kids getting along the best way they can or elderly people with few things of value left; hard-timers backed into tight corners and strong-willed women trying to help them out; all kinds of people facing all kinds of trouble, from the beaches of Hawaii to the great plains of Montana, to the Dixieland clubs of New Orleans, to the ravaged streets of Northern Ireland.

The one thing that pulls them through when everything else in life is trying to do them in, is that pride — manifesting itself in surprising ways at unexpected times, giving troubled, desperate people the mind and muscle needed to pull out, to make it, to get through another day, and hopefully get another chance. Because, ultimately, that's what life is all about — getting one more chance to do something right.

The people in these stories found that out.

Hopefully, so will the reader.

Clark Howard
Palm Springs, California
March 2000

HORN MAN

When Dix stepped off the Greyhound bus in New Orleans, old Rainey was waiting for him near the terminal entrance. He looked just the same as Dix remembered him. Old Rainey had always looked old, since Dix had known him, ever since Dix had been a little boy. He had skin like black saddle leather and patches of cotton-white hair, and his shoulders were round and stooped. When he was contemplating something, he chewed on the inside of his cheeks, pushing his pursed lips in and out as if he were revving up for speech. He was doing that when Dix walked up to him.

"Hey, Rainey."

Rainey blinked surprise and then his face split into a wide smile of perfect, gleaming teeth. "Well, now. Well, well, well, now." He looked Dix up and down. "They give you that there suit of clothes?"

Dix nodded. "Everyone gets a suit of clothes if they done more than a year." Dix's eyes, the lightest blue possible without being gray, hardened just enough for Rainey to notice. "And I sure done more than a year," he added.

"That's the truth," Rainey said. He kept the smile on his face and changed the subject as quickly as possible. "I got you a room in the Quarter. Figured that's where you'd want to stay."

Dix shrugged. "It don't matter no more."

"It will," Rainey said with the confidence of years. "It will when you hear the music again."

Dix did not argue the point. He was confident that none of it mattered. Not the music, not the French Quarter, none of it. Only one thing mattered to Dix.

"Where is she, Rainey?" he asked. "Where's Madge?"

"I don't rightly know," Rainey said.

Dix studied him for a moment. He was sure Rainey was lying. But it didn't matter. There were others who would tell him.

They walked out of the terminal, the stooped old black man and the tall, prison-hard white man with a set to his mouth and a canvas zip-bag containing all his worldly possessions. It was late afternoon: the sun was almost gone and the evening coolness was coming in. They walked toward the Quarter, Dix keeping his long-legged pace slow to accommodate old Rainey.

Rainey glanced at Dix several times as they walked, chewing inside his mouth and working up to something. Finally he said, "You been playing at all while you was in?"

Dix shook his head. "Not for a long time. I did a little the first year. Used to dry play, just with my mouthpiece. After a while, though, I gave it up. They got a different kind of music over there in Texas. Stompin' music. Not my style." Dix forced a grin at old Rainey. "I ever kill a man again, I'll be sure I'm on *this* side of the Louisiana line."

Rainey scowled. "You know you ain't never killed nobody, boy," he said harshly. "You know it wudn't you that done it. It was *her*."

Dix stopped walking and locked eyes with old Rainey. "How long have you knowed me?" he asked.

"Since you was eight months old," Rainey said. "You know that. Me and my sistuh, we worked for your grandmamma, Miz Jessie DuChatelier. She had the finest gentlemen's house in the Quarter. Me and my sistuh, we cleaned and cooked for Miz Jessie. And took care of you after your own poor mamma took sick with the consumption and died —"

"Anyway, you've knowed me since I was less than one, and now I'm *forty*-one."

Rainey's eyes widened. "Naw," he said, grinning again, "you ain't that old. Naw."

"Forty-one, Rainey. I been gone sixteen years. I got twenty-five, remember? And I done sixteen."

Suddenly worry erased Rainey's grin. "Well, if you forty-one, how old that make *me?*"

"About two hundred. I don't know. You must be seventy or eighty. Anyway, listen to me now. In all the time you've knowed me, have I ever let anybody make a fool out of me?"

Rainey shook his head. "Never, no way."

"That's right. And I'm not about to start now. But if word got around that I done sixteen years for a killing that was somebody else's, I'd look like the biggest fool that ever walked the levee, wouldn't I?"

"I reckon so," Rainey allowed.

"Then don't ever say again that I didn't do it. Only one person alive knows for certain positive that I didn't do it. And I'll attend to her myself. Understand?"

Rainey chewed the inside of his cheeks for a moment, then asked. "What you fixin' to do about her?"

Dix's light-blue eyes hardened again. "Whatever I have to do, Rainey," he replied.

Rainey shook his head in slow motion. "Lord, Lord, Lord," he whispered.

Old Rainey went to see Gaston that evening at Tradition Hall, the jazz emporium and restaurant that Gaston owned in the Quarter. Gaston was slick and dapper. For him, time had stopped in 1938. He still wore spats.

"How does he look?" Gaston asked old Rainey.

"He *look* good." Rainey said. "He *talk* bad." Rainey leaned close to the white club-owner. "He fixin' to kill that woman. Sure as God made sundown."

Gaston stuck a sterling-silver toothpick in his mouth. "He know where she is?"

"I don't think so," said Rainey. "Not yet."

"You know where she is?"

"Lastest I heard, she was living over on Burgundy Street with some doper."

Gaston nodded his immaculately shaved and lotioned chin. "Correct. The doper's name is LeBeau. He's young. I think he keeps her around to take care of him when he's sick." Gaston examined his beautifully manicured nails. "Does Dix have a lip?"

Rainey shook his head. "He said he ain't played in a while. But a natural like him, he can get his lip back in no time a 'tall."

"Maybe." said Gaston.

"He can," Rainey insisted.

"Has he got a horn?"

"Naw. I watched him unpack his bag and I didn't see no horn. So I axed him about it. He said after a few years of not playing, he just give it away. To some cowboy he was in the Texas pen with."

Gaston sighed. "He should have killed that fellow on this side of the state line. If he'd done the killing in Louisiana, he would have went to the pen at Angola. They play good jazz at Angola. Eddie Lumm is up there.

You remember Eddie Lumm? Clarinetist. Learned to play from Frank Teschemacher and Jimmie Noone. Eddie killed his old lady. So now he blows at Angola. They play good jazz at Angola."

Rainey didn't say anything. He wasn't sure if Gaston thought Dix had really done the killing or not. Sometimes Gaston *played* like he didn't know a thing, just to see if somebody *else* knew it. Gaston was smart. Smart enough to help keep Dix out of trouble if he was a mind. Which was what old Rainey was hoping for.

Gaston drummed his fingertips silently on the table where they sat. "So. You think Dix can get his lip back with no problem, is that right?"

"Tha's right. He can."

"He planning to come around and see me?"

"I don't know. He probably set on finding that woman first. Then he might not be *able* to come see you."

"Well, see if you can get him to come see me first. Tell him I've got something for him. Something I've been saving for him. Will you do that?"

"You bet." Rainey got up from the table. "I'll go do it right now."

George Tennell was big and beefy and mean. Rumor had it that he had once killed two men by smashing their heads together with such force that he literally knocked their brains out. He had been a policeman for thirty years, first in the colored section, which was the only place he could work in the old days, and now in the *Vieux Carre*, the Quarter, where he was detailed to keep the peace to whatever extent it was possible. He had no family, claimed no friends. The Quarter was his home as well as his job. The only thing in the world he admitted to loving was jazz.

That was why, every night at seven, he sat at a small corner table in Tradition Hall and ate dinner while he listened to the band tune their instruments and warm up. Most nights, Gaston joined him later for a liqueur. Tonight he joined him before dinner.

"Dix got back today," he told the policeman. "Remember Dix?"

Tennell nodded. "Horn man. Killed a fellow in a motel room just across the Texas line. Over a woman named Madge Noble."

"That's the one. Only there's some around don't think he did it. There's some around think *she* did it."

"Too bad he couldn't have found twelve of those people for his jury."

"He didn't have no jury, George. Quit laying back on me. You remember it as well as I do. One thing you'd *never* forget is a good horn man."

Tennell's jaw shifted to the right a quarter of an inch, making his mouth go crooked. The band members were coming out of the back now and moving around on the bandstand, unsnapping instrument cases, inserting mouthpieces, straightening chairs. They were a mixed lot — black, white, and combinations; clean-shaven and goateed; balding and not; clear-eyed and strung out. None of them was under fifty — the oldest was the trumpet player, Luther Dodd, who was eighty-six. Like Louis Armstrong, he had learned to blow at the elbow of Joe "King" Oliver, the great cornetist. His Creole-style trumpet playing was unmatched in New Orleans. Watching him near the age when he would surely die was agony for the jazz purists who frequented Tradition Hall.

Gaston studied George Tennell as the policeman watched Luther Dodd blow out the spit plug of his gleaming Balfour trumpet and loosen up his stick-brittle fingers on the valves. Gaston saw in Tennell's eyes that odd look of a man who truly worshipped traditional jazz music, who felt it down in the pit of himself just like the old men who played it, but who had never learned to play himself. It was a look that had the mix of love and sadness and years gone by. It was the only look that ever turned Tennell's eyes soft.

"You know how long I been looking for a horn man to take Luther's place?" Gaston asked. " A straight year. I've listened to a couple dozen guys from all over. Not a one of them could play traditional. Not a one." He bobbed his chin at Luther Dodd. "His fingers are like wood, and so's his heart. He could go on me any night. And if he does, I'll have to shut down. Without a horn man, there's no Creole sound, no tradition at all. Without a horn, this place of mine, which is the last of the great jazz emporiums, will just give way to —" Gaston shrugged helplessly "— whatever. Disco music, I suppose."

A shudder circuited George Tennell's spine, but he gave no outward sign of it. His body was absolutely still, his hands resting motionlessly on the snow-white tablecloth, eyes steadily fixed on Luther Dodd. Momentarily the band went into its first number, *Lafayette*, played Kansas City style after the way of Bennie Moten. The music pulsed out like spurts of water, each burst overlapping the one before it to create an even wave of sound that flooded the big room. Because Kansas City style was so rhythmic and highly danceable, some of the early diners immediately moved onto the dance floor and fell in with the music.

Ordinarily, Tennell liked to watch people dance while he ate; the moving bodies lent emphasis to the music he loved so much, music he had first heard from the window of the St. Pierre Colored Orphanage on Decatur Street when he had been a boy; music he had grown up with and would have made his life a part of if he had not been so completely talentless, so inept that he could not even read sharps and flats. But tonight he paid no attention to the couples out in front of the bandstand. He concentrated only on Luther Dodd and the old horn man's breath intake as he played. It was clear to Tennell that Luther was struggling for breath, fighting for every note he blew, utilizing every cubic inch of lung power that his old body could marshal.

After watching Luther all the way through *Lafayette*, and halfway through *Davenport Blues*, Tennell looked across the table at Gaston and nodded.

"All right," he said simply. "All right."

For the first time ever, Tennell left the club without eating dinner.

As Dix walked along with old Rainey toward Gaston's club, Rainey kept pointing out places to him that he had not exactly forgotten, but had not remembered in a long time.

"That house there," Rainey said, "was where Paul Mares was born back in nineteen-and-oh-one. He's the one formed the original New Orleans Rhythm Kings. He only lived to be forty-eight but he was one of the best horn men of all time."

Dix would remember, not necessarily the person himself but the house and the story of the person and how good he was. He had grown up on those stories, gone to sleep by them as a boy, lived the lives of the men in them many times over as he himself was being taught to blow trumpet by Rozell "The Lip" Page when Page was already past sixty and he, Dix was only eight. Later, when Page died, Dix's education was taken over by Shepherd Norden and Blue Johnny Meadows, the two alternating as his teacher between their respective road tours. With Page, Norden, and Meadows in his background, it was no wonder that Dix could blow traditional.

"Right up the street there," Rainey said as they walked, "is where Wingy Manone was born in nineteen-and-oh-four. His given name was Joseph, but after his accident ever'body taken to calling him 'Wingy.' The accident was, he fell under a street car and lost his right arm. But that boy didn't let a little thing like that worry him none, no sir. He learned to play trumpet *left-handed*, and *one-handed*. And he was good."

They walked along Dauphin and Chartres and Royal. All around them were the French architecture and grillework and statuary and vines and moss that made the *Vieux Carre* a world unto itself, a place of subtle sights, sounds, and smells — black and white and fish and age — that no New Orleans tourist, no Superdome visitor, no casual observer, could ever experience, because to experience was to understand, and understanding of the Quarter could not be acquired, it had to be lived.

"Tommy Ladnier, he used to live right over there," Rainey said, "right up on the second floor. He lived there when he came here from his hometown of Mandeville, Loozey-ana. Poor Tommy, he had a short life too, only thirty-nine years. But it was a good life. He played with King Oliver and Fletcher Henderson and Sidney Bechet. Yessir, he got in some good licks."

When they got close enough to Tradition Hall to hear the music, at first faintly, then louder, Rainey stopped talking. He wanted Dix to hear the music, to *feel* the sound of it as it wafted out over Pirate's Alley and the Cafe du Monde and Congo Square — they called it Beauregard Square now, but Rainey refused to recognize the new name. Instinctively, Rainey knew that it was important for the music to get back into Dix, to saturate his mind and catch in his chest and tickle his stomach. There were some things in Dix that needed to be washed out, some bad things, and Rainey was certain that the music would help. A good purge was always healthy.

Rainey was grateful, as they got near enough to define melody, that *Sweet Georgia Brown* was being played. It was a good melody to come home to.

They walked on, listening, and after a while Dix asked, "Who's on horn?"

"Luther Dodd."

"Don't sound like Luther. What's the matter with him?"

Rainey waved one hand resignedly. "Old. Dying, I 'spect."

They arrived at the Hall and went inside. Gaston met them with a smile. "Dix," he said, genuinely pleased, "it's good to see you." His eyes flicked over Dix. "The years have been good to you. Trim. Lean. No gray hair. How's your lip?"

"I don't have a lip no more, Mr. Gaston," said Dix. "Haven't had for years."

"But he can get it back quick enough," Rainey put in. "He gots a natural lip."

"I don't play no more, Mr. Gaston," Dix told the club owner.

"That's too bad," Gaston said. He bobbed his head toward the stairs. "Come with me. I want to show you something."

Dix and Rainey followed Gaston upstairs to his private office. The office was furnished the way Gaston dressed — old style, roaring Twenties. There was even a wind-up Victrola in the corner.

Gaston worked the combination of a large, ornate floor vault and pulled its big, tiered door open. From somewhere in its dark recess he withdrew a battered trumpet case, one of the very old kind with heavy brass fittings on the corners and, one knew, real velvet, not felt, for a lining. Placing it gently in the center of this desk, Gaston carefully opened the snaplocks and lifted the top. Inside, indeed on real velvet, deep-purple real velvet, was a gleaming, silver, hand-etched trumpet. Dix and Rainey stared at it in unabashed awe.

"Know who it once belonged to?" Gaston asked.

Neither Dix nor Rainey replied. They were mesmerized by the instrument. Rainey had not seen one like it in fifty years. Dix had *never* seen one like it; he had only heard stories about the magnificent silver horns that the quadroons made of contraband silver carefully hidden away after the War Between the States. Because the silver cache had not, as it was supposed to, been given over to the Federal army as part of the reparations levied against the city, the quadroons, during the Union occupation, had to be very careful what they did with it. Selling it for value was out of the question. Using it for silver service, candlesticks, walking canes, or any other of the more obvious uses would have attracted the notice of a Union informer. But letting it lie dormant, even though it was safer as such, was intolerable to the quads, who refused to let a day go by without circumventing one law or another.

So they used the silver to plate trumpets and cornets and slide trombones that belonged to the tabernacle musicians who were just then beginning to experiment with the old *Sammsamounn* tribal music that would eventually mate with work songs and prison songs and gospels, and evolve into traditional blues, which would evolve into traditional, or Dixie-style, jazz.

"Look at the initials," Gaston said, pointing to the top of the bell. Dix and Rainey peered down at three initials etched in the silver: BRB

"Lord have mercy," Rainey whispered. Dix's lips parted as if he too intended to speak, but no words sounded.

"That's right," Gaston said. "Blind Ray Blount. The first, the best, the *only*. Nobody has ever touched the sounds he created. That man hit notes nobody every heard before — or since. He was the master."

"Amen," Rainey said. He nodded his head toward Dix. "Can he touch it?"

"Go ahead," Gaston said to Dix.

Like a pilgrim to Mecca touching the holy shroud, Dix ever so lightly placed the tips of three fingers on the silver horn. As he did, he imagined he could feel the touch left there by the hands of the amazing blind horn man who had started the great blues evolution in a patch of town that later became Storyville. He imagined that —

"It's yours if you want it," Gaston said. "All you have to do is pick it up and go downstairs and start blowing."

Dix wet his suddenly dry lips. "Tomorrow I —"

"Not tomorrow," Gaston said. "Tonight. Now."

"Take it, boy," Rainey said urgently.

Dix frowned deeply, his eyes narrowing as if he felt physical pain. He swallowed, trying to push an image out of his mind; an image he had clung to for sixteen years. "I can't tonight —"

"Tonight or never," Gaston said firmly.

"For God's sake, boy, take it!" said old Rainey.

But Dix could not. The image of Madge would not let him.

Dix shook his head violently, as if to rid himself of devils, and hurried from the room.

Rainey ran after him and caught up with him a block from the Hall. "Don't do it," he pleaded. "Hear me now. I'm an old man and I know I ain't worth nothin' to nobody, but I'm begging you, boy, please, please, please don't do it. I ain't never axed you for nothing in my whole life, but I'm axing you for this: *please* don't do it."

"I got to," Dix said quietly. "It ain't that I want to; I *got* to."

"But why, boy? Why?"

"Because we made a promise to each other," Dix said. "That night in that Texas motel room, the man Madge was with had told her he was going to marry her. He'd been telling her that for a long time. But he was already married and kept putting off leaving his wife. Finally Madge had enough of it. She asked me to come to her room between sets. I knew she was doing it to make him jealous, but it didn't matter none to me. I'd been crazy about her for so long that I'd do anything she asked me to, and she knew it.

"So between sets I slipped across the highway to where she had her room. But he was already there. I could hear through the transom that he was roughing her up some, but the door was locked and I couldn't get in. Then I heard a shot and everything got quiet. A minute later Madge opened the door and let me in. The man was laying across the bed dying.

Madge started bawling and saying how they would put her in the pen and how she wouldn't be able to stand it, she'd go crazy and kill herself.

"It was then I asked her if she'd wait for me if I took the blame for her. She promised me she would. And I promised her I'd come back to her." Dix sighed quietly. "That's what I'm doing, Rainey — keeping my promise."

"And what going to happen if she ain't kept *hers*?" Rainey asked.

"Mamma Rulat asked me the same thing this afternoon when I asked her where Madge was at." Mamma Rulat was an octaroon fortuneteller who always knew where everyone in the Quarter lived.

"What did you tell her?"

"I told her I'd do what I had to do That's all a man *can* do, Rainey."

Dix walked away, up a dark side street. Rainey, watching him go, shook his head in the anguish of the aged and helpless.

"Lord, Lord, Lord —"

The house on Burgundy Street had once been a grand mansion with thirty rooms and a tiled French courtyard with a marble fountain in its center. It had seen nobility and aristocracy and great generals come and go with elegant, genteel ladies on their arms. Now the thirty rooms were rented individually with hotplate burners for light cooking, and the only ladies who crossed the courtyard were those of the New Orleans night.

A red light was flashing atop a police car when Dix got there, and uniformed policemen were blocking the gate into the courtyard. There was a small curious crowd talking about what happened.

"A doper named LeBeau," someone said. "He's been shot."

"I heard it," an old man announced. "I heard the shot."

"There's where it happened, that window right up there —"

Dix looked up, but as he did another voice said, "They're bringing him out now!"

Two morgue attendants wheeled a sheet-covered gurney across the courtyard and lifted it into the back of a black panel truck. Several policemen, led by big beefy George Tennell, brought a woman out and escorted her to the car with the flashing red light. Dix squinted, focusing on her in the inadequate courtyard light. He frowned. Madge's mother, he thought, his mind going back two decades. What's Madge's mother got to do with this?

Then he remembered. Madge's mother was dead. She had died five years after he had gone to the pen.

Then who —?

Madge?

Yes, it *was* her. It was Madge. Older, as he was. Not a girl any more, as he was not a boy any more. For a moment he found it difficult to equate the woman in the courtyard with the memory in his mind. But it was Madge, all right.

Dix tried to push forward, to get past the gate into the courtyard, but two policemen held him back. George Tennell saw the altercation and came over.

"She's under arrest, mister," Tennell told Dix. "Can't nobody talk to her but a lawyer right now."

"What's she done anyhow?" Dix asked.

"Killed her boyfriend," said Tennell. "Shot him with this."

He showed Dix a pearl-handled over-and-under Derringer two-shot.

"Her boyfriend?"

Tennell nodded. "Young feller. 'Bout twenty five. Neighbors say she was partial to young fellers. Some women are like that."

"Who says she shot him?"

"I do. I was in the building at the time, on another matter. I heard the shot. Matter of fact, I was the first one to reach the body. Few minutes later she came waltzing in. Oh, she put on a good act, all right, like she didn't even know what happened. But I found the gun in her purse myself."

By now the other officers had Madge Noble in the police car and were waiting for Tennell. He slipped the Derringer into his coat pocket and hitched up his trousers. Jutting his big jaw out an inch, he fixed Dix in a steady gaze.

"If she's a friend of yours, don't count on her being around for a spell. She'll do a long time for this."

Tennell walked away, leaving Dix still outside the gate. Dix waited there, watching, as the police car came through to the street. He tried to catch a glimpse of Madge as it passed, but there was not enough light in the back seat where they had her. As soon as the car left, the people who had gathered around began to leave too.

Soon Dix was the only one standing there.

At midnight George Tennell was back at his usual table in Tradition Hall for the dinner he had missed earlier. Gaston came over and joined him. For a few minutes they sat in silence, watching Dix up on the bandstand. He was blowing the silver trumpet that had once belonged to Blind Ray Blount; sitting next to the aging Luther Dodd; jumping in whenever he could as they played *Tailspin Blues,* then *Tank Town Bump,* then *Everybody Loves My Baby.*

"Sounds like he'll be able to get his lip back pretty quick," Tennell observed.

"Sure," said Gaston. "He's a natural. Rozell was his first teacher, you know."

"No, I didn't know that."

"Sure." Gaston adjusted the celluloid collar he wore, and turned the diamond stickpin in his tie. "What about the woman?" he asked

Tennell shrugged. "She'll get twenty years. Probably do ten or eleven."

Gaston thought for a moment, then said, "That should be time enough. After ten or eleven years nothing will matter to him except the music. Don't you think?"

"It won't even take that long," Tennell guessed. "Not for him."

Up on the bandstand the men who played traditional went into *Just a Closer Walk With Thee.*

And sitting on the sawdust floor behind the bandstand, old Rainey listened with happy tears in his eyes.

ALL THE HEROES ARE DEAD

The district director finished perusing the personnel file and shook his head dubiously. "Are you sure you've selected the right man for this assignment?" he asked his chief investigator. "We need someone to infiltrate a very close-knit bootlegging operation in Lasher County, Georgia. That's redneck country. This agent David Berry somehow doesn't seem the type for it. His background, I mean: political-science major at Yale, midwestern upbringing, interests in soccer and the theater —"

"His interest in the theater is precisely one of the reasons I selected Berry," the chief investigator said. "He's an amateur actor, belongs to a little-theater group in Alexandria. It's going to take someone who can put on a very good performance to fool those people in Lasher County."

"Maybe a better performance than you think," the director said. "The state authorities put an undercover man down there last year. He dropped out of sight and hasn't been heard from since. There are lots of deep woods and swamps in that part of Georgia. Good places to dispose of a body."

"I still feel Berry's the man for the job," the chief insisted.

"All right," the director said with a quiet sigh. "Have him come in."

The chief rose and summoned David Berry from an outer office. When the director saw him, his doubts were by no means assuaged. Berry's hair was styled, he wore a three-piece Brooks Brothers suit, and carried an attaché case. He belonged, the director thought, in the bank examiners section, not in illegal whiskey.

"Berry, you've been with Treasury for three years now," the director said. "According to your file, all of your assignments up until now have been desk work. Do you think you can handle an undercover job?"

"Yes, sir, I do," Berry replied. "I've been eager for field work for quite some time now." His voice was precise, educated.

"You've read the Lasher County file," the director said, "so you know what the case is all about. An estimated one hundred thousand gallons of liquor is being manufactured illegally somewhere down there every year. That's not what we consider a huge operation by any means. The government loses tax revenue on about two-and-a-half million dollars annually based on their selling price, which is around one-third the cost of legal liquor, so we wouldn't go broke if we let them operate indefinitely. But that's not the point. The issue here is a violation of the law — manufacturing liquor without a license and distributing liquor without a tax stamp."

"Most of their sales, as you know from the file," the chief said, "are to rural residents in south Georgia and Alabama, and northern Florida. People that are commonly known as 'rednecks.' They live in and around places like the Apalachicola Forest, the Osceola Forest, and the Okefenokee Swamp. That's where we think they've got their manufacturing plant — their whiskey still: in the Okefenokee."

David Berry nodded. "Yes, sir, I noticed in the file that at one point there was nearly a six-hundred-percent increase in the sale of Mason jars in the swamp communities."

The chief smiled. "That's how we pinpointed the manufacturing site. Normally they make runs about a hundred miles away for their Mason jars, but apparently they ran out of them from their regular suppliers and had to buy locally. It was a sure tipoff — you can't bootleg hooch without Mason jars."

The director, still looking worried, sat forward, and folded his hands on the desk. "Berry, I want to emphasize to you the potential peril of an assignment like this. You'll be going into a completely foreign environment, among people who are totally different from the kind you're accustomed to associating with."

"I know that, sir," Berry said. "I plan to spend a few weeks traveling around small towns in northern Georgia to learn how to act the part. I fully intend to prepare for the role."

"Your dress, your mannerisms, your speech — you'll have to change everything."

"Well, Ah don't think Ah'll have too much trouble with the speech, suh," Berry said, suddenly falling into a very good southern drawl. "Ah been listenin' to some dialect records over at that there linguistic department at the university an' Ah 'spects Ah'll have the talkin' down pat pretty quick like." Smiling, Berry reverted to his own speech pattern. "As for the clothes, visits to a couple of thrift shops and surplus stores will take care of that. And the mannerisms — well, just opening the beer can and drinking out of it ought to do for a start."

The chief flashed an I-told-you-so-smile at the director. "We've established a complete new identity for him," he said. "His name will be Dale Barber. We chose that surname because Barber is very common in the southeastern U.S. He'll have an Alabama driver's license, army discharge, social-security card, and two membership cards to private after-hours clubs in Tuscaloosa. We picked that city because it's far enough away from where he'll be operating to make it difficult for anybody to check up on him, and it's large enough — about a hundred fifty thousand — to throw them off if they do. I think we've got all the bases covered, sir."

"It certainly seems like it." But there was still a trace of doubt in the director's voice, a gut feeling of reluctance inside him, some instinct — perhaps based on his thirty years of law-enforcement experience — that told him not to give David Berry the Lasher County assignment. It was nothing he could put his finger on and he knew if he tried to explain it to his chief investigator he would sound as if he were procrastinating. Based on the chief's recommendation and Berry's apparent ability to discharge the assignment, he was left with no choice. "All right, Berry, the job's yours," he said.

He had a feeling that he would never see the young agent again.

Three weeks later, David Berry was cruising down Highway 441, which ran parallel to the Okefenokee Swamp. He was driving a '78 Chevy pickup with a roll-bar he'd bought with agency money in Tuscaloosa. A battered suitcase and a cardboard box containing his extra clothes rode in the rear bed along with a nearly bald spare tire, a lug wrench, an empty gas can, and a six-pack of Miller's beer. In one corner of the pickup's back window was a decal of a Confederate flag. Inside the cab was a rifle rack with a .22 pump on it. A Slim Whitman tape was playing in the dashboard deck.

When David got to DeSota, the little town that was halfway down on the edge of the swamp, he circled the tiny town square once and pulled up in front of Luther's Cafe.

Getting out of the truck, he stretched and twisted some of the stiffness out of his back and shoulders. He knew that several people sitting by the window in the cafe had already noticed him, his truck, the Alabama plates. His appearance, he knew, fit the picture — old faded Levi's, an inexpensive plaid cotton shirt, a blue denim vest, and a soiled yellow visor cap with an STP patch on it. The cap was pushed to the back of his now unstyled hair. On his feet he wore low-heel Frye boots.

Going inside, David sat at the counter and looked at the handwritten menu. A waitress came over to him — red headed, well built, a sexy wide mouth, too much mascara. She wore a white uniform that had "Tommy Sue" embroidered above her left breast.

"Hi," she said, setting a glass of water in front of him.

"Hi, Tommy Sue," he said reading her uniform. "Ah'll have three chicken wings, some coleslaw, an' fried okra. An' iced tea."

Their eyes met just long enough for them to realize it. Then David reached down the counter and retrieved the sports section of the Tallahassee *Democrat*. He pretended to read, but he was actually thinking about Eileen, his girl friend. She was working on her master's in history at Georgetown. Eileen was tall, slim, chic, and proper — almost too proper sometimes. She had not been at all pleased about this field assignment.

"*Georgia!*" she had said. "Really, David. Can't you get out of it somehow? The Clary's lawn party is coming up."

"I don't want to get out of it," he had told her. "This is my first opportunity in three years to get away from a desk."

"But *Georgia!* Couldn't you get an assignment someplace close?"

"There aren't many illegal whiskey stills in Bethesda or Arlington or Alexandria," he pointed out. "We have to go where the violation is. I'm sorry about the Clary's party."

Tommy Sue brought his food and David put the paper aside. He began to eat the chicken wings with his fingers. Out of the corner of his eye he saw the fry cook come out of the kitchen, wiping his hands on a greasy apron. "That your pickup with the 'Bama plates?" he asked.

"Tha's me," David said with his mouth full.

"Where 'bouts in 'Bama you from?"

"Tuscaloosa. Ax'ly Ah'm from Coker, a little piece north. But ain't nobody ever heard of Coker, so Ah say Tuscaloosa.

The fry cook nodded. "Jus' passin' through?"

David shook his head. "Lookin' for work. Heard up in Waycross that ya'll had a canning factory down here that might be hirin' on."

"Cannin' factory shut down last week. Soybeans done poorly this year. Nothin' to can."

David shook his head in disappointment and kept on eating. In a booth near the window sat three men he could sense listening with interest to his conversation with the fry cook.

"Know of anything else around?" he asked.

"Such as?"

Davis shrugged. "Ah ain't particular. Fillin' station, farm work, construction."

"Things is real slow right now. Maybe fu'ther south. Florida maybe."

David grunted. "Ah'm runnin' low on lookin' money. There a poolroom in town?"

"Right across the square. Leon's Pool Hall."

"Maybe Ah can pick up a couple dollars."

"Don't count on it," the fry cook said.

There was a motel called Harley's Motor Inn a mile out the highway: twelve units that usually filled up only during the legal fishing season. The season was past now and the alligators were breeding in the swamp waters, so there was no one at Harley's except a notions salesman who worked the territory between Macon and Orlando. The salesman was in Unit One, so Harley put David in Unit Two when David drove out after lunch and checked in.

"How long you be staying?" Harley asked.

"Couple of days, maybe. Lookin for work."

"Things is real slow around here. Be twelve-fifty a night, first night in advance. No playin' the television after midnight."

David carried his old suitcase and cardboard box into the room and unpacked. Then he pulled off his boots to stretch out on the bed for a while. It was funny about those boots. He had expected to hate them. His taste ran to Carranos: glove-leather, Italian-made. But the Frye boots, after a week of breaking in, were as comfortable as anything he'd ever put on his feet. It was the same with the Chevy pickup. In Washington he drove a low-slung Datsun 280-Z and rode close to the pavement. The cab of the pickup was up high, above everything except motor homes and tractor rigs. You saw a lot more in a pickup cab than in a sports car.

David spent the afternoon resting, then at sunset he showered, put on clean jeans and a striped shirt, and drove back uptown. He found a phone booth next to the post office and called the chief on a blind telephone number with a memorized credit-card number. "I'm settled," he said when the chief answered. "I should be able to spot the delivery truck tonight. Unless you hear from me to the contrary, I'm ready for stage two."

"I understand," the chief said. "Good luck."

David left the booth and walked across the street to Luther's cafe again. Tommy Sue was still on duty. "You work all the time?" he asked when she handed him the supper menu.

"Girl's got to make a living," she answered. While he studied the menu, she said, "I saw you in the phone booth. Calling your wife like a good little boy?"

"Don't have no wife. Let me have the fried catfish and hush puppies. Iced tea. Pecan pie for dessert."

"Calling your girl friend then?" she asked as she wrote down his order.

"Calling my mama. Your curiosity satisfied now?"

"Well 'scuse me for livin'," she said huffily.

Throughout his meal David occasionally caught her glancing at him. Whenever he did, he threw her a smile or a wink. She turned her nose up at him. When he paid his supper check, he said, "Next time Ah talk to Mama, Ah'll tell her you said hello."

"Don't bother."

"No trouble. Ah'll tell her Ah met this here little Georgia peach who's too pretty to even describe."

"You might's well save it, Alabama. You got off on the wrong foot with me with that curiosity crack. I was only makin' small talk."

Outside the window David saw a Buick drive up to Leon's Pool Hall, followed closely by a Dodge pickup. One man got out of the Buick, two out of the pickup, and they all went inside. They were the same three who had listened so intently to David's conversation with the fry cook at noon.

"Let's you and me start all over," David said, turning his attention back to Tommy Sue. "At breakfast."

"I don't work breakfast," she told him. "I come on at eleven-thirty."

"What time do you get off?"

"Nine-thirty — when we close. I work ten hours a day, four days a week. That way I get to spend three days a week with Lonnie."

"Lonnie?"

"My little boy. He's four. My mama keeps him for me, over in Talbot."

"Oh." David glanced out the window again and his thoughts went momentarily to the Dodge pickup. It looked like the right truck, he thought. The one the department had come so close to catching several times.

Tommy Sue, taking his silence for disinterest, handed him his change, shrugged, and started to walk away.

"Hey, wait a minute. What time did you say?"

"What's it matter? You turned awful cold soon's you found out I had a kid. But don't feel bad, it's happened before."

"I didn't turn cold, I simply became distracted," David said, lapsing into his normal speech before he realized it. Tommy Sue frowned, staring curiously at him. David locked eyes with her for a moment, then forced a smile. "That was Tony Randall. Ah can do Johnny Carson too." His awkward smile faded. "Can Ah come back at nine-thirty? Take you for a beer?"

She shrugged. "I guess," she said. But there was now a trace of reluctance in her voice.

David went back to his pickup and drove out of town. Cursing himself for his momentary lapse of cover, he drove up and down the back roads for an hour, until twilight came and grayness began to settle over the red dirt fields. Then he headed back uptown. It was fully dark when he parked in front of Leon's Pool Hall. Walking toward the door, he stopped at the Dodge, put his foot up on the back bumper, and pretended to pull a pebble out of his heel. While he was doing it, he palmed a miniature electronic transmitter with a magnet on the back of it, and attached it to the inside of the bumper. Then he went on into the pool hall.

Leon's was a prototype of every poolroom in every small town in the South. Six Brunswick tables so old their cushions could barely reject a ball. Drop pockets with net catchers. A shelf near each table holding a can of talcum for the cuestick shaft and blue chalk for its tip. A few rickety raised wooden benches for tobacco-chewing spectators. Half a dozen spittoons. Two pinball machines that paid off in free games that could be cashed in for money. A wooden bar with an illuminated beer-logo clock over the cash register behind it. And on the bar two large jars — one of pickled eggs, one of pig's feet. All under a cloud of gray smoke that hung at the ceiling because it had no place else to go.

David went to the bar and got a bottle of Bud. The three men who had driven up earlier were shooting nine-ball on a middle table. David stepped up on one of the benches and sat down to watch. Two of the men shooting were either twins or brothers very close in age. They wore jeans with leather belts that had their names tooled on the back of them — Merle and Earl. The latter, David noticed, also had E-A-R-L tattooed on the top joint of each finger on his right hand. The work didn't look professional. It was a jailhouse tattoo, David guessed. The third man was the oldest, probably fifty, with a pot-belly hanging over the waist of a pair of self-belted polyester trousers. He wore a shirt that had a western scene embroidered across the yoke. David sensed that he was studying him from under a pair of tinted lenses between shots.

David watched the progress of the game, waiting for an opportunity to interject a comment. To come right out with a remark would have been poor form and would have marked him at once as a total outsider, an "up-North" type. He had to be subtle about it. He waited until Earl, the one with the tattoos, missed a fairly easy straight-in corner shot, then he rolled his eyes toward the ceiling and groaned quietly. But not so quietly that Earl couldn't hear him.

"What's your problem, boy?" Earl said antagonistically. "Don't nobody ever miss a shot where you come from?"

"Not that kind," David said. Then he raised his hands, palms out. "Hey, Ah'm sorry, hear? Ah didn't have no call to remark. It just slipped out."

"You a pool player?" asked the older man, smiling across the table.

David shrugged. "Ah shoot a game ever' now and then." Which was a gross understatement. David had been president of the billiards club at college for five semesters.

The older man came around the table. He had a chaw of tobacco in one cheek, but instead of using a spittoon he kept a Dixie cup handy. "We heard you say at Luther's today that you hoped to win a little money over here. You care to shoot a game of rotation with Earl here? Say for twenty-five-dollars?"

David pursed his lips. "That's mighty temptin'."

The man in the polyester trousers smiled. "What's your name, boy?"

"Dale Barber. From Tuscaloosa, Alabama."

"I didn't ask where you was from. My name's Billy Roy Latham. My friends call me Billy Roy. You can call me Mr. Latham." He peeled twenty-five dollars off a roll and stuck it in one of the corner pockets. "Anytime you're ready."

David covered the bet and beat Earl 67 to 53. He could have run the balls and blanked him, but he didn't want to look like a slicker trying to skin the locals. Neither did he want his thumbs broken. So he laid back and just won by two balls, the six and the eight. As he was fishing his winnings out of the pocket, Earl's brother Merle said, "Lemme have a crack at him, Billy Roy."

Latham nodded and put another twenty-five in the pocket. Merle was about in the same league as Earl. David beat him a little more badly, 71 to 49, winning with the two, three, seven and ten balls.

After the game with Merle, Latham removed his tinted glasses and smiled an artificial smile at David. "Ah cain't decide if you're good or jus' lucky. How 'bout you and me shoot a game for the fifty you've won?"

David glanced around. A dozen men had idled up from the other tables and were gathered around watching. They were somber, leathery men, their eyes squinty from years in the bright sun of the fields. Maybe they worked for Latham, maybe they didn't. But David knew instinctively that even if he had wanted to there was no way he'd be allowed to walk out with the fifty he had won.

"How 'bout it, boy?" Latham pressed. "You an' me for fifty each."

"Whatever you say, Mr. Latham."

The balls were racked and Latham won the break. He made the six on the break, then ran the one, two and three, and dropped the twelve off the three-ball. David saw at once that Latham was a much better pool shooter than Merle and Earl.

On his first shot, David ran the four, five, seven, and eight, tying it up with twenty-four points each. Latham made the nine and ten, but scratched on the ten and had to spot it back on the table. David then made it in the side pocket but missed the eleven-ball. Latham made the eleven. David made the thirteen, to go three points ahead, 47 to 44. Latham made the fourteen, to move up to forty-eight. Then he missed the fifteen and it was David's turn.

The fifteen was the game-winning ball. It was dead on the side rail, midway down from the end pocket. Its position did not present a difficult shot, merely a tricky one — the cueball had to hit the rail and the fifteen-ball at the same time in order to run the fifteen straight along the cushion into the pocket. If the cueball hit the fifteen first, the fifteen would be brought out from the rail and go nowhere, leaving the opponent a good shot. If the cueball hit the rail first, the fifteen would roll straight along the rail but wouldn't have enough momentum to go all the way to the pocket.

David chalked his cue-tip and bent low over the far end of the table. Wetting his lips, he took dead-perfect aim and let go a slow shot that hit the fifteen and the cushion at the same time. The fifteen rolled along the rail — and stopped four inches from the pocket.

There was a general murmur of approval from the on-lookers: the stranger had lost. David shook his head and stepped back. Billy Ray Latham leaned casually over the side rail and eased the ball on in to win the game. He got more than a few pats on the back as he dug the fifty dollars out of the end pocket.

In the men's room, David and Latham stood side by side washing the talcum off their hands at a tin sink. "You could've made that last shot," Latham said quietly.

"Can't win 'em all," David said.

"You could've won that one. Why didn't you?"

David shrugged. "Your town, your people. No call to beat a man in his own town. 'Sides, Ah broke even,"

Latham studied him for a long moment as he dried his hands. Then he made up his mind about David and nodded to himself. "There's a place called Joe's Pit out on the highway that's got good barbecued ribs and ice-cold beer. How 'bout havin' a bite?"

"No offense," David said, "but Ah got other plans." He winked at Latham. "Tommy Sue over at the cafe."

Latham grinned. "You Alabama rednecks is all the same. After the sun goes down you only got one thing on your mind."

"Yep. Jus' like you Georgia rednecks." David bobbed his chin. "See you around."

He bought a cold six-pack at Luther's and drove away from the square with Tommy Sue. "Where do ya'll park around here?" he asked.

"Out by the cemetery. It's quiet there."

"Ah reckon it would be."

She showed him the way. When they were parked, David opened both doors of the pickup and two cans of the beer. They sat holding hands and sipping the beer. Someone had burned a stump during the day and there was still a smell of scorched wood in the air. It mixed with the fragrance of hackberry plants that grew wild along the side of the road. The result was an odd, almost sensual night scent. After they finished a can of beer each, David guided Tommy Sue onto the seat and put his lips on her throat. He found himself whispering things to her that he would never have dared say to Eileen. Things that made Tommy Sue draw in her breath and entwine her fingers in his hair.

It was later, when they were having their second beer, that she asked. "Who are you anyway?"

"Jus' plain ol' Dale Barber from Tuscaloosa, honey."

"You're not 'just plain old' anybody from anywhere," she said. "And that wasn't no Tony Randall imitation you were doing earlier. That was the real you."

David looked out at the moonlight and thought it over. "Suppose it was the real me? What would you do about it?"

"Depends on who you came here to hurt. I'm not from DeSota, I'm from Talbot, but the people here been good to me. I wouldn't stick nobody in the back."

"I wouldn't ask you to. Let's get to know each other a little better first. Then we can decide what's right and what's wrong." He kissed the tips of her fingers as he talked.

"You're so gentle," she said softly. "I can't imagine you hurting nobody." She turned her hand around. "Do that to the palm."

"Tell me about your little boy."

"I already told you. His name is Lonnie and he's four and my mama keeps him for me over in Talbot. He's just like any other little boy. Likes cowboys and trucks and beaches. I keep tellin' him we'll go down to the Florida beaches some weekend but, Lord, I never seem to find the time."

"Where's his daddy?"

"Ran off with another woman. Last I heard he was on welfare out in California. He left me with Lonnie to raise. I couldn't find no work in Talbot so I come over here to DeSota. A friend of Mama's sent me to see Mr. Latham. He gave me the job at Luther's and fixed the hours so I could spend three days a week back home."

"Billy Roy Latham? He owns Luther's?"

"Sure. Luther's. Leon's Pool Hall. DeSota Market. The filling station, the canning factory, even the undertaker's parlor. He owns just about everything in Lasher County."

"When he helped you out, did he make any moves on you?"

"Not one. He's been a perfect gentleman. He's good to lots of people, and most times he don't ask nothin' in return."

A Georgia godfather, David thought. He had guessed as much from the demeanor of the men in the poolroom. But he had not imagined that Latham owned the entire county. It would be interesting to see how he reacted the following day when his illegal whiskey operation began to fall apart.

But that was tomorrow and tonight was still tonight. David slipped his hand up Tommy Sue's back under her blouse. He felt nothing except flesh.

"Where do you stay the four nights you're in DeSota?" he asked.

"Out at Harley's Motor Inn. I rent Number Twelve by the week."

"I'm in Number Two," he told her.

She put her lips on his ear. "Small world," she said.

David started the pickup.

The next day when David drove up to Luther's for breakfast, Billy Roy Latham and one of the brothers, Merle, were drinking coffee in a booth and looking worried. David nodded a greeting and sat at the counter. The fry cook was in the kitchen doorway, moving a toothpick back and forth in his mouth. "Somethin' wrong?" David asked, bobbing his chin toward the somber men in the booth.

"Revenue agents caught that fellow's brother Earl with a load of bootleg last night. Got him just after he crossed the Florida line."

David nodded. "Oh." The fry cook's wife, who worked mornings until Tommy Sue came on, handed him a menu. "Just grits and sausage," David said.

While David was eating, Merle got up and left the booth. After he was gone, Latham waved David over to join him. "Bring your plate on over," he said hospitably. David carried his coffee and the rest of his meal over.

"How'd you make out with Tommy Sue last night?" Latham asked.

"Struck out," David lied. "She's a right proper girl."

"You got that right," Latham said. "Gonna make a fine little wife for some man someday." Latham sighed wearily and took a sip of coffee.

"Fry cook tells me you got problems this morning." David said.

Latham shot an irritated look over at the counter. "Fry cook's got a big mouth." Then he studied David for a moment. "But he's right. One of them boys you whipped at pool last night got caught in a revenue-agent trap." Latham narrowed his eyes. "You know anything about bootlegging?"

"A little," David admitted.

Latham tossed down his last swallow of coffee. "Come on, take a ride with me. Somethin' I want to show you."

They rode in Latham's Buick down Route 441 to a narrow country road that cut east into Okefenokee Swamp. Five miles along, Latham turned into a rutted dirt path barely wide enough for the car to negotiate. The farther they drove, the more the morning sunlight was shut out by the entangled treetops overhead and the more eerie the great swamp became. A bit of fog still clung to the ground on both sides of the car, looking wet and cold, making David think of the warmth he had left behind in Tommy Sue's bed. He shivered slightly and wished he was still there.

Before the road ended, Latham turned into a bog path and guided the car with a sure, practiced eye onto a log raft ringed with empty 55-gallon drums to keep it afloat. Sticking his head out the window, he whistled three times. Presently the raft began to float across the marsh to an island, being pulled along by an unseen rope under the murky water. The trip took only three or four minutes, then Latham, who had not even shut off the engine, drove the car onto the island and into a stand of tall pines. David saw the rope and pulley that were used to bring the raft over. A black man with enormous muscles was standing next to the pulley crank. "That's Mose," said Latham. "He can crush a man's skull between his hands." David didn't doubt it for a moment.

The car drove through the shade of the pines, and up ahead David could see the whiskey still. It consisted of several large wooden tubs and a couple of cast-iron vats with kerosene burners under them. Everything was connected by wires and tubes, and with the escaping steam and the bubbling surface in two of the vats it reminded David of the mad doctors' laboratories he used to see in the movies as a kid. Latham parked and they got out. "Come on," he said. "I'll give you the ten-cent tour."

He led David to the layout of tubs, where several lean sweating white men were pouring industrial alcohol from ten-gallon cans into the first tub, then straining it through a water-and-charcoal filter into a second one. "That's how we wash the noxious chemicals out of the alky," Latham said. "Over here in this here tub is where we mix water with the alky, then we run it into that iron vat and cook it some, put some caramel or butterscotch coloring in it to make it look good, then run it into the last tub there to simmer and cool." He grinned sheepishly. "I usually pour a fifth of bonded rye into the final batch to give it a little extra flavor. Like a taste?"

"Why not?" David said.

Behind the last vat were several young boys filling Mason jars with the freshly cooled liquor. Latham opened one of the jars and handed it to David. Although his taste ran to very dry martinis and good brandy, David knew he had to take a convincing drink of the bootleg stuff, as if he'd been drinking it all his life. He took a respectable swallow, prepared to forcibly hold back both cough and tears if necessary, but to his surprise the drink went down not only smoothly but with a tart good taste. He saw that Latham was smiling at him.

"Smooth, ain't it?"

"Sure is, man," David admitted. "And good too."

"Ah don't make nothin' but the best for my customers," Latham bragged. He nodded toward a picnic table and benches under a low weeping willow at the edge of the clearing. "Let's set a spell." As he spoke, Latham pulled back one side of his coat and for the first time David saw that he had a pistol stuck in his belt. Glancing around, he also now saw two men armed with rifles, one at each end of the compound. "Sure 'nuff, Mr. Latham," David said easily and followed him over to the table.

"You know," Latham said, sitting down and shaking a cigarette out of a soft pack, "I sometimes wonder what the ol' world's comin' to. I read in the papers and see on the evenin' news all the stories about crime in the streets, violence in the schools, poverty in the slums, crooks in gub'ment, all that sort of thing. Makes me realize more ever' day that things is changin' too fast to keep up with — and not necessarily for the better, neither. Hell, even all the heroes are dead. Harry Truman's dead. Audie Murphy's dead. John Steinbeck's dead. Ain't nobody around to admire no more. Nowadays all's a man can do is hope to keep his own little part of the world protected from outside influences that might corrupt it. You take Lasher County now. It's my own little corner of the earth and I try to look after it as best I can. I own nearly all there is to own from one end of it to the other, and ever'body except the postmaster and a couple of bankers works for me."

Latham leaned forward on the table and locked eyes with David.

"I run this county like the whole country ought to be run. We don't have no welfare recipients or food stamps down here 'cause we don't need 'em. Ever'body that *can* work *does* work. An' the ones that can't, why the others take care of 'em. Our old people and our sick people don't want for nothin'. Nobody sleeps cold in the wintertime, nobody goes hungry at suppertime, and nobody has to be afraid *anytime*. We ain't got no real crime in Lasher County — no robberies, burglaries, that sort of thing. People here *work* for what they want. They work for me — in my cafe, my pool hall, my grocery market, my filling station, my farms, my canning factory, and ever'thing else I own. My farms and canning factory are the economic backbone of this county. And when the economy don't stay up, when crops are bad or inflation keeps me from making enough to go around for ever'body, why then this whiskey bi'ness takes up the slack. It's this right here — " he waved an arm around " — that keeps the people of Lasher County free and independent of the rest of our dyin' and decayin' society." Now Latham's expression seemed to turn hard as stone. "And I'm here to tell you I'll do anythin' I have to do to keep it that way. Do you take my meanin'?"

David, his mouth as dry as old wood, managed to speak. "Yessir, Mr. Latham, I take your meanin'."

"Good," Latham said quietly. He sat back and seemed to relax a little, toying with the burnt-out-stick match he had used to light his cigarette. "I don't know," he said matter-of-factly, "if it was just a coincidence you comin' to town one day and Earl gettin' caught with a load that same night. I don't know if you're really Dale Barber from Tuscaloosa or if you're a revenue agent from Washington. I know that Tommy Sue is crazy about you — I talked to her on the phone after Harley called to tell me you'd left the motel. Incidentally, I admire the fact that you said you struck out with her instead of braggin' the other way; that's the mark of a good man.

Anyway, Tommy Sue says she thinks you're who you say you are."

She lied for me, David thought.

"But I'd like to hear it from you," Latham said. "For some funny reason I kind of like you. And I kind of trust you. Enough to give you the benefit of the doubt anyhow. I think I'll know if you lie to me. So I'll just ask you outright: who are you, boy?"

A montage of his own world saturated David's mind. Washington. Eileen. The Clary's lawn party. Dry martinis. Sports cars. Italian shoes. Styled hair. A career in government.

Then the montage dissolved into another world. Lasher County. Frye boots and Levi's. A Chevy pickup. Catfish and hush puppies. Tommy Sue's warm neck and the things he could whisper against it.

David met Billy Roy Latham's fixed stare with a calm sureness. "I'm Dale Barber, Mr. Latham. From Tuscaloosa."

The letter he wrote to the district director was brief and polite. He was sorry to resign so abruptly in the middle of a field assignment but he had been offered a job in private industry that he couldn't turn down. He wished the department luck in its pursuit of further leads in Lasher County even though based on his own investigation he didn't believe it would be possible to find an illegal whiskey still in the vast Okefenokee Swamp.

The letter he wrote to Eileen was also brief, and apologetic. He was leaving government service for private employment and he had to be honest and tell her he had become interested in another woman. He would always remember her fondly, he said, and was certain that, attractive, educated woman that she was, she would find someone who deserved her much more than he did.

He mailed the letters in the box outside the DeSota post office, then pulled up in front of Luther's just as Tommy Sue was leaving for the night. She was carrying a small suitcase.

"Hop in," he said. "I'll give you a lift."

"I'm fixin' to catch the ten o'clock bus to Talbot," she told him. "My three days off starts tomorrow."

"I'll give you a lift to Talbot," he said.

"You mean it?"

"Sure, I mean it. Get in."

She put her suitcase in the back and climbed into the cab.

"I start work for Mr. Latham on Monday," he told her.

Tommy Sue's eyebrows went up. "Doin' what?"

"Helping him run Lasher County, honey. He said a good ol' boy like me from Tuscaloosa would fit right in. Said that someday I might even take over and run it for him. How's that for a future?"

"Sounds like you've got the future all worked out. What about the past?"

"There isn't any past," David replied quietly. "There's just today. And tomorrow. Listen, let's pick up your little boy and drive down to Florida to the beach. Would you like that?"

"I'd like it just fine." Tommy Sue slid over close and curled up to him. "You're wrong about there bein' just today and tomorrow," she said.

"Am I? What else is there?"

"There's tonight."

The pickup drove out of town and into the Georgia night.

PUERTO RICAN BLUES

The first-class cabin of the Eastern flight to San Juan was only half full, so Cesar Navarez and his friend Bannion were able to talk without being overheard by other passengers

"What makes you think your brother will go along with the deal?" Bannion asked. He was a flat-faced man with cold eyes. No one in his right mind would have started trouble with him.

"I know my brother," Cesar said. "He's a *jibaro*, a Puerto Rican hillbilly. He works in the tobacco factory, rolling cigars for a living. But he's also got this little patch of dirt where he grows coffee beans. It's part of what used to be a plantation that produced some of the best coffee beans in the world. But that was long ago. Anyway, this brother of mine has had a dream all his life of restoring that little patch of land to its former condition and once again growing the best coffee beans in the world. He's a dreamer, my brother. Dreamers can be had, my friend, if they think what they do will help their dreams come true. He'll go along with the deal. I guarantee it."

"I hope you're right." Bannion said. Somehow, coming from the flat-faced man, it sounded almost like a threat. But it did not bother Cesar. He was not afraid of Bannion, or of anyone else. His many years in the South Bronx had conditioned him against fear. He was already carrying scars from two knife slashes and one gunshot wound. When his time came, he knew there would be nothing he could do about it. Until then he would survive.

"Another drink, gentlemen?" the cabin attendant asked.

"Why not?" said Cesar. Bannion ordered one also.

"Let me tell you a story about my brother," Cesar said after their fresh drinks arrived. "When we were little kids, when I was about ten and Jorge was twelve, Jorge picked up this stray dog and brought it home. It was just a dirty mongrel but it had stepped on a piece of glass and one of its paws was cut. Jorge asked our old man could he keep the mongrel and take care of it, and the old man said okay. At that time there were seven kids at home and we all lived in a little *bohio*. You know what a *bohio* is? It is a corrugated tin shack set up on a slab of concrete. Most *jibaros* live in them.

"So anyway, there's nine of us including my parents and we all live in this *bohio*. My old man works for the tobacco plantation for slave wages, you know, and we never have enough of anything — never enough clothes, never enough beds, never enough to eat. But my old man, he's a real chump, you know, a real loser. He tells Jorge, sure, you can keep the mongrel — he even helps him doctor the cut paw so it don't get infected. My old lady, who was a little more practical, says to my father, hey, we don't have enough food to feed no dog. But the old man says there's always scraps, the dog can eat scraps. So Jorge gets to keep the dog."

Cesar took a large swallow of his drink and stared unblinkingly at the seatback in front of him. He was no longer merely telling a story to Bannion — he was reliving it.

"That same week I had asked my old man for a couple of dollars to buy fishing line and bait. I wanted to fish the mountain streams for bass and see if I could sell it at the outdoor market in Jayuca, where we lived. But the old man wouldn't give it to me — he said there were too many people selling fish in the market already and I'd just get stuck with whatever I caught. I got really sore, you know, because Jorge got to keep that lousy mongrel and I didn't get my fishing line. I waited a month so nobody would be suspicious of me and one night when everybody was asleep, I put a burlap coffee-bean sack over that dog's head and smothered it."

Cesar paused for a moment, still staring straight ahead. His eyes had narrowed to slits and his face looked like a death mask. Bannion watched him, unmoved by the story — so Cesar killed a dog, so what? Finally Cesar sighed quietly and came out of his fixation. He tossed down the rest of his drink.

"Anyway, Jorge knew how upset I'd been over the fishing line, but even so he never suspected me for a minute. That's the way it is with dreamers — most of the time they live in a world all their own and they won't do nothing that'll let the real world in. It was easier for Jorge to blame somebody he didn't know. He ended up saying his dog was killed by wandering gypsies."

Cesar lighted a cigarette and blew an almost perfect smoke ring. "Jorge will go along with the deal, all right," he said confidently. "I know he will because he's still a dreamer."

While they were waiting for their luggage after the plane landed at San Juan's Isla Verde airport, Cesar went into the barber shop for a shoeshine. He was wearing shoes make of endangered alligator skin, which he had to buy illegally but which he felt gave him status. The rest of his wardrobe was equally expensive —- Italian silk suit, custom-made shirt, designer tie with a diamond stickpin.

While Cesar got his shoeshine, Bannion stood near the baggage conveyor waiting for their luggage. Looking around the airport, he noticed that a large number of locals seemed to be dressed in blue. Not just blue, but almost the same shade of blue, with very little variation. Almost as if it were a uniform. Bannion thought it odd but didn't have time to dwell on it because the bags began arriving.

They rented a Cadillac at the Avis counter and Cesar drove the eight kilometers into the city. As soon as they got into the metropolitan area, Bannion began seeing people dressed in identical blue again. He also noticed storefronts, doors, even entire homes painted in the same shade.

"What's with the blue?" he asked.

"That's the color of the statehood movement," Cesar explained. "People who want Puerto Rico to become the fifty-first state wear blue to show support and approval of the plan. They even paint their homes and businesses, as you can see. And their cars. There's an auto-painting place in the city that does cars in that color. It's a popular cause with about half the population."

"What about the other half?"

Cesar grunted and bobbed his chin at a large building they were passing. "Those people there are the other half," he said, indicating the parking lot, which was filled to overflowing with an incredible variety of old cars, trucks, station wagons, campers, and vans — most of them dented or rusted, missing a fender or a hood, a trunk-lid wired down, no wheel covers. Each vehicle had a male driver, sitting alone drinking beer from a can or standing outside talking to the man parked next to him or listening to disco music on a portable radio.

"For every man in the parking lot," Cesar said, "there's a woman on line inside to get *cupones* — food stamps. This is the half of the population that *doesn't* want statehood. The freeloaders. They get more welfare benefits as citizens of a territory than they would if Puerto Rico were a state. You notice none of *them* are wearing blue. They wouldn't be caught dead in blue."

At the hotel, they checked in and put their plan into motion. Cesar made a telephone call and, speaking in Spanish, arranged a meeting for Bannion in the hotel lounge in two hours.

"The woman you're meeting —" he started to tell Bannion, but Bannion interrupted him.

"Woman? The mule is a woman?"

"Why not, man?" said Cesar. "This is the age of equal opportunity, my friend. If women can be pilots and priests, they can be dope smugglers too. You'll meet her in the lounge at four. She'll be wearing a white-linen pantsuit with a coral blouse. She'll be carrying a shopping bag containing several packages with San Juan department-store wrappings on them. You two will have a drink together, you'll give her the shoebox full of money in the Lord and Taylor bag, she'll leave the shopping bag of packages with you and go. You stay and have another drink, then come back up to the room and start pouring the stuff into the special plastic bags we brought with us. Okay?"

"Okay. Does she speak English, this woman?"

"Like a native. She used to teach third grade in the New York City school system."

Cesar was putting on a fresh shirt and tie as he talked. "While you're taking care of the buy," he said, "I'll drive up in the mountains to Jayuca to see my brother and set up the rest of the deal. I'll be back in time for supper."

Cesar Navarez drove out of the city on the route that led up and over the Cordillera Mountains. Before the highway began its ascent, it made a straight line through the sweltering sugarcane fields in which Cesar had labored as an adolescent. Beyond the fields it bisected a jungle that began thinly but within a mile or so abruptly thickened into a dark, forbidding wilderness.

Above the jungle, however, after the highway had climbed out of it, the lower plateaus of the mountain were clear and open. At twelve hundred feet, the road was wet and Cesar knew it had been raining. Looking ahead at the higher elevation, he saw the once-familiar low-hanging chartreuse cloud formations, made that color by the sun reflecting off the *espigas*, the wild wheat of the uplands.

The barrio settlement of Jayuca set three miles off the main highway by way of a rutted asphalt road. The first thing Cesar thought when he drove into the village was how much smaller everything looked. Jayuca had once been to him the most exciting place on earth, but that was when he had been a barefoot kid who climbed guava trees for sport. Now Jayuca was no more than a single dirty street, with old men, neglected children, and loose chickens wandering around, while the unemployed young men of the town hung out at the pool hall and drank beer all day. A place for losers, Cesar thought. Losers like his old man had been. And like Jorge still was.

Cesar had no trouble driving directly to the *bohio* where he had grown up, and where Jorge, now with his own family, still lived. He was not surprised to find the *bohio* painted statehood blue. Jorge was probably the only *jibaro* in Jayuca who supported statehood.

Cesar parked the Cadillac in the dirt front yard and got out. Two children, a boy and a girl, stopped playing and stared at him. The boy reminded Cesar of himself twenty-five years earlier. They were obviously Jorge's children — the family resemblance was too striking for them not to be.

At the screen door of the *bohio*, Cesar knocked. Luz, Jorge's wife opened it. Her mouth dropped open at the sight of him.

"Hello, Luz," he said with a smile.

"Hello, Cesar." Luz was a slim woman with an exquisite mouth and wide, attractive shoulders. Her hair was black as a crow's wing, waist-length, and she let one side fall loosely across her face to partially hide a badly pockmarked left cheek.

"Those two yours?" Cesar asked, bobbing his chin at the children.

"Yes. The boy is Martin —" she pronounced it Mar-*teen* "— and the girl is Estelle." Luz held the door open. "Please — come in, Cesar."

The inside of the *bohio*, Cesar saw, had changed considerably. It was not as crowded with beds and cots as Cesar remembered it — there were a few pieces of discount-store furniture he had never seen before and Luz had made attempts to brighten up the place with variety-store wallpaper and a few plastic-framed prints. There were also several partitions placed to give the illusion of rooms. In the corner allotted as the kitchen, Cesar noticed that Luz was preparing *alcapurias* — dumplings made from banana plants. How many hundreds of times, he thought, had he and the whole family had nothing but *alcapurias* for supper? Now, after twenty years, Jorge and his family were still eating it.

"I'll call Jorge for you," Luz said. "He's out back in the field."

"Never mind," said Cesar. "I'll go out there and see him." He started out the back door but paused and turned back. "You look good, Luz." he said quietly. "As good as you did when you were fifteen."

Luz looked away, refusing to meet his eyes. She kept on with her work and did not respond.

Cesar found his brother a hundred yards in back of the *bohio*, tilling the dark-brown soil of a small patch of land on which were growing several rows of coffee-bean shrubs. The patch had once been part of the huge coffee-bean plantation for which their father had worked until the day he died. Now it was abandoned land, free to whoever wanted to use it. Mostly it was untended and its soil had become impure with erosion and rocks and waste. All except the patch Jorge Navarez kept. That patch was still cultivated and Jorge tended it lovingly. When Cesar walked up, Jorge was on his knees, tilling around the bushes with a hand tool. When he looked up and saw his brother, he stopped working and sat back on his heels.

"Hello, Cesar. You look prosperous."

"Hello, Jorge. You look tired."

Jorge shrugged. "I work hard. In the cigar factory at night, here in my coffee field during the day. But you know, Cesar, the more tired a man is from his work, the more blessed and wonderful rest is to him. Do you ever get so tired, Cesar, that the simple act of resting is luxurious?"

"Never," said Cesar. He smiled slightly. "Not from work, anyway. I see you have two kids now."

"Yes. The boy, Martin, reminds me a great deal of our little brother Felix when he was growing up. Remember how Felix was always building things with sticks? Martin is the same way."

"Where is Felix now?" Cesar asked.

"Dead. He was killed in Vietnam. I have a medal inside that they sent, if you'd like to see it."

"Maybe later," Cesar said. He decided not to ask about their other four brothers and sisters.

"Did you come back home to hide again?" Jorge asked. Once before, ten years earlier, Cesar had returned to Jayuca after he had killed a man in New York. He had a serious knife wound at the time. It had become infected and had taken a long time to heal.

"No, I haven't come to hide," Cesar said. "I'm here on business. I've come to offer you an opportunity to make some money."

Jorge shook his head. "I don't want your kind of money, Cesar. To get it, I have to live your kind of life and I cannot do that. I'm too honest. And too afraid."

"To get this money you do not have to live any kind of life except your own. You have only to work one day, doing the same thing you always do. You don't have to be dishonest and you don't have to be afraid. There's absolutely no way you can be caught. And you can earn five thousand dollars."

Jorge stared at his brother. Five thousand dollars, to Jorge, was an enormous amount of money. Not only could he buy many things he wanted for his family — a washing machine for Luz, real beds instead of cots for the children, a television set — but he could also purchase chemicals and some additional tools to properly restore his patch of coffee-bean land. He had done his best over the years using leftover fertilizer from the tobacco fields, tilling by hand, pruning with ordinary household scissors, but he knew the soil would never come back all the way without more expensive methods.

Jorge stood up and looked out over the small patch. "This is the field Papa used to tend, remember? When you and I were boys, Cesar, the coffee beans that grew on this field were so rich and choice the entire crop was reserved for the Vatican. Remember that?"

"Yes. Papa used to say every night that the Pope was drinking coffee made from beans that he grew. I remember too that Papa himself had to drink coffee made from waste beans."

"That didn't matter to Papa," said Jorge. "He was proud of the coffee beans he grew."

Sure, thought Cesar, Papa was proud and what did it get him? And you, Jorge, you're still the dreamer you've always been, and what has it got you? Losers and dreamers — they were all alike.

"Let me tell you how you can earn the five thousand dollars," Cesar said quietly, feeling the time was right.

It was a very simple plan, Cesar explained. He and his partner were buying a quantity of heroin in San Juan and needed a way to smuggle it back into New York. Each of them was allowed by U.S. Customs to bring back one hundred cigars. They had designed and had made for them before leaving New York a supply of plastic bags the size and shape of a ball point pen. As soon as they got the heroin, they would put it into these cylindrical bags and seal them. Then they wanted the bags rolled into cigars that would pass through Customs unsuspected. The tobacco odor would neutralize the detection prowess of the Customs narcotics dogs, which could sniff out heroin even through plastic.

"Can you roll two hundred cigars in one day?" Cesar asked.

Jorge shrugged. "If the tobacco leaf is good — not too dry but not too moist either."

"We'll let you buy the tobacco yourself at the market in Poco. We'll pick up four boxes of coronas in town, throw away the cigars, and use the boxes and wrappers for the ones you will roll. What do you say, brother?"

Jorge sighed and looked down at the ground. With the toe of one scuffed work shoe, he worried a broken twig lying there. "I don't know, Cesar," he said reluctantly. "Drugs are a bad thing."

"Drugs are a way of life for some people," Cesar said pragmatically. "People who want drugs will always get drugs. If not at one place, then at another."

"I know that. I just hate to think that maybe what I do is going to hurt some poor person I don't even know."

Cesar put a hand on his brother's shoulder. "Most likely you'll be helping, not hurting. Look, Jorge, you don't know how it is up there. In Spanish Harlem and the South Bronx it's another world, man. There aren't any happy smiling little kids playing barefoot in the dirt like you've got down here. Up there the kids are street-tough, street-hardened, street-smart. They live in a world of apartments without heat, a world of family court and social workers, a world of trouble — trouble in school, on the job, with the cops. Every day is a struggle, a battle, a war; and every night is a dark time to dread the next day. This stuff that I deal in, it helps people get through those nights."

Jorge was still not convinced. He wanted the money, but he also wanted to be able to continue living with himself. "I can't give you an answer without thinking about it, Cesar," he said at last.

"I can't wait long," Cesar warned. "This is Saturday, so you don't work tonight. I'll drive back up in the morning, after you've had time to think about it. If you decide to do it, we'll go to the Sunday market at Poco and buy the tobacco. You can do the rolling in our hotel room — there's a table and plenty of water. You have the tools you need, right?"

"Yes, I have my own tools for cutting and shaping and rolling. All right, Cesar, I will think about it and let you know in the morning."

Cesar left him there at the edge of his little coffee-bean patch and walked back to the *bohio*. Luz was still preparing the banana-plant noodles. "I just told Jorge a way to make some quick money," he said. "Encourage him to do it, will you?"

"Jorge is his own man," Luz said. "He will make up his own mind without my help.

Cesar went over and stood very close to her. "Have you ever told Jorge that I had you before he did?"

Luz closed her eyes tightly. "No."

"I haven't told him either," Caesar said pointedly. He patted her arm. "I will be back in the morning. Encourage him for me, Luz."

He left the *bohio* then and drove back down the mountain to San Juan.

That night in bed, lying up close to Jorge's back, the two of them like two spoons in a drawer, Luz said, "Are you going to tell me what Cesar asked you to do?"

"No," Jorge replied.

"Is it something bad?"

"Yes," Jorge said.

They fell silent. Across the *bohio*, in their own little partitioned areas, Martin and Estelle slept peacefully. Outside, the night sounds of the high jungle wafted in the air: a night hawk, a fox, a spider monkey at play.

"If you did what he wanted, would you be in any danger?" Luz asked.

"No." Jorge adjusted his position, and Luz did the same. "Why do you ask about danger? Do you think I should do it as long as there is no danger?"

"I know how badly you would like to have money for the land," she said.

"The land is a dream," he told her. "That's all it's ever been. A man needs a dream to keep going. If I got the money, most of it would go for the family."

"But some would go for your dream," she said.

Jorge smiled in the darkness. "Some," he admitted. "A little."

Luz hugged him tighter. "Good," she said, "because I like your dream. It is my dream too. And we are Puerto Rican Blues," she reminded him. "Someday, when statehood comes, all our dreams will come true."

"Statehood, yes," he said quietly, almost wistfully. "The end of the rainbow."

Once again they fell silent. Jorge could feel Luz's heart beating steadily against his bare back — her hand lay still on his shoulders, her breath was soft on his neck.

"Jorge, there is something I must tell you," she said at last. "It is something I have wanted to tell you for a very long time, but I have not had the courage to do so."

"Is it about you and Cesar?" he asked. At once he felt her heartbeat increase. "About you and Cesar sleeping together when you were fifteen?"

"He told you," she said bitterly.

"No. Someone else did. A long time ago."

"Why didn't you tell me you knew?"

"I thought it might hurt you to know I knew. You were so very young when I found out. And after a while, I just forgot about it."

"Didn't it matter to you, Jorge?"

"It mattered," he admitted. "But not enough."

He thought he detected warm tears on his back after that, but he wasn't sure.

Much later, just before she drifted to sleep, Luz asked, "Will you go with Cesar in the morning?"

"Yes," Jorge replied.

The next morning when Cesar drove through Jayuca, Jorge flagged him down halfway through town. "I came in to the metal shop to get my tools sharpened," he told Cesar, getting in.

"You're going to do the job for me then," Cesar said, smiling. "Good. I knew you would."

Cesar turned the Cadillac around and drove back toward San Juan. Just outside the city, he detoured to Poco, where a huge outdoor market was located. Farmers from the surrounding area bought their produce, poultry, sugarcane, tobacco, and other products to sell at stalls they rented from the town council. It was the only market allowed open on Sundays, and all stalls had to close between ten and eleven in the morning while the church across the square conducted Mass.

Cesar and Jorge got to Poco well before ten, and Jorge shopped for tobacco with the sure eyes of one who had handled the leaf for many years. He had been a stacker and bundler as a young boy, then a harvester as an adolescent, finally an apprentice cutter and roller as a young man. Now he was one of the best hand-shapers of cigars in the entire factory. He knew the leaf by texture, touch, aroma, and instinct. Luz had once marveled at how much he knew about tobacco when coffee was his first love. Jorge told her that a man learned what he *had* to learn to survive, but that he loved only what he *wanted* to love.

After Jorge had selected enough leaf for two hundred cigars and Cesar had paid for it, they put the bundle in the truck and drove the rest of the way into the city. Cesar parked the car in the hotel lot and Jorge carried the bundled leaf as they walked into the lobby. The tobacco was tightly wrapped in burlap, a parcel the size of an overnight bag.

As Cesar and Jorge waited for the elevator, four men dressed in suits crossed the lobby from outside and waited with them. They all boarded the elevator, but only Cesar pressed a button for a floor. He glanced nervously at the men as the car glided up to eleven. When the door opened, two of the men took his arms firmly while the other two did the same with Jorge.

"You're under arrest," one of the men said to Cesar. "Which is your room?"

"You're making a mistake," Cesar protested. "I'm a cigar importer in

San Juan on business —"

"You're a heroin smuggler, senor," the man said. He twisted Cesar's arm behind his back. "Now tell us which room you are in, and whether your partner is armed."

"All right," Cesar said as the pain shot into his shoulder. He was not afraid of pain — he merely decided that then was as good a time as any to start working on getting a light sentence. "Eleven-fourteen," he said. "He is not armed. Listen, I want to cooperate with you —"

Cesar and Jorge were handcuffed, and two of the men stayed with them while the other two went down the hall to eleven-fourteen to get Bannion and the heroin.

Jorge was back home by two o'clock that afternoon. "Did it go well?" Luz asked. Jorge had opened up to her about the plan that morning.

"Yes," he said. "I talked to the Jayuca constable this morning and he notified the federal officers. They followed us from the Poco market to the hotel. I was arrested along with Cesar and the other man. Then at the justice building we were all separated. They took some information from me and let me go."

"And the reward? How much will it be?"

"It will depend on how much heroin there was," Jorge told her. "Probably about a thousand dollars, they said. We'll get a check once it's decided."

Luz nodded. "And Cesar? What will happen to him?"

"He will go to federal prison in the States. They said he would probably get a long sentence because he had a bad record."

"Will he know you informed on him?"

"No. As far as he'll be concerned, they just let me go because there was no evidence against me. All I did was buy tobacco and walk into the hotel with it."

As they were talking, their young son Martin burst through the door.

"Papa! Papa! Come see what I found!"

Jorge allowed himself to be pulled by the hand out to the side of the *bohio*. There, cowering in some weed, was a little mongrel puppy, unwashed, trembling with fear and hunger.

"Where did it come from, Papa?" Martin asked, wide-eyed.

"He probably wandered away from his litter and got lost," Jorge said.

Martin gripped his father's hand tightly. "Papa, can I please keep him? Can he please be my puppy?"

Jorge looked down at his son and the years raced backward in his mind. He saw himself as a boy, saw his own father, saw a mongrel dog of another time. He felt a warmth in his chest.

"Yes, you can keep it, Martin." He scooped up the puppy and put it in his son's arms.

"Oh, Papa, isn't it a nice little dog!" Martin exclaimed.

"A very nice dog, son."

"Papa, did you ever have a dog when you were little?"

"Yes. Once."

"What happened to it?"

"Someone killed it one night."

"A bad man?"

"He became a bad man, yes."

"Did he ever get punished for it?"

Jorge nodded solemnly. "Oh, yes, Martin. He got punished."

Jorge led his son into the *bohio* to get a dish of milk for the new puppy.

CHALLENGE THE WIDOW-MAKER

They buried old Terangi in a small country cemetery several miles below the crater of Kaneakala volcano. It was a simple funeral. Most of Terangi's neighbors made the drive up-mountain from Lahaina Town to attend, and a few of his fellow merchants who had small stores near Terangi's surfboard shop on the waterfront also attended. Because there were no other family members, Terangi's widow, Marama, was escorted to the services by George Hill, her late husband's sole employee, who was like a son to them. George had been with Terangi when the massive heart attack struck. They had been sanding separate ends of a new competition board Terangi was making for one of the Maui surfers to use in the next big North Shore finals on Oahu.

When the services were over and the other mourners had left, Marama leaned her head against George's arm. "Life will seem very strange without him, Keoki," she said, using the Polynesian form of George.

"Yes, it will," George replied, just as quietly. "I hate to think what my life would have been like if it hadn't been for him. And you."

"You have been a great comfort to us, Keoki," she assured him. "You'll stay on and run the shop, won't you?"

"Yes," George shrugged. "I wouldn't know how to do anything else. All I've ever been was a soldier, a convict, and a surfboard maker."

"And a son," Marama reminded him, squeezing his arm. "You've been a son to two lonely people."

As they walked away from Terangi's grave, George noticed that not all the mourners had gone. A solitary figure stood well back at the edge of the cemetery, watching. Wearing a flowered Hawaiian shirt, his hands shoved into his pants pockets, he was a once-husky islander who had gone to fat. In one corner of his mouth was an ever-present toothpick. His name was Charley Kula. He was George Hill's parole officer from Oahu.

George drove Marama back down-mountain in Terangi's old Plymouth, which he supposed would now become his because Marama had never learned to drive. George had a lot on his mind at the moment. He was wondering how life was going to be without Terangi's wise counseling. He was wondering whether he could run the surfboard shop by himself. And he was wondering what was on Charley Kula's mind. In the rearview mirror he could see Kula following them down-mountain in the white state-owned pool car he used when he was on Maui. Kula was, in George's opinion, exactly what old Terangi had called him in private for years: *a baabaa na mea kino me ka banu ola*. Literally translated, it meant a low creature, unworthy of a name.

George had been under Charley Kula's thumb for five years, living with the constant threat of being returned to Oahu Prison on the whim of an unfavorable monthly report. For five years George had loaned Kula money — twenty dollars here, twenty dollars there — money that was never paid back; or given him free surfboards for his supervisor's kids; or fixed him up with one of the *wahines* from the Cloud Nine Massage Parlor, at George's expense; or bought his dinner, his lunch, his breakfast, his haircuts, his shoeshines. When Kula came over from Oahu once a month, George always paid for one thing or another.

"Never mind," Terangi had always counseled him "keep your *bu'ibu'i*." Your cool. "Don't let a robber like him upset you. Be happy. Take one of the boards and go surf for an hour."

For five years George had worked off his anger out on the waves. For five years he had kept his *bu'ibu'i*. But he had not been happy about it.

When George and Marama got back to Lahaina Town, to the little frame house on Lani Street where Terangi and Marama had lived for forty years, the ladies of the neighborhood were there with dishes of food and doses of comfort, so George only stayed a little while before telling Marama he was going to the shop for a couple of hours.

Then he left to go see what Charley Kula wanted.

Kula was in the bar of the old Missionary Inn, sipping a gin and tonic around his toothpick, shooting the breeze with the bartender. When George came in, he moved to a back table, taking his drink with him.

"Aloha, Georgie," he said with a smile. George sat down and a bored cocktail waitress in a sarong came over to take his order.

"Just a Coke," George said.

"I'll have another gin and tonic," Kula added. Then to George, he said, "Listen, have something stronger if you want it. I know how much you liked the old man."

George shook his head. "Just a Coke," he repeated. He remembered Terangi's words from the very first day of his parole: *Never let him get anything on you. Never break the rules, even if he tells you it's okay.* Parolees weren't allowed to drink alcoholic beverages.

"I guess the old lady wants you to stay on and run the shop, huh?" Kula asked when the waitress left.

"Yes."

"There's no other family, is there? They all died in that car wreck, didn't they?"

"Yes. I mean no, there's no other family."

"Well, that leaves you pretty well fixed, I guess. I mean, the shop will be all yours someday, won't it?"

"I suppose."

"Lucky day for you when old Terangi helped you make parole and gave you a job in his shop."

"Yes. Lucky day."

The waitress brought their drinks and George paid for them.

Kula sat back and patted his ample belly with both hands. "You know, what happened to old Terangi makes a man realize just how short life is. A man's a fool if he don't make the most of the time he's got left. Take me, for instance. Next month's my birthday. I'll be fifty-five. That makes me eligible for early retirement. Know what I'd like to do? Buy a little corn farm in Kansas."

George looked at him incredulously and Kula chuckled. "Yeah, I know that's funny. Probably half the people in Kansas would like to come here to retire, and I want to go back there." He leaned forward on his elbows. "But I'm sick of the islands. I'd like to get up in the mornings and know I can hop in my car and drive more that thirty miles without running into the ocean. I want to live someplace where they have seasons, not the same boring perfect weather all the time."

"But why a corn farm?" George asked.

"I like to grow things," Kula said, taking the toothpick out of his mouth for the first time. "I've got a little garden at home right now. Tomatoes, radishes, carrots. But you need a field for corn — all I've got is the patio of my bachelor apartment. I get this realty catalogue every month. It's got a section on rural properties, with photographs, in color. I'll tell you something: a field of growing corn is a real pretty sight." Kula sat back again, taking a sip of his drink. "Only thing is, it takes a hefty down payment to buy a decent-sized farm in Kansas."

George sat back, too, and drank some of his Coke. "What's on your mind, Mr. Kula?"

The parole officer smiled. "Know what I like about you, Georgie? You cooperate. You always cooperate." The smile faded and the voice lowered.

"I've got a parolee over on Oahu named Nicky Dade. Did five for burglary. Young guy, mid-twenties, real hip — he's a surfer, like you. The kid's old man was a locksmith. Nicky can pick damn near any lock there is."

George nodded. "So?"

"So there's a wholesale costume jewelry merchant on Oahu that gets a shipment of pearls from Hong Kong the first of every month. They're supposed to be fake, but they're not, they're *real* — the kind divers bring up from the ocean. Nobody knows they're real, of course — everybody assumes they're fake because the business is set up as a costume jewelry company. It's a perfect cover. The guy pays no import duty on the pearls, doesn't have to pay a big insurance premium, doesn't have to have fancy security at his offices. I mean, who's going to steal a few hundred bucks' worth of fake pearls, right?" Kula sat forward again and his voice became even lower. "This guy brings in between a half and three-quarters of a million dollars worth every month and nobody's the wiser. I only found out about it by accident, from this guy I know who works for the air courier service that brings the stuff from Hong Kong."

"What's the point?" George asked.

"The point is that my boy Nicky can pick the locks to this guy's office *and* his safe."

"Sounds like your boy Nicky's heading for trouble."

"Not at all," Kula said emphatically. "It's a walk-in, walk-out job, sixty minutes from start to finish. It's all set to go on the first of the month. All I have to do is find my boy Nicky a partner. A helper. Nothing heavy — a bag holder, lookout man, that sort of thing. Very easy work."

"Why don't you do it yourself if it's so easy?" George asked flatly.

"Me?" Kula said. There seemed to be genuine surprise in his expression. "Hell, Georgie, I couldn't do a thing like that. I'm no thief."

"Neither am I," George reminded him. "I did time for manslaughter, remember?"

Kula's eyes narrowed a fraction. "Like I said, Georgie, I like you because I figure you always cooperate. But maybe I'm wrong. Maybe I've been wrong writing good parole reports on you all these years."

Sighing quietly, George looked away for a moment. There was hurt in his eyes, and helplessness. Presently he looked back and said, "No, Mr. Kula, you aren't wrong. What do you want me to do?"

Charley Kula smiled.

Two days later, the girl came into his shop. She had what islanders called "mixed-up blood," and it was obvious from her appearance: the brown hair of the Portuguese, the blue eyes of the *keokeos*, the whites; the flat lips of the Tahitians, the wide nostrils of the Filipinos, and the long body of the Spaniards. She was almost pretty.

"Hi. You Georgie?" she asked.

"I'm George," he replied.

"I'm Mileka. Nicky's friend. He wants to see you."

"I'm right here," George said. He went on waxing the competition board he was working on.

"Not here," Mileka said. "Nicky doesn't talk business in rooms, only on beaches. He got sent to prison because of a microphone in a motel room." She jerked her head toward the ocean. "He's out surfing."

George thought about it for a moment, then put the board aside and reached under the counter for a printed sign that read: BACK IN TEN MINUTES. Terangi had used a felt-tip marker to cross out IN TEN MINUTES and in its place had hand lettered SOON.

"Let's go," George said, putting the sign in the door.

He and the girl walked down Front Street a couple of blocks, then cut over to where the beach began. Neither of them tried to make conversation. George was pushing thirty-six and the girl couldn't have been more than twenty, so each assumed they had nothing to say to each other. When they reached the sand, both took off their sandals and left them on the curb with a dozen other pairs. Then they walked along the beach, up away from the water, until they came to a couple of towels with a beach bag on them.

"Nicky's out there." The girl pointed to a figure lying flat on a surfboard on the water fifty yards out, waiting for a swell. As George looked seaward, Mileka dropped her shorts onto one of the towels and pulled her polo shirt over her head. When George looked back, she was stretched out on the towel in a yellow French-cut bikini that made her tanned body look like warm caramel. Sun bunny, George thought derisively.

He waited for five minutes until the figure on the board caught a soft wave and stood up to surf back onto the beach. As the surfer walked toward him, George saw that he was a typical young white islander: blond, golden-tanned, supple, muscular, handsome, confident. Like I used to be, George thought before he could help himself.

"I'm Nicky Dade," the young man said, not offering to shake hands.

"George Hill," said George.

"I thought we ought to meet once before the job," Nicky said easily. "I guess Kula told you it's a real piece of cake. All you'll really have to do is what I tell you to. I thought we ought to have a look at each other, but Kula says you're okay so that's good enough for me."

"He told me you were okay too," George countered. He didn't like being talked to as if he were a flunky.

"Of course I'm okay," Nicky retorted, annoyed. "It's my job, man. I'm the one that's doing it. Of course I'm okay."

"Of course."

Nicky stuck his surfboard upright in the sand. It was, George observed, one of the most expensive factory-made boards.

"Kula tells me you surf," Nicky said, seeming to get over his pique as quickly as it came.

"Yes."

"A little old for it, aren't you?"

"I do it anyway," George told him. He noticed that Mileka was leaning up on her elbows, looking curiously at him.

"Maybe we can go out together sometime," Nicky suggested, bobbing his head at the water. "Early in the morning, before you open your shop."

"I don't surf in the harbor," George said. He didn't even try to keep the disdain out of his voice.

"That right?" Nicky said, with a trace of amusement. "Where do you surf?"

"Kaanapali," said George.

Nicky frowned slightly. "*You* surf Kaanapali?"

"I surf Kaanapali."

"At your age?"

"At my age." George could feel himself blush. He wished the girl wasn't there. Or at least that she wasn't looking at him. He forced himself to smile. "The waves aren't big at Kaanapali, but they're tricky. Harbor surfing's too tame for me. Look, I've got to get back to my shop. You can find me there whenever you want me."

He knew their eyes followed him all the way off the beach.

At noon the next day, Marama, as usual, brought George his lunch, as she had always done for Terangi and him. "Couple of nice *opakapaka* sandwiches today," she said. George went into the bathroom at the back of the shop and washed his hands. When he came back out, Marama had his lunch set out on the desk behind the counter. As he started to eat, Mileka came in. Marama got up to leave. "I've got marketing to do, Keoki.

Don't be late for supper."

After Marama left, Mileka raised her eyebrows inquiringly. "Keoki?"

"Polynesian for George," he said. "You've got Poly blood — don't you know the dialect?"

"If I spoke the language of every kind of blood I've got in me, man, I'd be — what do you call it? — multilingual. I'm not real big on being a native girl. What's that you're eating?"

"*Opakapaka.* Pink snapper. Want some?"

"No, thanks. I'm strictly a hamburger-and-fries person. Listen, the reason I'm here is that Nicky wants to surf Kaanapali with you. He wants to know if tomorrow morning's okay."

"I'm too busy," George said. "I'm all alone in the shop now and I'm getting behind in the work." He saw that she had pursed her lips and was nodding knowingly.

"Nicky said you were probably all talk. I'll tell him you can't make it."

As she started to leave, George said. "Wait a minute. Tell him I'll be at Black Rock at daybreak."

"I'll tell him," she said, a little smugly. Walking out, she looked back over her shoulder. "Bye, *Keoki.*"

At sunrise, George was sitting on the beach at the foot of Black Rock, a dark outcropping of lava rock that stood eighty feet high and jutted into the sea like a driven fist, dividing the long beautiful beach into two lengths. Legend had it that Pele, the ancient fire goddess, had build the rock as a throne for herself. Terangi and Marama believed the story, so George believed it too. As he sat on the sand, a thick beach towel around his shoulders for warmth, his surfboard resting familiarly between his legs, he wasn't afraid of the shadows of the rock that seemed to shift and adjust as if they had life, or of the eerie noises the wind made as it dervished its way throughout the throne's crags and crevices.

The sun rose at the edge of Lanai, ten miles away on the horizon, and in an instant sent warm yellow light across the dark water, changing its surface from black to an azure blue that perfectly matched the lightening sky above it. George heard a whistle and turned to see Nicky Dade and Mileka walking down the beach toward him. He rose and was pulling his sweatshirt off over his head as they came up.

"Hello, Keoki," Mileka said pertly. George ignored her.

"These waves look kind of soft to me," Nicky said.

"Like I told you, they're not big but they're tricky." George looked at him. "You a wave counter?"

"What do you mean?"

"On this side of the island, every ninth wave is a good one. So we wait here on the beach for a good one to break, then we start out, counting the incoming waves as we go. When the ninth one is about to come in, we get up and go with it. Clear?"

"Yeah, sure," Nicky said. "Where'd you learn all that?"

"Here and there."

As they waited, Nicky studied George's board. It was a handmade, tapered, hollow board ten feet long and eighteen inches wide, with a skeg, or stabilizing fin, near its back. Etched in a curve across the upper front were the words CHALLENGE THE WIDOW-MAKER.

"What's that mean?" Mileka asked, seeing the inscription.

"The widow-maker is what the old merchant seamen used to call the ocean. The man who helped me make this board said every time a person goes out to ride the water on a piece of wood, that person is challenging the widow-maker. He wanted me to remember that, so he put it on the board." At that moment a good wave broke in the surf and George turned to Nicky. "Ready?"

"Ready, man."

"Let's go."

They walked into the water until they were chest-deep, then belly-flopped onto their boards and began paddling seaward. A low wave rolled in and they pushed easily through it. "That's number one!" George shouted. They kept paddling. Twenty yards, thirty. Another wave rolled in. "Number two!" Fifty yards, sixty. A third wave, perceptibly higher. "Three!"

They paddled in as straight a line as the sea would allow, their bodies flat on the narrow boards, their hands moving rapidly, their faces raised to the mass of water confronting them. In that juxtaposition, their relationship to the ocean was perilous and unpredictable, but at the same time almost carnal. Behind them, the safety of land grew farther and farther away. Ahead of them, the waves grew higher and began rolling and twisting as, far beneath the surface, the water encountered deep reefs and sandbars.

"Number six!"

One hundred eighty yards, one ninety.

Arm, shoulder, and neck muscles began to burn as if raw rope had been pulled across them.

"Seven!"

Two hundred ten yards. Two twenty.

The throat and groin began to react now, tightening, tensing, tickling oddly.

"Eight — !"

Two hundred and fifty yards away from the land, a six-foot wall of water rolled toward them.

"Number nine coming up!" George shouted. He leaped up-right and with his feet turned the board so that it was diagonally facing the beach in the path of the wave. In his peripheral vision, he saw Nicky do the same thing. Then both of them were being lifted and carried like feathers on the wind as the swell of ocean rolled, shifted to the right, and rolled some more, taking them back where they belonged. Knees bent, bodies arched, arms akimbo, hearts pounding, faces glowing with the thrill of it, they rode the ocean. It was exhilarating.

When their boards hit sand, they leaped off and grabbed them up, then stood panting and smiling. They had come as close as any mortal comes to walking on water.

"Man, I see what you mean about tricky!" Nicky exclaimed as they walked back to where Mileka waited. "But I did all right, didn't I!" It was a boast more than a question.

"You did okay," George allowed. "Good thing the wave wasn't any higher."

"What do you mean?"

"I'm not sure you could have handled a higher swell."

"Oh, yeah? Could you have?"

"Sure, I handle them all the time," George replied confidently. He noticed that Mileka was taking in every word.

"Oh, yeah? Where at?" Nicky demanded.

"Kahana," George said. "The other side of Black Rock."

"Okay, let's surf there tomorrow," Nicky said.

"Look, I've got a business to run."

"You chicken?" Nicky taunted. "Afraid I'll show you up?"

George didn't have to look at Mileka to know she was again appraising him. What the hell do you care? he asked himself. She's just another sun bunny — Lahaina Town was crawling with them. Nevertheless, he said, "Okay, Kahana tomorrow at sunrise."

As George walked away, he heard Nicky ask, "Did I look better than him out there?"

And he heard Mileka reply, "You both looked about the same to me."

George couldn't help smiling.

That night George met Nicky and Charley Kula at a small cafe in Wailea. Mileka was with Nicky, but he sent her to play the pinball machines while the men talked.

"You two getting acquainted?" Kula asked, shifting a toothpick from one side of his mouth to the other.

"Yeah, we're surfing buddies now," Nicky said. Something in his tone told George that Nicky didn't like the fat parole officer any more than he did.

"What do you think of my boy Nicky?" Kula asked George.

"Great guy," George replied blandly.

"I knew you two'd get on." Kula leaned forward. "Speaking of business, I checked on the pearl shipment. It'll be in right on schedule Friday afternoon." He looked at Nicky. "You ready to go to work Friday night?"

"I'm ready," Nicky assured him.

"Good. Now, remember, you have to be in and out of the building before eleven o'clock — that's when the night watchman comes on duty. I'll be at my house all evening, so I'll be able to provide an alibi for either of you on the outside chance you need one — I'll say you were with me all evening, helping me in my garden. After the job, you bring the pearls directly to me, Nicky. I'll hang on to them until it's safe to approach a fence to buy the stuff."

"How long before we get any bread out of this?" Nicky wanted to know.

"You'll get your cut as soon as I make the sale. A month probably. Georgie, I'll take care of you out of my share."

I can hardly wait, George thought. Just then a waiter brought their dinner and Nicky waved to Mileka to come join them. "I ordered you a steak and fries," he told her when she came over.

"Okay." She glanced at the plate that was set in front of George. Everyone had steak and fries except him. "What's that?" she asked.

"*Ahi*," he said. When she frowned, he translated, "Yellowfin. It's a tuna."

"You ought to try steak sometime, Keoki," she said.

"Keoki?" Nicky asked, raising his eyebrows.

"That's his Polynesian name."

"Cute," Nicky said dryly.

George felt himself turn red again. Silently he called Mileka a little bitch.

The next morning, George was waiting on Kahana beach when Nicky and Mileka got there.

"Hello Keoki," Mileka teased at once.

"Hello, Mildred," he replied.

Nicky's mouth dropped open. "Mildred?"

"That's what Mileka means in English." George told him. He looked innocently at Mileka, who was glaring at him. "I asked my foster mother last night."

Nicky looked at her incredulously. "I don't believe it. Mildred?" After a moment, he laughed. "That's funny, Mildred!"

"Oh, shut up!" she snapped. "I thought you came here to surf."

Nicky was still laughing as he and George walked down to the water's edge. George looked over his shoulder at Mileka and smiled. She made an obscene gesture at him.

After a good wave broke, George and Nicky put their boards in the water and began paddling out, counting waves as they went. "Remember," George reminded him, "these aren't as tricky as the ones at Kaanapali, they don't twist as much, but they're higher. You'll need a tighter crouch to keep your balance."

"I know how to surf, man," Nicky said.

Okay, big shot, let's see, George thought. He began to paddle a little faster, to get farther out before the ninth wave swelled. Nicky increased his own paddling to keep up. By the time eight waves rolled under them, they were nearly three hundred yards from shore. When number nine began to rise up in front of them, George yelled, "Looks like a ten-footer!"

Both of them stood and planted their feet firmly against the boards. Their arms extended like gulls spreading their wings. With the lift of the water, they turned, and as they felt themselves being lifted lightly with the swell they had a brief glimpse of Mileka, far away on the beach, standing with her hands on her hips, looking out at them.

Then they made the oblique shift to ride diagonally and she passed from their line of sight as they faced Kahana far to the right of where she stood. It *was* a ten-footer and it lifted them high and sped them along on its sheet of water as if it were frozen and they were city kids sliding on an icy sidewalk.

They rode in until the big wave broke, then maneuvered their boards into a calmer water and coasted until it was shallow enough to jump off.

"Great! That was great!" Nicky exclaimed as they waded in. "Man, it can't get any better than that!"

"Sure it can." George said.

"Huh? What do you mean?"

"At Kapalua," George told him. "Farther up the coast. There the waves are high *and* tricky."

"Let's go there, then." Nicky said at once. "Tomorrow."

George shrugged, "Why not?"

Mileka didn't say good-bye to George when she and Nicky left, but as they were walking away George heard Nicky ask, "How did I look out there?"

"You looked good," Mileka said. Then after a moment she added, "But he looked better."

Early that afternoon, Mileka came into the surfboard shop. Marama had already been there and George was eating his lunch.

"Fish again?" she asked. "What is it this time?"

"*Ono,*" he said. "The fishermen call it *wahoo.* It's a gray game fish."

"Do you eat fish all the time?"

"Yes. My foster father said if a man ate fish every day he'd become a better swimmer and surfer because he'd feel more at home in the ocean"

"Come on, you don't really believe that do you?"

"Yes, I do." Her tone irritated him. "What are you doing here anyway? Another message from Nicky?"

"No. Nicky's taking a nap." Now it was she who blushed slightly. "Look, I came to say I'm sorry. About the name business, teasing you like I was doing. I didn't realize how you felt until you did the same thing to me. Then I realized how dumb it was. Sometimes I can be really stupid."

George grunted softly. "Can't we all."

"Anyway, I'm sorry."

"Forget it," he said. He pushed his plate toward her. "Want half a *wahoo* sandwich?" She hesitated. "Go on, try it, you might like it."

"Okay." Mileka sat and joined him for lunch. Presently she asked, "So how'd you get Poly foster parents? Did they adopt you?"

"Kind of." George turned to gaze out the window, across Front Street at the harbor.

"Maybe I shouldn't have asked," she said when he didn't elaborate.

George shrugged. "It's no secret, really. Thirteen years ago I was in the army, stationed at Fort Shafter over on Oahu. I loved the army — I was going to be a thirty-year man. To me it was the perfect life: soldier all week, drink beer, surf, and get laid every weekend. Except that one weekend it didn't quite work out that way. Four of us were coming back from surfing the north shore and we'd had a little too much to drink. We were cruising along the Nimitz Highway in a convertible one of the guys owned when he lost control of the car, crossed the center line, and crashed head-on into an oncoming car.

"A Hawaiian couple and their two children were killed. My three buddies were killed, too. Seven dead — and I survived. I guess they wanted to make an example out of me as a warning to other servicemen stationed on the island, so they indicted me for manslaughter. I hadn't been driving — but I couldn't prove it. The prosecution couldn't prove that I *had*, but there was enough doubt for the jury to convict me. I got fifteen years. I did eight and then Terangi and Marama helped me get out. They offered to provide me with a job and a place to live, and talked to the parole board. The parole board was very impressed by their interest — because the woman killed in the other car had been their daughter. I guess the board figured that if Terangi and Marama could forgive me, so could they. So five years ago I got out and came here to Maui. Terangi and Marama treated me like a son from the first day."

"They sound like wonderful people," Mileka said quietly.

"The best," George said.

Mileka studied him for a moment, then asked, "You don't like being in on this job Nicky's doing, do you?"

He shook his head. "I'm in it because of Kula. I don't want to go back to prison."

"Neither does Nicky." She took one of his hands and held it for a moment. "It'll be okay, Keoki," she said, and this time she spoke his Polynesian name naturally, without teasing. "Things will work out all right."

Yes they would, George thought, nodding slightly.

Because he would *make* them work out all right.

Off Kapalua beach the next morning, George and Nicky paddled out a hundred yards, let a six-foot wave roll under them, and *then* began to count waves as they pushed farther out to sea. By the time they had counted eight waves, they were four hundred yards from the beach and facing a twelve-foot swell that was twisting forty degrees to their right. Getting upright on their boards, they turned almost fully around instead of diagonally, braced, crouched, sucked in air, and stopped breathing as the water lifted them like so much driftwood and seemed to hold them aloft for a split instant before rolling under them and rushing them back toward the beach. As their journey began, they breathed again, moving as if in flight, seemingly weightless, soaring along smoothly in defiance of magnetic gravity, marine physics, and mortal fear. For as long as they rode the crest of the wave, they were greater than other men.

When it was over, they waded back onto the beach and dropped to the sand, their chests heaving as the tension of the ride slowly gave way to the calm and safety of land.

"Man" said Nicky, "I never got a charge out of surfing like I get when I surf with you. There's something about the way you know the ocean — it's almost spooky." He propped up on one elbow and glanced at Mileka, who lay sunning farther up the beach. "Look, tonight's the job. When it's over, I figured we'd go our separate ways. But I been thinking. After the payoff, why don't we take a trip together? A surfing trip. We could head down to Peru for the season there, then move on to eastern Australia — hell, we could just follow the waves wherever they were breaking."

George sat up and hugged his knees. "What about her?" he asked, bobbing his chin at Mileka.

"I'll dump her," Nicky said without hesitation. "She's just a sun bunny — there'll be plenty like her wherever we go. Look, my share of tonight's job, and whatever Kula gives you for helping me, ought to last us a year, maybe a year and a half. And when it's gone, we'll find a way to get more. It's the chance of a lifetime, Georgie. What do you say, man?"

George seemed to ponder the proposition for a long moment, but presently he nodded and smiled at Nicky Dade. "Count me in."

"Far out!" Nicky all but cheered. Glancing toward Mileka again, he quickly lowered his voice. "Our little secret, right?"

George winked at him. "Right."

That evening, George flew to Oahu on the six o'clock Aloha flight. Nicky, who had gone over at noon, met him outside the airport in a rental car. When Nicky saw the look on George's face, he asked at once, "What's wrong, man?"

"We've got a problem," George said tensely. He handed Nicky the pink carbon of an airline ticket confirmation from a Maui travel agency. It was a one-way ticket on the next morning's Continental flight to San Francisco in the name of Charles Kula. Looking at it, Nicky frowned.

"I don't understand."

"A friend of mine works in the travel agency," George said. "He knows Kula's my parole officer. This afternoon he mentioned to me that Kula was flying to the mainland tomorrow. I had my friend get me a copy of the ticket confirmation, just to be sure." Nicky was now staring incredulously at George. "He's crossing us, man," George concluded simply. "It's a one-way ticket. He's taking the pearls and skipping."

Nicky's eyes scanned the confirmation again. "The dirty bastard," he whispered.

"We'll have to call off the job," George said.

"No!" Nicky snapped. "We're not calling off nothing! I'm not giving up my surfing trip because of this bastard. Besides, this job is too cushy to call off. We'll just do to him what he was going to do to us: take the pearls and skip."

"No good," George vetoed. "He'd find a way to finger us without involving himself. He's the law, remember, and we're ex-cons. We'd better call it off."

"No! We're going to pull this job, man, just like we planned!" Nicky was staring out the windshield as if transfixed. "After we pull it, I'll figure out how to handle Mr. Charles Kula."

Nicky pulled away from the airport and drove into Honolulu. He parked on a side street off busy Kalakaua Avenue, where the costume jewelry firm's office building was located. He and George walked around the area for an hour as Nicky briefed him. "Kalakaua's a big tourist street now: lots of shops, places to eat, lots of bars. There's usually people on the street until midnight or later. That's our building over there —"

George looked at a rather ordinary five-story structure that rose above a large drugstore. On one side of the drugstore was the entrance to an underground garage. Stretching beyond it was a string of souvenir shops: T-shirts, seashells, monkey-pod carvings, muumuus. Shoppers were everywhere.

Just before nine o'clock, Nicky said, "Okay let's go."

They returned to the car and Nicky drove directly to the building and into the underground garage. It was only about one-third full, most of the building's employees having left for the day. Nicky parked as close as he could to a door marked: ELECTRICAL ROOM — AUTHORIZED PERSONNEL ONLY. Opening the trunk of the car, he said, "Stay here. Bend over the trunk like you're looking for something. If anybody comes, drop the tire iron on the floor."

He walked away, pulling on a pair of gloves. George saw him take something from his pocket and briefly do something with the lock of the electrical room door. The door opened almost at once and Nicky disappeared inside. Waiting at the trunk, George began to sweat.

In less than five minutes, Nicky was back. "Okay, the alarm's crossed," he said. He took a briefcase from the trunk. "Come on."

They rode the elevator from the garage up to three. No one got on with them and they encountered no one in the hall. "I can't believe there's a fortune in pearls just lying around this place," George said in a tense whisper.

"I told you, it's a cushy job," Nicky whispered back. "Now you see why I wouldn't call it off?" They reached a door with lettering on a frosted-glass pane that read PACIFIC-ORIENT COSTUME JEWELRY CO., LTD. "Watch the elevator indicator," Nicky instructed. "If the light comes on, nudge me and we'll both walk away from the door. Same thing if anyone comes out of another office." He immediately went to work on the door's lock.

The elevator light did not come on and within a minute Nicky had the door open and was pulling George inside. Nicky had him wait just inside the door to listen for any sound from the hallway. He himself disappeared into one of the inner offices. George began to sweat again. At one point while he was standing there, he heard the sound of footsteps going by in the hall, and for a fleeting moment he thought he was going to be sick. He could challenge the widow-maker atop a rolling wave three times his height, but standing in a dark office at night was something else entirely.

Nicky seemed to take forever in the other room. Several times George heard vague metallic sounds and soft, muted tapping, but aside from that there was only silence. In the light from a nearby outside window, George could see a water cooler. It was sorely tempting as he felt his mouth go drier and drier, but he didn't want to leave his place at the door — somehow being next to the door seemed safer.

After what seemed like half the night, Nicky was suddenly back at his side. "Check the hall."

George opened the door a crack, using a handkerchief around the door knob. The hall was clear. They left quickly, walking briskly back down to the elevator. Waiting there, Nicky grinned and shook the briefcase once. It sounded as if it was full of dried peas.

Back in the car, Nicky handed the briefcase to George. "I'm gonna drop you at a taxi stand. Go back out to the airport and wait for me around the Aloha ticket counter."

"Where are you going?"

"To see Kula," Nicky smiled coldly. "I want to be the one to tell him that his trip to San Francisco tomorrow has been canceled."

"You sure you know what you're doing?" George asked.

"I know exactly what I'm doing, man."

At the Royal Hawaiian taxi queue, Nicky pulled over and left the engine running. For just an instant, he seemed to hesitate. George knew at once what he was thinking.

"Don't worry," he said easily. "I'll be at the airport when you get there." He patted the briefcase. "And so will this."

Nicky nodded and drove off.

George had to wait in the airport four hours. Then he and Nicky had to wait another two hours for the first early-morning commuter flight back to Maui. The sun was just breaking on the ocean horizon as the twin-engine Otter set down on the airstrip at Kahului.

Both men had been silent during the flight. The night's events lay heavily between them. When Nicky had arrived back at the Honolulu airport, George had immediately asked, "What happened?"

"It's all settled with Kula," Nicky had replied tightly.

"What happened?" George asked again. Nicky glanced around. They were sitting alone in a corner of the passenger terminal.

"I bashed his double-crossing head in with a tire iron," Nicky told him coldly. "Then I put him in the trunk and drove out to Kaneana. You know where that is?"

George nodded. "It's out the Farrington Highway. Out where the underwater caves are."

"Right. I dumped him off the cliff right above the caves."

George swallowed. "Sharks feed in those caves."

"All the time," Nicky had confirmed in a whisper.

Now they were walking out of the Kahului airport toward the parking lot where George had left the old Plymouth that used to belong to Terangi. Nicky, carrying the briefcase, put it on his lap when he got in the car. As George started the engine, he said almost to himself, "Man, I've got an edge on. I need to unwind. After I drop you, I'm hitting the waves."

"I'll go with you," Nicky said. "We'll just stop by and pick up my board."

George shook his head. "Not today. I need a real challenge. I'm going out to Mokolea Point."

"Where's that?"

"It's out past where the highway ends. Out past Lipoa, where the lighthouse is."

"What's out there?"

"Pipelines," George said. "You ever surf a pipeline?"

Nicky shook his head. Pipelines were the twelve-to-eighteen foot waves that rolled all the way over to form a moving channel of water through which a person could surf — if they were good enough. Fearless enough. Crazy enough.

"I'm going with you," Nicky said.

"You're not good enough to do a pipeline." George kept his tone clinical.

"Up yours," Nicky said. "I'm as good as you are. I'm going."

"Suit yourself," George told him.

They stopped at a little motel in Lahaina Town where Nicky and Mileka had been living. Nicky slipped in and out and got his board without waking her. Then George headed out Honoapiilani Highway and followed it past all the beaches they had surfed together — Kaanapali, Kahana, Kapalua — then on past Lipoa, where the lighthouse stood, and on around to where the paved highway ended and a dirt road began.

The road curved and wound around the natural lay of the craggy rock on which it rested, twisting and turning as if teasing the great ocean with its presence. George drove slowly, guiding the car carefully in tracks left by other vehicles. As on the plane, the two men did not talk, but George noticed that Nicky drummed his fingertips soundlessly on the briefcase that he again held on his lap.

Finally they arrived at a high point above the beach with a precarious path leading down to it. Beyond the beach, the ocean seemed angry. Great churning waves roiled up and rushed the shore as if in attack, not merely to erode but to shatter, to break apart this speck of rock that usurped its vastness.

Nicky put the briefcase of pearls under a blanket in the backseat and George locked the car, hiding the keys under a rock. Then the two men changed into their swim trunks and stood with their boards, looking out from the point.

"This is a *ubane lele*," George said quietly. "It's a sacred place where the souls of the dead leap into their ancestral spirit land."

"You don't really believe that bullshit, do you?" Nicky asked derisively.

"Yes, I do," George replied, staring at the sea.

Shaking his head disdainfully, Nicky started down the steep path. Then he turned back, eyes suspicious, and said, "You first." Containing a knowing smile, George led the way down to the beach.

There they waited for the next pipeline to break, then plunged in and started paddling. Even though the sea was turbulent, moving against the tide wasn't difficult — the slender boards pierced the oncoming water with almost no resistance, needling through the waves. When the ninth one broke before them, Nicky yelled, "It's not the pipeline!"

"The *ninth* ninth wave is the pipeline!" George yelled back. "We've got a long way to go!" Nicky was looking at him in astonishment. "Want to turn back?" George challenged.

"Not me, man! I'm in all the way!"

They kept paddling. And counting. The second ninth wave broke. The third ninth wave. Periodically they rested, letting several waves go past without paddling through or over them, moving their hands only enough to keep from losing distance, then they began thrusting again. The passed the fourth ninth wave, the fifth, the sixth and rested some more. Their upper arms burned, hot with fatigue. Their breath came in bursts.

"How far — out are we?" Nicky asked.

"About — eight hundred yards —"

"God!"

"It'll be — a great ride!" George bolstered. "Probably — half a mile!"

The seventh ninth wave broke.

The eighth.

Then it came. The pipeline, rolling up in front of them as if the ocean had been tilted on edge. A sixteen-foot wave that looped back to embrace itself and form a tunnel of spiraling water that skimmed toward landfall with unbridled power.

"Waaaa-hoooo!" George yelled as he rose upright on his board. He caught only a brief glimpse of Nicky, just long enough to see the terror in his face, then the pipeline was upon him and he was in the vortex of it. An embryo in the womb of mother ocean.

George rode the great whirlpool all the way back to the beach. And he was right: it *was* a mile high ride.

He sat on the bluff with a blanket around his shoulders for an hour but Nicky never came out of the water. Score one more for the widow-maker he thought.

He got the briefcase out of the car and opened it. The pearls lay spread inside like white caviar from some giant fish. They came from the ocean, they might as well go back to the ocean, he thought. Scooping up a handful, he flung them from the high bluff out into the water. Then he flung a second handful, a third. At some point, he began to laugh at what he was doing. It was a loud, uncontrollable laugh, growing in volume with each new handful of pearls he threw back to the ocean. He kept throwing and laughing, throwing and laughing. Finally the pearls were all gone and he put a couple of rocks in the briefcase and threw that off the edge too, watching it sink into the water.

From the glove compartment, he took the airline ticket he had bought in Charley Kula's name, and tore it into tiny pieces, releasing the bits to the sea breeze. Then he got into Terangi's old Plymouth and drove back toward Lahaina Town to open his shop.

ANIMALS

As Ned Price got off the city bus at the corner of his block, he saw that Monty and his gang of troublemakers were, as usual, loitering in front of Shavelson's drugstore. A large portable radio — they called it their "ghetto blaster" — was sitting atop a newspaper vending machine, playing very loud acid rock. The gang of six of them, all in their late teens, appeared to be arguing over the contents of a magazine that was circulating among them.

Ned started down the sidewalk. An arthritic limp made him favor his right leg. That, coupled with lumbago and sixty-six years of less than easy living, gave him an overall stooped, tired look. A thrift shop sport coat slightly too large didn't help matters. Ned could have crossed the street and gone around Monty and his friends, but he lived on this side of the street so he would have to cross back again farther down the block. It was difficult enough to get around these days without taking extra steps. Besides, he figured, he had at least as much right to walk down the sidewalk as they did to obstruct it.

When Ned got closer, he saw the magazine the gang was passing around was *The Ring* and that their argument had to do with the relative merits of two boxers named Hector "Macho" Camacho and Ray "Boom Boom" Mancini. Maybe they'd be too caught up in their argument to hassle him today. That would be a welcome change. A day without having to match wits with this year's version of the Sharks.

But no such luck.

"Hey, old man, where you been?" Monty asked as Ned approached. "Down to pick up your check?" He stepped in the middle of the sidewalk and blocked the way.

Ned stopped. "Yes," he said. "I've been down to pick up my check."

"You're one of those old people who don't let the mailman bring their check, huh?" Monty asked with a smile. "You know there's too many crooks in this neighborhood. You're smart, huh?"

"No, just careful," Ned said. If I was smart, he thought, I would have crossed the street.

"Hey, lemme ask you something," Monty said with mock seriousness. "I seen on a TV special where some old people don't get enough pension to live on an' they eat dogfood and catfood. Do you do that, old man?"

"No, I don't," Ned replied. There was a slight edge to his answer this time. He knew several people who *did* resort to the means Monty had just described.

"Listen, old man, I think you're lying," Monty said without rancor. "I myself seen you in Jamail's Grocery buying catfood."

"That's because I have a cat." Ned tried to step around Monty but the youth moved and blocked his way again.

"You got a cat, old man? Ain't that nice?" Monty feigned interest. "Wha' kind of cat you got, old man?"

"Just an ordinary cat," Ned said. "Nothing special."

"Not a Persian or a Siamese or one of them expensive cats?"

"No. Just an ordinary cat. A tabby, I think it's called."

"A tabby! Hey, tha's really nice."

"Can I go now?" Ned asked.

"Sure," Monty said, shrugging elaborately. "Who's stopping you, old man?"

Ned stepped around him and this time the youth did not interfere with him. As he walked away, Ned heard Monty say something in Spanish and the others laughed. A regular Freddie Prinze, Ned thought.

As Ned entered his third-floor-rear kitchenette, he said, "Molly, I'm back." Double-locking the door securely behind him, he hung his coat on a wooden wall peg and limped into a tiny cluttered living room. "Molly!" he called again. Then he stood still and a cold feeling came over him that he was alone in the apartment. "Molly?"

He stuck his head in the narrow Pullman kitchen, then pushed back a curtain that concealed a tiny sleeping alcove.

"Molly, where are you?"

Even as he asked the question one last time, Ned knew he would not find her. He hurried into the bathroom. The window was open about three inches. Ned raised it all the way and stuck his head out. Three stories below in the alley, some kids were playing kick-the-can. A ledge ran from the window to a back-stairs landing.

"Molly!" Ned called several times.

Moments later, he was out in front looking up and down the street. Monty and his friends, seeing him, sauntered down to where he stood.

"What's the matter old man?' Monty asked. "You lose something?"

"My cat," Ned said. He turned suspicious eyes on Monty and his friends. "You wouldn't have seen her, by any chance, would you?"

"Is there a reward?" Monty asked.

Ned gave the question quick consideration. There was on old watch of his late wife's he could probably sell. "There might be, if the cat isn't harmed. Do you know where she is?"

Monty turned to the others. "Anybody see this old man's cat?" he asked with a total absence of concern. When they all shrugged and declared ignorance, he said to Ned, "Sorry, old man. If you'd let the mailman deliver your check, you'd have been home to look after you cat. See the price you pay for being greedy?" He strutted off down the street, his followers in his wake. Feeling ill, Ned watched them all the way to the corner, where they turned out of sight. Pain from an old ulcer began as acid churned in his stomach.

"Molly!" he called and started walking down the block. "Molly! Here kitty, kitty."

He searched for her until well after dark.

Ned was up early the next morning and back outside looking. He scoured the block all the way to the corner, then came back the other way. In front of the drugstore, he encountered Monty again. The youth was alone this time, leaning up against the building, eating a jelly doughnut and drinking milk from a pint carton.

"You still looking for that cat, old man?" Monty asked, his tone a mixture of incredulity and irritation.

"Yes."

"Man, why don't you go in the alley and get another one? There mus' be a dozen cats back there."

"I want this cat. It belonged to my wife when she was alive."

"Hell, man, a cat's a cat," Monty said.

Shavelson, the drugstore owner, came out, broom in hand. "Want to make a half a buck sweeping the sidewalk?" he asked Monty, who looked at him as if he were an imbecile, then turned away disdainfully, not even dignifying the question with an answer. Shavelson shrugged and began sweeping debris toward the curb himself. "You're out early," he said to Ned.

"My cat's lost," Ned said. "She may have got out the bathroom window while I was downtown yesterday."

"Why don't you go back in the alley —"

Ned was already shaking his head. "I want *this* cat."

"Maybe the pound got her," Shavelson suggested. "Their truck was all over the neighborhood yesterday."

The storekeeper's words sent a chill along Ned's spine. "The pound?"

"Yeah. You know, the city animal shelter. They have a truck comes around —"

"It was here yesterday? On this block?"

"Yeah."

"Where do they take the animals they catch?" Ned asked out of a rapidly drying mouth.

"The animal shelter over on Twelfth Street, I think. They have to hold them there seventy-two-hours to see if anybody claims them."

Too distressed by the thought to thank Shavelson, Ned hurried back up the street and into his building. Five minutes later, he emerged again, wearing a coat, his city bus pass in one hand. Crossing the street, he went to the bus stop and stood peering down the street, as if by sheer will he could make a bus appear.

Monty, having finished his doughnut and milk, sat on the curb in front of Shavelson's, smoking a cigarette and reading one of the morning editions from the drugstore's sidewalk newspaper rack. From time to time he glanced over at Ned, wondering at his concern over a cat. Monty knew a few backyards in the neighborhood that were knee-deep in cats.

Presently it began to sprinkle light rain. Monty stood up, folding the newspaper, and handed it to Shavelson as the storekeeper came out to move his papers inside.

"You sure you're through with it?" Shavelson asked. "Any coupons or anything you 'd like to tear out?"

Monty's eyes narrowed a fraction. "Someday, man, you're gonna say the wrong thing to me," he warned. "Then you're gonna come to open up your store and you gonna find a pile of ashes."

"You'd do that for *me?*" Shavelson retorted.

The sprinkle escalated to a drizzle as the storekeeper went back inside. From the doorway, Monty looked over at the bus stop again. Ned was still standing there, his only concession to the rain being a turned-up collar. I don't believe this old fool, Monty thought. He goes to more trouble for this cat than most people do for their kids.

Tossing his cigarette into the gutter, he trotted down the block and got into an old Chevy that had a pair of oversize velvet dice dangling from the rearview mirror. Revving the engine a little, he listened with satisfaction to the rumble of the car's gutted muffler, then made a U-turn from the curb and drove to the bus stop.

"Get in, old man," he said, leaning over to the passenger window. "I'm going past Twelfth Street — I'll give you a lift."

Ned eyed him suspiciously. "No thanks. I'll wait for the bus."

"Hey, man, waiting for a bus in this city at your age ain't too smart. An old lady over on Bates Street *died* at a bus stop last week, she was there so long. Besides, in case you ain't noticed, it's raining." Monty's voice softened a touch. "Come on, get in."

Ned glanced up the street one last time, saw that there was still no bus in sight, thought of Molly caged up at the pound, and got in.

As they rode along, Monty lighted another cigarette and glanced over at his passenger. "You thought me and my boys did something with your cat, didn't you?"

"The thought did cross my mind," Ned admitted.

"Listen, I got better things to do with my time than mess with some cat. You know, for an old guy you ain't very smart."

Ned grunted softly. "I won't argue with you there," he said.

On Twelfth, Monty pulled to the curb in front of the animal shelter. "I got to go see a guy near here, take me about fifteen minutes. I'll come back and pick you up after you get your cat."

Ned studied him for a moment. "Is there some kind of Teenager of the Year award I don't know about?"

"Very funny, man. You're a regular, what's his name, Jack Albertson, ain't' you?"

At the information counter in the animal shelter, a woman with tightly styled hair and a superior attitude asked, "Was the animal wearing a license tag on its collar?"

"No, she —"

"Was the animal wearing an ID tag on its collar?"

"No, she wasn't wearing a collar. She's really an apartment cat, you see —"

"Sir," the woman said, "our animal enforcement officers don't go into apartments and take animals."

"I think she got out the bathroom window."

"That makes her a street animal, unlicensed and unidentifiable."

'Oh, I can identify her," Ned assured the woman. "And she'll come to me when I call her. If you'll just let me see the cats you picked up yesterday —"

"Sir, do you have any idea how many stray animals are picked up by our trucks every day?"

"Why, no, I never gave —"

"*Hundreds*," he was told. "Only the ones with license tags or ID tags are kept at the shelter."

"I thought all animals had to be kept here for three days to give their owners time to claim them," Ned said, remembering what Shavelson had told him.

"You're not listening, sir. Only the animals with license or ID tags are kept at the shelter for the legally required seventy-two hours. Those without tags are taken directly to the disposal pound."

Ned turned white. "Is that where they — where they — ?" The words would not form.

"Yes, that is where stray animals are put to sleep." She paused a beat. "Either that or sold."

Ned frowned. "Sold?"

"Yes, sir. To laboratories. To help offset the overhead of operating our department." Her eyes flicked over Ned's shabby clothing. "Tax dollars don't pay for *everything*, you know." But she had unknowingly given Ned an ember of hope.

"Can you give me the address of this — disposal place?"

The woman scribbled an address on a slip of paper and pushed it across the counter to him. "Your cat might still be there," she allowed, "if it was picked up late yesterday. Disposal hours for cats are from one to three. If it was a dog you'd be out of luck. They do dogs at night, eight to eleven, because there are more of them. That's because they're easier to catch. They trust people. Cats, they don't trust —"

She was still talking as Ned snatched up the address and hurried out.

Monty was waiting at the curb.

"I didn't think you'd be back this quick," Ned said, getting into the car.

"The guy I went to see wasn't there," Monty told him. It was a lie. All he had done was drive around the block.

"They've taken my cat to be gassed," Ned said urgently, "but if I can get there in time, I might be able to save her." He handed Monty the slip of paper. "This is the address. It's way out at the edge of town, but if you'll take me there I'll pay you." He pulled out a pathetically worn billfold, the old-fashioned kind that zipped around three sides. When he opened it, Monty could see several faded cellophane inserts with photographs in them. The photographs were old, all in black-and-white except for a paper picture of June Allyson that had come with the billfold.

From the currency pocket Ned extracted some bills, all of them singles.

"I don't have much because I haven't cashed my check yet. But I can at least buy some gas."

Monty pushed away the hand with the money and started the car. "I don't *buy* gas, man," he scoffed. "I quit buying it when it got to be a dollar a gallon."

"Where do you get it?" Ned asked.

"I siphon it. From police cars parked behind the precinct station. It's the only place where cars are left on a lot unguarded." He flashed a smile at Ned. "That's because nobody would *dare* siphon gas from a cop car, you know what I mean?"

They got on one of the expressways and drove toward the edge of the city. As Monty drove, he smoked and kept time to rock music from the radio by drumming his fingers on the steering wheel. Ned glanced at a scar down the youth's right cheek. Thin and straight, almost surgical in appearance, it had probably been put there by a straight razor. Ned had been curious about the scar for a long time. Now would be an opportune time to ask how he got it, but Ned was too concerned about Molly. She was such an old cat, nearly fourteen. He hoped she hadn't died of a stroke from the trauma of being captured and caged. If she was still alive, she was going to be so glad to see him, Ned doubted she would ever climb out the bathroom window again.

After half an hour on the expressway, Monty exited and drove them to a large warehouse like building at the edge of the city's water-treatment center. A sign above the entrance read simply: ANIMAL SHELTER — UNIT F.

F for final, Ned thought. He was already opening his door as Monty brought the car to a full stop.

"Want me to come in with you?" Monty asked.

"What for?" Ned wanted to know, frowning.

The younger man shrugged. "So's they don't push you around. Sometimes people push old guys around."

"Really?" Ned asked wryly.

Monty looked off at nothing. "You want me to come in or not?"

"I can handle things myself," Ned told him gruffly.

The clerk at this counter, a thin, gum-chewing young man with half a dozen ball-points in a plastic holder in his shirt pocket, checked a clipboard on the wall and said, "Nope, you're too late. That whole bunch from yesterday was shipped out to one of our lab customers early this morning."

Ned felt warm and slightly nauseated. "Do you think they might sell my cat back to me?" he asked. "If I went over there?"

"You can't go over there," the clerk said. "We're not allowed to divulge the name or address of any of our lab customers."

"Oh," Ned wet his lips. "Do you suppose you could call them for me? Tell them I'd like to make some kind of arrangements to buy back my cat?"

The clerk was already shaking his head. "I don't have time to do things like that, mister."

"A simple phone call," Ned pleaded. "It'll only take —"

"Look, mister, I said no. I'm a very busy person,"

Just then someone stepped up to the counter next to Ned. Surprised, Ned saw that it was Monty. He had his hands on the counter, palms down, and was smiling at the clerk.

"What time do you get off work, Very Busy Person?" he asked.

The clerk blinked rapidly. "Uh, why do you want to know?"

"I'm jus' interested in what kind of hours a Very Busy Person like you keeps." Monty's smile faded and his stare grew cold. "You don't have to tell me if you don't want to. I can wait outside and find out for myself."

The clerk stopped chewing his gum, the color disappeared from his face, leaving him sickly pale. "Why, uh — why would you do that?"

" 'Cause I ain't got nothing better to do," Monty replied. "I *was* gonna take this old man here to that lab to try and get his cat back. But if he don't know where it is, I can't do that. So I'll just hang around here." He winked at the clerk without smiling. "See you later, man."

Monty took Ned's arm and started him toward the door.

"Just — wait a minute," the clerk said.

Monty and Ned turned back to see him rummaging in a drawer under the counter. He found a sheet of paper with three names and addresses mimeographed on it. With a ball-point from the selection in his shirt pocket, he circled one of the addresses. Monty stepped back to the counter and took the sheet of paper.

"If it turns out they're expecting us," Monty said, "I'll know who warned them. You take my meaning, man?"

The clerk nodded. He swallowed dryly and his gum was gone.

At the door, looking at the address circled on the paper, Monty said, "Come on, old man. This here place is clear across town. You positive one of them cats in the alley wouldn't do you?"

On the way to the lab, Ned asked, "Why are you helping me like this?"

Monty shrugged. "It's a slow Wednesday, man."

Ned studied the younger man for a time, then observed, "You're different when your gang's not around."

Monty tossed him a smirk. "You gonna, what do you call it, analyze me, old man? You gonna tell me I got 'redeeming social values' or something like that?"

"I wouldn't go quite that far." Ned said dryly. "Anyway, sounds to me like you've *been* analyzed."

"Lots of times," Monty told him. "When they took me away from my old lady because it was an 'unfit environment,' they had some shrink analyze me then. When I ran away from the foster homes I was put in, other shrinks analyzed me. After I was arrested and was waiting trial in juvenile court for some burglaries, I was analyzed again. When they sent me down-state to the reformatory, I was analyzed. They're very big on analyzing in this state."

"They ever tell you the results of all that analyzing?"

"Sure. I'm incorrigible. And someday I'm supposed to develop into a sociopath. You know what that is?"

"Not exactly," Ned admitted.

Monty shrugged. "Me neither. I guess I'll find out when I become one."

They rode in silence for a few moments and then Ned said, "Well, anyway, I appreciate you helping me."

"Forget it," Monty said. He would not look at Ned; his eyes were straight ahead on the road. After several seconds, he added. "Jus' don't go telling nobody about it."

"All right, I won't," Ned agreed.

Their destination on the other side of the city was a large square two-story building on the edge of a forest preserve. It was surrounded by a chain-link fence with an entrance gate manned by a security guard. A sign on the gate read: CONSUMER EVALUATION LABORATORY.

Monty parked outside the gate and followed Ned over to the security-guard post. Ned explained what he wanted. The security guard took off his cap and scratched his head. "I don't know. This isn't covered in my guard manual. I'll have to call and find out if they sell animals back."

Ned and Monty waited while the guard telephoned. He talked to one person, was transferred to another, then had to repeat his story to still a third before he finally hung up and said, "Mr. Hartley of Public Relations is coming out to talk to you."

Mr. Hartley was a pleasant but firmly uncooperative man. "I'm sorry, but we can't help you," he said when Ned had told him of Molly's plight. "We have at least a hundred small animals in there — cats, dogs, rabbits, guinea pigs — all of them undergoing scientific tests. Even the shipment we received this morning has already been processed into a testing phase. We simply can't interrupt the procedure to find one particular cat."

"But it's *my* cat," Ned insisted. "She's not homeless or a stray. She belonged to my late wife —"

"I understand that, Mr. Price," Hartley interrupted, "but the animal *was* outside with no license or ID tag around its neck. It was apprehended legally and sold to us legally. I'm afraid it's just too late."

As they were talking, a bus pulled up to the gate. Hartley waved at the driver then turned to the security guard. "These are the people from Diamonds-and-Pearls Cosmetics, Fred. Pass them through and then call Mr. Draper. He's conducting a tour for them."

As the bus passed through, Hartley turned back to resume the argument with Ned, but Monty stepped forward to intercede.

"We understand Mr. Hartley," Monty said in a remarkably civil tone. "We're sure you'd help us if you could. Please accept our apology for taking up your time." Monty offered his head.

"Quite all right," Hartley said, shaking hands.

Ned was staring incredulously at Monty; Macho had suddenly become Milquetoast.

"Come along, old fellow," Monty said, putting an arm around Ned's shoulders. "We'll go to a pet store and buy you a new kitty."

Ned allowed himself to be led back to the car, then demanded, "What the hell's got into you?"

"You're wasting your time with that joker," Monty said. "He's been programmed to smile and say no to whatever you want. We got to find some other way to get your cat."

"What other way?"

Monty grinned. "Like using the back door, man."

Driving away from the front gate, Monty found a gravel road and slowly circled the fenced-in area of the Consumer Evaluation Laboratory. On each side of the facility, beyond its fence, were several warehouses and small plants. In front, beyond a feeder road, was a state highway. Growing right up to its rear fence was the forest preserve: a state-protected wooded area.

Monty made one full circuit of the complex occupied by the laboratory and its neighbors, then said, "I think the best plan is to park in the woods, get past the fence in back, and sneak in that way."

"You mean slip in and *steal* my cat?" Ned asked.

Monty shrugged. "They stole her from you," he said.

Ned stared at him. "I'm sixty-six years old," he said. "I've never broken the law in my life."

"So?" said Monty, frowning. He did not see any relevance. The two men, one young, one old, each so different from the other, locked eyes in a silent stare for what seemed like a long time.

They were parked on the shoulder of the gravel road, the car windows down. The air coming into the car was fresh from the morning rain. Ned detected the scent of wet earth. Some movement a few yards up the road caught his eye and he turned his attention away from Monty. The movement was a gray squirrel scurrying across the road to the safety of the nearby woods. Watching the little animal, wild and free, made Ned think of the animals in he laboratory that were not free — the dogs and rabbits and guinea pigs.

And cats.

"All right," he told Monty. "Let's go in the back way."

Monty parked in one of the public picnic areas. From the trunk, he removed a pair of chain cutters and held them under his jacket with one hand.

"What do you carry those things for?" Ned asked, and realized at once that his question was naive.

"To clip coupons with, man," Monty replied. "Coupons save you money on everyday necessities."

The two men made their way through the trees to the rear of the laboratory's chain-link fence. Crouching, they scrutinized the back of the complex. Monty's eyes settled immediately on a loading dock served by a single-lane driveway coming around one side of the building. "We can go in there," he said. "Overhang doors are no sweat to open. But first let's see if there's any juice in this fence." Keeping his hands well on the rubber-covered handles, he gently touched the metal fence with the tip of the chain cutters. The contact drew no sparks. "Nothing on the surface," he said. "Let's see if there's anything inside. Some of these newer chain-links have an insulated circuit running through them." Quickly and expertly, he spread the cutters and snipped one link of the metal. Again there were no sparks. "This is going to be a breeze."

With a practiced eye, he determined his pattern and quickly snipped exactly the number of links necessary to create an opening large enough for them to get through. Then he gripped the cut section and bent it open, like a door, about eight inches. The chain cutters he hid nearby in some weeds.

"Now here's our story," he said to Ned. "We was walking through the public woods here and saw this hole cut in the fence, see? We thought it was our civic duty to tell somebody about it so we came inside looking for somebody. If we get caught, stick to that story. Got it?"

"Got it," Ned confirmed.

Monty winked approval. "Let's do it, old man."

They eased through the opening and Monty bent the cut section back into place. Then they started toward the loading dock, walking upright with no attempt at hurrying or hiding. Ned was nervous but Monty remained very cool; he even whistled a soft little tune. When he sensed Ned's anxiety, he threw him a grin.

"Relax, old man. It'll take us forty, maybe fifty seconds to reach that dock. The chances of somebody seeing us in that little bit of time are so tiny, man. And even if they do, so what? We got our story, right?"

"Yeah, right," Ned replied, trying to sound confident. But as Monty predicted, they reached the loading dock unobserved and unchallenged. Once up on the dock, Monty peered through a small window in one of the doors. "Just a big room with a lot of work tables," he said quietly, "Don't look like nobody's around. Hey, this service door's unlocked. Come on."

They moved inside into a large room equipped with butcher-block tables fixed to a tile floor. A number of hoses hung over each table, connected to the ceiling. As the two men stood scrutinizing the room, they suddenly heard a voice approaching. Quickly they ducked behind one of the tables.

An inner door opened and a man led a group of people into the room, saying, "This is our receiving area, ladies and gentlemen. The animals we purchase are delivered here and our laboratory technicians use these tables to wash and delouse them. They are then taken into our testing laboratory next door, which I will show you next. If you would, please take a smock from the pile there, to protect your clothes from a possible contact with any of the substances we use in there."

Peering around the table, Ned and Monty watched as the people put on smocks and regrouped at the door. As they were filing out, Ned nudged Monty and said, "Come on."

Monty grinned. "You catching on, old man."

The two put on smocks and fell in at the rear of the group. They followed along as it was led through the hall and into a much larger room. This one was set up with a series of aisles formed by long work counters on which stood wire-grille cages of various sizes. Each cage was numbered and had a small slot containing a white card on its door. In each cage was a live animal.

"Our testing facility, we feel, is the best of its kind currently in existence," the tour guide said. "As you can see, we have a variety of test animals: cats, dogs, rabbits, guinea pigs. We also have access to larger animals, if a particular test requires it. Our testing procedures can be in any form. We can force-feed the test substance, introduce it by forced inhalation, reduce it to a dermal form and apply it directly to an animal's shaved skin, or inject it intravenously. Over here, for instance, are rabbits being given what is known as a Draize test. A new hairspray is being sprayed into their very sensitive eyes in order to gauge its irritancy level. Just behind the rabbits you see a group of puppies having dishwashing detergent introduced directly into their stomachs by a syringe with a tube attached to a hand pump. This is called an Internal LD-50 test; the LD stands for lethal dose and the number fifty represents one-half of a group of one hundred animals on which the test will be conducted. When half of the test group has died, we will have an accurate measurement of the toxicity level of this product. This will provide the company marketing the product with evidence of safety testing in case it is later sued because some child swallowed the detergent and dies. During the course of the testing, we also learn exactly how a particular substance will affect a living body, by observing whatever symptoms the animal exhibits: convulsions, paralysis, tremors, inability to breathe, blindness as in the case of the rabbits there —"

Ned was staring at the scene around him. As he looked at the helpless, caged, tortured animals, he felt his skin crawl. Which were the animals: the ones in the cages, or the ones outside the cages? Glancing at Monty, he saw the younger man was reacting the same way — his eyes were wide, his expression incredulous, and his hands were curled into fists.

"We can test virtually any substance or product there is," the guide continued. "We test all forms of cosmetics and beauty aids, all varieties of detergents and other cleaning products, every food additive, coloring, and preservative, any new chemical or drug product — you name it. In addition to servicing private business, we test pesticides for the Environmental Protection Agency, synthetic substances for the Food and Drug Administration, and a variety of products for the Consumer Products Safety Commission. Our facility is set up so that almost no lead time is required to service our customers, As an example of this, a dozen cats brought in this morning are already in a testing phase over here —"

Ned and Monty followed the group to another aisle where the guide pointed out the newly arrived cats and explained the test being applied to them. Ned strained to see beyond the people in front of him, trying to locate Molly.

Finally the tour guide said, "Now, ladies and gentlemen, if you'll follow me, I'll take you to our cafeteria, where you can enjoy some refreshments while our testing personnel answer any questions you have about how we can help Diamonds-and-Pearls Cosmetics keep its products free of costly lawsuits. Just drop your smocks on the table outside the door."

Again Ned and Monty ducked down behind a workbench to conceal themselves as the people filed out of the room. When the door closed behind the group, Ned rose and hurried to the cat cages. Monty went over to lock the laboratory door.

Ned found Molly in one of the top cages. She was lying on her side, eyes wide, staring into space. The back part of her body had been shaved and three intravenous needles were stuck in her skin and held in place by tape. The tubes attached to the needles ran out the grille and up to three small bottles suspended above the cage. The were labeled: FRAGRANCE, DYE and POLYSORBATE 93.

Ned wiped his eyes with the heel of one hand. Unlatching the grille door, he reached in and stroked Molly. "Hello, old girl," he said. Molly opened her mouth to meow, but no sound came.

"Dirty bastards," Ned heard Monty whisper. Turning, he saw the younger man reading the card on the front of Molly's cage. "This is some stuff that's going to be used in a hair tint," he said. "This test is to see if the cat can stay alive five hours with this combination of stuff in her."

"I can answer that," Ned said. "She won't. She's barely alive now."

"If we can get her to a vet, maybe he can save her," Monty suggested. "Pump her stomach or something." He bobbed his chin at the back wall. "We can get out through one of those windows — they face our hole in the fence."

"Get one open," Ned said. "I'll take Molly out."

Monty hurried over to the window while Ned gently unfastened the tape and pulled the hypodermic needles out of Molly's flesh. Once again the old cat looked at him and tried to make a sound, but she was too weak and too near death. "I know old girl," Ned said softly. "I know it hurts,"

Near the window, after opening it, Monty noticed several cages containing puppies that were up and moving around, some of them barking and wagging their tails. Monty quickly opened their cages, scooped them out two at a time, and dropped them out the window.

"Lead these pups to the fence, old man," he said as Ned came over with Molly.

"Right," Ned replied. He let Monty hold the dying cat as he painfully got his arthritic legs over the ledge and lowered himself to the ground. "What about you?" he asked as Monty handed down the cat.

"I'm gonna turn a few more pups loose, an' maybe some of those rabbits they're blinding. You head for the fence — I'll catch up."

Ned limped away from the building, calling the pups to follow him. He led them to the fence, bent the cut section open again, and let them scurry through. As he went through himself, he could feel Molly becoming even more limp in his hands. By the time he got into the cover of the trees, her eyes had closed, her mouth had opened, and she was dead. Tears coming again, he knelt and put the cat up against a tree trunk and covered her with an old red bandanna he pulled out of his back pocket.

Looking through the fence, he saw that Monty was still putting animals out the window. Two dozen cats, dogs, rabbits, and guinea pigs were moving around tentatively on the grass behind the laboratory. He's got to get out of there or he'll get caught, Ned thought. Returning through the opening in the fence, he hurried back to the window.

"Come on," he urged as the younger man came to the window with a kitten in each hand.

"No!" Monty tossed the kittens to the ground. "I'm going to turn loose every animal that can stand!"

Old man and young man fixed eyes on each other as every difference there had ever been between them faded.

"Give me a hand up, then." Ned said.

Monty reached down and pulled him back up through the window.

As they worked furiously to open more cages and move their captives out the window, they became aware of someone trying the lab door and finding it locked. Several moments later, someone tried it again. A voice outside the door mentioned a key. The two inside the lab worked all the faster. Finally, a sweating Monty said, "I think that's all we can let go. The rest are too near dead. Let's get out of here!"

"I'm going to do one more thing first," Ned growled.

Poised by the open window, Monty asked, "What?"

Ned walked toward a shelf on which stood several plastic gallon jugs of isopropyl alcohol. "I'm going to burn this son-of-a-bitch down."

Monty rushed over to him. "What about the other animals?"

"You said yourself they were almost dead. At least this will put them out of their misery without any more torture." He opened a jug and started pouring alcohol around the room. After a moment of indecision, Monty joined him.

Five minutes later, just as someone in the hall got the lab door open and several people entered, Ned and Monty dropped out the open widow and tossed a lighted book of matches back inside.

The laboratory became a ball of flame.

While the fire spread and the building burned, Ned and Monty managed to get the released animals through the fence and into the woods, Sirens of fire and police emergency vehicles pierced the quiet afternoon. There were screams and shouts as the burning building was evacuated. Monty retrieved the chain cutters and ran toward the car. Ned limped hurriedly after him, but stopped when he got to where Molly was lying under the red bandanna. I can't leave her like that, he thought. She had been a good, loving pet to Ned's wife, then to Ned after his wife died. She deserved to be buried, not left to rot next to a tree. Dropping to his knees, he began to dig a grave with his hands.

Monty rushed back and saw what he was doing. "They gonna catch you, old man!" he warned.

"I don't care."

Ned kept digging as Monty hurried away.

He had barely finished burying Molly a few minutes later when the police found him.

Ned's sentence, because he was a first offender and no one had been hurt in the fire, was three years. He served fourteen months. Monty was waiting for him the day he came back to the block.

"Hey, old man, ex-cons give a neighborhood a bad reputation," Monty chided.

"You ought to know," Ned said gruffly

"You get the Vienna sausages and crackers and stuff I had sent from the commissary?"

"Yeah." He did not bother to thank Monty; he knew it would only embarrass him.

"So how you like the joint, old man?"

Ned shrugged. "It could have been worse. A man my age with a game leg, there's not much they could do to me. I worked in the library, checking books out. Did a lot of reading in between. Mostly about animals."

"No kidding?" Monty's eyebrows went up. "I been learning a little bit about animals, too. I'm a, what do you call it, volunteer down at the A.S.P.C.A. That's American Society for the Prevention of Cruelty to Animals."

"I know what it is," said Ned. "Good organization. Say, did that Consumer Evaluation Laboratory ever rebuild?"

"Nope," Monty replied. "You put 'em out of business for good, old man."

"Animal shelter still selling to those other two labs?"

"Far as I know."

"Still got their addresses?"

Monty smiled. "You bet."

"Good," Ned said, nodding. Then he smiled too.

SCALPLOCK

Rita saw the young man as he came out of the Las Vegas bus depot and stood at the curb looking at the brilliant lights of the Union Plaza Hotel and Casino. She was working across the street because the Union Plaza security guards did not permit street girls near the hotel. Normally, Rita would have ignored the young man; he looked too country to risk crossing the street for: old faded Levi's, worn Western boots, a khaki shirt like gas-station attendants wore, cheap suitcase. He appeared to be deeply tanned under a straw Western hat, so she figured he was a cowboy or construction worker. Probably didn't have two twenties to fold together. Still, you never knew. Business had been such a bitch all night long. Plus which she was on her own now, had been for a week, since Greg, her boyfriend, had taken off for San Francisco. She decided to take a chance and cross the street.

Keeping a wary eye out for Union Plaza security, Rita sauntered across Main toward the depot. She had lost some weight the past few weeks — the heat of August in the desert, she guessed. Her mini-skirt did not fit as snugly as she would have liked. For that same reason, she now had to open an additional button on her blouse to show any cleavage at all. Still, she knew she looked better than most girls on the street. Her main problem was making sure her true age didn't show — she had to appear at least eighteen or it spooked customers.

"Hi, there," she said, stopping next to the young man at the curb.

"Hello," he replied, with only a glance. Rita saw now that he wasn't suntanned at all; his skin was naturally clay-colored, and his hair under the straw hat, his eyebrows, even his eyeballs, were black and shiny. Maybe he's Mexican, she thought.

"Waiting for somebody?" she asked.

He glanced at her again. "No."

"Looking for a cab? A bus maybe?"

"No."

Rita nodded resignedly. "Okay. You're going to stand here all night, right?"

He fished a slip of paper out of his shirt pocket. "Do you know where this is at?"

Rita looked at the paper. On it was written the address of some low-rent apartments on West Sahara Boulevard. "Sure, I know where it's at." Thinking quickly, she said, "Listen, if you're not in any big hurry to get there, I have an apartment a couple of blocks from here. Maybe you and I could — "

"I would like to go to this place as soon as I can," he said, taking back the slip of paper. "Will you tell me how to get there?"

Wonderful, Rita thought. She had taken a chance of being shagged by Union Plaza security to play Travelers Aid. "Okay," she said, a little exasperated. "Go down to the corner there and take a bus that has 'Las Vegas Strip' on the front — "

"Tell me how to walk there, please," he interrupted.

"*Walk* there? In this heat? This is the *desert*. It's six or seven miles."

"I will walk. Tell me, please."

Rita shrugged and gave him directions. Main to Wyoming and Highland to Sahara, then turn right and look for the number.

"Wyoming?" he said, looking surprised. "There is a street here named Wyoming? Is there one named Montana?"

"Not that I know of."

"Oh." He seemed disappointed. "Thank you for your help," he said and started to walk away.

"Listen," Rita said quickly, "you could leave your suitcase here. I mean, it *is* a long walk. You could leave your suitcase in a locker in the bus depot."

He paused and turned back, frowning. "A locker?"

"Yeah, sure. Come on, I'll show you."

She led him into the brightly lighted waiting room and over to a bank of coin-operated baggage lockers. "You'll need two quarters." He picked two quarters out of some change from his pocket and Rita showed him where to deposit them. She held the locker door open while he put his bag inside and locked it for him. "You can leave it there twenty-four hours, then you have to put two more quarters in. And don't lose this key or they'll make you fill out all kinds of papers to get your suitcase back. I have to go now. It was nice meeting you."

She went into the ladies room and held the door open a crack to watch him. For a moment he studied the key she had given him, then buttoned it securely in his shirt pocket and left the depot. Rita followed him outside, waited until he was well down the block, then went back inside to get his suitcase. Every evening she invested fifty cents in a locker just to get a key she could switch with a likely victim if one should come along. Tonight she figured she had blown the fifty cents again. But you never knew. This guy had acted awfully funny. Maybe he was on something; there might be drugs in the suitcase she could sell. Or use. She could stand a little speed; lately she had been dragging. She was sure she was anemic. Tomorrow she had a doctor's appointment for a checkup.

As casually as if it were hers, Rita got the suitcase out of the locker and started home with it.

The young man with the key in his shirt pocket was not bothered by the temperature as he walked. Las Vegas was high desert, the heat was very dry, and he was accustomed to both higher humidity and longer walks. The distance to the address on West Sahara Boulevard was only half as far as the girl at the bus depot had said it was and the young man was there in less than an hour. It was a large, tacky apartment complex with uncut grass and tight little patios crowded with bicycles, portable barbecues, and forgotten toys. A variety of noises came through walls too thin for privacy. The manager, who occupied a corner apartment, was a heavyset man who looked as if he had a bad taste in his mouth. Before the young man even spoke he said, "We require first and last month's rent in advance, plus fifty dollars deposit on utilities. An extra hundred deposit if you got kids. You got kids?"

"I don't want an apartment," the young man told him. "My name is George Wolf. I am the brother of Amalie Wolf. I have come for her belongings."

"Oh." The manager's eyes flicked over George's frame, assessing. "There's a week's rent owed. Eight days, actually."

George Wolf nodded. "I will pay. How much."

The manager picked up a pocket calculator from his desk and pressed a few keys. "Make it seventy dollars. I won't charge you for utilities."

George paid him and the manager took a cardboard box from a closet and handed it to him. Suddenly the manager seemed uncomfortable. "That's all there was left. The guy she was living with took most of the big stuff: the TV and stereo and stuff."

George didn't open the box. He wanted desperately to see the things his sister had left behind, to touch something that she had touched, but he would not do it in front of a stranger, particularly a white stranger. "Where did he go, the man my sister lived with?" he asked quietly.

The manager shrugged. "If I was to tell you and you done some harm to him, why, I could get in trouble."

"Is there a reason for me to do harm to the man?" George asked. His eyes never left the manager's face and he did not blink once.

"Depends on how you look at it," the manager said, a little nervously. "Your sister died of a drug overdose. The cops didn't hold the guy she was living with, so it stands to reason they don't blame him for it. But the way the cops think and the way her own brother thinks, there could be a lot of difference. Especially since —" He shrugged again, letting his words trail off.

"Especially since I am an Indian, is that what you mean?"

"I didn't say nothing like that."

George smiled a slight, cold smile. "I may not be white, but I know some of the white man's ways." He put several bills in front of the manager. "Give me the name and address of the man my sister lived with. I will tell no one I found out from you. That is my promise."

The manager pushed a scratch pad and ball-point at him, and told him what to write down. "It's about a mile from here, straight down Sahara. But you won't find him at home now. He works nights as a stick man at a craps table. He probably won't be home until morning."

"I will wait," George said.

His words expressed no emotion at all. The manager was afraid of him nevertheless and was relieved when he left.

Rita was back on the street when George returned to the bus depot. She had put his suitcase in another locker and had the new key in her purse. The suitcase, which she had carefully searched in her apartment, had contained nothing of value: a few changes of clothes, a magazine-sized leather pouch — empty, with some kind of Indian-looking markings on it — a long strip of rawhide or something similar, and a return bus ticket to Lame Deer, Montana. No money, no drugs, not even any jewelry she could hock.

When she saw George walking back into the bus depot, she hurried across the street to intercept him. Her intent was to tell him that she had given him the wrong locker key by mistake, the key he had was to a locker she was using, and she would trade keys with him. That way, he had no beef against her — his suitcase, with all its contents, was intact. But as she trotted into the depot, she saw that George wasn't headed toward the coin lockers at all; he had gone to a nearby bench in the waiting room and sat down. He had a cardboard box on his knees and was going through its contents. From where she stood, Rita could see that the young man's stolid, dark face had turned soft with sadness.

Edging around the side of the waiting room, Rita worked her way behind him and unobtrusively moved to where she could look over his right shoulder. Watching, she saw him take one article at a time out of the cardboard box and examine it thoughtfully, almost lovingly. There was an obviously cheap gold-colored bracelet that he turned over and over in his hands; a hairbrush from which he drew a long black hair that he caressed gently and then put back; a polyester scarf that he held briefly to his nose; a makeup compact with a little mirror that he opened and stared at for a long time. It was while he was staring at the mirror that Rita moved around the bench and sat down next to him.

"Hi again," she said.

George looked at her and then back at the mirror. "I heard a story when I was a boy that if you stare at a mirror long enough, you can see the last image that the mirror saw." The sorrow in his face took on a melancholy smile. "It is not true."

"Who's image are you looking for?"

"My sister's. She's dead. I had not seen her in a long time." He put the compact back and closed the box. "It doesn't seem right that a piece of glass saw my sister before she died and I did not."

"Life's not always right," Rita said knowingly. She had the other locker key in her closed hand — her palm was becoming moist around it. "Are you going to take a bus back where you came from now?"

George shook his head, his eyes narrowing a fraction. "No. There is something I must do first. In the morning."

"Well," she said, seizing the opportunity, "you'll want your suitcase so you can find a place to stay." Before he could protest, Rita had unbuttoned the flap of his shirt pocket and fished out the locker key she had seen him put there. "You wait here with your sister's things and I'll get it for you."

She clicked across the waiting-room floor in her spike heels, switching the keys as she went, found the right locker, and removed his bag.

"Here you go," she said when she got back to the bench with it.

"You have been very kind to help me," George said. "You are a good person."

"Yeah, well," Rita said, feeling herself blush. She forced an embarrassed smile. "Listen, I've got to run. You take care, hear?"

"Before you go, can you tell me which way it is to the nearest woods?"

"The nearest what?"

"Woods. Forest. I will sleep among the trees tonight."

"I already told you once, this is the *desert*," Rita replied. "There aren't no woods." She sighed dramatically. "There's a cheap hotel across the street, the Sal Sagev — that's Las Vegas spelled backwards. You better get a room there."

"I have no money for a room." George said. "I had to pay rent that my sister owned. And I had to give a man money to tell me where someone was."

"Who?"

"Someone I must see tomorrow."

"Well, lookit," Rita said, "there just aren't no woods and you can't sleep in the desert, it's full of scorpions." She began tapping one foot like an impatient mother. "If you try to sleep here in the bus depot, the cops'll bust you for vag."

"What's that?"

"Being broke. Don't you know it's a crime not having no money? What kind of place do you come from anyway?"

George shrugged. "A place where it's not a crime to have no money."

"Well, you'd better go back there as soon as you can," Rita advised cynically.

"I will. Tomorrow."

Rita tilted her head, studying him. "You have to stay until tomorrow?"

"Yes."

Looking up at the big waiting-room clock, Rita thought, what the hell, the night was shot anyway. She was too bushed to even think about another trick. Tomorrow, she was sure, she was going to find out she was anemic.

"Come on," she said, smoothing her skirt over her thin hips, "you can crash on my couch for the night. But you'll have to split early — I have a doctor's appointment at nine."

Chump, she thought as she led him out to the street. Getting soft in your old age. By the time you're seventeen, you'll be a real patsy.

Later that evening, Rita came into her postage-stamp living room wearing a ratty terrycloth robe and trying to comb wet tangles out of her hair. "You can use the shower now if you want," she told George, who was sitting on her tired velour sofa, once again going through the box of his dead sister's belongings.

"Thank you," he said. "I was hoping to find something of my sister's that I could give you for being so kind to me. But I am afraid there is nothing of value."

Peering into the box, Rita said, "That little bracelet looks like it might be worth something."

George shook his head. "If it was worth anything," he said darkly, "the man she lived with would have taken it." Then he added, "But if you would like it —"

"No, you better keep it, being your sister's and all," Rita said. Taking something that a dead person had worn gave her the creeps anyway.

She sat on the arm of the sofa, tugging at her hair with a large comb. "How'd your sister end up in Vegas?" she asked curiously.

"Because of something that happened more than a hundred years ago," George said. "Do you know the story of General Custer and the Little Bighorn?"

"The Custer massacre? When I was a little girl back in Milwaukee, my stepfather used to take me with him to this neighborhood tavern where they had a big picture of it behind the bar. What's that got to do with your sister?"

"There were many tribes which fought Custer at the Little Bighorn, and when it was over those tribes had to run away because the Army sent thousands of soldiers to hunt them down and kill them. Sitting Bull, the great Sioux medicine man, took his people north into Canada where the white soldiers couldn't follow. Some of the Shahiyena tribe, which the whites called the Cheyenne, went with the Sioux. Crazy Dog took a band to Canada — so did Rock Forehead, Little Robe, Wolf Tooth, and others. Wolf Tooth was my great-grandfather. My full name is George Wolf Tooth."

Hell, Rita thought, he's not even a Mexican, he's an *Indian*. And I brought him home for the night. Your porch light's getting dim, kid.

"Many Shahiyena were not able to escape to Canada, to the north, and had to flee south," George continued. "They went down into what is now Wyoming and Colorado but were not part of the United States at the time. Some went over into Nebraska, which *was* a state. Because the Shahiyena spread out in so many directions, the tribe never got back together again as one people. Even today we are known by the part of the country in which we live. I am a Northern Cheyenne — we live mostly in Montana. But those of us who live in the North have uncles and cousins who are Southern Cheyennes or Western Cheyennes."

He gazed off at nothing for a long moment, his clean features dissolving into despair. He was really kind of nice-looking, Rita thought. Not a hunk like Greg had been, but still not bad.

"My sister grew weary of our life in the North," George said at last. "It is a very simple life and often young people my own age find it dull and tiresome, so they go away. Amalie went to live with our cousins in Ogallala, Nebraska. She got a job as a waitress in a cafe on the big Interstate highway that comes out here to Las Vegas and goes on to California. One day a man came through driving a big shiny car —"

"You don't have to say another word," Rita interrupted, "I *been* there. I can even describe the guy for you. Nice tan, sunglasses, gold chain around his neck, shirt unbuttoned halfway down. And he prob'ly told her he had 'connections' in Las Vegas."

George shrugged. "I don't know what he told her. I only know that she went with him. And now she is dead from using drugs." He lowered his head. "We didn't even find out about her until after the time had passed for claiming her body. She had already been cremated. They didn't even keep the ashes for her people."

Rita stopped combing her hair.

"Our way of burial would have been different," George said. "First she would have been wrapped in a cloak of white rabbit fur and placed on a raised travois on the bank of the Rosebud River. The travois would have been made of cedar and ash and pine, all freshly cut so that their fragrances would surround her. We would have prayed around the travois for a day and a night. Then she would have been put on a bed of wildflowers — yellow primroses, white wild lilies, red coralroot, and blue lobelias — in a canoe made of white birch. Her body would have floated down the Rosebud to our sacred burial ground. There the women would have placed her in the ground and covered her resting place with the flowers from the canoe. When those flowers died, their seeds would have taken root and new blossoms would grow every spring."

Rita was enraptured. "That's beautiful," she said. "I never heard anything so beautiful before. I'm sorry you didn't get here before they cremated her." Then something occurred to her. "This thing you have to do in the morning — you're going to see the guy who brought your sister out here, aren't you?"

"Yes."

"Hey," she cautioned, "I hope you're not planning to do anything dumb. I mean, they've got a state prison up in Carson City that's like *ancient*. I know a guy that did time up there. The cells are like *dungeons*, you know what I'm saying? You don't want to end up in a joint like that."

George shook his head. "No."

"Okay. So you're not going to do anything dumb, right?"

He shook his head again. "No, nothing dumb."

"Smartest thing you can do," she lectured, "is forget that guy and get on a bus out of here in the morning. This town is a scab, believe me, and it never heals." She bobbed her chin toward the tiny bedroom and bath. "Go on now and take your shower like a good kid."

Listen to me, will you, she thought as George left the room. The guy's at least four or five years older than me and I'm playing Mommy to him. I ought to be seeing a shrink tomorrow instead of an MD.

While George was in the shower, Rita went to her stash and got a couple of joints to smoke after she had closed her bedroom door.

Closed it and *locked* it.

Just in case.

When Rita dragged out of the bedroom the next morning, feeling as if she had not rested at all, George was at the sink in the tiny kitchenette, slowly gliding the blade of a bone-handled pocketknife across the smooth surface of a four-inch-square whetstone. Every few strokes he would hold the blade under the faucet, which was running a thin stream of water. Rita mustered enough energy to become angry.

"Wonderful," she snapped. "You promised last night you weren't going to do anything dumb."

George looked at her, frowning. "I promised nothing."

"You're going over there to murder that man, aren't you?"

"No, I am not." George rinsed the blade, dried it on his shirttail, and closed the knife. "I am only going to take his scalplock."

Rita winced. "His what?"

"Scalplock." Turning off the faucet, George wrapped the whetstone in a square of soft leather and put it in his pocket. "It is a piece of his scalp. Four inches wide, from the top of his forehead in front to the top of his neck in back. That is all."

"That's *all* ? You don't call that murder?" she asked incredulously.

"No. He will not die. It will be no worse than if he suffered a bad burn."

Rita grimaced, confused. "I thought when people got scalped it killed them."

The young Indian smiled tolerantly. "Only in the white man's movies. Usually a soldier, or a warrior — the white man scalped, too — was dead before his hair was taken, killed by a bullet or a saber, an arrow or a warclub. Scalps were taken when the fighting was over. There have been many instances when a man was thought to be dead and his scalp was taken — his whole scalp, not just the scalplock — and even after he was fully scalped he recovered to tell about it. My own great-grandmother, Wolf Tooth's middle wife, Fox Eye, was scalped by a soldier and survived. It is told that her hair grew back more beautiful than ever."

"I don't believe this conversation." Rita walked wearily into the living room and sat down. George, seeing that he had upset her, followed and knelt on the floor in front of her.

"Let me try to explain something to you. In our tribe, we have an elder, a very old man, who is called the Keeper of the Sacred Arrows. In his home he has a section of buffalo hide which contains six arrows that have been used in battle against the Shahiyena's six traditional enemies: the Crow, the Ute, the Shoshone, the Pawnee, the Blackfeet, and the white man. These arrows remain sacred, and our people maintain their tribal honor only as long as none of our traditional enemies commits an offense against us. If one of them does commit an offense, if one of them steals from us, cheats us, lures away one of our women —"

"Wait," Rita interrupted. "That's why you're going to cut off this man's hair? Because he lured your sister to Las Vegas? Don't you think *she* was partly to blame? I mean, she could've said no."

"Yes, the council of elders took that into consideration. Amalie went with the white man of her own free will. That is why I've been sent for his scalplock instead of his life. It was felt that this man took advantage of my sister's free will. He was much wiser and more worldly than she and influenced her beyond a point which was acceptable. Had it not been for him, she wouldn't have become involved with the drugs that killed her." George studied Rita closely for a moment. "Do you understand?"

"No, I don't. But what difference does it make?

"It makes a lot of difference." He took her hands in his. "You have been kind to me; it's important to me that you do not feel that I have lied to you or broken a promise. You are my friend — I want you to understand."

"The only thing I understand is that you're about to get yourself into something very heavy." She sniffed as if trying to hold back tears. "I just hate to see you do it, that's all."

George squeezed her hands. "There will be no trouble," he assured her. "It will be over very quickly and I will be gone like the morning mist when the sun rises. You are good to worry about me." Suddenly he frowned. "Rita, why are you alone? You are so young to be alone."

She shrugged and sniffed again. "I had a boyfriend until last week. He took off."

"Where are your people?"

"Milwaukee. That's in Wisconsin." She became embarrassed. "I don't keep in touch no more. The stepfather I told you used to take me to the neighborhood tavern with him? Well, he used to take me other places, too. Like into the bedroom when my old lady was at work. I didn't know how to tell her. So I just left."

"Will your boyfriend come back?" George asked with obvious concern.

Rita forced herself to brighten up. "Oh, sure, he'll be back any day now. Probably bring me a nice present." What the hell, she thought, why let the guy worry about her when he had problems of his own. As for Greg, he was gone for good. Guys like Greg never came back. They just drained all a person had, then went on to the next one.

"I am happy you will not be alone for long." George stood up. "I must go now."

She managed a smile. "Yeah — me too. I can't be late for the doctor. Listen, you take care."

"I will. You too." At the door, with his suitcase and the cardboard box, George paused. "Thank you for everything." he said.

He went to the bus station and put the suitcase and box in a locker, then he walked back through the increasing morning heat to Sahara Boulevard and started following the numbers on the apartment buildings, carrying in one hand the slip of paper on which he'd written the name — Nick Gordon — and address of the man his sister had been living with. From time to time, waiting to cross a street, George would look at the name, wondering what Nick Gordon would be like. How big would he be, how strong? Would he fight hard or give up easily? In the pocket with his knife, George carried a slip-tie of the kind used to capture wild ponies. The previous night, while Rita slept, he had fashioned it out of the length of rawhide from his suitcase. It resembled a lariat made of leather. With a quick jerk, the intricate slipknot could hold a man's wrist or foot as tautly as a steel chain. George had been using slip-ties since he was eight — he was very good with them.

When he found the right address, he looked on a bank of mailboxes and located Nick Gordon's apartment number: 308. All apartment doors were outside, on walkways that ringed the building on each floor. It was a large building and George saw a few people coming and going, but no one paid any attention to him. Unobtrusively, he made his way up two flights of cement steps and along the walkway to 308. At the door, he took the slip-tie from his pocket and enlarged the restraining loop to about twice fist-size. Holding it at his side, he knocked.

The door was opened by a man about thirty-five who had a nice suntan and thick black hair with long sideburns. Except for his eyes, he was handsome. His eyes were somehow offensive — they flicked over George, top to bottom.

"Mr. Nick Gordon?" George asked.

"Yeah, what do you want?"

"I was told to give you this." George held out the rawhide slip-tie.

Nick Gordon instinctively reached for it, and when his right hand was at the proper angle, George expertly flipped the loop around his wrist and jerked it tight. "Hey, what the hell?"

That was all the protest Gordon could voice before George spun him around, twisting his arm behind him, and pushed him back inside the apartment. Elbowing the door shut after them, he put a foot in front of Gordon and tripped him to the floor. Grabbing the other man's left foot, he bent it up behind him and looped the thong once around the ankle. Drawing it tight, he had him face down with his right hand held to his left foot.

"What the hell are you doing, man!" Gordon said, half in anger, half in fear. "You want my money, its on the dresser!"

"I'm not a thief," George said with quiet indignation. Drawing the thong upward, he threw a loop around Gorton's neck and with one knee in the middle of the helpless man's back he held it firmly in place across his throat, cutting off his voice. The next instant, he had his pocket knife out and with his teeth opened its honed blade. Closing his eyes, he silently intoned the Shahiyena scalping prayer. When his lips stopped moving, he held the blade at the top of Nick Gordon's head, entwined the fingers holding the thong in Gordon's thick black hair, and pulled it to tauten the scalp for slicing.

But it did not tauten. The hair, all of it, came off in George's hand — a great round mass of it — leaving the top of the man's head bald and shiny.

George got to his feet, staring at the thing in his hand. On the floor, the loop slipped from around Gordon's neck and he twisted and struggled until his foot was loose. "You crazy son of a bitch!" he said.

George looked at him, then back at the bowl of hair in his hand. He didn't understand. This man was wearing a scalp!

"Try to choke me, will you?" Gordon sputtered. "I'll kill you!" Jerking open an end-table drawer, he snatched out a small revolver and pushed the cylinder free. From a box of cartridges, he fumbled to load it. At the sight of the gun, George's eyes widened in fear. Still holding the patch of hair, he wrenched open the apartment door and fled.

In the examining room, the doctor, whose name was Franken, asked, "How old are you really, Rita?"

"Twenty-one — like the form says," Rita replied with practiced annoyance. She chastised herself for not wearing more makeup. She had tried to dress like some of the young women she saw pushing shopping carts with toddlers in the child seat in the supermarket. They always seemed to be wearing slacks, blouses, sandals, and shoulder-strap bags. They were all scrubbed-looking — the effect Rita had wanted today — but apparently she had not achieved it.

"Do you have any identification that proves your age?" the doctor wanted to know.

"You sound like a bartender," Rita grumbled.

The doctor, a short man with a beard, said, "Rita, we've got a problem, you and I. If you're under eighteen, and I suspect that you are, I'd like to get in touch with your parents."

"Forget it," she told him firmly. She studied the look of concern on the doctor's face. "Is there something wrong with me?"

"You have gonorrhea, Rita."

She looked relieved. "Is *that* all? Oh, look, I've had it twice before. It's no big deal. Just start me on penicillin shots."

"I'm afraid it *is* a big deal this time, Rita," he said gravely. "Do you know what AIDS is?"

The color drained from her face. "Oh, no."

"You can understand why it's imperative that your family be notified," Dr. Franken said. "We also have to contact your school so that any boys you've been intimate with can be referred to their own doctors."

"I don't go to — school," Rita said, her mouth suddenly dry. Her confidence was gone now, her eyes wide with fright. "I'm a hooker, see? A runaway and a hooker."

The doctor's expression reflected a fleeting moment of incredulity, but he quickly composed himself. "I see. Well, it's important that we contact as many of your clients as possible, Rita."

She shook her head. "I work the street, Doc. My tricks don't leave calling cards. But I can tell you where I probably got the AIDS." She gave the doctor Greg's full name. "He's bi. We lived together for about six months. He took off for San Francisco last week with some guy who was down for the weekend." She swallowed tightly and asked, "What's going to happen to me?"

"There's a Public Health Service hospital in Phoenix I could send you to," the doctor said. "It wouldn't cost you anything and they have the personnel and facilities to work up a complete prognosis on your condition."

"AIDS kills people, doesn't it?" she asked bluntly. Tears were trying to escape her eyes but she wouldn't let them.

"AIDS itself doesn't kill people," Dr. Franken explained. "AIDS is a condition known as Acquired Immunodeficiency Syndrome. It's a condition that helps other conditions kill people. The gonorrhea you have that was so simply cured for you twice before, for instance, could develop this time into meningitis that could affect your spinal column and brain, or endocarditis that could affect the membranes of your heart."

"Okay, okay," Rita interrupted. "I don't want to hear no more. How do I get into that hospital you mentioned?"

"I'll telephone and arrange admittance. Do you have bus fare to Phoenix?"

"Sure I do. I'm not a charity case, you know. I got my own checking account."

"Fine," Dr. Franken said. He circled Greg's name on his pad. "The San Francisco health authorities will have to look for your boyfriend."

"Ex-boyfriend."

"All right, ex-boyfriend. Now, before you go there's one thing I'd like you to do for me. Let me call the county health department to send a representative over to get you. They'll want to take your photograph and show it around areas where you worked to try and find some of the men you've been with."

Rita shrugged. "Why not? I'm not going to be around no more anyhow."

"Good." Dr. Franken rose. "You wait here in the examining room while I make arrangements."

After he left and Rita was alone in the quiet stillness of the room, she lay back down on the examining table, closed her eyes, and sighed as wearily as if she were a tired old woman. Finally she let the tears come.

It was just after noon when Rita got back to her apartment and found George sitting outside her door. "Oh, no," she said. "Look, man, I've got this big problem right now, okay?" Seeing the hairy object in his hand, she looked away. "Is that what I think it is?"

"He was wearing a scalp," George told her incredulously. "It came off in my hand."

Rita looked back at it. "That's a *toupee*, you dummy. Oh, I don't need this." She put the key in the lock and opened the door.

"What is a two-pay?" George asked. "Not a scalp?"

"No." Snatching it from him impatiently, she turned it inside-out and showed him the sewn lining. "It's for guys that lose their hair."

"From scalping?"

"No — for guys whose hair falls out!" Thrusting it back at him, she said, "Look, I'm sorry but you gotta go. I'm trying to deal with something really heavy right now."

"I'll go," George said. "I'm sorry, I didn't mean to upset you again." From his shirt pocket he took the scrap of paper and looked at the address again. "I must go see this man again."

"What? Are you crazy?" She glared at him. "He's probably got the cops over there waiting for you."

George shook his head. "He's not the kind who calls the police. He has his own gun."

"Wonderful. Look, you've got his hair — that's what you came for, isn't it?"

George glanced scornfully at the toupee. "It isn't really his hair. I must take his scalplock — "

"But he doesn't *have one!* Gimme a break here!"

"He has hair in the back and on the sides, and in front of his ears," George said stubbornly.

Rita shook her head in amazement. "You're crazy, you know that? Look, read my lips: You — are — crazy."

"I do what is necessary," George informed her. He started to turn away.

"Wait a minute," she said quickly. "Look, it's your business, okay? Who am I to stop you. But I want you to do me a favor first. You owe me a favor, am I right?" He nodded. "Okay. I have to go out of town, see, on personal business. Wait for me to pack and carry my suitcase to the bus depot for me, will you? It's right on your way. I mean, it's so hot out there I don't think I can make it by myself. Will you help me?"

"Of course," said George.

"Super. Go in and sit down while I run get my suitcase from the landlady. I let her borrow it last week to visit her brother in Reno."

George sat and waited, folding and unfolding the scrap of paper with Nick Gordon's address on it. Rita was gone nearly twenty minutes. When she returned, she had two uniformed policemen with her.

"That's him," she said pointing at George. "He tried to rape me."

George stood up, bewildered, as the officers swiftly descended on him, one of them pinioning his arms behind him and handcuffing his wrists, the other patting him down in a body search and relieving him of his pocketknife. George stared at Rita in wide-eyed disbelief, but she refused to look at him. Presently one of the policeman took George down to sit in the caged back seat of the radio car while the other officer remained with Rita to do the paperwork. It took ten minutes to fill out the arrest form and complaint, both of which Rita signed. The officer, handing her a copy, said, "Be at the address on the form for arraignment court at nine in the morning."

"Right."

She watched out the window as they drove George away. When the car was out of sight, she went to her stash and rolled a joint. Smoking it, she dragged out an old Samsonite overnighter and started packing. It occurred to her that the assortment of things she was carelessly tossing into the bag weren't a whole lot different from the things in the cardboard box that had belonged to George's sister. Too bad we didn't know each other, she thought. Maybe I could have helped her, given her a few tips. As soon as the thought manifested, she grunted softly. Listen to me. The blind leading the blind.

She finished the joint and her packing, and started to leave. On the way out, she noticed a scrap of paper on the floor. It was the address George had had with him. He must have dropped it when the police grabbed him. Rita picked it up and studied it. She pursed her lips and tapped the toe of one sandal. Then she shrugged and thought, Why not? Why the hell not?

Sixty days later, George walked out of the county jail and stood indecisively for a moment on the hot Las Vegas sidewalk. In one hand he had his suitcase, in the other the box containing his sister's belongings. The police, finding the key when George was booked, had gone to the bus depot and opened the locker. Finding nothing incriminating, they had put the suitcase and box in the jail property room to be held for his release. He had been given back the rest of his things, even his pocketknife, which was under the legal blade length. In a shirt pocket, he had his return bus ticket to Lame Deer, Montana. He no longer had the piece of paper with Nick Gordon's address on it, but that didn't bother him. He was sure he could find the place again.

As he started down the street toward the bus station to check his suitcase and the box in a locker again, he heard a voice behind him call, "Hey, wait a sec!"

Turing, he saw Rita hurrying toward him. His first reaction was anger. Then, as she got closer, a sudden pity came over him. She looked terrible: pale, very thin, her eyes hollow. Nevertheless, when she reached him he said stiffly, "You should not have done what you did. I almost went to prison."

"You didn't either," she retorted. "There was no complaining witness 'cause I didn't show up. I never intended to."

"Well," he said sullenly, "they put me in jail for two months for vagrancy."

"They didn't either. They gave you thirty days for vag. The other thirty you got for trying to make a break from the courtroom. Hot head."

He looked away. "You shouldn't have done it anyhow," he muttered.

"Come on," she pulled on his arm, "let's get out of the sun."

They walked to the bus depot, got two glasses of iced tea in the self-service coffee shop, and sat at a tiny table.

"Guess where I've been," she said. George shrugged. "In the hospital," she told him. "Down in Phoenix, Arizona. I've been part of some experiments. Very important *medical* experiments. I've got Kaposi's sarcoma," she added almost aloofly.

"What's that?"

"Well, let's just say it's not the twenty-four-hour flu. It's here to stay." She found it too embarrassing to describe the ugly purple lesions growing on the surface of her thighs, stomach, and lower back. "Anyway," she went on excitedly, "I was the very first one picked to test a new drug called Ribavirin, which was previously used only on some kind of fever down in Africa. It didn't work, but it was kind of an honor to be picked first."

George nodded gravely. "It is always an honor to be picked first for something important."

She bit her lower lip. "You're probably wondering why I'm here, right?"

George shook his head. "You're still my friend. I know why you did what you did. But it does not change what *I* must do."

"But it does," Rita told him anxiously. "That's what I ran away from the hospital for and came here to tell you. That guy Nick Gordon is down there in the same hospital I was in, only he's over in the men's building. He checked in about five weeks ago. He's almost dead. Seems he had sex with someone who had the same thing I've got."

She remembered for a fleeting moment how easy it had been. He'd opened the door and she had said, "Hi, there. Listen, could I trouble you to use your phone? My girlfriend and I want to rent an apartment here and she was supposed to meet me with the deposit, you know, but she hasn't showed. I want to call and see if she's left yet." She had pulled the top of her blouse out and fanned herself. "It's so hot! I can't wait to get my hands on a nice cold beer." He had invited her in and from there on it had been a piece of cake.

"You say he's dying? How do you know?" George asked suspiciously.

"He was a cocaine user," Rita explained. "Over the years, the lining of his nose weakened from snorting the stuff. After he picked up what I've got, he developed something called *Candida albicans*, which is like a fungus, really gross, that grows in the nose, mouth, and throat. There's no way to stop it. The man is practically *finito*." She saw mistrust in George's eyes. "Don't you believe me?" she asked indignantly.

"I wonder if you are only trying again to keep me out of trouble."

Rita reached across the table and took his hand. "I'm not," she said, the simple phrase coming out with a quaver. "I'm dying, too," she told him. "I wouldn't lie to you, not now. The man can't speak, can't swallow, can't breathe through his nose or throat. He's got a dozen tubes in him. If you want to, you can go to Phoenix and see for yourself, but he'll probably be dead before you get there. He might be dead already."

George's direct, penetrating black eyes studied her across the table for several long moments, his intense concentration muting for him the sounds of the coffee shop around them. When he finally spoke, he said, "I believe you, Rita."

Relief showed in her hollow eyes, her drawn expression. Sniffing, she took back her hand and dabbed at her eyes with a paper napkin. "Look at me, will you?" she said. "Blubbering like some dumb kid. No shame at all."

"Where will you go now?" George asked. "Back to the hospital?"

"Not on your life," she announced. "Me and that place are quits. I'm in my final stage, so they won't use me for no more experiments. All's I do is live in a separate ward until — well, you know."

"What will you do?" he asked with concern. "Who will look after you?"

"I can look after myself," she assured him. "I'm not no charity case. I got my own checking account. I'll get a room somewheres. No problem."

Now it was he who took her hand. "Would you like to come back home with me?"

She had thought to play coy if he asked her, but it was too important. She seized on the offer as if it were salvation. "Could I?" she asked like a desperate child pleading. "Could I, please?"

"Yes, I will take you. You will be my sister for the time you have left."

"And when it's all over?" she asked. "Will I have the cloak of white rabbit fur and the bed of wildflowers and float down the river in a canoe made of white birch?"

"Yes," he said solemnly, "you will have that." He rose and picked up his suitcase and the box. "Come, sister," he said.

THE DAKAR RUN

Jack Sheffield limped out of the little Theatre Americain with John Garfield's defiant words still fresh in his mind. "What are you gonna do, kill me?" Garfield, as Charley Davis, the boxer, had asked Lloyd Gough, the crooked promoter, at the end of *Body and Soul*. Then, challengingly, smugly, with the Garfield arrogance, "Everybody dies!" And he had walked away, with Lilli Palmer on his arm.

Pausing outside to look at the *Body and Soul* poster next to the box office, Sheffield sighed wistfully. They were gone now, Garfield and Lilli Palmer, black and white films, the good numbers like Hazel Brooks singing "Am I Blue?" Even boxing — real boxing — was down the tubes. In the old days, hungry kids challenged seasoned pros. Now millionaires fought gold-medal winners.

Shaking his head at the pity of things changed, Sheffield turned up his collar against the chilly Paris night and limped up La Villette to the Place de Cluny. There was a cafe there called the Nubian, owned by a very tall Sudanese who mixed his own mustard so hot it could etch cement. Every Tuesday night, the old-movie feature at the Theatre Americain changed and Jack Sheffield went to see it, whatever it was, and afterward he always walked to the Nubian for sausage and mustard and a double gin. Later, warm from the gin and the food, he would stroll, rain or fair, summer or winter, along the Rue de Rivoli next to the Tuileries, down to the Crazy Horse Saloon to wait for the chorus to do its last high kick so that Jane, the long-legged Englishwoman with whom he lived, could change and go home. Tuesdays never varied for Sheffield.

How many Tuesdays, he wondered as he entered the Nubian, had he been doing this exact same thing? As he pulled out a chair at the rickety little table for two at which he always sat, he tried to recall how long he had been with Jane. Was it three years or four? Catching the eye of the Sudanese, Sheffield raised his hand to signal that he was here, which was all he had to do; he never varied his order. The Sudanese nodded and walked with a camel-like gait toward the kitchen, and Sheffield was about to resume mentally backtracking his life when a young girl came in and walked directly to his table.

"Hi," she said.

He looked at her, tilting his head an inch, squinting slightly without his glasses. When he didn't respond at once, the girl gave him a wry, not totally amused look.

"I'm Chelsea," she said pointedly. "Chelsea Sheffield. Your daughter." She pulled out the opposite chair. "Don't bother to get up."

Sheffield stared at her incredulously, lips parted but no words being generated by his surprised brain.

"Mother," she explained, "said all I had to do to find you in Paris was locate a theater that showed old American movies, wait until the bill changed, and stand outside after the first show. She said if you didn't walk out, you were either dead or had been banished from France."

"Your mother was always right," he said, adding dryly, "about everything."

"She also said you might be limping, after smashing up your ankle at Le Mans two years ago. Is the limp permanent?"

"More or less." He quickly changed the subject. "Your mother's well, I presume."

"Very. Like a Main Line Philadelphia doctor's wife should be. Her picture was on the society page five times last year."

"And your sister?"

"Perfect," Chelsea replied, "just as she's always been. Married to a proper young stockbroker, mother of two proper little girls, residing in a proper two-story Colonial, driving a proper Chrysler station wagon. Julie has *always* been proper. I was the foul-mouthed little girl who was too much like my race-car-driver daddy, remember?"

Sheffield didn't know whether to smile or frown. "What are you doing in Paris?" he asked.

"I came over with my boyfriend. We're going to enter the Paris-to-Dakar race."

Now it Sheffield who made a wry face. "Are you serious?"

"You better believe it," Chelsea assured him.

"Who's your boyfriend — Parnelli Jones?"

"Funny, Father. His name is Austin Trowbridge. He's the son of Max Trowbridge."

Sheffield's eyebrows rose. Max Trowbridge had been one of the best race-car designers in the world before his untimely death in a plane crash. "Did your boyfriend learn anything from his father?" he asked Chelsea.

"He learned plenty. For two years he's been building a car for the Paris-Dakar Rally. It's finished now. You'd have to see it to believe it — part

Land Rover, part Rolls-Royce, part Corvette. We've been test-driving it on the beach at Hilton Head. It'll do one hundred and ten on hard-packed sand, ninety on soft. The engine will cut sixty-six hundred RPMs."

"Where'd you learn about RPMs?" he asked, surprised.

Chelsea shrugged. "I started hanging out at dirt-bike tracks when I was fourteen. Gave mother fits. When I moved up to stock cars, she sent me away to boarding school. It didn't work. One summer at Daytona, I met Austin. We were both kind of lonely. His father had just been killed and mine —" she glanced away "— well, let's just say that Mother's new husband didn't quite know how to cope with Jack Sheffield's youngest."

And I wasn't around, Sheffield thought. He'd been off at Formula One tracks in Belgium and Italy and England, drinking champagne from racing helmets and Ferragamos with four-inch heels, looking for faster cars, getting older with younger women, sometimes crashing. Burning, bleeding, breaking —

"Don't get me wrong," Chelsea said, "I'm not being critical. Everybody's got to live their life the way they think best. I'm going my own way with Austin, so I can't fault you for going your own way without me."

But you do, Sheffield thought. He studied his daughter. She had to be nineteen now, maybe twenty — he couldn't even remember when her birthday was. She was plainer than she was pretty — her sister Julie had their mother's good looks, poor Chelsea favored him. Lifeless brown hair, imperfect complexion, a nose that didn't quite fit — yet there was something about her that he suspected could seize and hold a man, if he was the right man. Under the leather jacket she had unzipped was clearly the body of a woman, just as her direct grey eyes were obviously no longer the eyes of a child. There was no way, Sheffield knew, he could ever make up for the years he hadn't been there, but maybe he could do something to lessen the bad taste he'd left. Like talking her out of entering the Paris-Dakar Rally.

"You know, even with the best car in the world the Paris-Dakar run is the worst racing experience imaginable. Eight thousand miles across the Sahara Desert over the roughest terrain on the face of the earth, driving under the most brutal, dangerous, dreadful conditions. It shouldn't be called a rally, it's more like an endurance test. It's three weeks of hell."

"*You've* done it," she pointed out. "Twice."

"We already know I make mistakes. I didn't win either time, you know."

A touch of fierceness settled in her eyes. "I didn't look you up to get advice on whether to enter — Austin and I have already decided that. I came to ask if you'd go over the route map with us, maybe give us some pointers, but if you're too busy — "

"I'm not too busy," he said. Her words cut him easily.

Chelsea wrote down an address in Montmartre. "It's a rented garage. We've got two rooms above it. The car arrived in Marseilles by freighter this morning. Austin's driving it up tomorrow." She stood and zipped up her jacket. "When can we expect you?"

"Day after tomorrow okay?"

"Swell. See you then." She nodded briefly. "Good-night, Father."

"Good-night."

As she was walking out, Sheffield realized that he hadn't once spoken her name.

On Thursday, Sheffield took Jane with him to Montmartre, thinking at least he would have somebody on his side if Chelsea and Austin Trowbridge started making him feel guilty. It didn't work. Jane and Chelsea, who were only ten years apart in age, took to each other at once.

"Darling, you look just like him," Jane analyzed. "Same eyes, same chin. But I'm sure your disposition is much better. Jack has absolutely no sense of humor sometimes. If he wasn't so marvelous in bed, I'd leave him."

"He'll probably save you the trouble someday," Chelsea replied. "Father leaves everyone eventually."

"Why don't you two just talk about me like I'm not here?" Sheffield asked irritably.

Austin Trowbridge rescued him. "Like to take a look at the car, Mr. Sheffield?"

"Call me Jack. Yes, I would. I was a great admirer of your father, Austin. He was the best."

"Thanks. I hope I'll be half as good someday."

As soon as Sheffield saw the car, he knew Austin was already half as good, and more. It was an engineering work of art. The body was seamless, shaped not for velocity but for balance, with interchangeable balloon and radial wheels on the same axles, which had double suspension systems to lock in place for either. The steering was flexible from left-hand drive to right, the power train flexible from front to rear, side to side, corner to corner, even to individual wheels. The windshield displaced in one-eighth-inch increments to deflect glare in the daytime, while infrared sealed beams could outline night figures fifty yards distant. A primary petrol tank held one hundred liters of fuel and a backup tank carried two hundred additional liters. Everywhere Sheffield looked — carburetor, generator, distributor, voltage regulator, belt system, radiator, fuel lines — he saw imagination, innovation, improvement. The car was built for reliability and stability, power and pace. Sheffield couldn't have been more impressed.

"It's a beauty, Austin. Your dad would be proud."

"Thanks. I named it after him. I call it the 'Max One.' "

Nice kid, Sheffield thought. He'd probably been very close to his father before the tragedy. Not like Chelsea and himself.

After looking at the Max One, Sheffield took them all to lunch at a cafe on the Boulevard de la Chapelle. While they ate, he talked about the rally.

"There's no competition like it in the world," he said. "It's open to cars, trucks, motorcycles, anything on wheels. There's never any telling who'll be in — or on — the vehicle next to you; it might be a professional driver, a movie star, a millionaire, an Arab king. The run starts in Paris on New Year's Day, goes across France and Spain to Barcelona, crosses the Mediterranean by boat to Africa, then down the length of Algiers, around in a circle of sorts in Niger, across Mali, across Mauritania, up into the Spanish Sahara, then down along the Atlantic coast into Senegal to Dakar. The drivers spend fifteen to eighteen hours a day in their vehicles, then crawl into sleeping bags for a short, badly needed rest at the end of each day's stage. From three to four hundred vehicles start the run each year. About one in ten will finish."

"We'll finish," Chelsea assured him. "We might even win."

Sheffield shook his head. "You won't win. No matter how good the car is, you don't have the experience to win."

"We don't have to win," Austin conceded. "We just have to finish, well — respectably. There are some investors who financed my father from time to time. They've agreed to set me up in my own automotive-design center if I prove myself by building a vehicle that will survive Paris-Dakar. I realize, of course, that the car isn't everything — that's why I wanted to talk to you about the two rallies you ran, to get the benefit of your experience."

"You haven't been racing since you hurt your ankle," Chelsea said. "What have you been doing, Father?"

Sheffield shrugged. "Consulting, training other drivers, conducting track courses—"

"We're willing to pay you for your time to help us," she said.

Sheffield felt himself blush slightly. God, she knew how to cut.

"That won't be necessary," he said. "I'll help you all I can." He wanted to add, "After all, you *are* my daughter," but he didn't.

As he and Jane walked home, she said, "That was nice, Jack, saying you'd help them for nothing."

"Nice, maybe, but not very practical. I could have used the money. I haven't made a franc in fourteen months."

Jane shrugged. "What does it matter? I earn enough for both of us."

It mattered to Sheffield.

Sheffield began going to Montmartre every day. In addition to talking to Austin about the route and terrain of the rally, he also helped him make certain modifications on Max One.

"You've got to put locks on the doors, kid. There may be times when both of you have to be away from the car at once and there are places along the route where people will steal you blind."

Holes were drilled and locks placed.

"Paint a line on the steering wheel exactly where your front wheels are aligned straight. That way, when you hit a pothole and bounce, or when you speed off a dune, you can adjust the wheels and land straight. It'll keep you from flipping over. Use luminous paint so you can see the line after dark."

Luminous paint was secured and the line put on.

A lot of Sheffield's advice was practical rather than technical. "Get rid of those blankets. It gets down to twenty degrees in the Sahara at night. Buy lightweight sleeping bags. And stock up on unsalted nuts, granola bars, high-potency vitamins, caffeine tablets. You'll need a breathing aid too, for when you land in somebody's dust wake. Those little gauze masks painters use worked fine for me."

Most times when Sheffield went to Montmartre, Chelsea wasn't around. Austin always explained that she was running errands or doing this or that, but Sheffield could tell that he was embarrassed by the excuses. His daughter, Sheffield realized, obviously didn't want to see him any more than necessary. He tried not to let it bother him. Becoming more friendly each visit with Austin helped. The young man didn't repeat Chelsea's offer to pay him for his time, seeming to understand that it was insulting, and for that Sheffield was grateful. No one, not even Jane, knew how serious Sheffield's financial predicament was.

No one except Marcel.

One afternoon when Sheffield got back from Montmartre, Marcel was waiting for him at a table in the cafe Sheffield had to pass through to get to his rooms. "Jack, my friend," he hailed, as if the encounter were mere chance, "come join me." Snapping his fingers at the waiter, he ordered, "Another glass here."

Sheffield sat down. At a nearby table were two thugs who accompanied the diminutive Marcel everywhere he went. One was white, with a neck like a bucket and a walk like a wrestler's. The other was *cafe au lait*, very slim, with obscene lips and a reputation for being deadly with a straight razor. After glancing at them, Sheffield drummed his fingers silently on the tablecloth and waited for the question Marcel invariably asked first.

"So, my friend, tell me, how are things with you?"

To which Sheffield, during the past fourteen months anyway, always answered, "The same, Marcel, the same."

Marcel assumed a sad expression. Which was not difficult since he had a serious face, anyway, and had not smiled, some said, since puberty. His round little countenance would have reminded Sheffield of Peter Lorre except that Marcel's eyes were narrow slits that, despite their owner's cordiality, clearly projected danger.

"I was going over my books last week, Jack," the Frenchman said as he poured Sheffield a Pernod, "and I must admit I was a little surprised to see how terrible your luck has run all year. I mean, horse races, dog races, prizefights, soccer matches — you seem to have forgotten what it is to pick a winner. Usually, of course, I don't let anyone run up a balance so large, but I've always had a soft spot for you, Jack."

"You know about the car in Montmartre, don't you?" Sheffield asked pointedly.

"Of course," Marcel replied at once, not at all surprised by the question. "I've known about it since it arrived in Marseilles." Putting a hand on Sheffield's arm, he asked confidentially, "What do you think of it, Jack?"

Sheffield moved his arm by raising the Pernod to his lips. "It's a fine car. Once of the best I've ever seen."

"I'm glad you're being honest with me," Marcel said. "I've already had a man get into the garage at night to look at it for me. He was of the same opinion. He says it can win the rally."

Sheffield shook his head. "They're a couple of kids, Marcel. They may finish — they won't win."

Marcel looked at him curiously. "What is a young man like this Austin Trowbridge able to pay you, anyway?"

"I'm not being paid."

Marcel drew back his head incredulously. "A man in your financial situation? You work for nothing?"

"I used to know the kid's father," Sheffield said. Then he added, "I used to know his girlfriend's father, too."

Marcel studied the American for a moment. "Jack, let me be as candid with you as you are being with me. There are perhaps two dozen serious vehicles for which competition licenses have been secured for this year's rally. The car my associates and I are backing is a factory-built Peugeot driven by Georges Ferrand. A French driver in a French car. Call it national pride if you wish, call it practical economics — the fact is that we will have a great deal of money at risk on a Ferrand win. Of the two dozen or so vehicles that will seriously challenge Ferrand, we are convinced he will outdistance all but one of them. That one is the Trowbridge car. It is, as you said, a fine car. We have no statistics on it because it did not run in the optional trials at Cegry-Pontoise. And we know nothing about young Trowbridge himself as a driver — whether he's capable, has the stamina, whether he's *hungry*. The entire entry, car and driver, presents an unknown equation which troubles us."

"I've already told you, Marcel — the car can't win."

The Frenchman fixed him in an unblinking stare. "I want a guarantee of that, Jack." He produced a small leather notebook. "Your losses currently total forty-nine thousand francs. That's about eight thousand dollars. I'll draw a line through the entire amount for a guarantee that the Max One will not outrun Ferrand's Peugeot."

"You're not concerned whether it finishes?"

"Not in the least," Marcel waved away the consideration. "First place wins, everything else loses."

Sheffield pursed his lips in brief thought, then said, "All right Marcel. It's a bargain."

Later, in their rooms, Jane said, "I saw you in the cafe with Marcel. You haven't started gambling again, have you?"

"Of course not." It wasn't a lie. He had never stopped.

"What did he want, then?"

"He and his friends are concerned about Austin's car. They know I'm helping the kid. They want a guarantee that the Max One won't ace out the car they're backing."

Jane shook her head in disgust. "What did you tell him?"

"That he had nothing to worry about. Austin's not trying to win, he only wants to finish."

"But you didn't agree to help Marcel in any way?"

"Of course not." Sheffield looked away. He hated lying to Jane, yet he did so regularly about his gambling. This time, though, he swore to himself, he was going to quit — when the slate was wiped clean with Marcel, he had made up his mind not to bet on anything again, not racing, not boxing, not soccer, not even whether the Eiffel Tower was still standing. And he was going to find work, too — some kind of normal job, maybe in an automobile factory, so he could bring in some money, settle down, plan for some kind of future. Jane, after all, was almost thirty; she wouldn't be able to kick her heels above her head in the Crazy Horse chorus line forever.

And his bargain with Marcel wouldn't matter to Austin and Chelsea, he emphasized to his conscience. All Austin had to do to get his design center was finish the race, not win it.

That night while Jane was at the club, Sheffield went to a bookstall on the Left Bank that specialized in racing publications. He purchased an edition of the special Paris-Dakar Rally newspaper that listed each vehicle and how it had performed in the optional trials at Cergy-Pontoise. Back home, he studied the figures on Ferrand's Peugeot and on several other cars which appeared to have the proper ratios of weight-to-speed necessary for a serious run. There was a Mitsubishi that looked very good, a factory-sponsored Mercedes, a Range Rover, a Majorette, a little Russian-built Lada, and a Belgian entry that looked like a VW but was called an Ostend.

For two hours he worked and reworked the stats on a pad of paper, dividing weights by distance, by average speeds, by days, by the hours of daylight which would be available, by the average wind velocity across the Sahara, by the number of stops necessary to adjust tire pressure, by a dozen other factors that a prudent driver needed to consider. When he finished, and compared his final figures with the figures he had estimated for Austin Trowbridge's car, Sheffield reached an unavoidable conclusion: The Max One might — just *might* — actually win the rally.

Sheffield put on his overcoat and went for a walk along the Champs-Elysees and on into the deserted Tuileries. The trees in the park were wintry and forlorn, the grass grey from its nightly frost, and the late-November air thin and cold. Sheffield limped along, his hands deep in his pockets, chin down, brow pinched. Marcel had used the word "guarantee" — and that's what Sheffield had agreed to: a guarantee that the Max One wouldn't win. But the car, Sheffield now knew, was even better than he'd thought: it *could* win. In order to secure his guarantee to Marcel, Sheffield was left with but one alternative. He had to tamper with the car.

Sheffield sat on a bench in the dark and brooded about the weaknesses of character that had brought him to his present point in life. He wondered how much courage it would take to remain on the bench all night and catch pneumonia and freeze to death. The longer he thought about it, the more inviting it seemed. He sat there until he became very cold. But eventually he rose and returned to the rooms above the cafe.

The following week after conceiving and dismissing a number of plans, Sheffield asked Austin, "What are you going to do about oil?"

"The rally supply truck sells it at the end of every stage, doesn't it? I thought I'd buy it there every night."

"That's okay in the stages where everything goes right," Sheffield pointed out. "But the rally supply truck is only there for a couple of hours and then starts an overnight drive to the next stage. If you get lost or break down or even blow a tire, you could miss the truck and have to run on used oil the entire next day. You need to carry a dozen quarts of your own oil for emergencies."

"I hate to add the weight," Austin said reluctantly.

"I know of a garage that will seal it in plastic bags so you can eliminate the cans," Sheffield said. "That'll save you a couple of pounds."

"You really think it's necessary?"

"I'd do it," Sheffield assured him. Austin finally agreed. "Tell me the grade you want and I'll get it for you," Sheffield said.

Austin wrote down the viscosity numbers of an oil density that was perfect for the Max One's engine. On his way home, Sheffield stopped by the garage of which he had spoken. Before he ordered the bags of oil, he drew a line through some of Austin's numbers and replaced them with figures of his own — lower figures which designated less constancy in the oil's lubricating quality.

Several days later, the garage delivered to the rooms above the cafe a carton containing the bagged oil. Jane was home and accepted the delivery. The garageman gave her a message for Sheffield.

"Our mechanic said to tell Monsieur that if this oil is for a rally vehicle, it should be several grades lighter. This viscosity will reduce engine efficiency as the air temperature drops."

When the garageman left, Jane saw taped to the top bag the slip of paper with the viscosity numbers altered. When Sheffield returned from

Montmartre, she asked him about it.

"Yes, I changed them," he said, his tone deliberately casual. "The oil Austin specified was too light."

"Does he know you changed his figures?"

"Sure."

"Are you lying to me, Jack?" She had been exercising and was in black leotards, hands on hips, concern wrinkling her brow.

"Why would I lie about a thing like motor oil?" Sheffield asked.

"I don't know. But I've had an uneasy feeling since I saw you with Marcel. If you're in some kind of trouble, Jack —"

"I'm not in any kind of trouble," he said, forcing a smile.

"You're not trying to get back at Chelsea for the way she's acting toward you, I hope."

"Of course not."

"Jack," she said, "I called Austin and said I thought the garage made a mistake. I read him your numbers and he said they were wrong."

"You *what?*" Sheffield stared at her. The color drained from his face. Jane sighed wearily and sat down.

"I knew it. I could feel it."

Sheffield felt a surge of relief. "You didn't call Austin."

She shook her head. "No." Her expression saddened. "Why are you doing it, Jack?"

Sheffield poured himself a drink and sat down and told her the truth. He told her about the lies of the past fourteen months, the money he'd bet and lost, the circle of desperation that had slowly been closing in on him. "I saw a way out," he pleaded.

"By hurting someone who trusts you?"

"No one will be hurt," he insisted. "Austin doesn't have to win, all he has to do —"

"Is finish," she completed the statement for him. "That's not the point, Jack. It's wrong and you know it."

"Look," he tried to explain, "when Austin uses this heavier oil, all it will do is make the Max One's engine cut down a few RPMs. He probably won't even notice it. The car will slow down maybe a mile an hour."

"It's wrong, Jack. Please don't do it."

"I've *got* to do it," Sheffield asserted. "I've got to get clear of Marcel."

"We can start paying Marcel. I have some savings."

"No." Sheffield stiffened. "I'm tired of being kept by you, Jane."

"*Kept* by me?"

"Yes, kept! You as much as said so yourself when you told my daughter I was marvelous in bed."

"Oh, Jack — surely you don't think Chelsea took me seriously!"

"I took you seriously."

Jane stared at him. "If you think you're going to shift onto me some of the responsibility for what you're doing, you're mistaken."

"I don't want you to take any of the responsibility," he made clear, "but I don't expect you to interfere, either. Just mind your own business."

Jane's eyes hardened. "I'll do that."

In the middle of December, the Crazy Horse closed for two weeks and Jane announced that she was going back to England for the holidays. "Dad's getting on," she said, "and I haven't seen my sister's children since they were toddlers. I'd invite you along but I'm afraid it would be awkward, our not being married and all."

"I understand," Sheffield said. "I'll spend Christmas with Chelsea and Austin."

"I rather thought you would." She hesitated. "Are you still determined to go through with your plan?"

"Yes, I am."

Jane shrugged and said no more.

After Jane was gone, Chelsea seemed to feel guilty about Sheffield being alone for Christmas. "You're welcome to come here," she said. "I'm not the greatest cook, but —"

"Actually, I'm going to England," he lied. "Jane telephoned last night and said she missed me. I'm taking the boat train on Christmas Eve."

What he actually took on Christmas Eve was a long, lonely walk around the gaily decorated Place de la Concorde, past the chic little shops staying open late along Rue Royale. All around him holiday music played, greetings were exchanged and the usually dour faces of the Parisiennes softened a bit. When his ankle began to ache, Sheffield bought a quart of gin, a loaf of bread, and a small basket of cold meats and cheese, and trudged back to his rooms. The cafe downstairs was closed, so he had to walk around to the alley and go up the back way. A thin, cold drizzle started and he was glad it had waited until he was almost inside.

Putting his food away, he lighted a little space heater, opened the gin, and sat trying to imagine what the future held for him. The telephone rang that night and several times on Christmas Day, but he did not answer it. He was too involved wondering about the rest of his life. And he was afraid it might be a wrong number.

Sheffield finally answered the telephone the following week when he came in one evening and found it ringing. It was Jane.

"I thought I ought to tell you, I'm staying over for a few days longer. There's a new cabaret opening in Piccadilly and they're auditioning dancers the day after New Year's. I'm going to try out. Actually, I've been thinking about working closer to home for a while. Dad's —"

"Yes, I know. Well, then. I wish you luck."

"No hard feelings?"

"Of course not. You?"

"Not anymore."

"Let me know how you make out."

"Sure."

After he hung up, Sheffield got the gin out again. He drank until he passed out. It was nearly twelve hours later when he heard an incessant pounding and imagined there was a little man inside his head trying to break out through his left eye with a mallet. When he forced himself to sit upright and engage his senses, he discovered that the pounding was on his door.

He opened the door and Chelsea burst in. "Austin's arm has been broken!" she announced, distraught.

On their way to Montmartre, she gave him the details. "We decided to go out for dinner last night, to celebrate finishing the last of the work on the car. We went to a little cafe on Rue Lacaur —"

"That's a rough section."

"Tell me about it. On the way home, we were walking past these two guys and one of them made a comment about me. Austin said something back, and before I knew it both of them jumped him. They beat him up badly and one of them used his knee to break Austin's arm like a stick of wood. It was awful!"

In the rooms over the garage, Austin was in bed with an ice compress on his face and his right arm in a cast. "Two years of work down the tubes," he said morosely.

"It could have been worse," Sheffield told him. "People have been shot and stabbed on that street."

"I thought for a minute one of them was going to slice Austin with a razor," Chelsea said.

"A razor?" Sheffield frowned. "What kind of razor?"

"One of those barber's razors. The kind that unfolds like a pocket knife."

"A straight razor," Sheffield said quietly. An image of Marcel's two bodyguards came into focus. The thin one carried a straight razor, and the other one looked strong enough to break arms.

Sheffield managed to keep his anger under control while he tried to reconcile Austin and Chelsea to the fact that it wasn't the end of the rally for them. He gave Austin the names of four drivers he knew who weren't signed up for Paris-Dakar this year and might consider an offer to make the run. Two were here in Paris, one was in Zurich, and the other at his home in Parma. "Call them and see what you can do," he said. "I'll go back to my place and see if I can think of any others."

As soon as he left the garage, he went to a telephone kiosk around the corner and called Marcel's office.

"You son of a bitch," he said when the Frenchman came on the line. "We had an arrangement that I was to keep Austin Trowbridge from winning."

"That is not precisely correct," Marcel said. "You agreed to take care of the *car*. I decided, because of the amount of money at risk, that it would be best to protect your guarantee with an additional guarantee."

"That wasn't necessary, you son of a bitch!"

"That's twice you've called me that," Marcel said, his tone icing. "I've overlooked it up to now because I know you're angry. Please refrain from doing it again, however. For your information —" his voice broke slightly "— my mother was a saint."

"I don't think you had a mother," Sheffield said coldly. "I think you crawled up out of a sewer!" Slamming down the receiver, he left the kiosk and stalked across the street to a bar. He had a quick drink to calm himself down, then another, which he drank more slowly as he tried to decide what to do. There was no way he could turn in Marcel's thugs without admitting his own complicity to Austin and Chelsea. And it was Marcel he wanted to get even with. But Marcel was always protected. How the hell did you take revenge on someone with the protection he had?

As Sheffield worried it over, the bartender brought him change from the banknote with which he'd paid for his drinks. Sheffield stared at the francs on the bar and suddenly thought: *Of course.* You didn't hurt a man like Marcel physically, you hurt him financially.

Leaving the second drink unfinished, something Sheffield hadn't done in years, he left the bar and hurried back to the rooms over the garage.

Austin and Chelsea were at the telephone.

"The two drivers here turned us down," Austin said. "I'm about to call the one in Zurich."

"Forget it," Sheffield said flatly. "I'm driving the Max One for you."

It wasn't even dawn in the Place d'Armes where the race was to start, but a thousand portable spotlights created an artificial daylight that illuminated the four lines of vehicles in eerie silver light. A hundred thousand spectators jammed the early-morning boulevard on each side, waving flags, signs, and balloons, cheering select cars and select drivers, the women throwing and sometimes personally delivering kisses, the men reaching past the lines of gendarmes to slap fenders and shout, "*Bon courage!*"

Young girls, the kind who pursue rock stars, walked the lines seeking autographs and more while their little brothers and sisters followed them throwing confetti. Everyone had to shout to be heard in the general din.

The Max One was in 182nd starting position, which put it in the forty-sixth row, the second car from the inside. Chelsea, in a racing suit, stood with Austin's good arm around her, both looking with great concern at Jack as he wound extra last-minute tape over the boot around his weak ankle.

"Are you absolutely sure about this, Jack?" the young designer asked. "It's not worth further damage to your ankle."

"I'm positive," Sheffield said. "Anyway, we'll be using Chelsea's feet whenever we can." Looking up, he grinned. "You just be in Dakar to receive the trophy."

"That trophy will be yours, Jack."

"The prize money will be mine," Sheffield corrected. "The trophy will be yours."

There was a sudden roar from the crowd and a voice announced through static in the loudspeaker that the first row of four vehicles had been waved to a start. The rally had begun.

"Kiss him good-bye and get in," Sheffield said, shaking hands with Austin, then leaving the couple alone for the moments they had left.

Presently father and daughter were side by side, buckled and harnessed in, adrenaline rushing, their bodies vibrating from the revving engine, their eyes fixed on the white-coated official who moved down the line and with a brusque nod and a wave started each row of four vehicles five seconds apart.

Sheffield grinned over at Chelsea. "I wonder what you mother would say if she could see us now?"

"I know exactly what she'd say — 'Birds of a feather.'"

"Well, maybe we are," Sheffield said.

"Let's don't get sentimental, Father," Chelsea replied. "Driving together from Paris to Dakar doesn't make a relationship."

Looking at her determined young face, Sheffield nodded. "Whatever you say, kid."

A moment later, they were waved away from the starting line.

From Paris to Barcelona would have been 850 kilometers if the road had been straight. But it wasn't. It wound through Loiret, Cher, Creuse, Correze, Cantal, and more — as if the route had been designed by an aimless schoolboy on a bicycle. Nearly all the way, the roadsides were lined with cheering, waving, kiss throwing well-wishers shouting, *"Bonne chance!"* From time to time flowers were thrown into the cars as they bunched up in a village and were forced to slow down. Farther south, cups of *vin ordinaire*, slices of cheese, and hunks of bread were shared. The farther away from Paris one got, the more relaxed and cheerful were the French people.

Sheffield and Chelsea didn't talk much during the trip south. She was already missing Austin, and Sheffield was concentrating on finding ways to relieve pressure on his weak ankle by holding his foot in various positions. These preoccupations and the increasingly beautiful French countryside kept them both silently contemplative. The Paris-to-Barcelona stage of the rally was a liaison — a controlled section of the route in which all positions remained as they had started — so it wasn't necessary to speed or try to pass. A few vehicles invariably broke down the first day, but for the most part it was little more than a tourist outing. The real race would not begin until they reached Africa.

It was after dark when they crossed the Spanish border and well into the late Spanish dinner hour when they reached Barcelona. As the French had done, the Spaniards lined the streets to cheer on the smiling, still fresh drivers in their shiny, unbattered vehicles. Because of the crowds, and the absence of adequate crowd control, the great caterpillar of vehicles inched its way down to the dock, where the Spanish ferry that would take them to Algiers waited. It was midnight when Sheffield and Chelsea finally drove onto the quay, had their papers examined, and boarded the boat. The first day, eighteen and a half hours long, was over.

Crossing the Mediterranean, Sheffield and Chelsea got some rest and nourishment and met some of the other drivers. Sheffield was well known by most of them already. He had asked Chelsea ahead of time how she wanted to be introduced. "I don't have to say I'm your father if you'd rather I didn't," he told her.

She had shrugged. "It makes no difference to me. Everyone knows we don't choose our parents."

"Or our children," Sheffield added. He introduced her simply as Chelsea and told everyone she was the vehicle designer's girlfriend.

Ferrand, the French driver, Vera Kursk, a shapely but formidable-looking Russian woman, and Alf Zeebrug, a Belgian, all expressed great interest in the Max One's structure configuration. They were, Sheffield remembered from his computations, the three favorites to win the rally: Ferrand in his Peugeot, Vera Kursk in a Lada, Zeebrug in the Volkswagen look-alike called an Ostend.

As they studied the Max One, Ferrand winked at Sheffield and said, "So you've brought in — what do you Americans call it, a ringer?"

Vera nodded her head knowingly. "I see why you passed up the trial races, Jack. Foxy."

"Let us look under the hood, Jack," pressed Zeebrug, knowing Sheffield wouldn't.

In the end, Ferrand spoke for them all when he said, "Welcome back, Jack. It's good to race with you again." Vera gave him a more-than-friendly kiss on the lips.

Later, Chelsea said, "They all seem like nice people."

"They are," Sheffield said. "They're here for the race, nothing else — no politics, no nationalism, no petty jealousies. Just the race." Ferrand, Sheffield was convinced, knew nothing about Marcel's machinations in favor of the Peugeot. Had he known, Ferrand — an honorable man and an honest competitor — would have withdrawn and probably sought out Marcel for physical punishment.

Another comment Chelsea made just before they docked was, "They all seem to like you, Father."

"There are some quarters in which I'm not a pariah," he replied. "Believe it or not."

In Africa, the first stage was Algiers to Ghardaia. Sheffield stuck a hand-printed list to the dashboard between them. It read:

Ferrand — Peugeot
Kursk — Lada
Zeebrug — Ostend

Sakai — Mitsubishi
Gordon — Range Rover
Smythe — Majorette

"These are the drivers and cars to beat," he told Chelsea. "I had a Mercedes on the list, too, but the driver was drinking too much on the ferry and bought a bottle of scotch to take with him when we docked. I don't think we'll have to worry about him."

Chelsea looked at him curiously. "I thought we were only in this to finish, so that Austin can get his design center."

Sheffield fixed her in a flat stare. "I'm a racer, kid. I enter races to *win*. This one is no exception. If you don't want to go along with that, you can get off here."

Chelsea shook her head determinedly. "Not on your life."

Sheffield had to look away so she wouldn't see his pleased smile.

During the first stage, it seemed to Chelsea that every car, truck, and motorcycle in the rally was passing them. "Why aren't we going faster?" she demanded.

"It's not necessary right now," Sheffield told her. "All these people passing us are the showboats — rich little boys and girls with expensive little toys. They run too fast too quickly. Most of them will burn up their engines before we get out of Algeria. Look over there —"

Chelsea looked where he indicated and saw Ferrand, Vera Kursk, and the other experienced drivers cruising along at a moderate speed just as Sheffield was doing. "I guess I've got a lot to learn," she said.

At Ghardaia, their sleeping bags spread like spokes around a desert campfire, the drivers discussed the day. "Let's see," Zeebrug calculated, "three hundred forty-four vehicles started and so far one hundred eighteen have dropped out."

"Good numbers," Ferrand said.

Vera Kursk smiled. "This could turn into a race instead of a herd."

Chelsea noticed that the Russian woman and Sheffield shared a little evening brandy from the same cup and that earlier, when the sleeping bags were spread, Vera had positioned hers fairly close to Sheffield's. Commie slut, she thought. When no one was paying any attention, Chelsea moved her own sleeping bag between them.

It took a week to get out of Algeria — a week in which Sheffield and the other experienced drivers continued to drive at reasonable, safe speeds that were easy on their engines, tires, and the bodies of both car and driver. All along the route, vehicles were dropping out — throwing pistons, getting stuck in sand, blowing too many tires, sliding off soft shoulders into gullies, dropping transmissions, or the exhausted drivers simply giving up. The Mercedes quit the second day — its driver, as Sheffield had predicted, drinking too much liquor for the heat he had to endure and the stamina required to drive. A surprise dropout was the Mitsubishi. Driven by the Japanese speed-racer, Sakai, it had hit a sand-concealed rock and broken its front axle. "One down, five to go," Sheffield said, drawing a line through Sakai's name on the dashboard list.

By the time they crossed into Niger, an additional sixty-three vehicles had dropped out. "That leaves one hundred sixty-three in," said Smythe, the Englishman driving the Majorette, when they camped that night. He was feeling good about the dropouts. At noon the next day, he joined them when the Majorette burned up its gearbox.

"Two down, four to go," Sheffield told Chelsea, and drew another line.

After camping one night in Chirfa, Chelsea noticed the next morning that Sheffield and Ferrand and the others shook hands all around and wished each other good luck. "What was that all about?" she asked.

"Everyone will be camping alone from now on." he said. "The socializing is over." Sheffield pointed toward a band of haze on the horizon. "We go into the Tenere Desert today. Now we start racing."

The terrain they encountered that day was hell on a back burner. The Max One was in ashlike sand up to its axles, plowing along like a man walking against a gale wind. The stink of the desert decay was unexpected and appalling to Chelsea. She gagged repeatedly. Huge white rats the size of rabbits leaped at the car windows. This stage of the rally that crossed the Tenere was a nightmare in glaring daylight no newcomer was ever prepared for.

Camped alone that night in some rocks above the desert floor, Chelsea saw Sheffield massaging his foot. "How's that ankle?" she asked.

"Just a little stiff. It'll be okay."

"Let's switch places tomorrow," she suggested. "I'll drive and you relieve." Up to then, Sheffield had done eighty percent of the driving. "Tomorrow," Sheffield told her, "we go over the Azbine Plain. Its like driving across a huge corrugated roof."

"Let me drive," she said quietly. "I can manage it."

He let her drive — and she took them across the rough terrain like a pilgrim determined to get to Mecca. Along the way, they saw Zeebrug lying at the side of the road, a rally first-aid team inflating a splint on his leg. The Ostend was nearby, upside down in a ditch, one wheel gone.

"Three and three," Sheffield said. He handed Chelsea the marker and she crossed off Zeebrug's name.

Into the second week of the race, both Jack and Chelsea began to feel the strain of the collective pressures: the usually unheated, quickly eaten food that wreaked havoc with their digestion, the constant jarring and jolting of the car that pummeled their bodies, the freezing nights sleeping on the ground, the scorching, glaring sun by day, the sand and dirt in their mouths, ears, eyes, noses, the constant headaches and relentless fatigue that the short rests could not remedy. Depression set in, underscored by the begging of poverty-stricken Africans everywhere they stopped.

"*Cadeau,*" the black children pleaded as Sheffield adjusted his tire pressure. "*Cadeau,*" they whined as Chelsea filled the radiator from a village stream.

"We have no gifts," Sheffield told them in English, in French, and by a firm shaking of his head. "Try to ignore them," he advised Chelsea, and she did try, but her eyes remained moist. As did his.

Just over the border in Mali, their physical and mental distress was displaced in priority and urgency by problems the Max One began to develop. A fuel line cracked and split, and they lost considerable petrol before Chelsea noticed the trail it was leaving behind them and they stopped to repair it. The lost fuel had to be replaced at a township pump at exorbitant cost. Later the same day, for no apparent reason, a center section of the windshield bubbled and cracked. Sheffield patched it with some of the tape he had brought for his ankle. The very next day, the odometer cable snapped and they were unable to monitor their distance to the end of the stage.

"Austin's damned car," Chelsea seethed, "is falling apart."

"It's holding up better than most," Sheffield bobbed his chin at two cars, two trucks, and a motorcycle that had dropped out at the side of the road. By then seventy-one more vehicles had quit the rally, leaving ninety-two still in.

Near Timbuktu, Sheffield and Chelsea happened on a small water pond that no one else seemed to notice. Behind a high rise, it had a few trees, some scrub, and even a patch of Gobi grass. "We've died and gone to heaven," Chelsea said when she was in the water. She began undressing. "I hope you're not modest."

"Not if you aren't."

The took their first bath in two weeks, and when they were clean they applied salve to their hips and shoulders where the Max One's seatbelts and harnesses had rubbed the skin raw.

"Mother never went with you when you raced, did she?" Chelsea asked reflectively.

"No."

"Who took care of you when you got hurt?"

"Whoever was around," Sheffield said. He looked off at the distance.

Chelsea patted his head maternally. "If you get hurt in this race, *I'll* take care of you," she assured him. Then she turned away to dress, as if her words embarrassed her where her nakedness had not.

After Mali, they crossed into Mauritania. The topography of the route seemed to change every day. One stage would be a mazelike, twisting and turning trail along a dry-riverbed, in turn sandy and dusty, then suddenly muddy where an unexpected patch of water appeared. Then they would encounter a long miserable stage of deep ruts and vicious potholes, then a log-and-rock-strewn track that shook their teeth and vibrated agonizingly in Sheffield's weak ankle.

With each kilometer, his pain grew more intense. During the day he swallowed codeine tablets. At night Chelsea put wet compresses on his ankle and massaged his foot. Those days they came to a stage that was open, flat straightaway, Chelsea did the driving and Sheffield enjoyed temporary respite from the pain.

Nearly every day they caught glimpses of Ferrand, Vera Kursk, and the Australian in his Range Rover. There were no smiles, waves, or shouted greetings now — just grim nods that said, so you're still in it, are you? Well, so am I.

Into the third grueling week, the pain, fatigue, and depression evolved into recrimination. "How in hell did I let myself get into this mess anyway?" Sheffield asked as he untaped his swollen ankle one night. "I don't owe Austin Trowbridge or you anything."

"How did *you* get into it! How did *I* get into it! Chelsea shot back. "I'm making the same damned mistake my mother made — getting mixed up with a man who thinks speed is some kind of religion."

"I could be back in Paris going to old movies," Sheffield lamented, "eating sausages with homemade mustard, drinking gin."

"And I could be in Philadelphia going to club meetings and playing tennis with your *other* daughter."

They caught each other's eyes in the light of the campfire and both smiled sheepishly. Chelsea came over and kneeled next to her father. "I'll do that," she said, and tended to his ankle.

Later, when he got into his sleeping bag and she was preparing to stand the first two-hour watch, flare gun at the ready, she looked very frankly at him. "You know," she said, her voice slightly hoarse from the dryness, "if we weren't blood relatives, I might find myself attracted to you."

Sheffield stayed awake most of the two hours he should have been sleeping. This was one race he would be very glad to have over — for more reasons than his swollen ankle.

From Mauritania, the route cut north across the border of the Spanish Sahara for a hundred or so kilometers of hot sand, between the wells of Tichia in the east and Bir Ganduz in the west. During that stage, with 71 vehicles of the original 344 still in the race, there was much jockeying for position, much cutting in, out, and around, much risky driving on soft shoulders, and much blind speeding as the dust wake of the vehicle in front reduced visibility to the length of your hood. It was a dangerous stage, driven with goggles and mouth masks, clenched jaws, white knuckles, tight sphincters, and the pedal to the metal, no quarter asked, none given.

In a one-on-one, side-by-side dash to be the first into a single lane between two enormous dunes, Chelsea at the wheel of the Max One and Gordon in his Range Rover were dead even on a thousand-yard straightway, both pushing their vehicles to the limit, when Gordon glanced over at the Max One and smiled in his helmet at the sight of the girl, not the man doing the driving. He had the audacity to take one hand off the wheel and wave good-bye as he inched ahead.

"You bastard," Chelsea muttered and juiced the Max One's engine by letting up on the accelerator two inches, then stomping down on it, jolting the automatic transmission into its highest gear and shooting the car forward as if catapulted. With inches to spare, she sliced in front of Gordon to the point where the dunes came together, surprising him so that he swerved, went up an embankment, and immediately slid back down, burying the Range Rover's rear end in five feet of what the nomad Arabs, translated, called "slip sand": grains that, although dry, held like wet quicksand. The Australian would, Sheffield knew, be stuck for hours, and was effectively out of the race as far as finishing up front was concerned.

"Nice work, kid," he said. Now they had only Ferrand and Vera Kursk with whom to contend.

That night they camped along with the other remaining drivers around the oasis well at Bir Ganduz. When the rally starts for the day were announced, they learned that seventeen more vehicles had fallen by the wayside on the Spanish Sahara stage, leaving fifty-four competitors: thirty-eight cars, ten trucks, and six motorcycles. Ferrand was in the lead position, one of the cyclists second, Vera Kursk third, and one of the trucks fourth, another cyclist fifth, and the Max One sixth.

"Are you disappointed we aren't doing better?" Chelsea asked as they changed oil and air filters.

Sheffield shook his head. "We can pass both cyclists and the truck anytime we want to. And probably will tomorrow. It'll come down to Ferrand, Vera, and us."

"Do you think we can beat them?"

Sheffield smiled devilishly. "If we don't, we'll scare hell out of them." For a moment then he became very quiet. Presently he handed Chelsea a plastic jar. "Hustle over to the control truck and get us some distilled water."

"The battery wells aren't low — I just checked them."

"I want some extra anyway, just in case. Go on."

As soon as she was out of sight, Sheffield reached into the car and got the flare gun. Turning to a stand of trees in deep shadows twenty feet from the car, he said, "Whoever's in there has got ten seconds to step out where I can see you or I'll light you up like the Arch of Triumph."

From out of the darkness stepped Marcel's two thugs. The one who carried a razor had a sneer on his gaunt brown face. The one with the bucket neck simply looked angry as usual. "We bring greetings from Marcel," said the thin one. "He said to tell you he is willing to be reasonable. Forget what has gone before. You and he will start fresh. He will cancel your debt and give you one-hundred thousand francs if you do not overtake Ferrand."

"No deal," Sheffield replied flatly.

"I am authorized to go to a hundred and fifty-thousand francs. That is twenty-five thousand dollars —"

"I can add. No deal."

The other man pointed a threatening finger. "To double-cross Marcel is not very smart —"

Sheffield cocked the flare gun. "You're the one who broke my friend's arm, aren't you? How'd you like to have a multicolored face?"

"No need for that," the thin one said quickly, holding up both hands. "We delivered Marcel's message, we have your answer. We'll go now."

"If I see you again," Sheffield warned them, "I'll tell the other drivers about you. They won't like what they hear. You'll end up either in a sandy grave or a Senegalese prison. I don't know which would be worse."

"Perhaps the young lady has an opinion," the thin man said, bobbing his chin toward the Max One, off to the side of Sheffield. It was the oldest ruse in the world, but Sheffield fell for it. He looked over to his left, and when he did the thin man leaped forward with enough speed and agility to knock the flare gun to the ground before Sheffield could resist. Then the man with the bucket neck was there, shoving him roughly until his back was against the car and driving a boot-toe hard against his painful ankle. Sheffield groaned and started to fall, but the other man held him up long enough to deliver a second brutal kick.

"That's all!" his partner said urgently. "Come on."

They were gone, leaving Sheffield sitting on the sand clutching his ankle, tears of pain cutting lines on his dry cheeks, when Chelsea got back. She ran over to him. "My God, what happened?"

"I must have stepped in a hole. It's bad —"

The ankle swelled to thrice its normal size. For several hours, Chelsea made trips to and from the public well to draw cold water for compresses. They didn't help. By morning, Sheffield couldn't put any weight at all on the foot.

"That does it, I guess," he said resignedly. "Ferrand and Vera will have to fight it out. But as least Austin will get his design center; you can drive well enough for us to finish."

"I can drive well enough for us to win," Chelsea said. She was packing up their camp. "I proved that yesterday."

"Yesterday was on a flat desert straightway. From here down the coast to Dakar are narrow, winding roads full of tricky curves, blind spots, loose gravel."

"I can handle it."

"You don't understand," Jack said, with the patience of a parent, "this is the final lap. This is for all the marbles — this is what the last twenty days of hell have been all about. These people still in the run are serious competitors —"

"I'm serious too," Chelsea asserted. "I'm a racer, I'm in this run to win. If you can't accept that, if you don't want to drive with me, drop off here."

Sheffield stared incredulously at her. "You're crazy, kid. Ferrand, Vera, and the others will run you off a cliff into the Atlantic Ocean if they have to."

"They can try." She stowed their belongings on the rear deck and closed the hatchback. "You staying here?"

"Not on your life," Sheffield growled. He hopped over to the car. The passenger side.

The last lap into Dakar was a war on wheels. All caution was left behind on the Spanish Sahara. This was the heavyweight championship, the World Series, and the Kentucky Derby. No one who got this far would give an inch of track. Anything gained had to be taken.

As soon as the stage started, the Max One dropped back to eighth, losing two positions as a pair of motorcycles outdistanced them. Chelsea cursed but Sheffield told her not to worry about it. "This is a good stretch for cycles. We'll probably be passed by a few more. They start falling back when we reach Akreidil; the track softens there and they can't maneuver well. Keep your speed at a steady ninety."

Chelsea glanced over. "I don't want advice on how to finish, just how to win."

"That's what you're going to get," Sheffield assured her. "You do the driving, I'll do the navigating. Deal?"

Chelsea nodded curtly. "Deal."

Sheffield tore the piece of paper from the dash and looked at the names Ferrand and Vera Kursk. Crumbling it, he tossed it out the window.

"Litterbug," she said.

"Shut up and drive, Chelsea."

"Yes, Daddy."

They exchanged quick smiles, then grimly turned their attention back to the track.

By midmorning the Max One was back to eleventh, but Ferrand and Vera had also fallen behind, everyone being outrun by the six daredevil cyclists still in the rally. This was their moment of glory and they knew it. They would lead the last lap of the run for three magnificent hours, then — as Sheffield had predicted — start falling behind at Akreidil. From that point on, the four-wheeled vehicles overtook and passed them one by one. Ferrand moved back into first place, Vera pressed into second, and the Max One held fourth behind a modified Toyota truck. They were all sometimes mere feet apart on the dangerous track along the Mauritanian coast.

"Blind spot," Sheffield would say as they negotiated weird hairpin turns. "Hug in," he instructed when he wanted Chelsea to keep tight to the inside of the track. "Let up," he said to slow down. "Punch it," to speed up. "Drop one," to go into a lower gear as he saw Ferrand's car suddenly nose up a grade ahead.

Two of the nine trucks behind them started crowding the track south of Mederdra, taking turns ramming into the Max One's rear bumper at ninety kph. "Get ready to brake," Sheffield said. Watching in a sideview mirror, he waited for exactly the right second, then yelled, "Brake!" Chelsea hit the brake and felt a jolt as one of the trucks ricocheted off the Max One's rear fender and shot across the rocky beach into the surf.

"The other one's passed us!" Chelsea shouted.

"I wanted it to," Sheffield said. "Watch."

The truck that had displaced them in fourth place quickly drew up and challenged the truck in third. For sixty kilometers they jockeyed and swerved and slammed sides trying to assert superiority. One kilometer in front of them, Ferrand and Vera held the two lead positions; behind them, Sheffield and Chelsea kept everyone else in back of the Max One to let the trucks fight it out. Finally, on the Senegal border, the crowding truck finally forced number three off the track and moved up to take its place.

"Okay!" Sheffield yelled at Chelsea. "His body's tired but his brain is happy because he just won. The two aren't working together right now. Punch it!"

Chelsea gunned the Max One and in seconds laid it right next to the victorious truck. The driver looked over, surprised. Sheffield smiled at him. Then Sheffield put his hand over Chelsea's and jerked the steering wheel sharply. The Max One leaped to the right, the truck swerved to avoid being hit, the Max One crossed the entire track, and the truck spun around and went backward into a ditch.

"Now let's go after Vera," Sheffield said.

"With pleasure," Chelsea replied.

It became a three-car race. For more than four hundred kilometers, speeding inland along Senegal's gently undulating sandy-clay plains, the Peugeot, the Lada and the Max One vied for position. Along straightaways, it became clear that Austin Trowbridge's car was superior in speed to both the French and Russian vehicles. Chelsea caught up with and passed them both. "Yeeeeoh!" she yelled as she sped into the lead.

"Don't open the champagne yet," Sheffield said.

When the straightaway ended and they again encountered a stretch of the great continental dunes, the experienced drivers once more out-maneuvered and outdistanced the Max One.

"What am I doing wrong?" Chelsea pleaded.

"Hanging out with race-car drivers."

"That's not what I mean!" she stormed, her sense of humor lost in the face of her frustration.

"We'll be on a sandstone flat when we cross the Saloum River," Sheffield calmed her. "You'll have a chance to take the lead again there."

When they reached the flat, Chelsea quickly caught up with Vera Kursk and passed her, and was pressing Ferrand for first place when the accident happened. A pack of hyenas, perhaps a dozen, suddenly ran in front of the Peugeot. Seasoned professional that he was, Ferrand did not swerve an inch as he felt the impact of his grille on the animals he hit and the rumble of his tires on those he ran over. Then one of the hyenas was spun up into the wheel well and in a mangle of flesh and blood jammed the axle. Ferrand's front wheels locked and his vehicle flipped end over end, landing a hundred feet out of the flats, bursting into flames.

"Stop the car!" Sheffield ordered, and Chelsea skidded to a halt on the shoulder. They unharnessed and leapt out, Sheffield grabbing the portable fire extinguisher, Chelsea helping him to balance upright on his swollen ankle. As they ran, hobbling, toward the burning car, they became aware that the Lada had also stopped and Vera Kursk was getting out.

At the fiery Peugeot, Sheffield handed Chelsea the extinguisher. "Start spraying the driver's door!" Chelsea pointed the red cylinder and shot a burst of Halon up and down the door. It immediately smothered the flames on that side and Sheffield was able to reach through the window, unstrap Ferrand, and drag him out of the car. Sheffield and Chelsea each took a hand and, Sheffield limping agonizingly, dragged the unconscious man far enough away so that when the Peugeot exploded none of them was hurt.

From overhead came the sound of a rotor. Looking up, Sheffield and Chelsea saw a rally control helicopter surveying a place to land. Paramedics wearing Red Cross armbands were in an open hatch waiting to touch down.

"They'll take care of him," Sheffield said. He stood up, holding onto Chelsea for support, and they looked across at the Max One and the Lada parked side by side. Vera Kursk was beside the Lada, peering down the track, where several kilometers back came the surviving vehicles. Smiling, she threw Sheffield and Chelsea a wave and quickly got into her car.

Chelsea started running, dragging Sheffield, with her. "The bitch!" she said.

"I'd do the same thing in her place," Sheffield groaned.

By the time they were harnessed back into the Max One, the Lada was half a kilometer ahead and the rest of the pack was moving up behind them very quickly. "We're almost to Dakar," Sheffield told his daughter. "If you want to win, you'll have to catch her."

Chelsea got back on the track and shot the car forward like a bullet. Into the African farming communities she sped, watching for animals, people, other vehicles, always keeping the Lada in sight. "Am I gaining on her, do you think?" she asked.

"Not yet."

Through the farmland, into the nearer outskirts, past larger villages, a soap factory. "Am I gaining?" she shouted.

"Not yet."

Past a power station, a cotton mill, small handicraft shops at the side of the road, a huge open-air market, increasing lines of spectators in marvelously colored native garb. "Am I gaining?"

"Not yet."

"*Goddamn!*"

Then into the city of Dakar itself and on to the far end of Gann Boulevard, a wide, tree-lined thoroughfare roped off a mere one hour earlier, when the control aircraft advised the city that the first of the rally vehicles was approaching. The boulevard led straight to the finish line in the Place de l'Independence. The Lada was still half a kilometer ahead. "Punch it!" Sheffield yelled. He beat his fist on the dashboard. "Punch it! Punch it!"

Chelsea punched it.

The Max One drew up dead even on the right side of the Lada. The two women exchanged quick, appraising glances, saw only unyielding determination in the other, and as if choreographed, both leaned into their steering wheels and tried to push their accelerators through the floorboards. "Come *on!*" Chelsea muttered through clenched teeth.

The Max One pulled forward an inch. Then two. Then three. Vera Kursk glanced over again, desperation in her eyes. Sheffield yelled, "All right!"

The cars sped down to the finish line next to the war memorial in the great plaza. Thousands cheered them on from a vast crowd that was but a blur of color to the drivers. Stretched across the end of the boulevard, a great banner with FINIS lettered on it fluttered in the breeze. The Max One was less than a car length ahead, the Lada's windshield even with the American vehicle's rear bumper. Then Vera punched the Lada.

"She's pulling up!" Sheffield cried.

Chelsea saw Vera's face moving closer to the sideview mirror. In seconds, the Russian woman was next to her again. Biting down hard enough on her bottom lip to draw blood, Chelsea punched the Max One again.

The Max One crossed the finish line one and a half seconds ahead of the Lada.

At the banquet that night in the Saint Louis Hotel, Chelsea and Vera Kursk hugged each other and Austin Trowbridge read everyone a cable he had received congratulating him on the Max One and advising him that a bank account had been opened for five million dollars to start the Trowbridge Automotive Design Center. "I'd like you to come back to the States and be my partner," the young man told Sheffield. "Between the two of us, we can come up with cars nobody's ever imagined."

"I'll think about it, kid," Sheffield promised.

At midnight, Sheffield rode with Chelsea and Austin in a taxi out to Grand Dakar Airport, where they watched the Max One being rolled into the cargo hold of a Boeing 747 bound for Casablanca and New York. The young couple had seats in the passenger section of the same plane.

"Austin and I are going to be married when we get home," Chelsea told Sheffield. Austin had gone ahead, giving them time to say good-bye. "And we're going to start having babies. The first boy we have, I'm naming Jack. After a guy I met recently."

"Do yourself a favor," Sheffield said. "Raise him to be a doctor."

She shook her head. "Not on your life." She kissed him on the cheek. "Bye, Daddy."

"See you, kid."

Sheffield watched the plane rumble down the runway and climb into the starry African sky. Then he sighed and limped slowly off the observation deck and back into the terminal. When he reached the glass exit doors, he was met by the familiar face he'd been expecting.

"Hello, Marcel."

The Frenchman's two thugs were standing nearby.

"The Max One was pressing Ferrand when he crashed," Marcel

accused. "You were racing to win."

"I always race to win," Sheffield replied evenly.

"Do you think you can get away with double-crossing me?" The Frenchman's eyes were narrowed and dangerous.

Sheffield merely shrugged. "What are you going to do, Marcel, kill me?" He cocked his head in the best John Garfield tradition. "Everybody dies," he said arrogantly.

Pushing through the doors, he walked painfully out into the Senegalese night.

CUSTER'S GHOST

The old man learned of the anniversary ceremony entirely by accident. One of the previous night's patrons had left a newspaper on the bar, and it was still there when the old man came in early the next morning to clean up. Wiping down the bar, he had picked up the paper to throw it away, but his still-quick eyes had caught a glimpse of two words that he recognized beneath a picture on the open page. The picture, of an old man like himself, meant nothing to him, but the two words beneath it had been etched in his mind for fifty years.

Stopping his work, he studied the words carefully to be certain he was not mistaken. He could not read, so he studied each letter, all fourteen of them. They spelled: WENDELL STEWART. When the old man was absolutely sure that the letters and words were the same as he remembered, he carefully folded the newspaper and put it in the pocket of his old, worn coat, which he had hung inside the door. Then he resumed his job of cleaning up the saloon.

Three hours later, when his work was done, the old man locked up the saloon, put on his frayed coat, and limped down the little New Mexico town's main street to a combination cafe-pool hall above which he had a room. He went into the kitchen of the cafe and showed the newspaper to Elmo, the black fry cook.

"Read this for me, please, Elmo," he said.

"I can't read, John," the black man said without embarrassment. "Ask Stella."

The old man took the newspaper to Stella, the white waitress, who was filing her nails on a stool behind the cash register.

"Will you read this for me, please, Stella?" he asked.

"Sure, John. Which one? This one? Sure." Stella cleared her throat. "It says, 'Ceremony Planned for Fiftieth Anniversary of Custer Battle.' You want me to read the whole story?"

John nodded. "Yes, please."

"Sure. 'A ceremony co-mem-mor-ating the fiftieth anniversary of the Battle of the Little Bighorn and the defeat and death of General George A. Custer and his Seventh Cavalry has been scheduled for June 25, 1926, at the Custer Battlefield National Monument near Hardin, Montana. Being honored at the ceremony will be former cavalry corporal Wendell Stewart, one of the survivors of A Company, commanded by Major Marcus Reno, which was also nearly annihilated on a ridge three miles away after the Custer massacre. Stewart, one of twenty men who received the Congressional Medal of Honor for bravery that day, is believed to be the sole survivor of the Custer regiment. He is seventy-three years old.' " Stella paused and studied the old man to whom she was reading. "Say, John, you must be about the same age as him, aren't you?"

"I am almost seventy summers," John answered.

Stella cracked her chewing gum. "You sure talk funny sometimes, John. Want me to read the rest?"

"No, that is enough. Can you tell me what is the number of today?"

"You mean the date? Sure. This is yesterday's paper, so today must be Thursday, June 16, 1926."

"How many days is it until the day the newspaper speaks of?"

"Well, let's see, that would be —" Stella counted on her fingers "— nine days, not counting today." She tilted her head, raising one eyebrow curiously. "Why? You're not thinking of going up there, are you, John? It's a mighty long way."

"How long a way?"

Stella shrugged. "I don't know. A *long* long way. That's Montana and this here is New Mexico. I can tell you this: we're at the bottom of the map and that's at the top."

Two customers came in and Stella went to wait on them. John folded the newspaper and went back into the kitchen.

"How far is it to Montana?" he asked Elmo.

The fry cook smiled. "Now you asking the right man," he said proudly. "I ain't never learned to read, but, brother, I done hoboed all over this here country, top to bottom, and side to side. 'Tween here and Montana you got Colorado and you got Wyoming. I expect you got about twelve hundred miles. A good, long piece, my friend."

"Thank you, Elmo," the old man said.

He went to the kitchen door and limped up the back stairs, favoring his right leg. There were three rooms above the cafe. Elmo lived in one, an old Mexican with a government pension lived in another, and John occupied the third. Because John had dark skin, most people thought he was also Mexican, or at least part Mexican. But he was not.

In his little room, John spread the newspaper on top of a faded old bureau in which he kept his few clothes. From the bottom drawer he removed an odd-looking pouch, shaped like but slightly larger than a saddlebag, from the bottom of which hung what appeared to be, and in fact was, a brown, hairy tail. The pouch itself was also hairy, except in spots where the hair had worn off, leaving a shiny brown skin. It was a buffalo bag, and it was almost as old as John himself.

Opening the flap, John pulled out a faded blue cavalry campaign hat, its brim bent and broken, its crown crushed and lifeless. The old man straightened it out as best he could and placed it upside down next to the picture in the newspaper. On the inside band of the hat, just barely legible after so many years, were the same fourteen letters and two words that he had found in the newspaper: WENDELL STEWART.

John shifted his eyes to the newspaper and stared at the face above the name. As he did so, he reached down and rubbed the dull, constant pain in his right leg.

So, he thought, the spirits have finally brought you to me.

After fifty years.

For many years he had used the name John Walker, but once he had been Walks-across-Prairies, a young Oglala warrior and a follower of Crazy Horse, his chief. His people had been members of the seven tribes which made up the great Teton Sioux Nation. He had ridden a pony bareback across the vast High Grass, the plain that stretched from the foot of the Black Hills all the way to the Rosebud in the place the bluecoats called Montana.

Child, boy, and young man, he had been a Sioux.

When the spell of the moment was over, and he no longer stared hypnotically at the photo of Wendell Stewart, the old man reached into his buffalo bag again and drew forth a crudely made but structurally solid and well-crafted stone and pine hatchet. It was his war club of long ago, and the wood of the pine handle was so old it had petrified nearly as solid as the smooth rock that was its head. He closed his still-strong right hand around the handle and held the club diagonally across his chest.

In the cracked mirror above the bureau, he looked at his old, lined face, its skin now similar in texture to the buffalo bag itself. His hair, though still thick, was white like a summer cloud. The line of his mouth had relaxed with the passage of time and no longer served to advise others of the arrogance and defiance that once burned inside him. He knew that much of the fire had gone out of him, but he was pleased to see that his eyes were still clear and alert. The spirits, he thought, always knew what they were doing. His grandfather, Many Leaves, had taught him that, when he was a boy living in the tipi of one of his father's wives.

"If the great spirits did not know in which direction to go, they would not move at all," Many Leaves had told him. And added quietly, "Unlike human beings."

It was obvious to John what the spirits now wanted him to do. The picture and the words in the white man's newspaper had been his sign. He was to return to the great battlefield and meet the bluecoat called Wendell Stewart, the soldier who had wounded John's right leg with a long, shiny saber and given him his limp.

For fifty years of pain, he was to kill Wendell Stewart.

The next morning when the sun began to rise, John turned his right shoulder toward the light and began walking. His buffalo bag was slung over one shoulder, and he also carried an old carpetbag he had stolen years earlier from a drummer of needles and thread. On his feet he wore his hightop white-man's shoes, but in the buffalo bag he carried the last pair of moccasins he had made for himself some ten years earlier. When he got to the High Grass, he would put on the moccasins. He walked down the street of the little New Mexico town where he had made his home for more than nine years and, without a backward glance or a regret, began his journey north.

The first day, he passed through towns called Hatch, Arrey, Caballo, and Chuchillo, and by dusk was in a place called Socorro. He did not know addition and subtraction as such, so he had no way of figuring that he had to travel 130 miles in each of the nine days he had in order to arrive at the battlefield on the day of the ceremony. He knew only that it was north and far away, and since the spirits wanted him to get there in time, he *would* get there in time.

His leg hurt as he walked, as it always did, but it was advantageous in a way because his limp provided him with many rides. Farmers in wagons gave him lifts, country people driving buggies stopped for him, salesmen in Model T cars took him from town to town so they could have someone to talk to.

"Yessir, I paid three hundred and fifty dollars for this little buggy," one of them said the second day, north of Albuquerque. "Never thought I'd pay that much money for *any* car. But it's worth it. Got a self-starter — don't even have to crank it."

John merely grunted. The cost meant nothing to him. He seldom had more than a little money. Mostly he earned only enough for food, shelter, and clothing. But that had always been enough — his needs were few and simple.

His travel day began at the first hint of sunup. As soon as he was able to tell direction, he was up and moving. During the day he ate berries and other wild fruit — at night he stole corn and melons from the fields when he could and picked up stray chickens here and there. He would have trapped small game for his meals, but he was in too much of a hurry. Nights he slept in haystacks or woods. The second night it rained and he slept under a country bridge. It had been a long time since he had slept outdoors — it was good to see the stars last thing before going to sleep.

John was pleasantly surprised that he did not dream during his journey. For fifty years, since the long-ago day of the battle, he had dreamed sporadically of Custer. Long Hair, as he had been called by Crazy Horse. Long Hair often came to him in his dreams — buckskin-clad, yellow hair flowing from under the wide-brimmed white leather hat. In the dreams, Custer would walk directly toward him, eyes fixed, arms swinging slightly, pistols stuck in the belt of his buckskin coat. He would keep coming, growing larger and larger, seeming bent on trodding over John. Finally he would fill the boundaries of John's mind, become too big for the dream itself, and that was when John would wake up.

John was convinced that his dream image was Custer's ghost, and he hated and feared the dream. As the trip back took him closer and closer to the only place where he had ever seen Long Hair, he had presumed he would be troubled by the dream every night. But he was not, and that made him even more sure of the spirits that had planned his journey.

Even without the dreams, however, he found himself thinking of Custer as he traveled.

The time of the battle was as fresh in John's mind in 1926 as it had been immediately after it happened, in 1876. There had been 12,000 in their vast camp on the banks of the Little Bighorn back then. Tipis stretched for three miles on both sides of the river. Totanka Yotanka, the great Uncpapa medicine man, whose name translated to Sitting Buffalo, but whom the bluecoats called Sitting Bull, had summoned every tribe on the northern plains to come forward and council with him about the encroachment of the whites onto land that had been ceded to them by the Ft. Laramie Treaty of 1868.

All of South Dakota west of the Missouri River, including the sacred Black Hills and all of the Powder River country of Montana, was supposed to be theirs.

It was known as the Great Sioux Reservation and Hunting Ground. There they had lived in peace with all tribes — except the unworthy Crow, of course — for eight years. Then someone had found gold in the Black Hills, and the greedy whites had swarmed in like ants to an anthill. The Sioux had lashed out to protect what the white chief had ceded to them. And the white chief had ordered his bluecoats in to subdue them. When the soldiers began their marches, from faraway places called Omaha and St. Paul, Sitting Bull sent word for all tribes to join him at the Little Bighorn.

For the first time ever, they came together as one people. The Uncpapa, Oglala, Miniconjou, Sans Arc, Blackfoot, Brule, even the austere, high-minded Northern Cheyenne, who considered themselves the Superior Ones. For the first time ever, their leaders, Crazy Horse, Low Dog, Gall, Black Moon, Big Road, Two Moon, and Hump, were all disenchanted with the white man at the same time. Twelve thousand people gathered to hear Sitting Bull's medicine, and of that number 4,000 were of fighting age.

Walks-across-Prairies had just turned nineteen. Since he had been a boy of eleven, there had been peace with the white eyes. Walks-across-Prairies had never counted a coup, except among the shiftless Crow, and that certainly was no honor to boast about. When he complained to his grandfather, Many Leaves, about it, Many Leaves had said, "A worthy enemy is a valuable thing. But no enemy at all is even more valuable. Count coup with the buffalo, my grandson, so that an old man like me might have a new robe before the snows come."

Walks-across-Prairies had taken his grandfather's advice, and for a while he was content with his lot. But when the call came from Sitting Bull, and Crazy Horse ordered the camp struck and moved to the Little Bighorn, the young brave felt a new kind of excitement in his breast.

An excitement that meant warpaint.

On the third day of his journey, John made it into Colorado and was picked up by an oil-truck driver going from Alamosa to Mineral Hot Springs.

"Know anything about this feller Tunney they got matched with the champ?" the man asked.

John shook his head. He did not know what the man was talking about.

"I seen a pitcher of him," the trucker said. "Looks pretty fancy to me. Ain't even got much of a beard. You know, that Dempsey, why, he's got such a rough beard he can draw blood with it."

"This Dem-see, he is a warrior?" John asked.

"I'll say!" the truck driver laughed.

It did not bother John that even after fifty years he knew so little about the ways of the white man's world. He had not tried to learn more than he knew. He felt it was enough that he could now speak the language. Until he was twenty-five, he spoke only Sioux, because after the great battle he had followed Crazy Horse and Sitting Bull into exile in Canada. The great chiefs knew that the white government would not tolerate their great victory over the bluecoats.

"When the white-eyes defeat us, it is a victorious campaign," Many Leaves had said. "But when we defeat them, it is a massacre. The white-eyes are clever with words."

Following the battle, great trails of tribes had moved north into Saskatchewan. The chiefs knew that the bluecoats could not follow them there — some treaties they would *not* break. They planned to live on the Canadian side and return secretly to the Montana plain to hunt buffalo, which was not plentiful in Canada. But the bluecoats, ever spiteful over the "massacre," put up intense patrols all along the border — in effect, sealing it. They themselves killed buffalo for sport, but would not permit the Indian to kill it for food and hides.

Walks-across-Prairies remained in Canada for six years. For nearly all of the first year he was practically helpless from his severely wounded right leg. The women cared for him until he could walk again. The first time he realized that he would limp the rest of his life, he cried. Then he imagined what Many Leaves, by then dead, would have said. Something like: "A man is not judged by how straight his legs are, but by how straight his heart is." That was the first of many times to come when, to bolster his spirit, he would imagine something his grandfather probably would have said.

A year after the Custer battle, he saw Crazy Horse lead one thousand of his people down to Ft. Robinson, Nebraska, and take them onto the reservation because he could not feed them. Others began to straggle after him — Gall, with his people, then Two Moon, then Low Dog. Finally, after five long years, Sitting Bull led the last forty-three tattered, starving families down to Ft. Buford, Montana, and surrendered.

Walks-across-Prairies remained in Canada another year, living alone, hunting small game to survive, fishing, occasionally making his way north to Moose Jaw to steal necessities such as rifle cartridges and salt to cure meat. When the loneliness began to gnaw at him, he left Saskatachewan, and walked into Manitoba. He walked all the way across that province and entered the United States again at Pinecreek, Minnesota. For ten long but uneventful years he wandered mid-America. He crossed to Wisconsin, went over the top of Michigan, down into Indiana, over to Ohio — so far from the High Grass that at times he thought he was in another world.

Gradually he adopted the white man's dress and began to do white man's work. He toiled in the fields for white farmers, fished off boats on Lake Huron for white fishermen, cut trees in white timber camps, herded milch cows for white dairymen. He was surprised to find that as time went by, the white-eyes regarded him with less and less animosity — and even more surprised to realize that he was beginning to feel the same about them. At all times, for years, he kept his war club handy, but he never had to hit anyone with it. It was a strange life he led, but he slowly became used to it.

Traveling now on his journey back to the Little Bighorn reminded John of his incredible lifelong pilgrimage around the United States. The little town in New Mexico where he had lived for nine years was the longest he had ever stayed in one place since his wanderings began.

At thirty-five he had been in the Midwest, at forty and forty-five in the Deep South where he learned to pick cotton. At fifty he had been shoveling coal in the engine room of a New Orleans paddleboat up and down the Mississippi. At fifty-five he had been a cook's helper on a cattle drive in Texas. At sixty he worked in the oil fields in Oklahoma, where his employer was a Cherokee millionaire.

A couple of years later he had wandered down into the desert of New Mexico because his bones had begun to ache when it rained or snowed, and he remembered Many Leaves once saying, "After a man passes his sixtieth summer he should look for a warm place to die so that he will not feel the chill of death so strongly." John found his warm place in a little desert community where he got the job cleaning up the saloon in the morning and the cafe-pool hall at night. For just enough money for food, clothing, and shelter. All a man needed.

When the oil-truck driver let him out in Mineral Hot Springs, John waved and said, "I hope your warrior Dem-see wins his battle." The driver laughed and drove away.

That night, John found a bubbling hot spring outside town and soaked his tired old body in it for three hours. It made him feel strong again. The spirits still knew what they were doing.

On the fourth day, he passed through Poncha Springs, Colorado, walking; Buena Vista, riding a hay wagon; Leadville, on an ore truck; Dowd, walking. Day five took him out of Colorado and into Wyoming. He passed the welcome sign at the sate line — he could not read it, but he knew he was making progress because for the first time in many years he saw purple prairie clover growing at the edge of fields. He collected some and put it into his buffalo bag to dry. He also found some wild currant flowers that day and picked fifty of their small blue-black berries.

That night, near Saratoga, he trapped a young rabbit, roasted and ate its legs, and stretched the rest of the meat out, crushed the berries all over it, poured fat from the cooked meat of the rabbit on top of that, and pounded all of it together with a rock. Then he laid it out to dry by his campfire. By morning it would be pemmican, a dry emergency food much like beef jerky he could carry with him the rest of the trip. Afterward, he steeped the purple prairie clover in water he boiled in a tin cup and make himself some wonderful tea to warm his old bones against the night air.

On the sixth day, he made it to within twenty miles of Casper, and the next morning was given a ride on a Baptist revival bus all the way to Sheridan — more than 150 miles. With half of the day still left, he walked out of Sheridan and by late afternoon came suddenly upon the Tongue River and knew he was in the High Grass country again. Montana.

He made his bed that night on the bank of the Tongue, and for the first time in many years he dreamed not just of Custer, but of Custer's death.

"Today is a good day to fight, and a good day to die," Chief Low Dog told his warriors, who sat on the ground gathered around him the morning of the battle. Walks-across-Prairies stood nearby with Crazy Hose and other Oglalas.

"Low Dog is a fool," Crazy Horse said quietly to his group. "No day is a good day to die, but every day is a good day to fight and live. I think Low Dog has given his brain to the white man's picture box." The Sioux chief was highly contemptuous of all the Sioux leaders who, for a few worthless trinkets, had allowed themselves to be photographed during the years of the peace. Crazy Horse himself had never permitted a picture to be taken of him. "I want no one to see my face if I cannot see theirs," he gave as his reason.

It was noon that day when Sioux scouts brought them word that Custer's regiment was crossing the plain.

"Long Hair has split his bluecoats into three forks," the leader of the scouts reported. "The captain called Ben-teen has taken one hundred twenty-five men and turned toward the foothills of the Wolf Mountains. They are moving well away from Long Hair. The other captain called Ree-no has taken one hundred forty men and crossed Rosebud Creek. He now moves in the same direction as Long Hair, who has two hundred fifteen men on the other side of the creek."

"How soon will they reach the Little Bighorn River?" Crazy Horse asked.

"When the sun is there," the scout replied, pointing to mid-sky in the west. By three o'clock.

Gall, who was obnoxious and a braggart, spat on the ground. "Long Hair is a fool," he announced. "He will ride right into our midst."

Crazy Horse, tall and regal, with a single white feather in his hair, grunted quietly. "Long Hair is no fool. A better bluecoat does not live. But his judgment fails him when he chooses scouts. He relies on information given him by the idle-minded, no-account Crow. They are too lazy to scout more than three miles ahead of the bluecoats." He smiled. "We will lie in wait four miles ahead. We will lure Ree-no and his soldiers away when they reach the fork of the creek. Then we will meet Long Hair at the Little Bighorn."

And that was the way it happened. A party of forty warriors rode up on Reno's column four miles from the Little Bighorn. Custer ordered Reno to pursue them with full strength. Reno led his 140 men galloping after the forty warriors. The warriors led them three miles across the plain — where one thousand more warriors waited for them behind a knoll. Reno and his men were immediately cut off and driven up onto a bluff where they took cover and dug in.

Custer was now alone with 215 men, riding along one side of the creek that ran into the Little Bighorn. Crazy Horse, at the head of another army of one thousand warriors, waited in a low valley on the other side of the river. When the cavalry column was where Crazy Horse wanted it, the Oglala and his warriors rode up the grassy bank and across the shallow river. Custer and his men were totally, completely — and fatally — surprised.

"No white man or Indian ever fought as bravely as Custer and his men," Oglala chief Low Dog would say in an interview at the Standing Rock Agency five years later, after he had returned from Canada and surrendered. "The white soldiers stood their ground bravely and none of them made any attempt to get away. Our warriors were told not to mutilate the head white chief, for he was a brave warrior and died a brave man, and his remains should be respected."

When all but fifty of his men lay dead around him, Custer ordered his remaining soldiers to follow him to a small hill that formed the highest point on the immediate plain. There the legendary "Last Stand" took place. Crazy Horse's Sioux abandoned their ponies at this point and fought on foot, with rifles and war clubs, swarming up the low hill on all sides.

Walks-across-Prairies had counted six coup on his way up the hill. His bare chest and arms were drenched in his enemy's blood. He saw a white man in civilian clothes take a blow to the back of the head from a war club and fall dead. He didn't know until later that it was Custer's brother, Boston Custer, who had been traveling with the Seventh Cavalry as a civilian historian. A few minutes later, when there were just a few bluecoats left, perhaps a dozen, he saw a very brave captain standing shoulder-to-shoulder with Long Hair, both of them firing pistols with both hands, until finally a rifle bullet struck him in the throat and he died. That brave captain had been Tom Custer, another brother of Long Hair.

Many historians were to speculate over the decades that followed whether Custer was the last to die that afternoon. Most conclusions were that it was highly unlikely. But unlikely or not, Walks-across-Prairies knew it to be true. Custer lasted the longest that day because his men, who idolized him, fought closely around him, and took the early bullets and blows meant for him. Walks-across-Prairies had been thirty feet from Long Hair when he took the fatal bullets that killed him. It would have been good, he thought later, if Crazy Horse could have been the one to kill him — a chief deserved to die at the hand of another chief — but that was not the way that day. Walks-across-Prairies vividly remembered that Long Hair was killed by two warriors: Mud-between-the-Toes shot him in the right breast, and Two Dogs shot him in the left temple.

After Custer fell, Crazy Horse stood by the corpse and said, "Long Hair's body is sacred. It shall not be cut."

And it had not been.

On the last day of his journey, John awoke on a low bluff near a tiny village called Lodge Grass. There was a water hole directly below the bluff, and it was for that reason that John had chosen to sleep there. He knew that in the early morning the buffalo would come to water, and he could watch them. He awoke when he heard the bulls snorting at each other, and splashing as the calves ran playfully into the water.

John sat up and for an hour watched the big, thick, somehow majestic animals as they started their day. There were about thirty of them, including the young — just enough, John remembered, to make a good tipi for winter. It took about twenty dressed hides to make a fifteen-foot tipi, another ten for ground covering and sleeping robes.

Watching them, the old Indian nodded fondly. Then his eyes became sad. Once, he thought, there would have been a hundred or more in the herd that watered here. Now there were thirty. He sighed a deep, quiet sigh. The buffalo and the Sioux, he thought, have gone the same way. Soon both would be only memories.

When the sun was midway in the morning sky, John prepared for the day. Now that he knew where he was, he knew also how long it would take him to get where he was going. He had about three hours easy walk across the High Grass. From his buffalo bag, he removed his moccasins and put them on, then packed the rest of his belongings.

Before he left the bluff, he searched for and found a cluster of white Dakota snowberries, and nearby some thriving bloodroot plants. Securing a quantity of each, he put them on separate flat rocks and squeezed the juices from their flowers and roots. When he was finished, he had two small portions of dye, one red and one white.

He wished he could paint his face, but he knew that a painted Indian, even an old one, would have little if any chance of getting past the modern-day bluecoats who guarded the battlefield. So he removed his shirt and streaked only his chest — one horizontal white line across the top, as he would have done his forehead, and three vertical lines drawn down from that, which would have covered his nose and each cheek. It was the Sioux symbol of life, the white line being the tribe, and three red lines being the stages of life: child, warrior, Old Person.

For the first time ever, John thought of himself as an Old Person. If life had gone on as it should have, if the whites had stayed off their land and left them alone, today he would be considered a respected elder, and would be treated with honor and dignity. Instead of having to clean out a saloon every morning.

But soon, he thought, taking the war club from his bag, he would make a place for himself in the last tales to be told around Sioux campfires. He would count one more coup — and drive the ghost of Custer from his head.

As he walked toward the half-century-old battlefield that day, John Walker, once again Walks-across-Prairies, thought about the man he would kill.

He knew almost nothing about Wendell Stewart. They had met for only a brief, fleeting instant an hour after the Last Stand. Walks-across-Prairies and some of the other young, eager Oglalas had joined Low Dog in his assault against Major Marcus Reno and the soldiers who had been lured away from Custer. By that time, Captain Frederick Benteen and the contingent Custer had sent toward the Wolf Mountains had hurried back to reinforce Reno. The young Oglalas who had fought Custer were still fresh — it had taken them only forty-five minutes to win that battle. By then it was only four o'clock on that June afternoon. Still plenty of daylight left for fighting.

It was while Walks-across-Prairies was helping fight Reno and Benteen that a young blond-haired corporal had seized the saber of a fallen officer and slashed the right calf of Walks-across-Prairies as he had ridden through in a pony charge. Walks-across-Prairies had swung at the soldier with his war club, felt it glance off bone, and whipped his pony away with the soldier's hat caught on his war club. They had never seen each other again.

Now, after fifty years, their fight would resume.

By noon, John stood at the edge of the old battlefield where the anniversary ceremony was to take place. There were already a number of people there. They had come in Model T cars, wagons, buggies. John looked around but he didn't see anyone who resembled the newspaper picture of Wendell Stewart. He waited patiently. Under his shirt, the war paint was dry and hard on his chest. In his buffalo bag was the war club.

As he waited, the old man studied the battlefield. There were small marble stones marking where each cavalryman's body had been found. The stones formed a weaving line that snaked its way up the hill. At the top of the hill was a large monument. John walked up and stood beside a schoolboy who was looking at it.

"Is this the grave of Cus-ter?" he asked the boy.

The boy shook his head. "General Custer's not buried here. They took him back to West Point to bury."

John shook his head briefly. That was a sad thing. Long Hair would have wanted to sleep with his soldiers. John had never heard of this "West Point." He hoped it was a place of honor.

"Who lies here?" he asked the boy, touching the monument.

"The last fifty men who died with Custer," the boy said. He pointed to a cluster of markers on one side of the hill. "Those are where the last fifty died. The one at the top there is General Custer's. Just behind his is his brother's, Captain Tom Custer. Right next to that is Captain Myles Keogh. His horse Comanche was the only survivor, man or animal, in this whole battle. 'Cept for Indians, of course. And see the marker way down at the bottom? That was General Custer's other brother, Boston Custer." The boy squinted up at the old Indian. "Anythin' else you want to know?"

John shook his head. "No. Thank you for helping me."

When the boy left, John walked over to the crest of the hill, to Custer's marker. He could still see him: white buckskin field uniform, wide-brimmed white leather hat, flowing yellow silk scarf, saber on his belt, pistol in each hand, firing down into the wall of Sioux coming up the hill, missing Mud-between-the-Toes and Two Dogs, who raised their rifles simultaneously —

"Ladies and gentlemen," a voice said through a megaphone at the bottom of the hill, "our anniversary ceremony will begin shortly. Will everyone please gather in front of the museum building."

John watched the visitors move in small groups over to the brick building at the edge of the battlefield. His eyes searched the crowd but still did not see Wendell Stewart. Frowning, he made his way back down the rise and walked around the edge of the group, studying faces but recognizing none. Finally he had gone all the way around the crowd and found himself at a side door of the small museum building. There was a young soldier there with a rifle.

"May I help you, sir?" he asked.

John's frown deepened. "Sir" was the title of respect the bluecoats used when addressing their chiefs. Why would this young soldier use it when speaking to him? Perhaps his old ears had played a trick on him.

"I am looking for the old soldier called Wen-dell Stew-art," John said.

"The guest of honor," said the soldier. "He's still inside. Use the front door, right around there."

John nodded. "Thank you."

"You're welcome, sir."

There, he had said it again. This time John was certain of it. The soldier had called him "sir." He had spoken to him with respect.

Still frowning, John went around to the front of the museum and entered. There were a few stragglers still inside, looking at maps and photographs and displays of uniforms and other memorabilia from the great battle. John's eyes swept the faces — and suddenly stopped, locking on the face of Wendell Stewart. The old white soldier was sitting down. A man, woman, and young girl were standing around him, their backs to John. Although it might have been his imagination, John was almost certain that the instant he recognized Stewart, he felt a sharp surge of pain where the saber had cut the tendons of his right calf.

Fifty years, and the spirits had brought them together again. For the final battle.

John's hand went into the buffalo bag and slipped the war club out. He held it at his side, handle gripped tightly. As he eased toward the small cluster of people, he made up his mind to hit Stewart at the top of the head rather than in the face. A soldier who had lived as long as Stewart had did not deserve to have his face destroyed. I will leave him his dignity and take only his life, John decided.

Slowly, he edged nearer to the man, woman and young girl, catching only glimpses of the seated Stewart when the people around him shifted their positions. John moved past the back of the man, then the woman, then stepped easily around the young girl to face his old enemy.

And there he stopped.

Wendell Stewart was in a wheelchair. He had no right leg.

Inside John's head, he heard what he imagined Many Leaves would have said. "It is better to have a leg that hurts for fifty years than to have no leg at all."

Wendell Stewart and the three people standing with him all stopped talking and stared at John. Stewart's eyes flicked down to the war club he held. The old white soldier tensed.

Softening, John stepped forward and held the club out to the man in the wheelchair. "I hit you in the head with this a long time ago," he said simply.

Stewart stared harder at him, frowned, then parted his lips incredulously. "And I cut your leg with Lieutenant Gibson's saber."

John nodded. "It has hurt for fifty years." He pulled the old campaign hat out of his bag. "This is yours."

Stewart took the hat and ran his fingers over it. Tears came to his eyes. The young girl knelt and gave him a handkerchief. "Here, Granddad."

"Where did you lose your leg?" John asked.

"On that same bluff with Reno and Benteen," the old soldier replied, wiping his eyes. "About an hour after you and I met. I was a little dizzy from the blow on the head you gave me. I didn't get out of the way fast enough and a Sioux warrior ran a lance through my thigh. By the time we got back to Ft. Lincoln two days later, I had gangrene and the post surgeon had to take it off."

"I am sorry you lost it." John said.

Stewart nodded. "I'm sorry, too, that your leg has hurt for so long."

They were next to a wide window that looked out on the markers, the hill, and the great plain beyond.

"There was room enough for everyone, red *and* white," John said.

"Yes. Yes, there was."

The young girl touched John's arm. "What's your name, sir?"

"Sir" again. John almost smiled, but checked it in time. He must maintain his dignity among these strangers, and smiling was not dignified at his age.

"I am Walks-across-Prairies," he said proudly. "Of the Oglala."

"Would you like to push my grandfather outside for the ceremony?" she asked.

"It would be a great honor."

As the old Sioux pushed the old cavalryman to the gathering outside, he asked quietly, "Do you ever dream about Custer's ghost?"

"No," Stewart replied. "I dream about Crazy Horse's ghost."

Walks-across-Prairies nodded solemnly. The spirits *did* know what they were doing.

THE PLATEAU

Tank Sherman felt his daughter Delia's hand shaking him gently. "Tank, Tank, wake up. Bruno's dead."

Tank sat up, moving his legs off the side of the cot where he had been napping, fully clothed except for his boots. Bruno? Bruno dead?

"You mean Hannah," he said, automatically reaching for his boots.

"No, Tank, I mean Bruno. Hannah's still alive. It's Bruno that died."

Tank frowned. That was not the way it was supposed to happen. He pushed first one foot, then the other, into black Atlas boots with riding heels. He had owned the boots for eighteen years, and they were as soft as glove leather. After he got them on, he sat staring at the floor, still confused. Bruno dead? How could that be? Bruno was young; Hannah was old. And it was on Bruno that the lottery had been held.

"What happened?" he asked Delia.

"I don't know. Doc Lewis is on his way over to check him." She crossed the little one-room cabin to the stove and turned on a burner under the coffee pot. Getting out a cup, she poured a shot of peach brandy into it. "Will they still have the hunt, do you think? Since it's Hannah and not Bruno?"

"No," Tank said emphatically, "they couldn't. Hannah's too old. It wouldn't be a hunt; it would be a target shoot."

When the coffee was ready, Delia poured it in with the brandy and brought it to him. As he sipped it, Tank studied his daughter. She had the dark hair of her mother: thick and black as a crow's wing. And the high cheek-bones of her mother's people, the Shoshone. Her light half-breed coloring and blue eyes she got from him. All her life she had called him Tank instead of Daddy. At nineteen, her body was round and strong. She lived in her own mobile home down the road, and dealt blackjack for a living in an illegal game behind the Custer's Last Stand restaurant. Tank himself still lived in the cabin where Delia had been born. He had been alone for a year, since Delia left; and lonely for six years, since her mother had died of bone disease.

"Are you going down to the concession?" Delia asked.

"In a minute." He held the coffee cup with both hands, as if warming his palms, and smiled at his daughter. "Remember how your ma used to raise hell when she caught you lacing my coffee with brandy?"

"Yes," Delia smiled back.

"She always wanted me to make something of myself, your ma. Always wanted me to do something important. But I guess it just isn't in the cards. If Hannah had died first, like she was supposed to, why, I could have done something important for the first time in my life. Important to your ma, at least, if she was still alive. And to Bruno. But Bruno ups and dies first, so I'm left with nothing important to do. If your ma was still alive, she'd swear on her medicine bag that I arranged it this way."

Shaking his head wryly, Tank drank a long swallow from his cup. At fifty, he was a rangy, well-worn man with not an ounce of fat on him. His face showed the results of a hundred fists, maybe more. Twenty years earlier he had come to town as part of a traveling boxing show, whites against Indians. Dan Sherman, his name had been, but they billed him as Tank because he was so tough. Tank Sherman, after the Sherman tank. A hide like armor. Took punches like Jake LaMotta. But he had taken too many by then. In their little Montana town, a Northern Cheyenne who hated whites had beaten him to a pulp, and when the outfit moved on it took the Northern Cheyenne with it and left Tank behind. Delia's mother had found him sitting behind the 7-Eleven trying to eat some crackers and Vienna sausage he had bought with his last dollar. His lips were swollen so grotesquely he could barely chew, his eyes puffed to slits through which he could hardly see. Delia's mother took him home with her. They were never to part. Delia was their only child.

"Let's go on down to the concession," Tank said, when he finished his coffee.

His cabin was on the slope of a low hill, and as Tank and Delia walked down its path they could see a small crowd already beginning to gather at the concession's corral. The concession itself was nothing more than a small barn next to the corral, with a gaudy red sign over its door which read: LAST TWO LIVING BUFFALO — ADMISSION $1. Tourists bought tickets and lined up around the corral, then the barn doors were opened and Bruno and Hannah were driven out to be viewed. They were the last two remaining buffalo in North America.

Now there was only one.

Old Doc Lewis, the reservation veterinarian from the nearby Crow agency, had just finished examining Bruno when Tank and Delia eased their way through the crowd to him.

"What killed him, Doc?" asked Tank, looking down at the great mass of animal spread out on the ground.

"Stroke," the vet said, brushing off his knees. "He was carrying too much weight. Must have been upwards of two thousand pounds."

Tank nodded. "Can't run off much fat in a corral," he observed.

Doc Lewis was making notes in a small book. "How old was he, do you know?"

"Nine," Tank said. "My wife helped deliver him." His scarred boxer's face saddened as he noticed his daughter reach out and pat the dead buffalo's massive head. Then he glanced over to the corral and saw Hannah, standing quietly, watching. Unlike Bruno, a young bull, Hannah was a cow and much older: at least thirty. She had thinner, lighter hair than most buffalo, and a triangular part of her neck and shoulder cape was almost blonde, indicating the presence somewhere in her ancestry of a white buffalo. Much smaller than Bruno, she stood only five feet at her shoulders, and weighed a shade over seven hundred pounds.

"I guess this means the big hunt is off, doesn't it, Doc?" Tank asked. It was the same question Delia had asked Tank, and Doc gave the same answer.

"Of course. There wouldn't be any sport at all going after Hannah. She's much too old."

The three of them walked over to Hannah and, as if compelled by some irresistible urge, all patted her at once. "Well, old girl," Doc said. "you made the history books. The last North American Plains buffalo."

"Maybe they'll put her on a stamp or something," said Delia.

"Maybe," Doc allowed. "They already had the buffalo on a nickel, but that was before your time."

From the barn, a pretty young woman in the tan uniform of a state park ranger walked over to them. White, educated, poised, she was everything that Delia was not. "Hello, Dr. Lewis, Mr. Sherman," she said. "Hello there, Delia." She snapped a lead rein onto the collar Hannah wore. "I just got a call from headquarters to close down the concession. And to trim Hannah's hooves. Isn't it exciting?"

Doc and Tank exchanged surprised looks. "Isn't what exciting?" Doc asked, almost hesitantly. Instinctively, both he and Tank already knew what her answer would be.

"The hunt, of course. Oh, I know it won't be the same as it would have been with Bruno as the prey. But it will still be the last buffalo hunt ever. That's history in the making!"

"That," Doc rebuked, "is barbarism."

"Are you saying the hunt's still on?" Tank asked. "With Hannah as the prey?"

"Of course." She shrugged her pretty shoulders. "I mean, how else can it be? The tickets have been sold, the lottery had been held. You don't expect the state to go back on its word, do you?"

"No," Delia said, "definitely not. Never. Not the state."

"Well, there you are," the young ranger said, missing Delia's sarcasm entirely. "But, listen, they have changed the rules a little to make it fairer. Bruno was only to be given a twelve-hour start, remember? Well, Hannah gets a full twenty-four." She smiled, apparently delighted by the allowance.

Doc Lewis turned and walked away, thoroughly disgusted. Tank and Delia left also. Walking back up the path to Tank's cabin, Delia said, "Looks like you're getting our chance to do something important, after all."

Tank, thinking about his dead wife, nodded. "Looks like."

When it had become clear that the Plains buffalo had finally reached the threshold of extinction, when it was absolutely certain that no new calves would be born because the remaining cows were too old to conceive, the state had immediately done two things: penned up the few remaining members of the species and put an admission on their viewing; and devised a nationwide lottery to select the persons who would be allowed to hunt, and take the head and hide, of the last American buffalo. Both moves proved enormously successful. The Last Remaining Buffalo concession, let by the state to one of its own departments, the Bureau of Parks, was open nine months of the year. Managed by park rangers, it operated under very low overhead, and was the most profitable tourist attraction in the state. All around the corral where the buffalo were exhibited, there were coin-operated machines where for a quarter visitors could purchase cups of processed food pellets to toss into the corral for the buffalo to eat. Like peanuts to caged monkeys. Except that the buffalo refused to do tricks. Despite considerable effort in the beginning, including the use of a whip, the buffalo had remained stoic and refused to be trained. Finally the park rangers had to resign themselves to simply leading their charges into the corral and letting them stand there while small children pelted them with synthetic food. The attraction, nevertheless, was popular.

As profitable as the concession was, however, its earnings were modest compared to the proceeds of the lottery. In a scheme devised by one of the General Accounting Office's young financial wizards, two million numbered tickets had been sold throughout the state and through the mail nationally, for five dollars per chance. The ticket supply was exhausted within a month, and the state had made a quick ten million dollars. Even people who had no interest whatever in hunting bought a ticket for investment speculation. Even before the drawing, advertisements had already been run by people offering to buy a winning thicket from anyone whose number was picked.

The drawing, wherein three winners were selected, was by the use of a single, predesignated digit each day from the total shares traded on the New York Stock Exchange. The lucky ticket holders were a piano tuner in Boston, a waiter in Memphis, and a ranch hand in Nevada. The piano tuner sold his ticket for ten thousand dollars to Gregory Kingston, the actor. The waiter sold his for eighty-five hundred to best-selling author Harmon Langford. Lester Ash, the ranch hand, kept his, deciding that the head and hide would be worth far more than the ticket. He was counting on being a better hunter and shot than the actor and author.

Within two hours of the untimely death of Bruno, the three registered owners of the winning tickets were notified to come claim their prize. Hannah, the last surviving Plains buffalo, would be released fifty miles out on the prairie at noon on Friday.

At noon on Saturday, the three lottery winners would be free to hunt her.

By midnight on Thursday, Tank Sherman was ready to go. Hitched to the rear of his Ford pickup truck was a double stall horse trailer from which he had removed the center divider, creating one large stall. Parking the rig on the prairie some one hundred yards behind the concession corral, he and Delia slipped through the quiet night to the barn, snipped the padlock with bolt-cutters, and led Hannah out. The old buffalo cow was as docile as a rabbit and made no noise whatever as Delia fed her a handful of fresh meadow grass, and Tank slipped a braided halter over her head.

After walking the buffalo aboard the trailer and quietly closing her in, Tank handed Delia an envelope. "Here's the deed to the cabin and lot. And the passbook to your ma's savings account. She had six hundred and forty dollars saved when she died; it was supposed to be yours when you were twenty-one. Oh, and the title to the pickup is there too, just in case. Guess that's about all."

Delia got a paper bag and thermos jug from her jeep.

"Sandwiches," she said. "And coffee. With, uh —"

"Yeah. With brandy." He put the bag and jug on the seat of the pickup, and sniffed once as if he might be catching cold. But he wasn't catching cold. "Listen, take care of yourself, kid," he said brusquely, and started to get into the truck. Then he turned back. "Look, I know I ain't never won no Father-of-the-Year prize, and I never gave you no place to live but that cabin, and I never sent you to college or nothing; but those things don't have nothing to do with caring. You understand?"

"Sure," Delia said. She shrugged. "After all, you did teach me when to fold in poker. And how to change a flat. And how to get a squirrel to eat out of my hand. Lots of girls never learn those things." She had to struggle to control her voice. She was not able to control her tears. But she knew that Tank could not see the tears in the darkness.

"Okay," he said. "I'll be hitting the road then."

He eased the door of the pickup shut, quietly started the engine, and slowly pulled away without headlights.

Behind him, Delia waved in the darkness and said, "'Bye — Daddy."

When he reached the highway, turned on his headlights, and increased speed, Tank thought: *Okay, Rose, this is for you, honey.*

Rose was Tank's dead wife, the woman who had always wanted him to do something important. Her Shoshone name was Primrose, given to her by her father because she had been born on a day in early July when the evening primrose had just blossomed. Later, when she moved into town and took up the ways of the white woman, she shortened it to Rose.

Tank always remembered Rose as being beautiful, but she was not; she was not even pretty. Her face was very plain, her eyes set too close together, her nose too long, and one cheek was pitted with pockmarks. Only her hair, lustrous as polished onyx, could truly be called beautiful. But Tank saw so much more of her than was outside; he saw her hopes and dreams, her pride, her nakedness when they made love, her secret joys. He saw everything about her, and it was all those things combined which made her beautiful to him.

The first time she had shown him the buffalo was three months after she had taken him to live with her. After she had nursed him back to health from the beating he had taken. They got up early one morning on Rose's day off from the sugar beet processing plant, and in her old Jeep they drove thirty miles out onto the raw prairie. There, on an isolated meadow, was a small buffalo herd: three bulls, a cow, six calves. They were the beginning of the last migration, when the ocean of tourists had started driving them north and west from the Black Hills.

"See how noble they look," Rose had said. "See the dignity with which they stand and observe." Her eyes had become watery and she added, "They are watching their world come to an end."

Once, Rose explained to him, there had been sixty million Plains buffalo. Their presence on the Northern Plains had been the greatest recorded aggregation of large land animals ever known to man. To the red man of the prairie, the vast herds had been the mainstay of his economy. That single species provided food, clothing, shelter, and medicine for an entire race: the only time in history that such a natural balance between man and beast had ever been achieved.

"Then, of course, the whites came," Rose said. "At first, they killed the buffalo for meat and hides, as our people did, and that was acceptable because the herds were many. Later they killed them only for hides, leaving the carcasses to rot in the sun. Even that act, although it was without honor, could have been tolerated. But then they began killing them for what they called sport. Sport. Fun. Recreation. They killed them first by the tens of thousands. The butcher Cody, whom they called Buffalo Bill, personally recorded more than forty-two thousand kills in one seventeen-month period. Soon they were being slaughtered with total wantonness, by the hundreds of thousands. Today there are only a few hundred left. Most of them are in the Black Hills. But they are slowly migrating back up here again."

"Why?" Tank asked, fascinated by the tale.

"They know the end is nearing for them. A species can tell, you see, when their breed is running out. Each year they see fewer and fewer calves, the herds become smaller and smaller. So they look for a place to end their line. They look for a grassy meadow unspoiled by humans. A place to lie down and die with dignity."

For all the years Tank Sherman knew and lived with the Shoshone woman Rose, she had loved the great buffalo and mourned its diminishing number. As much as Tank missed her in death, he was glad that she had not lived to see Bruno and Hannah, the last two of the breed, penned up and put on display. Or known about the lottery for the privilege of hunting the survivor.

So this is for you, honey, he thought as he headed southeast with Hannah in the horse trailer. He would have about five hours headstart. Possibly two hundred fifty miles. Maybe it would be enough.

Maybe not.

Two hours after dawn, a tall, very handsome man, livid with anger, was stalking back and forth in the empty concession corral.

"What the hell do you mean, missing? How can something as large as a buffalo be missing?" His name was Gregory Kingston. An Academy Award-winning actor, he was not acting now, he was incensed.

"The state guaranteed this hunt," said a second man. Smaller, plumper, not as handsome, but with a good deal more bearing, this was Harmon Langford, internationally known best-selling author. Like Kingston, he was dressed in expensive hunting garb, carrying a fine, hand-tooled, engraved, foreign-made rifle. "Exactly who is in charge here?" he quietly demanded.

A third man, Lester Ash, the ranch hand from Nevada, stood back a step, not speaking, but observing everything. He wore hard working clothes, denim, twill, roughout leather.

"Gentlemen," a Bureau of Parks spokesman pleaded, "please believe me, we are trying to get to the bottom of this as quickly as we can. All we know right now is that some person or persons apparently abducted Hannah sometime during the night. The highway patrol has been notified and a statewide search is getting under way at this very moment —"

"Why in hell would anyone want to abduct a *buffalo?*" Kingston inquired loudly of the world at large, throwing his arms up in bewilderment. Now he *was* acting.

"Oh, come, Kingston," said Harmon Langford, "we're not talking about *a* buffalo, we're talking about *this* buffalo. Unlike ourselves, there are those," and here he glanced at Lester Ash, "who are interested in this animal not for sport, but for profit." Lester Ash grinned but remained silent. Langford continued, "At any rate, we cannot waste time on *why*; we must concentrate on *where*. Where is our great hairy prize? And how do we get to it?"

The Bureau of Parks man said, "We should be hearing from the highway patrol anytime now. Every road in the state is covered —"

"What do we do now?" asked Gregory Kingston, directing the question at Langford.

"We must be prepared to get to the animal as quickly as possible after it is located," the author declared, "before some outsider decides to take an illegal shot at it. This part of the country is crawling with would-be cowboys, you know. Pickup trucks, rifle racks in the back window, old faded Levi's: that sort of thing. I'm sure there are a few of them who would like to be remembered as the man who gunned down the last buffalo —"

"Like you, you mean?" Lester Ash said, speaking for the first time.

A smirk settled on Langford's lips. "Yes," he acknowledged. Adding, "And you."

They locked eyes in a moment of mutual understanding, and then Langford said, "What we need, of course, is fast, flexible transportation." He turned to the Parks man. "How far is the nearest helicopter service?"

"Fifty miles."

"I suggest we start at once. If we have a helicopter at our disposal by the time the buffalo is located, we can hurry there at once. I presume the state would have no objection to that?"

The Parks man shrugged. "Not so long as all three of you get an equal start. And don't shoot it from the air."

"Of course not. We aren't barbarians, after all." He looked at Kingston and Lester Ash. "Are we agreed?"

"Agreed," said the actor.

"Let's go," said Ash.

Three hours earlier, Tank had parked the pickup and trailer in a stand of elm and gone on foot deeper into the trees where Otter had his cabin. It had still been dark; the eerie void before dawn. He knocked softly at Otter's door.

"Who disturbs this weak old man at such an hour?" a voice asked from within. "Is it someone evil, come to take advantage of my helplessness?"

"Otter, it is Sherman," said Tank. "Your daughter's man before she passed."

"What is it you want?" asked Otter. "I am destitute and can offer you nothing. I have no money or other valuables. I barely exist from day to day. Why have you come to me?"

"For your wisdom, Otter. For your words."

"Perhaps I can give you that, although I am usually so weak from hunger that each breath could well be my last. How many others have you brought with you?"

Tank smiled in the darkness. "I am alone, Otter." Maybe now the old scoundrel would stop acting.

"You may enter," Otter said. "There are candles by the door."

Inside the front door, Tank lighted a candle that illuminated patches of an incredibly dirty and impoverished room. In one corner, an ancient cot with torn, sagging mattress; in another a rusted iron sink filled with dirty pots and pans; in a third an old chifforobe with a broken door hanging loose to reveal a few articles of ragged clothing. Everywhere in between there was dirt, grime, clutter.

Tank did not even pause in the room. He lit his way directly to a door which led to a second room, and in that room he found Otter sitting up in a king-size bed, a cigar in his mouth, a bottle of whiskey at his side. As Tank closed the door behind him, the old Indian uncocked a double-barrel shotgun on the bed beside him and put it on the floor. "How are you, Soft Face?" he asked. The first time he had seen Tank, the young fighter's face had been beaten to pulp. Otter had called him Soft Face ever since.

"I'm okay," Tank said. "You look the same."

The old Indian shrugged. "There is no reason for something perfect to change."

Tank grinned and glanced around the room. It was a self-contained little world, holding everything Otter needed or wanted for his personal comfort. Portable air conditioner, color television, microwave oven, upright freezer, power generator, small bathroom in one corner, indoor hot tub and Jacuzzi in another. "How's the bootlegging business?" Tank asked.

"My customers are loyal. I make ends meet." Otter got out of bed and put a Hopi blanket around his shoulders. "Is my granddaughter still dealing cards in the white man's game?"

"Yes."

"Does she cheat them when the opportunity presents itself?"

"Yes, if they are tourists."

Otter nodded in approval. "That is good. Even a half Indian should cheat the whites whenever possible." At a two-burner hot plate, Otter set water to boil. "Sit here at the table," he said. "and tell me your problem."

Tank quietly explained to the old Indian what he had done, and why. When he got to the part about Rose and her love for the buffalo, Otter's eyes became misty. When Tank stopped talking, Otter rose, poured coffee and brandy for them, and brought it to the table. "How can I help you?" he asked.

"I need a safe place to put the old buffalo. Someplace where she can live out her days in peace, without fear of being hunted and shot. Someplace where she will be able to die with dignity, like your daughter Primrose would want her to die."

Otter sipped his coffee and pondered the problem. Several times he shook his head in silence, as if first considering, then dismissing, a possibility. Finally he tapped a forefinger on the table and said, "Do you remember the place where Ditch Creek runs beside Bear Mountain?"

"In the Black Hills?" said Tank. "Where you used to take us on picnics when Delia was a little girl?"

"That is the place. There is a grassy meadow far above Ditch Creek that belongs to the few remaining people of the Deerfield tribe. It is within the Black Hills National Park, but the federal government deeded it to the Deerfields because there was no road into it and they must have figured the tourists would not be able to get to it anyway. The Deerfield use it for religious ceremonies; it is sacred ground to them. The buffalo would be protected once it got there. But there are only dirt paths leading up to the meadow. I don't know if the buffalo could climb it or not."

"How high is it?" Tank said.

"About seven thousand feet. There is a gravel road to about six thousand, but the rest of the way would be on footpaths. It would have been better if you had stolen a mountain goat. You were never very smart, Soft Face."

"Can you draw me a map?" Tank asked

"Of course. I am a man of many talents."

Otter got paper and pencil and from memory sketched a map and gave it to Tank. It was daylight now and the two of them walked out to the horse trailer and Tank backed Hannah out to exercise and feed her.

"She is a fine old buffalo," Otter observed. "Only your people would even think of shooting her."

"Just because they're the same color doesn't mean they're my people," Tank replied.

Tank tethered the buffalo to a tree and returned to the cabin with Otter. The old Indian cooked breakfast and they ate together. Then it was time for Tank to leave. Otter walked back to the rig and helped him load Hannah. After Tank got in and started the truck, Otter put a hand on the door.

"In each man's life, there is a plateau," he said quietly. "Every man reaches that plateau. He may be there for a day or a year, or only for a moment. But his time there is the meaning of his life. It is the reason the Great One put him here on earth. I think, Soft Face, that your plateau might be that grassy meadow above Ditch Creek." He touched Tank's shoulder. "Go with the wind, son."

Tank swallowed dryly, nodded and drove off.

The helicopter was flying a checkerboard search pattern two hundred miles from where the buffalo had been stolen. Harmon Langford sat next to the pilot. Gregory Kingston and Lester Ash occupied jump seats behind them.

All three men scanned the ground below with binoculars.

"This is maddening," Kingston muttered. He tapped Langford on the shoulder. "Tell me again!" he yelled through the noise of the rotor. "Why are we looking in this direction?"

The author yelled back, "The highway patrol reported that a pickup truck pulling a horse trailer filled up with gas in Dayton at four o'clock this morning! The station attendant said the animal in the trailer had a blanket over it and the man driving the truck said it was a rodeo bull! But he thinks it was our buffalo! They were headed toward Gillette! We're searching the area south of Gillette!"

The actor shrugged, as if it were all totally meaningless to him. Lester Ash leaned close to his ear and said, "Highway patrol thinks he might be headed toward Thunder Basin! That's a big grassland area; be a perfect place to set a buffalo loose!"

"I see!" Kingston said, smiling. "Now *that* makes sense!" He patted Ash fondly on the knee. Ash drew back suspiciously.

The helicopter continued to checkerboard, its pilot crossing out squares on a plot map on the console. They flew well into the grasslands, twenty miles deep, and began a random searching pattern, following shadows, wind movement, wild game — anything that attracted their attention. But they did not find what they were looking for. They searched for another hour.

"We'll have to land for fuel soon," the pilot advised Langford.

No sooner had he spoken than they received a radio message from the Parks man back at the concession. "The trailer has been sighted by a Civil Air Patrol scout plane. It's on Route 16, south of Osage, heading toward the Black Hills. It's sure to make it across the state line, so we're requesting the South Dakota state police to set up road-blocks. I'll keep you advised."

"How far is Osage?" Langford asked the pilot.

"Fifty miles, give or take."

"Can we make it?"

"Yes sir, but that'll be the limit. We'll have to refuel in Osage."

"Go," Harmon Langford ordered.

Tank had his CB turned to the law enforcement band, so he heard the South Dakota state police order go out for roadblocks. They were being set up in Custer, Four Corners, and at the junction of Routes 85 and 16. Pulling onto the shoulder of the road, Tank shifted to neutral and unfolded a map he had picked up at a service station near Sundance, where Otter lived. When he had stopped at the station, the tarp flaps on the trailer had been down so no one could see inside; he was sure it had not been the station attendant who put the law on him. Probably that low-flying two-seater that had come in over him outside Osage.

Studying the map, Tank saw that the locations selected for the road-blocks gave him considerably more leeway than he had expected. Apparently they thought he was going to try to drive well into the Black Hills. He was not; he needed to penetrate them only a few miles before reaching a secondary road that ran north and then east to Ditch Creek. Smiling, he saw that he would miss all three roadblocks. Getting out of the truck for a moment, he lifted one of the trailer flaps and reached in to pet Hannah's thick, hairy cape.

"We're going to beat the sons of bitches, old girl," he said happily.

It had not occurred to him that they might use a helicopter.

At Osage, Harmon Langford conferred by telephone with the authorities responsible for the roadblock. "Of course, I very much appreciate your help in containing this man, Captain, and I assure you that when I write my bestseller about this incident, you and your men will be prominently featured. Now if you'd just be good enough to keep your forces in place and let my associates and me handle it from here, I think justice will be properly served. We really don't consider this a criminal matter; it's more mischief than anything else; a nuisance, but we can handle it —"

Then he talked with the pilot of the scout plane. "Are you keeping him in sight?"

"Yes, Mr. Langford. He's moving up a secondary road toward a place called Ditch Creek."

"Fine. Keep circling and don't lose him. We'll be airborne again in a few minutes and should be there shortly to take over. Of course, I'll expect to see you after this is all over, for photographs and such. The national publicity, you know. Over and out."

As Langford turned to face them, Kingston and Lester Ash saw a look of gleeful triumph on his face. Almost an evil look.

"In a very short while, gentlemen," he said, "we should be in position to take our buffalo back. I trust both of you are prepared to deal with this abductor if he resists us?"

Kingston frowned. "What do you mean?"

Langford did not answer. Instead, he picked up his rifle and jacked a round into the chamber.

Watching him, Lester Ash smiled.

Turning off the secondary road into the inclining gravel road, Tank was aware that the patrol plane was following him. But he was not overly concerned. The two men in the light plane could not get to him: no place in the surrounding hills they could land. All they could do was radio his position. And he was too close to his goal now for that to matter. He knew where the roadblocks were: no one from there could catch up with him. Only one obstacle remained in his way.

The thousand feet of footpath from the end of the gravel road up to the meadow.

Frowning, he wondered if old Hannah was going to be able to make it. A lot would depend on how steep the trail was, and what kind of footing it offered. Good dirt footing was what he hoped for; Hannah's freshly trimmed hooves would slide too much on rock.

At the end of the gravel road, Tank drove the rig as far into the trees as he could. Part of the trailer still stuck out and he knew it could be seen from the air. No matter, he thought, they can't catch us now.

"Come on, old girl," he said as he backed Hannah out of the trailer and rubbed her neck. Studying the terrain above them, he selected the least steep path he could find and gently pulled Hannah onto it. Moving about four feet ahead of her, he drew the halter rope tight and urged her forward. She stepped nimbly up the trail and followed him without resistance.

This might be easier than I thought, Tank told himself hopefully.

The helicopter rendezvoused with the scout plane an hour after Tank and Hannah began their climb.

"Where are they?" Langford asked the air patrol pilot on the radio.

"In those trees on the side of the mountain, sir. You can't see them right now because of the overgrowth. They're probably about halfway up to that grassy meadow on the plateau there."

Langford praised the two men in the plane for exemplary work, dismissed them, and turned to the helicopter pilot. "Set down on the grassy meadow," he ordered.

"I can't do that, sir," said the pilot, who was half Nez Perce. "That's sacred land belonging to the Deerfield tribe. Outsiders are not permitted there."

Langford shifted the barrel of his rifle until it pointed toward the pilot. "I really do want you to land," he said pointedly.

The Nez Perce breed smiled. "I'd be careful with that rifle if I were you, sir. Unless you or your friends know how to fly one of these babies. They go down mighty fast."

Pursing his lips, Langford shifted the barrel back. He reached into his pocket, extracted a roll of currency, and peeled off five one-hundred-dollar bills. "If you could just hover a few feet from the ground. Long enough for us to drop off."

"That," the pilot said, taking the money, "I can do."

The last few hundred feet were the worst, for both the man and the buffalo. The trail, after an easy beginning, had become narrow, steep, rutted, and treacherous. Three times Hannah's hooves slipped on loose rocks or concealed roots, and the big animal went sliding back fifteen or twenty feet, dragging Tank with her. Each time she rolled over onto her side and mooed anxiously as dirt from above displaced and shifted down to half bury her. Each time, Tank had to stroke and soothe her, help her dig out and regain her balance, and patiently urge her forward again.

Twice Tank himself slipped badly, the leather of his old boots reacting just as Hannah's hooves did to the hostile ground under them. The first time he fell, his left foot came out from under him and he pitched onto both knees, puncturing one trouser leg on a sharp rock and cutting his knee badly enough to bleed. The second time, he lost his balance completely and went plunging downhill, sliding helplessly past Hannah, his face, shirt, boots catching the avalanche of loose dirt that followed him. He had the presence of mind to let go of the halter rope, however, and did not upset Hannah with his spill. He slid forty feet; when he straightened himself, he was filthy with dirt stuck to his sweaty clothes and body, and his face and hands showed nicks and cuts seeping blood through the dirt. Cursing mightily, Tank clawed his way back up to where Hannah, watching him curiously, waited with infinite patience.

Late in the climb, perhaps two hundred feet from the plateau, Tank thought he heard the roar of a motor. It was hard to tell, with the thick treetops insulating the ground from noise, and the constant wind whipping about now that they were so high. Maybe it was that light plane coming in low to search the meadow. If so, he thought craftily, they would find nothing there.

We're beating them, Rose. Hannah and me. And it's important. Important that we beat them. Important that we make that plateau.

They kept climbing, the man and the buffalo, struggling against the total environment around them: the height aloof above them, the ground resistant under them, the air thin and selfish, the dirt and dust, the rocks and roots. Blood and sweat burned their eyes, both of them, for Hannah now had cuts on her old face as well. Foam coated the buffalo's lips, saliva and tears wet the man's cheeks.

They climbed until their muscles came close to locking, their lungs close to bursting, their hearts close to breaking. With no resource left but blind courage, they climbed. Finally, they made it to the top and together crawled onto the edge of the grassy meadow.

The three hunters were waiting there for them.

Only when he saw the hunters did Tank Sherman realize that the motor roar he heard had not been the scout plane, but a helicopter. As he and the buffalo struggled together to drag their bodies over the lip of the plateau, both had fallen onto their knees: Tank pitching forward so that he was on all fours, Hannah with her front legs bent, great head down. Both were panting, trying to suck enough oxygen out of the thin air to cool lungs that felt as if they had been singed. For one brief instant, as they knelt side by side, Tank's shoulder brushing Hannah's neck, both their heads hung, it was as if man and beast were one.

Then Tank looked up and saw the hunters. They stood in a row, the sun reflecting on their rifles.

"No," he said softly, shaking his head. "No," a little louder as he got to his feet. "No!" he yelled as he walked toward them.

Harmon Langford, standing in the middle said, "Stop where you are! Come any closer and we'll shoot!"

Eyes fixed like a mad man, jaw clenched like a vise, his big fists closed, Tank stalked toward them. "No!" he kept shouting. "No! No! No!"

"You've been warned!" snapped Langford.

Tank kept coming.

"All right, shoot him!" Langford ordered, shouldering his own rifle and aiming.

No shots were fired. Langford lowered his rifle and looked frantically from Kingston to Lester Ash. "Shoot! Why don't you shoot!"

"Why don't you?" Lester Ash asked evenly.

Langford did not have time to reply. Tank reached him, snatched the rifle from his hands, and hurled it away. Then he drove a crushing right fist into Langford's face, smashing his nose and lips, sending him reeling back in shock.

As Langford fell, Tank turned on Gregory Kingston, "Now just a minute," the actor pleaded. "I had no intention of shooting you —" He threw down his rifle as evidence of his sincerity, but that did not deter Tank Sherman. The old fighter dug a solid right fist deep into Kingston's mid-section and the actor folded up like a suitcase, the color draining from his face, his eyes bulging. Dropping to his knees, he pitched forward onto his face, the juicy meadow grass staining it green.

When Tank looked for the third man, he found that Lester Ash, experienced hunter that he was, had flanked his adversary and moved around behind him. It was now Tank, standing on the meadow, Lester Ash facing him with his back to the sun.

"We can do it the easy way or the hard way, bud," said Lester. "Either way, that buffalo's mine."

Tank shook his head. "No." He moved toward Ash.

"I ain't no loudmouth writer or sissy actor, bud," the Nevadan said. Mess with me and I'll put you in the hospital. That buff is mine."

"No." Tank kept coming.

"Please yourself," Lester said disgustedly. He snapped the rifle to his shoulder and fired.

The round ripped all the way through the fleshy part of Tank's left thigh and knocked him off his feet. Instincts two decades old still lived in his mind, and as if someone were counting ten over him, Tank rolled over and got back up. Clutching his thigh, he limped toward Ash.

"You're a damned fool, bud," said Lester Ash. He fired again.

The second slug tore a hole in Tank's right thigh and he was again spun to the ground. He moaned aloud, involuntarily, and sat up, one hand on each wound. Pain seared his body, hot and relentless, and he began to choke, cough, and cry. I'm done for, he thought.

Then at his feet he saw something white and yellow. Pawing the tears from his eyes, he managed to focus. It was a clump of wildflowers: white petals with yellow nectaries. Primroses.

Tank dragged himself up one last time. He started forward again, weaving and faltering like a drunk man. His eyes fixed on Lester Ash and held.

"Okay, bud," said Lester, "now you lose a kneecap —"

Before Lester could fire, Hannah charged. Massive head down, hooves almost soundless on the thick meadow grass, she was upon Lester Ash before he realized it. Catching him from the left side, her broad forehead drove into his chest, crushing his left rib cage, collapsing the lung beneath it. With his body half bent over her face, Hannah propelled him to the edge of the plateau and hurled him over the side.

Lester Ash screamed as his body ricocheted off the first three trees, then was silent for the rest of the way down.

The Deerfield tribe marshal and his deputy, who rode up to the meadow on horseback at the first sound of gunfire, secured the area and arranged for Harmon Langford and Gregory Kingston to be escorted down to the reservation boundary. They were released with a stern warning never to violate Deerfield land again. Some men with a rescue stretcher retrieved Lester Ash's body, and his death was officially attributed to an accidental fall from the plateau.

A Deerfield medicine man named Alzada, who resided in a lodge back in the trees next to the meadow, was consulted by the marshal as to the disposition of the buffalo.

"If the Great One put the buffalo here," Alzada decreed, "then the buffalo must be sacred. It shall be allowed to graze on the sacred meadow until the Great One summons it back."

The marshal looked over at the edge of the meadow where Tank sat under a tree, exhausted and bleeding.

"What about the man?"

"What man?" said Alzada. "I see no man. I see only a sacred buffalo, grazing contentedly. If you see something else, perhaps it is a spirit."

The marshal shook his head. "If Alzada sees nothing, then I also see nothing. Only Alzada can see spirits."

The marshal and his deputy rode back down the mountain.

When they had gone, the medicine man went over and helped Tank into the trees to his lodge.

SPLIT DECISIONS

Roy Britt was sitting in the doorway drinking milk from a carton when old Rainey arrived to open the poolroom

"No work on the docks this morning?" Rainey asked. He was an old black man with cotton tufts for hair and a face like shiny saddle leather.

"Ice storm up in the Midwest," Roy said, standing. "Lots of the big rigs are waiting for the Interstates to be cleared, I guess. They didn't put on no day help at all this morning."

"Come on in, then," Rainey said, unlocking the front door. "You can sweep the floor and brush down the tables."

"Okay. Thanks, Rainey."

Rainey did not acknowledge the thanks as he led Roy into the stale, musty air of the poolroom and began turning on lights. Roy finished his milk and tossed the carton into a trash can. He was a middleweight, slightly over the one-sixty limit, with scar tissue along the flesh just under each eyebrow. With a twenty-and-fourteen record, he had other scars too, some that showed, some that didn't. He hadn't had a fight in eight months, which was why he showed up at the docks every morning to try for day work unloading trucks.

"Start with the floor, let's get these stinking cigarette butts out of here," Rainey told him, unlocking an old brass National cash register and checking his drawer of starter cash. As Roy got a broom out of the utility closet, Rainey asked, "You in the mood for Wingy or Bix this morning?"

"Wingy sounds good," Roy replied.

Finishing with the register, Rainey turned to an old beat-up hi-fi record player behind the counter and put on a 78 rpm of "St. James Infirmary" as written by W. C. Handy and rendered by Wingy Manone, a cornet player from right there in New Orleans who had lost an arm as a kid when he was run over by a streetcar named Burgundy. He had gone on to become a world-class Dixieland musician anyway.

As the achy blues of the number wafted in the dingy poolroom, Roy Britt closed his fighter's hands around the broom handle and began to sweep.

It was almost ten when the phone rang and Rainey turned from a racing form he was studying to answer it. "Pool hall."

Roy was at a back table, slowly dragging a soft-bristled brush across the green felt of the playing field. It pleased him to see how he could work the nap into a smooth, even texture completely devoid of fuzz or roughness that might throw a good shot off a thirty-second of an inch. As he worked, he heard the soft click-click of pool balls from another table where a hustler named Bumper was practicing with a custom stick. Backing that sound was another Dixieland record Rainey had put on. Everything considered, Roy liked the poolroom. There was something warm and cozy about it, like the locker rooms in some athletic clubs where he'd boxed as a kid. Seedy, shabby, but homey, too.

"Okay, I'll tell him," Roy heard Rainey say into the phone. The old black man hung up and shuffled back to where Roy was and said quietly, "Jack Kono wants to see you." He squinted suspiciously. "You ain't in no trouble, are you?"

"Not that I know of," Roy replied.

"Why Jack Kono sending for you, den?"

"Maybe he's got a fight for me," Roy said. "He's been putting together some matches for Legion Hall."

"If he wanted you for a fight, how come he didn't say so?" Rainey wanted to know.

Roy shrugged. "Who knows? Kono's got Cajun in him. They don't think like you and me." He picked some lint off the brush he was using. "Where does he want to see me?"

"Blue Creole at noon. He eatin' lunch there."

Nodding, Roy resumed brushing down the table. Old Rainey shuffled away, muttering, "Sho' hope you ain't in no trouble with Jack Kono."

When he finished the tables, Roy left the poolroom and walked down Canal Street to Sam's 24-Hour Grill. Sam, a rail-thin man with jailhouse tattoos on both forearms, was behind the counter filling saltshakers. "Hey, Roy," he said, bobbing his chin. "Benny's in the kitchen."

"Hey, Sam. Thanks."

Back in the kitchen, slicing tomatoes, was a young woman who would have had a drop dead figure if she'd been twelve pounds lighter, but with the extra weight was kind of roundy. She had freckles that started from her hairline and, when she was dressed, disappeared between her breasts. When she was undressed, they didn't disappear at all. Her hair was a reddish color that Crayola hadn't named yet.

"Hi, baby," she said as Roy walked in.

"Verbenia, you don't owe no money to Jack Kono, do you?" Roy asked without preliminary.

"Lord, no." She rolled her eyes toward the ceiling. "You know I don't borrow at street rates. Why?"

"He wants to see me."

"Jack Kono?"

"Yeah. I thought maybe you run short of money or something without telling me."

"Well, think again."

"You haven't been betting the dogs or nothing, have you?"

"Roy." She stopped slicing and put one fist on her hip, the thin-bladed knife still in it. "Read my lips. I said I haven't borrowed from none of Jack Kono's loan sharks. Period." She resumed slicing. "Did you go see about that job? In the ad I cut out?"

Roy looked down at the tomatoes. "I was going to, but then I got the message that Kono wanted to see me, an' I thought if you didn't owe him nothing, then maybe he had a fight for me or something —"

Benny stopped slicing again, her eyes becoming weary and knowing at the same time. "Roy, I thought we agreed you'd give up fighting and find a regular steady job so maybe you and me and Sugar can get out of the Quarter, move out to that new tract by the airport —"

"I know," he said. "But I got to see what Kono wants first, don't I? What do you want me to do, ignore the man, Verbenia?"

"Roy," she asked impatiently, "why can't you call me 'Benny' like ever'body else does? Why do you insist on calling me 'Verbenia'?"

Roy shrugged. "I like 'Verbenia.' I think it's pretty."

Benny shook her head in exasperation. "Well, I wish you could have knowed my daddy. Y'all would have got on real fine. Only two people in the world ever liked the name 'Verbenia.'" She pointed the slicing knife at the door. "Go on, get out of here; I got to finish getting ready for the lunch crowd."

"Okay. I'm gonna run home and put on my good shirt."

"Look around the neighborhood for Sugar while you're there," Benny said. "I got a feeling she's ditching school again."

"Okay. See you later." Roy kissed her on the cheek and sneaked in a quick feel of one thickset breast.

"Oh, stop it —"

"Bye," he said, going out the back door, "Verbenia."

They had a kitchenette apartment in a horseshoe-shaped building that had once been a high-class brothel in the days when customers arrived by carriage. There was still a long pole in front where the horses had been tethered. The courtyard was cobblestone set by slaves, and in its time had been a vine-covered and magnolia-filled place of gas-lit shadows, full of strange, alluring aromas that conjured up visions of the flesh, and fleeting glimpses of mysterious women behind numbered doors. That courtyard now, as Roy Britt walked briskly across it, was a dead, trash-littered place, uninviting and dreary by day, unlighted and dangerous by night.

When he let himself in, Roy found Sugar sprawled in front of the television, spreading mayonnaise on bread while she watched with riveted eleven-year-old eyes some dreadful horror special effects on the screen before her.

"Hey, Roy," she said with only a glance.

"Hey, Sugar. What you watching?"

"Vampire Vixens of Venus. What you doing home?"

"Changing shirts." He was already at the creaky chifforobe the three of them shared, unbuttoning his denim work shirt and replacing it with a wine-colored Western sport shirt with fake pearl buttons that Benny had given him for Christmas.

Now Sugar tore her eyes away from the television. This was not part of the regular drill around here. "What are you putting on your good shirt in daytime for? You only wear that shirt at night when you and Mama go out drinking."

"I'm going to see a man about some work," Roy said. He bobbed his chin at the television. "What's she doing to that poor guy?"

"Sucking his blood out through his thumb. It's called erotic horror. What kind of work?"

"A fight maybe."

"Really?" Her young face showed excitement. It was a face totally different from her mother's, with a *cafe au lait* complexion, light blue albino eyes, and tightly wired pitch-black hair that curled in a cluster on her head like a skullcap. "Who are you gonna fight?"

"Don't know. Not even sure that's what it's about."

Sugar sat up, cross-legged, still spreading mayonnaise. "I'd like to see you rematched with Sonny Boy Newton. I still think you whipped him that night. The judges giving him a split decision really sucked."

Roy shrugged. "Could've gone either way, I guess. I thought I whipped him, too. I really hate split decisions, you know? People think, hey, it's the best way to lose, because it was so close, one judge for you, two judges for the other guy. But it's really the worst way to lose, 'cause you know you came so near to winning. Makes you mad at yourself for not trying harder. I really hate split decisions." Roy was looking at himself in a yellow-stained mirror on the chifforobe door. A record of twenty-and-fourteen, and six of his fourteen losses had been split decisions. For a while, a few years back, they had even introduced him as "Roy 'Hard Luck Kid' Britt."

"You'll kick his ass next time, Roy," said Sugar.

"You watch your language," he chastised. " 'Member, you're a young lady." Roy knelt next to her and took a bite of the mayonnaised bread. "Stay off the streets until after school's out," he cautioned. From his pocket he pulled several crumpled dollar bills and gave her one. "See you later, Sugar."

"See you later, Roy," she said, and turned back to the television.

One got to the Blue Creole Cafe by entering a dark, damp passageway off Decatur Street and following it to an alley, then crossing the alley and going through a rusty wrought-iron gate and down a few cement stairs to a forbidding-looking metal fire door with a spring-hinged knocker on it. One could only enter by membership or invitation; it was a place where the bankers and other businessmen of respectable New Orleans took their secretaries and mistresses to lunch or dinner before going to bed somewhere for an hour or two.

When the door was opened for Roy Britt, he said to a massive black doorman who looked like Sonny Liston reincarnated, "I'm here to see Jack Kono."

"He ax you to come?"

"Yeah."

At a nod of the black man's head, Roy entered and was left waiting in an alcove furnished with several expensively upholstered love seats arranged under ornately framed prints of partly nude Tahitian women originally painted by Gauguin. A nervous young blond woman sat on one of the love seats, her knees pressed closely together, worrying the strap of her cheap purse.

She wouldn't be carrying a cheap purse much longer, Roy thought. He leaned on the wall as far away from her as he could, so as not to make her any more nervous about her rendezvous than she already was.

The black doorman returned after a moment and nodded for Roy to follow him. He led Roy through a dining room of private, draped booths and secluded tables concealed by large potted plants and folding screens. Roy noticed that the understated music backgrounding the room was the same kind Rainey played in the poolroom: the softer, slower Dixieland. At a back booth, with the drapes open, Jack Kono sat eating crab cakes and drinking *Pouilly-Fuisse*.

"Sit down, Roy," he said, bobbing his chin at the opposite bench. "You want to eat?"

"I ate early, thanks," Roy lied. For some reason his stomach had suddenly knotted up. Jack Kono frequently had that effect on people. He had reptilian eyes in an otherwise softly Cajun face, very white, hairless hands, and a reputation for easy murder. There were some who referred to him as the Antichrist of the French Quarter. No one, it was said, had ever successfully lied to him.

"I need you to do something for me, Roy," said Kono. "You know my baby sister Angela?"

"Seen her around," said Roy. "Don't really know her."

"Well, I'm having a problem with her. She turned eighteen a few months ago and she's getting unruly on me. Quit the private school I had her going to, moved out of our mother's house, got a job as a shoe clerk." Kono stared at a bite of crab cake, sighed quietly, and shook his head. "I've tried talking some sense into her head but she won't listen. Says she's a grown woman —" he grunted softly, "a grown woman at *eighteen*, can you imagine?"

Roy shrugged. What the hell did this have to do with a fight for him, he wondered.

"I recently," Kono continued as he chewed, "found out she's running around with a guy named Denny Boyle. He's a shanty Irish auto mechanic at a place called Sports Car Heaven across the river in Gretna. You happen to know the guy?"

Roy shook his head. "No."

"I didn't think it was likely you did. I had him checked out and as far as I can tell, nobody really knows the guy. He came down from Birmingham a year or so ago and went to work tuning sports car engines. Customizes cars on the side. Apparently wants to save some money and open his own custom shop some day. A real yokel, right?"

Roy shrugged and looked away. He wished now that he'd gone to answer the ad Verbenia had cut out for him instead of going to the poolroom and getting Kono's message.

"This Denny Boyle is not the kind of guy I want my sister running around with, know what I mean?" Kono said. "He's strictly a dirt-under-the-fingernails type, no class, no future. I want him to stop seeing Angela."

Roy nodded resignedly. No fight at the Legion Hall, he guessed. "You want me to have a talk with him, is that it?"

Kono smiled a barren smile. "If I thought talking would solve the problem, I'd do it myself, Roy."

"So what do you want?"

"I want the guy worked over. But not by hooligans. I don't want it to look to Angela like it was arranged. I want the guy to get in a street fight with somebody who looks like just another guy. But somebody who'll bust him up good and proper for me. Somebody like you, Roy."

Roy shook his head. "That's not my line. I'm not a street fighter; I'm a pro. I mean, I'm *licensed*. I could get sent up for using my fists outside the ring."

"You won't get sent up, I guarantee it. You probably won't even get caught. But if you do, I'll put the fix in. I can buy any judge in Gretna."

"I don't know," Roy said, still shaking his head.

"I'd consider this a personal favor," Jack Kono told him quietly, pointedly. "And there's five hundred in it for you."

Roy stared off at a section of embossed red wall covering. "I was hoping you'd called me over to offer me a fight on one of your cards," he said with soft honesty, keeping his eyes averted.

Kono frowned. "A fight? I didn't even know you were still active. I thought you retired after you lost two or three split decisions in a row. Somebody told me they saw you sweeping out old Rainey's poolroom. That's why I called you there."

"Yeah, well, I do that and I work the truck docks, too, but on'y because I haven't been able to get no fights."

"So, what do you want? You want to box again? Fine. Do this favor for me and I'll see that you get back in the ring."

Roy drummed his thick fingertips soundlessly on the brocaded place mat in front of him. Two or three good wins could put him into a main event, he thought. And a good main event might get him a TV fight on ESPN. And if he could beat a ranked contender on TV, with that kind of exposure, who knows, it might catapult him into a title shot. The middleweight division was currently wide open; anything could happen.

"Do you think you could get me a rematch with Sonny Boy Newton?" Roy asked. "I lost a split decision to him in eight last April, but I thought I beat him."

"Newton's boxing the hotel circuit now," Kono said. "You willing to go up to Atlantic City?"

"Sure," Roy replied eagerly.

"Can you make one-sixty?"

"Easy. A week's training."

"Okay, you take care of this little matter for me and I'll match you with Sonny Boy within ninety days. And I'll still give you the five bills. Deal?"

Roy bit his lip briefly, then nodded determinedly. "Deal."

That evening, Roy, Benny, and Sugar walked down to one of the *Vieux Carre* waterfront cafes for catfish. As soon as they were seated at one of the picnic-bench tables with their basket of breaded fillets and pitcher of iced tea, Benny started in on both of them.

"How was school today, Sugar?"

"Just thrilling, Mama. A real adventure."

"Don't you smart-mouth me, young lady. What did you learn?"

"That the possibility of life exists on the planet Venus."

Benny raised her eyebrows. "Well, that's interesting. I didn't know that." Her eyes shifted to Roy. "Tell me again what Kono said today."

"He said he'd get me a rematch with Sonny Boy Newton," Roy told her. "But first he wants me to have one tune-up bout across the river, a card he's putting on in Gretna."

"I didn't know they had fight cards in Gretna," Benny said.

"This is the first one. They're trying it out. Anyways, I get five hundred for a tune-up six-rounder, and if I win, Kono'll make the rematch with Sonny Boy."

"You'll kick his ass this time, Roy," said Sugar.

Benny's eyebrows immediately pinched together and she fixed her daughter in a laser stare. "I cannot believe what I just heard," she said dramatically. "May I inquire where you are learning such talk?"

"School, I guess, Mama," Sugar replied innocently. "You ought to hear how some of those kids talk! They even use the "F" word."

"That is disgusting. Roy, we have got to get out of this Quarter and into that tract of homes out by the airport. I refuse to allow Sugar to go to school down here next year."

"I like the Quarter, Mama," Sugar protested, realizing too late what she might have done.

"I don't care what you like. Be quiet. How much did you say you were getting for the tune-up in Gretna?" she asked Roy.

"Five hundred."

"We can get into a nice little two-bedroom, two bath, twelve hundred-square-foot patio home for three thousand down. Only thing is, you'd have to have a steady job. No bank is going to lend money to an unranked fighter who don't even have a manager. Do you think you could get Rainey to say you run the poolroom for him? If you could get him to say you'd worked there five years, and I could get Sam to say I'd worked at the cafe five years, why, I bet we could finance a patio home. What do you think?"

"I bet we could," Roy agreed. He tried never to disagree with Verbenia at mealtime. It made for serious indigestion. Breaking open a fillet with his fingers, he squeezed lemon juice all over it to absorb the catfish taste without neutralizing the catfish flavor, and laced it with salt and pepper.

"I could get a job delivering papers," Sugar suggested.

"You most certainly cannot," Benny squelched her. "You are to come directly home from school every day and stay inside, young lady. I do not want you on the streets of the Quarter. Roy, when is the Gretna fight?"

"Uh, I'm not sure yet. Next week sometime."

"All right. You'll probably be training this weekend, so Sugar and I will take the airport bus out to that new tract and pick us out a place." She patted her daughter's hand. "Won't that be fun, Sugar?"

"Yeah, Mama. A real thrill."

On Saturday afternoon, Roy took the Jackson Street ferry across the Mississippi River to Gretna and hoofed it along used-car row on Route 18 until he spotted Sports Car Heaven squeezed between a recreational vehicle lot and a motorcycle repair shop. A couple of sailors were browsing among the sports cars, birddogged by a salesman with a belly that hung over double-knit slacks. There was a lone mechanic in the garage, working on a teal-blue Jaguar. Roy strolled in.

"Help you?" the mechanic asked. He was wearing a grease-stained jumpsuit with "Denny" over the chest pocket.

"You got a phone book I can look at?" Roy asked.

"Sure. Right in the office there." He pointed. "Hanging by the pay phone."

"Thanks."

Roy stepped through an open door into a small, windowed office where the pay phone was on the wall between a water cooler and a Dr. Pepper machine. Pretending to look up a number, Roy peered over the top of the telephone directory and studied Denny Boyle. He was a nice-looking young man, twenty-five maybe, the clean-cut lines of his face interrupted only by a nose that was slightly crooked. The sleeves of his jumpsuit had been cut off and Roy could see that the mechanic had good biceps but no real muscle tone; he would be strong but slow. The arms were slightly long, so he'd probably have a couple of inches advantage over Roy in reach. Roy guessed his weight at one-seventy.

Overall, no problem, Roy decided. He could move in quick on the guy, get inside the reach, hook a few quick lefts to the body to bring the guy's hands down, then start busting his face open with straight rights and lefts. Ten, twelve shots ought to do it. The guy would feel like his head had been dragged behind a train.

Putting the directory down, Roy stepped back into the garage. "Thanks a lot," he said.

"No problem," Denny Boyle replied. "Need directions or anything?"

"No, I just needed the number." Roy walked over to him. "What's a car like that cost?" he asked, bobbing his chin at the Jag.

"This model new runs about fifty-five and change," Boyle replied. He stopped working and wiped his hands on a chamois. "I wouldn't buy one, I was you."

"No? Why not?"

"Repair record stinks. Costs a fortune to maintain. You want your money's worth, get a Corvette. Can't go wrong with a 'Vette."

Roy nodded. "You know a lot about cars, huh?"

Denny Boyle smiled. "Cars and nothing else. I been tinkering with engines since I was ten. What do you drive?"

"Nothing right now. But I been thinking about buying one —"

As Roy spoke, a BMW sports car pulled up outside and a young woman got out and came into the garage. "Hi, honey," Denny Boyle said.

"Hey," she greeted him, then went over to his workbench to wait for him to finish talking.

Roy got a good look at her as she passed. She had the same soft Cajun features that Jack Kono had, without the reptilian eyes; hers, instead were wide, lugubrious, almost frightened-looking. Her lips, too, were different: prominent, healthy, even suggestive. There was no question that it was Angel Kono, Jack Kono's "baby" sister — though from the way her body moved when she walked, there was nothing babyish or childlike about her; physically, Roy thought, she looked every bit the woman that Verbenia was. Roy had seen her around the Quarter, at Tradition Hall and a couple of the smaller Dixieland clubs, but this was the first time he had been this close to her. Now he knew why her brother was concerned. With that body and those lips, she was a magnet for sex.

Roy decided to move on. "Listen, I got a friend needs some work on an old Gran' Prix he's got. You fix those?"

"I fix anything with an engine," Denny said. "And I'll work days, nights, Sundays, anytime." He grinned again. "I'm saving so me and my girl there can get married and have our own custom shop."

"That's great," Roy replied. "What time you close during the week?"

"I try to get out by six, but I can stay if there's work. Send your friend around anytime."

"I'll do that," Roy said.

"Nice talking with you," Denny Boyle said as Roy walked away.

That night they had supper at a chili-dog joint because on Saturdays it was Sugar's turn to pick where they ate. Benny complained about it every week.

"I swear, this chili is nothing but grease with a few beans and a little ground beef to give it color. Can't you pick some place different for a change?"

"I like this place," Sugar replied steadfastly. Sugar never relinquished a perk once she got it.

"The chili's not bad if you dip your dog in it," Roy said. Which, of course, caused Benny to turn on him.

"Should you be eating that kind of stuff with a fight coming up? Shouldn't you be eating a salad or something healthy?"

"They don't serve healthy food here," Sugar pointed out. "Just good food."

"This won't hurt me," Roy said, shrugging.

"Just when is the fight anyway?"

"Monday night."

"Are you getting tickets for me and Sugar?"

Roy had been expecting her to ask and was prepared. He shook his head. "It's just club fights, Verbenia. They're holding 'em in a warehouse. It's no place for a woman and a little girl."

"I'm not a little girl, for God's sake," Sugar said crossly.

"Watch that mouth, young lady," Benny warned. "Roy, we have got to get her out of the Quarter and into a decent neighborhood. I wish to God I could find her daddy and get the eight years' worth of child support he's behind with." Benny leaned forward to impress urgency. "Listen, Sugar and me went out to that new tract by the airport today; it's called Lazy Acres, isn't that cute? The salesman out there was a really sweet guy named Lance, wore one of those spiffy gold pinkie rings. Anyway, he said if we wanted one of the units — that's what the salesmen call the houses: units — anyway, Lance said we should get a down payment in as soon as possible 'cause the units are selling like hotcakes on a frosty morning. So, what I thought was, Sam at the cafe said he'd advance me five hundred on my wages, and take twenty-five a week out until it was paid. Then I thought I'd ask my sister Dewanda to ask her husband, Melvin, if they could see their way clear to letting me have a loan of two thousand. Melvin's doing real good now; he's on the road selling manure to plant nurseries and he's pulling in twelve hundred a week commission, so I know they can afford it —"

"I'm not borrowing no money from your relatives," Roy said firmly.

"Well, I know *that*," Benny retorted. "First off, they wouldn't loan you no money; it'll be me that's borrowing. Reason I think they'll do it is to help Sugar. They've always felt sorry for her —"

Sugar stuck a finger in her mouth. "You're going to make me barf, Mama —"

"Sugar, I'm going to slap you silly if you don't behave," Benny threatened.

"*They* feel sorry for *me*? Roy, you ought to see *their* kids. Two grossly fat girls and a boy who's a retarded nerd —"

"Melvin, Junior, is *not* retarded, Sugar!" her mother stormed. "He's just a little slow —"

"Slow! He's s*topped*."

"That's e-*nough*, Sugar!"

The girl fell silent. Benny turned her attack back to Roy.

"All I want to know is if I can count on that five hundred from you on Monday?"

"Yeah," Roy assured her. "Yeah, you can, Verbenia."

On Sunday morning, Roy went around to Jack Kono's private social club, a storefront on Royal Street with the windows painted black and a MEMBERS ONLY sign on the door. As he was walking up to knock, the door flew back and Angela Kono came striding out with an angry look on her face, muttering what sounded to Roy like obscenities. She glanced at him in passing, then paused, frowning, to stare at him. Roy, feeling himself turn red, knowing she probably recognized him from the previous day, turned away from her, caught the door before it closed, and hurried inside.

Kono was at the bar, watching a replay of the previous night's NBA game, looking very irritated. Roy took a stool beside him.

"Well?" Kono inquired at once.

"Well, I seen the guy," Roy told him. "At Sports Car Heaven, over to Gretna, just like you said."

"And?"

"And I don't see no problem," Roy shrugged. "He's bigger'n me and looks to be pretty strong, but I'll be able to handle him."

"I don't want him just 'handled,'" Kono said grimly. "I want the son of a bitch wrecked. My baby sister Angela was just in here to tell me her and that guy Boyle are talking marriage. She wants to bring him around to meet our mother!"

"You know, he don't seem like all that bad a guy," Roy said tentatively. Kono gave him a withering look.

"Don't try to second-guess me on this, you hear? This is a family matter. My sister is *not* going to marry some Gretna grease monkey who don't even have Cajun blood. Am I clear on that?"

"You're clear," Roy replied.

"Fine. When are you going to do it?"

"Tomorrow night, I guess," Roy decided. "Might as well get it over with. He quits work at six. I'll catch him on the car lot as he's leaving and pick a fight with him. All's I need is about sixty seconds max to do it."

"I want his jaw broken. And his nose," Kono specified. "Work on his kidneys, too, so's he'll pass blood for a while. That'll give him something to think about."

"Okay," Roy said, looking away. He suddenly felt like a man eating tainted food. An urge stirred in him to get up and walk away from the deal. But he had promised the five hundred to Verbenia.

"So you'll do it around six tomorrow?" Kono confirmed. Roy Britt nodded.

"Yeah. Six tomorrow."

"You'll be coming back on the seven o'clock ferry, then?"

"Yeah, probably."

Kono patted Roy's arm and smiled a scant smile. "Good deal."

When Roy left Kono's club, he had walked only a few doors down Royal when Angela Kono suddenly stepped from somewhere onto the sidewalk and confronted him.

"Who the hell are you?" she demanded. "Do you work for my brother?"

"I don't know what you're talking about," Roy said. He tried to move around her, but she blocked his way. Her wide, dark Cajun eyes, looking like ripe plums, were seething with anger.

"You know what I'm talking about," she accused. "I saw you in Gretna yesterday, talking with Denny Boyle. What the hell's going on?"

"Nothing. Nothing's going on. You got the wrong guy, miss —"

"My brother is Jack Kono. You just came out of his club. And yesterday you were in Gretna talking to my boyfriend, Denny Boyle. Did my brother hire you to do something?"

Roy felt like a stagecoach surrounded by Apaches. Angela Kono was right in his face. Two people walking by gave them curious looks. Down at the corner he could see a police cruiser turning into Royal.

"Look, miss, I'm a fighter, see? I went to talk to Jack Kono about getting a fight, that's all. And yesterday I only stopped in at that garage to look up somebody in the phone book. Then the mechanic and me got to talking after. If one of 'em's your brother and the other's your boyfriend, that's got nothing to do with me. I'm just doing my own thing, see? Now, why don't you let me go about my business?"

"You'd better not try anything with Denny Boyle," Angela Kono warned. "If my brother hired you to hurt him, you'd better think twice about doing it, because you won't get away with it. I'll go to the police. I'll tell them about both of you. You'll go to jail."

Roy shook his head wryly. "Miss, do you have any idea how many things the police have been told about your brother? Has he ever gone to jail for any of them?"

Angela Kono parted her sensuous lips to speak, to hurl a retort back at this thug with the lumpy scar tissue over each eye, but her words never reached sound. Because there was no retort, and they both knew it. In the Quarter, Jack Kono was above the law.

Turning her face away, Angela swallowed tightly. Roy looked awkwardly down at his shoes. He sucked in on his upper lip for a moment. Why, he wondered, didn't this girl understand that her brother was just trying to look out for her, trying to protect her? Jack Kono was her older brother; not only that, but with their father dead, he was the head of the Kono family. She should listen to him.

"Look," he said after a moment. "I'm sorry you got troubles, you know? But I got some of my own. I gotta go now."

He was glad she did not try to stop him when he stepped around her and hurried along the street.

Roy slept until nine-thirty on Monday morning. He might have slept longer but the bedroom window shade had a crack in it that allowed the morning sun to come in. It woke him and then he could not get back to sleep because he started thinking about what he had to do that night.

Getting up, he pulled on a pair of jeans and a sweatshirt, and went barefoot into the living room. Sugar, in her school clothes, was stretched out on the floor in front of the TV. Her schoolbooks were on the floor by the door.

"Better hurry, Sugar, or you'll be late for school," Roy cracked as he went over to the Pullman kitchen.

"Very funny," the girl said crossly. "I already *went* to school. Mama insisted on walking me there. I had to hide in the girls rest room for fifteen minutes and then walk all the way back."

"You must really be wore out," he said wryly, opening the half-size kitchenette refrigerator and surveying its contents. "You eat yet?"

"Uh-huh."

"What'd you eat?"

"Mama made me eat cornflakes before we left. When I got back, I had a fried-tomato-and-peanut-butter sandwich and a Cherry 7-UP."

Roy shook his head. "You must have a cast-iron stomach, Sugar." He got out butter and peach preserves, spread some of each on two slices of sourdough bread, and poured a glass of milk. Going back into the living room, he sat on the couch to eat. "What are you watching?" he asked, frowning at the gory scene on the screen.

"Dr. Jekyll Meets Jack the Ripper," Sugar said.

"Which one is he?" Roy asked, bobbing his chin at the character on the screen.

"That's the Ripper."

"What's he doing?"

"Eviscerating a victim."

"Doing what?"

"Disemboweling her."

"What's that mean?"

"Cutting her open and taking out her insides, Roy," the girl said patiently.

"Isn't there anything else you can watch?" he asked, grimacing.

"Sure," Sugar replied cheerfully. "I can watch the news: war in Bosnia, starving kids in Somalia, riots in South Africa, drive-by killings in Los Angeles, gang rapes in New York —"

"Never mind," said Roy. "Watch what you're watching. At least it's not real."

When he finished eating, Roy went back to the little alcove kitchen and got out detergent to do a sink full of dirty dishes that had been left. Benny never did dishes. "I'm around dirty dishes all day; I can't cope with them at night," was her excuse. Now and then Sugar did them, but mostly it was left to him. Mother and daughter both knew he'd do them because he hated the sight of them.

While he was cleaning up, Sugar came over and lounged against the fridge. "You think you'll like living in Lazy Acres?"

Roy shrugged. "Don't know. Haven't never lived outside the city before."

"I won't like it," Sugar declared. "I'll hate it. There's no place to hang out. No bowling alley, no donut shop, no bus station —"

"Maybe you ought to try school again," he suggested.

"No, school's out for me," the girl replied analytically. "The teachers are boring, the classes are dull, the other girls are unbelievably silly, and the boys aren't interested in anything except looking up dresses. You should see how they purposely drop things on the floor so they can bend down to get them, then turn and look up the nearest dress while they're doing it. They're so juvenile."

"That's 'cause they're young," Roy said.

"Really? Golly, Roy, I never thought of that."

He looked steadily at her. "Your mother's right. We need to get you out of the Quarter."

"Well, if we move to Lazy Acres, I've made up my mind to run away. I'm going to Spain and become a flamenco dancer." She found a towel and began drying the dishes. "Who you fighting tonight?"

"Some dude, I don't even know his name," Roy lied.

"I hope he's got a weak jab. I hate it when that right eye of yours gets opened up."

"It's no worse than one of those movies you're always watching."

"It is worse, Roy. It's you." She put an arm around is waist and gave him a quick hug. "I love you, Roy. I wish you were my daddy."

"Good thing I'm not. I let you get away with too much." He rinsed the sink and dried his hands on the dishtowel Sugar was using. "Promise me you won't run away without talking it over with me first."

Sugar shook her head. "Running away has to be spontaneous or it won't be any fun."

"What does 'spontaneous' mean?"

"Impulsive. You know, spur of the moment."

"Promise me you won't do that. It would hurt your mother too much."

"I can't promise that."

"Promise," he insisted.

"Roy-ee! No — "

"Promise!" His voice turned harsh and he gripped her arm.

"All right, Roy, let go!" She decided to concede. Somewhere in the depths of her young mind she remembered her mother saying to another waitress, "Roy's kind and gentle most of the time, but let me tell you, there's a temper underneath it all. Roy Britt is a guy you never want to push too far."

"Promise?" he asked for verification.

"Yes, Roy, I promise. I do."

"Okay."

He let go of her arm.

By five-thirty that evening, Roy was on the recreational vehicle lot next to Sports Car Heaven, browsing around as if he were a customer. A salesman had approached him when he first got there, but Roy had put him off by saying he was just waiting for his wife to pick him up. From where he stood, he could see Denny Boyle finishing up some kind of work on the engine of a black Datsun 280Z. A light was on in the sports car lot sales office, but there was no salesman to be seen. Roy walked around among the recreational vehicles, looking in driver-side windows, kicking tires, always keeping the open repair-garage door clearly in sight.

It was already getting dark, the thin winter air cooling rapidly after the sun went down, a chilling wetness coming in from the waters of the muddy Mississippi and ankle-level fog crawling along the ground from the Gulf. The kind of spooky night that made people seek out jambalaya and gumbo and Dixieland music. Roy realized without knowing why that he really liked New Orleans, liked the French Quarter, more than anyplace he'd ever lived. He'd bummed around the Gulf Coast a lot before settling there — places like Mobile, Biloxi, Panama City, Port Arthur — but no place had ever suited him before. Maybe it had something to do with Verbenia and Sugar being there, he didn't know. All he was sure about was that it now felt like home. Maybe, he thought, if he and Sugar did some real fast talking, they could persuade Verbenia to consider buying an older house there in the Quarter that he could fix up a room at a time —

"So you were lying." A cutting female voice split the silence of his thoughts like a crack of lightning, startling the hell out of him. Roy whirled around to see Angela Kono standing six feet away, eyes riveted on him. "You're here to do something to Denny, aren't you? Did my brother hire you to kill him?"

Roy's mouth dropped open. "*Kill* him? I wouldn't kill nobody — "

"What are you going to do then, cripple him?" Break his fingers so badly that he won't be able to work on engines anymore?"

"Hey, I don't do stuff like that!" Roy declared. "What do you think I am, anyway?"

"I don't know," the fierce-looking young woman said. "Why don't you tell me. What are you?"

"I'm a fighter. I told you that yesterday — "

"Oh, yes, I remember. A fighter. What kind of a fighter?"

"A fighter," he repeated impatiently. "In the ring."

"Oh, I see. You mean you fight other fighters?"

"Yeah — "

"Except tonight you're going to fight an automobile mechanic, right?"

Roy felt his face become hot and knew it had turned red. It was almost as if he was a kid and this young woman, who was little more than a kid herself, had caught him doing something nasty and was shaming him for it.

"Listen, this whole thing is your fault, you know, not mine!" he accused. "If you'd listen to your older brother like you should, neither one of us would be in this fix!"

Angela Kono nodded knowingly. "Oh. Listen to my big brother, huh? Is that what I should be doing?"

"Yeah, it is!"

She got right in his face. "Do you know what incest is?" she asked in the coldest voice he had ever heard.

Frowning, Roy turned his face away, not answering. He hated admitting to anyone but Sugar when he didn't know what a word meant.

"You don't, do you?" Angela challenged. "You don't know what incest means." She stepped to the side where he had turned his face, and locked onto his eyes again. "Let me tell you what it means. Incest is where a parent has sex with one of their children. Or," she paused a beat for dreadful effect, "when a brother has sex with his sister."

Roy's face went blank, as if his mind had reset at zero and he was being given his very first piece of knowledge. Then, as he stared at the pretty young woman with the sad eyes, his memory kicked back in and began to help him think. Over the years he had heard dirty rumors now and again of a thing like that but he wasn't sure he had ever really believed them. To him, it just didn't seem possible that a girl's father, or her brother —

Well, it just didn't seem possible, that's all. Why, he wasn't even Sugar's real father, wasn't actually related to her at all; yet she *seemed* like his child, and he knew she thought of him as her daddy. But the mere idea of him doing anything like that to Sugar —

It was disgusting. Sickening. Enough to make him puke.

"You find it hard to believe, don't you?" Angela asked, and now her voice lost its sharpness, its cruel edge, and took on a tone that matched her cheerless eyes. "Well, it's true," she assured him forlornly. "Since I was twelve years old. There were only the three of us left in that big old family house: my mother, who was quite old — I was a late-life baby; Jack, who was nineteen when I was born; and me. Everybody else had died or moved away, and that big old house had all those rooms in it — so many rooms. Sometimes I tried to hide from Jack, but he always found me. He said what we were doing was all right, as long as nobody else knew, as long as I didn't tell anybody. So it went on until I was thirteen, and fourteen, and fifteen, and —"

Her voice broke off and she looked down at the asphalt of the recreational vehicle lot that showed between the wisps of fog, and shook her head in dismal helplessness. Roy felt awful, worse even than at the end of his toughest ten-round split-decision loss. If it hadn't been for Verbenia and Sugar, he'd have wished he was a million miles away.

"I'm sorry, miss," was all he could say. Then he found the words to add, "I didn't know nothing about that. I just thought your brother was, you know, looking out for you."

"I understand," she told him, looking up now, forcing a hint of a smile. "That's what everyone thinks: my mother, our neighbors, the nuns at school. You're not to blame for trying to help him."

"Well, I ain't helping him now," Roy said resolutely. He touched her arm, tentatively, briefly, then quickly pulled away. "You and your boyfriend don't have to worry none about me. I won't lay a hand on him."

"Thanks," she said. "We're getting out of here tonight. Denny's got a friend in Oklahoma City that's going to give him a working partnership in a shop there. It's our chance."

"A chance is all most people need," Roy told her quietly. "Good luck."

On impulse, Angela Kono leaned forward and kissed him on the cheek. Then she hurried off the lot toward the garage next door, toward her future.

Jack Kono was waiting on the Jackson Street ferry dock when the seven o'clock boat from Gretna moored and Roy came off with other passengers. Kono had a slick young hood named Shimmy with him, a younger guy who modeled himself after Kono in dress and attitude, and who was known to carry a switchblade stiletto to protect his boss with. The two of them fell in with Roy as he started up the dock.

"Well?" Kono asked.

Roy did not answer or look at him.

"How'd it go?" Kono demanded.

Roy still didn't answer or stop walking.

"Wait a goddamn minute, you!" Kono ordered, stepping in front of Roy to stop him. Seizing Roy's right wrist, Kono pulled up his hand and looked at it. It was clear that Roy's knuckles had not hit anything that night. Kono's face darkened. "What happened?"

"I changed my mind." Roy stepped around him and started walking. Kono quickly got in front of him and blocked his way again.

"Something happened," he accused. "What was it?"

"Nothing you don't already know about, Kono. Now leave me alone."

Again Roy stepped around him and continued on his way. The single, solitary thing he wanted in life at that moment was just to get home to Verbenia and Sugar.

But Jack Kono wasn't going to let him have that. He stepped in front of Roy again.

Roy's eyes turned mean. "I ain't going to move around you again, Kono," he said evenly.

"You won't have to, pug," said Kono, his reptilian eyes narrowing to slits. "Take him, Shimmy," he ordered.

Shimmy's right hand started out of the coat pocket where he carried his blade. But he wasn't even close to being quick enough. Roy pivoted to his left and drove an arcing, plowing right fist low and deep to Shimmy's groin. Shimmy felt his insides shrivel and turn hot as he dropped to his knees, lower body momentarily paralyzed. Then Roy turned back to Jack Kono.

"You low-life scum son of a bitch," he said in quiet, angry words.

Roy's experienced fists went to work in machinelike fashion, went to work on Jack Kono as they were supposed to have worked on Denny Boyle. A left jab set up a straight right that broke Kono's nose and sent a fire-hydrant rush of blood down the front of his silk suit. A right to the liver made Kono bend to that side and half turn, leaving the soft spot over one kidney unprotected. Roy drilled four hard lefts to that spot, all illegal blows had they been in the ring. *See how you like passing blood, you bastard,* he thought. As Kono stumbled backwards, Roy stayed right on him. The last punch he threw was a perfectly timed, perfectly placed right hook that generated a barely audible, brittle snapping sound that told Roy he had broken Jack Kono's left jawbone just under the ear.

Miraculously, Kono was still on his feet, staggering around the dock like a drunk man, holding his kidney area with one hand, trying to catch the blood from his broken nose with the other. Shimmy, groaning, was still on his knees.

Roy hurried past several people who had stopped to watch.

"Guys tried to rob me," he said in passing.

He walked away fast until he reached the mouth of an alley, then he turned in and ran like hell.

Benny's expression was as barren as a winter desert.

"You mean you've been lying to me, Roy? Everything you told me about the fight in Gretna was a lie?"

"He didn't lie about the money, Mama," Sugar interjected as a plea.

"Sugar," her mother said with rare harshness, "you stay out of this!" Then back to Roy, "It was all a lie?"

"Yeah," Roy admitted. "All except the five hundred, like Sugar said —"

"And you didn't even get that!" Benny fumed.

Roy unwrapped a towel that had four ice cubes in it from around his right hand. His index knuckle was swollen to about twice its normal size and was beginning to take on a greenish-purple color. Roy had known he hurt it from the way his fist impacted on Jack Kono's jawbone; but he also knew the knuckle was not broken, because he could still bend and unbend his finger.

"Want a dry towel, Roy?" Sugar asked, her young face looking older with concern.

"No, Sugar, I gotta get going," he said, putting the icy wet towel in the sink.

"Going? Going where?" Benny demanded.

"I don't know where," Roy told her. "Anywhere. Just out of New Orleans."

"Oh, don't be silly, for God's sake," Benny said. "I'm not *that* mad at you."

Roy and Sugar looked at her incredulously. In some ways she was more a child than Sugar was.

"Verbenia, I'm not leaving 'cause you're mad at me," Roy said patiently. "Right about now, Jack Kono's in some hospital getting his jaw wired. He's gonna have some gorillas after me before midnight. People die for what I done, honey. I gotta get out of town."

He went to the chifforobe in the bedroom and got out the few extra clothes he had and put them in his zippered gym bag. Sugar quickly got his shaving gear from the bathroom, put it in a plastic Baggie, and brought it to him. "I want to go with you, Roy," the girl whispered, her eyes tearing up.

"Don't start," he whispered back. "You got to stay with your mother."

Sugar pouted for a moment, but quickly gave it up and asked, "Don't you have any idea where you're going to?"

Roy glanced at an alarm clock on Benny's nightstand. It was almost nine. "There used to be a bus for Houston left about ten-thirty. I'll prob'ly try for that if it's still running." He put the hand that wasn't swelling under her chin. "Listen, wherever I end up, I'll send a postcard to old Rainey at the poolroom. I'll sign it 'Wingy,' like in 'Wingy Manone' —"

She knew at once. "The one-armed cornet player."

"Yeah. Then you'll know I got away all right. Okay?"

"Okay. But won't we never see each other again, Roy?" The tears left her eyes now and streaked her pale cheeks.

" 'Course we will," he assured her, knowing it was probably a lie. "I'll figure out something. You just take care of your mother, okay? Promise?"

Sugar promised, but her child's face reflected that it was the most miserable thing she had ever had to do. Standing in the bedroom door, watching him go out to speak to her mother, Sugar's chest trembled with sobs she would not permit herself to release.

"Verbenia, I'm sure sorry about all this," Roy said to Benny, who was sitting at their little breakfast table drumming her nails on its oilcloth covering.

"I know, Roy. I am too," Benny replied without looking up.

"Listen, I hate to ask." He lowered his voice, hoping Sugar would not hear. "But I've on'y got a few bucks, and well —"

"Sure, Roy." Benny rose and got her purse. "I borrowed the five hundred from Sam today. I'll give you a hundred of it, and that's all —"

"That's plenty," Roy said. He noticed Sugar hurry back into the bedroom and kneel at her chifforobe drawer.

"Fall for a guy and end up giving him money to skip town," Benny muttered as she took the money from her purse. "Story of my life. At least this one's not leaving me pregnant."

She gave him the hundred. He started to kiss her good-bye, but she waved him away. "Just go, Roy."

"Okay." He turned away, hurt.

Before he got to the door, Sugar came running out to him and pressed some tightly folded currency into his hand. "Twelve dollars," she said. "I've been lagging quarters with some kids in Louis Armstrong Park. I win nearly every day."

"Louis Armstrong Park!" her mother exclaimed, overhearing. "Why, that's all the way up to Rampart Street! What in the world were you doing up there, young lady?"

"Please take the money," Sugar begged Roy, ignoring her mother. "So I'll know I helped you get away. Please, Roy, it's important."

Smiling a slight smile, Roy took the money. He rubbed his painful knuckles briefly against her cheek. "Know something?" he said. "It's important to me, too."

Then he was gone.

The ten thirty-five Greyhound to Houston via Baton Rouge and Beaumont was still running. Roy bought a one-way ticket and sat in a far corner of the terminal, back to the wall, drinking hot black coffee from a nearby vending machine as he watched the street entrance for anyone entering who looked like they might work for Jack Kono. When the departure was announced over the loudspeaker an hour later, Roy was the first passenger to board. He took a window seat about halfway back where he could see through the open boarding-platform doors into the passenger terminal. Settling back, his bag on the overhead rack, he shifted his eyes from the terminal to the other passengers, scrutinizing each one as they boarded. None of them looked threatening in any way. When they were all on board, the bus was only about half full. Least I'll be able to get comfortable, Roy thought. Maybe get some shut-eye. He kept his eyes on what he could see of the passenger terminal.

Two minutes before the bus was due to depart, Benny and Sugar came hurrying onto the boarding platform lugging a couple of beat-up suitcases and looking like a pair of magpies with both their mouths going at once. Benny had Sugar get on to make sure Roy was aboard, then they gave their tickets to the driver and maneuvered their suitcases down the aisle to where Roy stood to meet them.

"Don't even ask," Benny said peremptorily with a wave of her hand. "I couldn't explain this in a million years. Let's just say I'm crazy."

"This isn't very smart, Verbenia," he said, taking the suitcase she handed him.

As Benny slid into a seat, Sugar punched Roy on the muscle. "Don't you blow this, Roy," she whispered a warning. "I went through hell getting her here."

"Still not very smart."

"Just put the suitcases up."

Sugar sat across the aisle, leaving the seat next to her mother for Roy. She noticed as Roy sat down that Benny took his arm and leaned her head on his shoulder. Sugar smiled.

"I gave Sam back three hundred of the five and promised we'd send him the rest," Benny said.

"Okay, honey," said Roy, patting her head.

The driver got behind the wheel. The big passenger door closed with a pneumatic hiss. Several seconds later there was the choking of a diesel engine firing up and a sigh of air brakes being released. The bus began to move.

As the Greyhound pulled back from the boarding platform, Roy looked past Benny out the window and saw Shimmy, the punk he had encountered earlier with Jack Kono. Shimmy was with another hood, bigger and meaner looking. Both stood on the platform and stared hard at the Houston-bound bus as it swung away and left.

Roy wet lips that suddenly went dry. They must have followed Verbenia and Sugar, he thought.

Well, that's all she wrote, he told himself. There'd be somebody waiting every place the bus stopped, watching for him to get off. They had him, and that was that.

He thought about it in the dim light of the moving bus for a while, and finally decided he'd wait until Verbenia and Sugar went to sleep, then get off at the next stop. That way, at least the two of them wouldn't be involved. He didn't want them with him when Kono's hoods caught up with him. He didn't want them to see what would happen.

If they got away, he thought, this was one split decision he would win.

MEXICAN TRIANGLE

The men arrived at Villahermosa aboard a faded yellow bus that had once transported school children before it was phased out as being too antiquated and unsafe. The prison department took it over then, had some bars welded on the windows, and used it for a while to haul convicted men from the Mexico City courts out to Lecumberri Prison. But now that Pemex, the national petroleum company, had begun a pipeline operation in the state of Tabasco, the bus was used to transport *contratistas* — contract prison laborers — from Lecumberri down to the oil fields.

There were fourteen men in this latest shipment — twelve Mexican nationals and two *Norteamericanos*. When they got off the bus, they were lined up in front of a prefab field office. A Mexican police captain addressed them from the porch.

"You men have all volunteered to work in the government oil fields to earn a sentence reduction. All of you are serving two years or le.˜ for crimes of a non-violent nature. If you perform well in the fields, your respective sentences will be reduced by one half. In addition, you will receive sixty pesos a week for canteen supplies." Sixty pesos was about five dollars. It was better than nothing.

As the captain was speaking, two Anglos in work clothes came out onto the porch. They were sunburned, weathered men; thickarmed and thick-wristed; narrow-eyed from years of squinting; oil-field men. As the captain spoke, they studied the prisoners.

"Some of you might have volunteered for this job in order to escape," the captain continued. "If so, you will find it relatively easy to do. But when you are captured — as you probably will be — your original sentence will be doubled, and you will be required to serve it at Santa Marta Acatitla."

There was a wave of low muttering at the mention of Santa Marta. The federal prison just outside Mexico City was considered the country's worst hellhole. "I leave you now to *Señor* Waters, the field foreman, who will give you your labor assignments."

The captain retired to the shade of the field office and one of the Anglos stepped down off the porch. "My name's Glenn Waters," he said in Spanish. "I'm the field foreman. The gentleman there" — he nodded at the older, heavier Anglo — "is Mr. Clyde Madden, the field supervisor. First off, do either of you *Norteamericano* prisoners speak Spanish?"

A young man named Tommy Kerry raised his hand. Waters walked over to him. "What are you in for?"

"Smuggling."

"Smuggling what? Dope? Guns? Young girls? What?"

"Dope. Marijuana. I was down here on vacation and decided to take a kilo back with me. They caught me at the airport."

"What'd you get?"

"Two years."

"Any criminal record in the States?"

"No." Kerry shrugged as if embarrassed. "This was the first time I ever tried anything like, you know, criminal."

"Well, it only takes once, kid," Waters said tonelessly. "Step out of line and wait for me by the porch. The rest of you men turn left and follow me in single file."

Tommy Kerry waited by the porch. Clyde Madden, after staring at him for a minute, went back into the little field office with the captain. Kerry, hot and tired from the long bus ride looked around, saw no one who could object, and sat down on the steps. He was twenty-six but had a baby face that made him look younger. Large dark eyes and soft, almost feminine lips made most women want to mother him. He had a reputation for being charming.

Waters returned in a little while and said, "Okay, kid, come with me." He led Tommy to a supply shack. "Give this man three sets of new khakis," he ordered the supply man. While the order was being filled, he said, "Kid, this must be your lucky day. You're going to work in Mr. Madden's house as a helper for his wife. The guy she had run off the other day. Got caught and shipped up to Santa Marta. Mrs. Madden don't speak Mex, so she needs somebody to talk to the help for her. You're it."

Kerry studied Glenn Waters as he talked. Waters was about forty, Kerry figured. A younger version of Clyde Madden: no belly yet, no red veins in his nose from too much tequila, no persistent rivulets of sweat down his neck. Not yet.

"Where you from, Mr. Waters?" Kerry asked as he was handed his khakis.

"Waco, Texas. Why?"

"I thought I recognized your drawl. I'm from Lubbock."

"Lubbock, huh? Good place to be *from*. What are you doing down here

— besides smuggling pot, I mean."

Kerry shrugged. "I just got out of the army. Met this girl at a party and she invited me to come to Mexico with her and some of her friends. It sounded better than going back to Lubbock, so —"

"So you came along," Waters finished the story for him. "And when you got ready to go back, somebody suggested taking enough pot along to pay for the trip. You drew straws or rolled dice or something to see who'd carry it —"

"Cut cards."

"— and you were the lucky winner. But the marijuana dog was on duty at the airport that day and sniffed you out of line, right? So you got busted and your friends flew back home to the good old U.S. of A., leaving you holding the bag — or in your case, the kilo."

"Sounds like you've heard the story before."

"That one and a dozen others, kid." They left the supply shack and walked down the rutted dirt road. "I been working the fields for twenty years, kid, since I was younger than you. I've worked 'em in Texas, Oklahoma, Alaska, Iran, Kuwait, just about any place you can name that's got oil underneath it. And one thing I learned a long time ago: if a man's smart, he don't break no law in no foreign country. Doing time is bad enough — but doing time in a foreign slammer is the pits. You're lucky you got this labor deal, otherwise you'd have to do your whole two years at Lecumberri. Things can get pretty rough on a *gringo* at *el Palacio Negro*."

"At what?"

"El Palacio Negro. That's what they call Lecumberri — the Black Palace. Except for Santa Marta, it's the worst prison in Mexico. Nearly a hundred years old. Rat-infested. Built to hold 800 men — and it's got more than *two thousand* crammed into it. *Frijoles* and rice at every meal, every day. And if you get out of line they turn you over to a gun called *El Turko*, who used to work in one of them Istanbul prisons. They say *El Turko* is an expert at teaching prisoners how to behave properly."

"I guess I'm lucky to be out of there." Kerry said.

"Double lucky," said Waters. "Lucky not to be in Lecumberri, and lucky to get the job in Mr. Madden's house."

After Kerry cleaned up and dressed in a new set of khakis, Waters took him over to the Madden house. They went in through the back door and waited in the kitchen where two *campesinos* — local people — were cooking and cleaning. Presently Clyde Madden and his wife Lorna came in. Lorna was younger than Kerry expected, probably a couple of years under forty. Plain, angular, bony-hipped, she also had perfect calves and wide attractive shoulders.

Madden sat down at the table and hollered for two cold beers to be brought over for him and Waters. "All right, boy," he said to Kerry, "lemme tell you 'bout the kind of work them other cons on the bus with you's gonna be doing. They gonna be tarring our drilling pipe. For twelve hours a day they'll be working with boiling tar. So hot it'll burn your skin right off, so shiny black that it half blinds you, so stinking the smell of it stays in your nose permanent. We give 'em a ghost cream, a kind of white paste, to put on their faces to protect 'em from splatters, and we give 'em 'spestos gloves for their hands. That makes the job a little easier, but not much. The only thing that'll keep our drilling pipe from corroding is that hot tar when it dries. Putting it on is the worst job in the fields — that's why we give it to the cons. I want you to 'member all that when you're doing this nice clean work up here for my wife. Understan' me?"

"Yes, sir, I do," Kerry said. "I appreciate the job, sir." He glanced over at Lorna Madden. "I'll do everything I can to help Mrs. Madden." Their eyes met, held for an instant, parted.

"There's three domestics," Madden said. "A cook, a cleaning woman, and a handyman. Miz Madden will give them their daily orders through you, an' you'll be responsible for seeing that ever'thing gets done. Keep your nose clean and stay in line, understan'?" Madden studied Kerry for a moment. "You ain't got no sex offenses on your record, have you?"

"No, sir," Kerry replied emphatically. "Not me, sir. Just dope smuggling, is all."

Madden got up and walked over to Lorna. "All yours, sweetie," he said, patting her on the rear. Kerry heard her say, "Clyde, please," and pushed his hand away.

"Let's go, Glenn. See you later, sweetie."

Madden and Waters left. Tommy Kerry remained standing next to the back door until finally Lorna looked at him and said, "Well, come on over here and get yourself some coffee if you want to."

"Yes, ma'am. Thank you, ma'am."

Kerry came over to the stove. While the cook poured his coffee, he held out his hand to Lorna Madden. "It's nice to meet you, Mrs. Madden."

Lorna shook hands with him. Kerry held onto her hand for just a second longer than necessary. And they both knew it.

Kerry's work around the Madden household was easy enough. He translated to the three domestics whatever instructions Lorna Madden had for them; checked periodically throughout the day to make sure they were doing their jobs properly; and the rest of the time he just made himself generally useful. For a while he kept busy painting the outside trim around the windows, and the railing around the front porch. He stripped and stained a couple of old straightback chairs, making them look like new; and sanded the runners of two dresser drawers that stuck. He even put new shelves in the pantry and built vegetable and fruit bins under the bottom one.

"My you *are* handy," Lorna praised. "Where in the world did you learn to do all those things?"

"My granddad, mostly," Kerry told her. "He raised me on his farm out in west Texas. When you grow up on a farm you pick up a lot about mending, and building, and fixing. Seemed like there was always something that needed repair."

Sometimes Lorna asked him to help with her flowers. She had a planter box outside every window and experimented with anything she thought might grow. "I'm always surprised when a new variety blooms," she admitted. "Sometimes I wonder how anything beautiful can flourish in this awful place."

"You don't like it here very much, do you?" Kerry asked.

"No, I'm afraid I don't. Not any more. I used to. When Mr. Madden first brought me here, why this valley was one of the loveliest places you can imagine. It was a lush tropical landscape where all sorts of wildflowers and fern and ivy grew. And the little village was quiet and sleepy, just like on a picture postcard."

Lorna paused and looked past her front yard, at the sprawling oil field beyond. Her expression tightened. "Then the chainsaw operators came in — an army of them. They cut down everything in sight, everything that grew. After them came the bulldozers to shave off the stumps and leave the land flat. Then the diggers, the drillers, the pipelayers. They turned the village into a shantytown filled with cheap little cantinas and sleazy streetwalkers. They made the town square a little dump of paper and plastic and aluminum cans. They brought in a caravan of peddlers selling digital watches, transistor radios, imitation Swiss Army knives, and a lot of other junk to keep the workers from getting home with their wages." She shook her head wryly. "All for the oil. The petroleum. The black gold. The Mexican crude."

"If you hate it so much, why do you stay?" Kerry asked.

Lorna answered softly, almost as if she were speaking to a slow child, "I'm thirty-eight years old, Tommy. I have been married to Mr. Madden since I was sixteen. For twenty-two years I've never been anything but his wife. I'm completely dependent on him for everything — the food I eat, the clothes on my back, the roof over my head. To answer your question, I stay because I have no choice. It's not easy. I have a bottle of sleeping pills in my bathroom. When I can't stand it any longer, I take two or three of them and go to sleep. It's not much of an escape, but it's the only one I've got."

Before Kerry could say anything further, they both noticed Clyde Madden's pickup coming down the road in front of a funnel of dust. They looked at each other for a moment, then Lorna sighed.

"You'd better get on around back. Mr. Madden wouldn't like us working together like this."

That night in the barracks Kerry asked his friend Paco, who bunked next to him, how far it was to the nearest U.S. border station. Paco laughed. "Oh, not so far, *amigo*. Only about eleven or twelve hundred kilometers."

"How far is that in miles?"

Paco shrugged. "I'm not sure. I think about seven hundred." His expression turned serious. "Too far, amigo," he said quietly.

Kerry was lying on his bunk. As usual he tried not to breathe too deeply because of the pervading smell of petroleum in the air. It was a constant thing, that smell; it got into a man's nostrils and mouth, throat and lungs; you could taste it with every word spoken or every bite taken. The only time Kerry ever got away from it was in the air-conditioned cleanness of the Madden house.

Getting up, Kerry stuck his head out the glassless window to see if there was any breeze outside. There was not. All he got was a breath of night air thick with the fumes of natural gas burnoff from the wellheads. In the distance the otherwise dark sky had an orange glow from the burning. As Kerry stared at the glow, he saw above it in the black upper sky a minute light moving slowly from south to north. A plane. Turning, he sat on the edge of Paco's bunk.

"How far to the nearest commercial airport?"

Paco thought for a moment. "I think that would be Gutierrez. It's about a two-hour drive south."

"Good road?"

"Narrow," said Paco, "but paved all the way."

"Do you know where they have air service to?"

"Mexico City. Maybe Vera Cruz and Campeche, I don't know."

"But Mexico City for sure?"

"*Si*. That's the one place you can always get to. But listen, *amigo*, you'd be a fool to try it. A *gringo* like you, all alone —"

"Maybe I won't be alone," Kerry murmured.

The next time Kerry was helping Lorna Madden with her flowers, he said matter-of-factly, "I've decided to escape, Lorna."

She stared at him incredulously; he was not sure whether it was because he had told her he intended to run, or because he had called her by her given name.

"You're crazy," she said after a few moments.

"Maybe I am. But I'm going to try anyway. I've made up my mind,"

"If they catch you, you'll get put back in prison with a double sentence."

"*If* they catch me."

"They catch nearly everybody that runs. The few who do make it are Mexes. No white man has ever escaped from these fields.

Kerry shrugged. "Maybe I'll be the first. Anyway, if I do get caught, it'll still be better than being here." Seeing a frown come to Lorna's face, Kerry quickly took her hand. "I didn't mean that the way it sounded. It's wonderful being here with you. You're the only good thing that's happened to me since I got out of the army and came down to this damned country. But I've begun to feel about these fields as you do; I've begun to hate them as you do. The smell of petroleum, the dust, the ugliness. Then there's — well, never mind, that's no concern of yours —"

"What?" she asked, squeezing is hand. "I want to know."

Kerry looked away, refusing to meet her eyes. "The Mexes in the barracks are jealous because I've got such an easy job. They — they've been talking about ganging up some night and dragging me into the shower room. I don't know how much of it is just talk —" He shrugged and still did not look at her.

"My god," Lorna said softly.

They stood in silence for a little while, their hands still together; it was her holding his hand now — the older woman comforting the younger man. He seemed so vulnerable with his large dark eyes and soft, almost feminine lips. Lorna thought about the shower room and shuddered.

"Come on in the kitchen," she said. "Let's have some coffee and think this out.

The cook had gone to the market and the cleaning woman was upstairs, so they had the kitchen to themselves. Lorna brought in a bottle of Clyde Madden's brandy and laced their coffee.

"I want you to help me, Lorna," Kerry said. "I won't ask you to do anything that would involve you directly, that would get you into any kind of trouble, but I'd like to be able to count on you for a little information."

"What kind of information, Tommy?"

Their eyes held for a moment. There way something about the way she said his name.

"It would be a big help if I knew when Madden was going to be away for the day — so I could get a good headstart before I was missed. And I'd appreciate knowing the shortest way across the fields to the road to Gutierrez."

"Gutierrez? You're making for the airport then?"

"Yes. I'm going to try and stow away on a cargo plane. I found out that the drums of barite drilling mud are flown in from south Texas and then trucked up here. The empty barrels are flown back to Texas. I figure if I can slip onto one of those return planes —"

"How do you plan to get to the airport? It's a hundred miles."

"I'll hitchhike."

"That's crazy — a white man, hitchhiking on a Mexican highway. How far do you think you'd get?"

"I'm going to steal some wet coffee grounds from your kitchen and darken my face. I think I'll have a good chance."

Lorna shook her head. "You won't get twenty miles."

Kerry shrugged. "Maybe not. But I'm going to try. I've *got* to try."

From outside came the sound of Clyde Madden's pickup again. Lorna quickly took their cups to the sink and rinsed them. Kerry started out the back way. When he got to the door, Lorna's voice stopped him.

"Tommy?"

Kerry looked back at her.

"I'll help you," she said. "We'll do it together."

Kerry nodded. As he went out the back door, he smiled a knowing smile.

That evening, as Kerry walked down the road that led to his barracks, Glenn Waters pulled up alongside him in a company Jeep. "Hop in," he said. Kerry climbed into the passenger seat. Waters threw him an unsmiling look. "You sure put one over on me, didn't you, kid?"

"I don't know what you mean."

"Like hell you don't. Lecumberri Prison sent me a copy of your record today. The Texas authorities tracked you down here and put an extradition hold on you. You're an escapee from Huntsville and you've got a record as long as my arm."

Kerry fished a cigarette out of his shirt pocket and lighted it. "What do you figure to do about it?"

"I haven't decided yet," Waters replied.

Kerry smiled the same kind of knowing smile again. "While you're making up your mind, you'd better be thinking about how Mr. Madden's going to feel when *he* finds out about my record. We both know how particular he is about who you pick to work in his house. I don't imagine that he's going to be too pleased that you let me work around his wife for two months — especially with the rape conviction I've got. Could cost you your job."

Waters pulled over to the side of the road and parked. "Pretty smart, aren't you, kid? I didn't know they grew 'em that smart in Lubbock."

"Just a shade smarter than they grow 'em in Waco," Kerry said. He locked eyes with Waters. "Do we make a deal or do we butt heads?"

"What kind of deal did you have in mind?"

"I want to get out of here."

Waters shook his head emphatically. "If I got caught helping you escape, *I'd* end up in Santa Marta prison. No, thanks. I'd rather lose my job."

"You don't have to get directly involved," Kerry assured him. "I already have a plan. All I need from you is capital. If you could arrange to leave some money where I'd find it —"

"How much money?"

"A thousand dollars."

Again the emphatic shake of the head. "I don't have that much — and you don't *need* that much. I'll give you five hundred. Take it or leave it."

Kerry quickly nodded. "It's a deal. But I'll need one other thing — a company ID badge to get out the gate. An old one will do — one turned in by an ex-employee."

"Okay. But that's all. And I don't want to know any of the details — not how or when or anything. Understood?"

They worked out a plan. On the next payday Waters would get three hundred in U. S. dollars and two hundred in Mexican pesos, and leave the money and the ID badge in a manila envelope under a drainage pipe at the side of the road. Kerry would pick it up on his way to work.

Kerry told Lorna he would be ready to go anytime after payday. "A couple of guys owe me a few dollars. I want to collect before I go."

"That'll be perfect," said Lorna. "The day after payday Clyde will be gone all day. He has to drive over to the west field and inspect the new rigs that just went up. It's a three-hour drive each way. If we leave thirty minutes after he does , we can get to the airport in Gutierrez and be on a plane for Mexico City before —"

"We?" Kerry interrupted.

"Yes," Lorna said firmly. "I'm going with you." She took hold of his arm with both hands. "Look, I know I'm twelve years older than you, and not very pretty either, so I don't expect you to stay with me. But if we could just help each other get out of here, and maybe stay together until I can find some kind of work —"

"I'll stay with you," Kerry promised. "And I'll take care of you."

"Tommy, don't say that if you don't mean it. I'm so scared of being alone —"

"You won't be alone," he told her. "Stop worrying. Tell me how you want to do it."

Lorna composed herself. "Clyde will be taking Glenn Waters, his field foreman, with him. They usually take Glenn's Jeep because it does better on the field roads. Clyde's pickup will be left here. As soon as they leave, I'll pack my clothes, take all the household money, and be ready to go. You can come in and put on some of Clyde's clothes — they'll be a little big but you can get by. Then you can hide under a tarp in the back of the truck until we get past the gate and out to the Gutierrez highway. It should work all right." She looked quizzically at him. "Shouldn't it?"

"Yeah." Kerry said. "It should work fine."

On the day after payday Kerry was washing windows at the back of the house when Glenn Waters drove up and parked his Jeep next to Clyde Madden's pickup. On his way into the house Waters paused and looked inquiringly at Kerry. The young convict nodded almost imperceptibly, just enough to let Waters know that he had picked up the manila envelope with the money and the ID badge. The envelope was tucked neatly under his khaki shirt.

Waters knocked and went into the kitchen. A few minutes later he came back out, accompanied by Clyde Madden. The two of them got into the Jeep. Neither man even glanced at Kerry as they drove away.

Kerry continued to wash the windows for several minutes, and then the cook and the cleaning woman emerged from the house and started toward the company store on errands. The handyman was already gone — Kerry had sent him over to the carpenter shop to get a chair leg repaired.

When he was certain no one was around, Kerry went into the house. Lorna was at the breakfast counter, nervously sipping coffee. "Everyone's gone," Kerry said. "Let's get moving."

Lorna put down her cup and swallowed hard. "Upstairs," she said. "Everything's ready."

As they left the kitchen, Kerry slipped a carving knife from the wall holder and held it concealed at his side.

Lorna led the way to the master bedroom. From the closet she handed Kerry some clothes. "These are some things Clyde wore a few years ago when he wasn't so heavy. They'll probably fit you better." Then she saw the knife in his hand. "Why do you have that?" she asked."

Kerry didn't answer. Instead he asked, "Where's the household money?"

"It's in the bureau."

"Get it." Kerry put down the knife and undressed to change clothes. He watched Lorna closely as she got a roll of bills from the bureau.

"You're not taking me, are you?" Lorna asked quietly.

"You guessed it, lady."

"I thought we were going to help each other."

"You were only half right." He took the money from her hand and began counting it.

"You need me to get out the gate," she said.

"I don't need you for anything. All I need is that pickup out there." He put the money on a chair with the manila envelope and the knife. Then he had a sudden thought. His eyes swept down to Lorna's perfect calves. Wetting his lips, he glanced at the clock. "On second thought, maybe I do need you for something —"

Stepping over to Lorna, Kerry put both hands on the front of her dress and ripped it open.

"Just hold it right there, punk," said Glenn Waters from the bedroom door. Kerry whirled around and froze. Waters had a pistol leveled at his chest. "Back up against the wall," he ordered.

Lorna hurried over to Waters. "I was afraid you weren't going to make it on time."

"Everything's right on schedule, honey," he said, kissing her briefly on the cheek. "But this next part is going to be hard."

Lorna took a step away from him. "Do it, Glenn," she said determinedly.

Waters hesitated.

"Do it!" Lorna ordered.

Waters shifted the gun to his left hand, closed his right fist, and punched her solidly in the jaw. Lorna dropped to the floor in a heap.

Kerry stared incredulously at Glenn Waters. "What the hell's going on, man?"

Waters gave him a slight smile. "Seems like there was an escape attempt this morning," he said matter-of-factly. "The convict assigned to Supervisor Madden's house. The supervisor and I had started out for the west field when he noticed he'd forgotten his inspection log. We drove back to get it. Madden came inside and caught you attacking his wife. There was a struggle and you stuck that kitchen knife in him. His wife ran upstairs. You caught her in the bedroom. I was waiting in the Jeep outside and heard her yell just before you slugged her. I got my pistol out of the utility chest and came inside. You rushed me with the knife and —" Waters shrugged.

Kerry's eyes narrowed. "So it's been you and her all along."

"You got that right, kid. Me and her and old Clyde's company insurance policy. You know that Pemex insures its field supervisors for two hundred thousand?"

"Where's Madden now?"

"Lying on the kitchen floor where I left him, dead to the world. Lorna put six of her sleeping pills in his coffee this morning." He smiled. "It won't matter though, because there won't be an autopsy; not in a stabbing death, not out here. I'll finish him off later."

On the floor, Lorna rolled over and groaned. Glenn Waters looked down at her, taking his eyes off Kerry for a split-second. But that split-second was long enough. Kerry snatched a lamp from the bedtable and hurled it in Glenn's face, knocking him backward. Then he leaped across the bed for the knife on the chair. Desperately his fingers closed on the handle. Turning he saw Waters on the floor, groping for his fallen gun. Kerry dove on him with the knife just as Waters rolled over and pulled the trigger.

Glenn Waters' bullet drilled Tommy Kerry in the center of the forehead, and Tommy Kerry's knife plunged directly into Glenn Waters' heart.

When Lorna woke up, it was not difficult for her to figure out what had happened.

Men, she thought. They couldn't be depended on to do anything right.

Quickly she revised her story. Clyde came back for his inspection log and caught Kerry attacking her. There was a struggle in the kitchen and Kerry stabbed Clyde. She ran upstairs. Kerry followed her, ripped her dress, punched her in the face —

Gently she touched her swelling jaw. At least you did that right, Glenn.

— anyway, Glenn came running into the bedroom with the gun. Kerry stabbed Glenn, and Glenn shot Kerry.

Lorna pursed her lips. Yes, that sounded fine. She looked around the room. Everything was perfect — except for one last little detail. She wet her lips. This was something she had not counted on. She wondered if she could do it.

Glancing out the window, she saw the barren, brown oil field in all its ugliness. She thought of the twenty-two years she had spent with Clyde. And she thought of freedom. Freedom and two hundred thousand dollars.

Lorna smiled. She could do it, all right.

Wrapping the knife handle with a handkerchief, she pulled it out of Glenn's chest and went down to the kitchen.

THE DUBLIN EYE

Kilkenny heard the phone ring as he was unlocking his office door. He hurried in to answer it.

"Kilkenny," he said.

"Is this Mr. Royal Kilkenny?" a hesitant female voice asked. The caller sounded very young. "Mr. Royal Kilkenny, the query man?"

"Yes. How can I help you?"

"Mr. Kilkenny, my name is Darlynn Devalain. I'm the daughter of Joe Devalain, of Belfast."

An image mushroomed in Kilkenny's mind. Not of Joe Devalain, but of the woman Joe had married. Of Sharmon. This girl on the phone was probably Sharmon's daughter.

"How is your dad, then?" Kilkenny asked. "And your mother?"

"My dad's not so good, Mr. Kilkenny," the girl replied, and Kilkenny, though he had never laid eyes on her, could almost see her lip quivering as her voice broke. "He's been in a bad accident. An explosion in his shop. They've got him over at St. Bartholomew's Hospital, but it's not known if he'll live or —"

"Did your mother tell you to call me?" Kilkenny asked, frowning. It had been eighteen years since Sharmon Cavan had picked Joe Devalain over him and he had gone off to America to try and forget her.

"No, she doesn't even know I'm after calling you," Darlynn Devalain said. "Me dad told me once that he knew you before you went to America. When he heard you'd come back and set up as a query man down in Dublin, he told me you were a man he could always count on. He said if I should ever find myself in serious trouble of any kind to get hold of you and tell you I'm the daughter of Joe Devalain. You'd help me just as if I were your own. So that's why I'm calling, sor. Not for me, but for me dad. He needs somebody to look out after his interests. The police, they don't seem to care much about who blew up his shop."

"How badly was he hurt in the explosion?" Kilkenny asked.

"As badly as one can be and still be called alive," the girl said. "Oh, Mr. Kilkenny, he's in terrible shape. Can you come, sor? Please."

The girl's voice reminded Kilkenny of Sharmon. Sharmon, with her deep rust-colored hair and dancing emerald eyes, the smile that showed crooked teeth that somehow made her even prettier, the wide, wide shoulders, and the strong peasant thighs that even at sixteen could lock a man where she wanted him, for as long as she wanted him there.

"Yes, I'll come," Kilkenny said. "I'll take the train up and meet you at the hospital this evening."

Kilkenny bought a first-class seat on the *Enterprise Express*, which made the Dublin-Belfast run in two hours and twenty minutes. Dundalk, an hour north of Dublin, was the last stop in the Irish Free State. After Dundalk, the train crossed into Armagh County, which was part of Northern Ireland.

At Portadown, the first stop in Armagh, British soldiers boarded the coaches and checked all passengers. From Portadown on into Belfast an armed British soldier rode at each end of every coach. Most passengers didn't leave their seats even to go to the lavatory during that leg of the journey.

At Belfast Central the passengers stood for a pat-down, baggage search, and questioning at a British Army checkpoint in the middle of the station.

"Identification, please," a pink-cheeked young lieutenant requested. Kilkenny handed over his billfold. "What's your business in Belfast, sir?"

"To see a friend who's in hospital."

"What's the duration of your stay, sir?"

"I don't know. No more than forty-eight hours, I shouldn't expect."

"Your occupation is listed as a 'personal enquiries representative.' What is that, exactly?"

"I'm a private investigator. A detective."

The young officer's expression brightened. "You mean like one of those American private eyes? Like that Magnum bloke?"

"Yes, sort of. Less hectic, though."

The lieutenant frowned. "Not armed, I hope."

"No." Kilkenny wondered why he asked. A sergeant had already patted Kilkenny down and two privates had rummaged though his overnighter.

"Pass through," the officer said, returning Kilkenny's billfold.

Outside the terminal Kilkenny got into a square black taxi. "St. Bartholomew's Hospital," he said.

The driver glanced at him in the rearview mirror, then looked out the side window at the darkening late-afternoon sky. "That's in the Flats," he said.

"The Flats?"

"Aye. Unity Flats. The Catholic section. I'll take you in, but I can't wait for you or come back to get you. I'm not Catholic, so I can't risk being in the Flats after dark."

"Just drop me at the hospital," Kilkenny said. "That'll be fine."

On the way through the city, it started to rain — one of those sudden, blustery rains that seemed to be forever blowing in off the North Channel and turning the already dreary grey streets a drearier black. Kilkenny hadn't thought to bring a raincoat — it had been so long since he'd been to Belfast he had forgotten how unpredictable the weather could be.

"Bit of a heavy dew out there," he said.

"Aye," the driver replied, turning on the wipers. He made no attempt at further conversation.

Kilkenny wasn't familiar with the section called Unity flats. He, Joe Devalain, and Sharmon Cavan had grown up in a slum known as Ballymurphy. It was a savagely poor place, worse than anything Kilkenny had seen during his ten years as a New York City policeman. In New York he had worked both Spanish Harlem and the South Bronx, and neither of them was nearly as poor, ugly, or deprived as Ballymurphy. Ballymurphy wasn't the gutter, it was the sewer. Both Kilkenny and Joe Devalain had sworn to Sharmon that they would take her away from the life of poverty in which they had all grown to adolescence.

It had not been Kilkenny Sharmon picked to do it. "I've decided in favor of Joe," she told Kilkenny one night after they had made love under the back stairs of Sharmon's tenement building.

"I thought you loved *me*," Kilkenny had said.

"I love you both," Sharmon had answered. "Do y'think I'd do this with the two of you if I didn't love you both? It's just that I can't *have* you both, so I must choose, mustn't I? And I've chosen Joe."

"But why? Why him and not me?"

"Lots of reasons," she said lightly. "I like the name Sharmon Devalain better than I like Sharmon Kilkenny. And I think Joe will do better in life than you. He's got a good job at the linen plant — someday he'll probably be a foreman. While you've done nothing at all to better yourself."

"I go to school," Kilkenny protested. "I want to be a policeman someday —"

"I don't like policemen," she said loftily. "They're a smug lot. Anyway, Joe'll earn lots more when he works his way up to plant foreman than you'll ever earn being a policeman."

Kilkenny had been sick with disappointment. "If it's just the money, maybe I could be something else —"

"It's not just that," she said.

"What else, then?"

"Well, y'see," she replied with a little reluctance. "Joe is — well, *better* at — well, you know —" She sighed impatiently. "He's a bit more of a man, if y'know what I mean."

Kilkenny had thought he would never get over that remark. It left him impotent for six months. Only after leaving Ireland, going to Southampton and boarding a ship for America, and meeting on board a fleshy Czech girl just beginning to feel her new freedom after escaping from behind the Iron Curtain, was he able to function physically as a man again. He had never had a problem since — but he had never forgotten Sharmon's words.

"Here you are," the driver said. "St. Bartholomew's."

Kilkenny collected his bag and got out. The driver made change for him, glanced up at the waning daylight again, and sped off.

From the front steps of the hospital Kilkenny looked around at what he could see of Unity Flats. It was a slum, as Ballymurphy had been, though not quite as stark and dirty. But definitely a ghetto. Sharmon hadn't made it very far with Joe, he thought.

In the hospital lobby, a young nun, wearing the habit of the Ulster Sisters of Charity, consulted a name file and directed Kilkenny to a ward on the third floor. He waited for the lift with several women visitors. The women in the north were not as attractive as the women down south, he noticed. Most of them wore white T-necks that clearly outlined their brassieres, wide-legged, baggy slacks or skirts that were too short, no stockings, and shoes with straps that made their ankles look thick. Their hair seemed to be combed and in control only down to their cheeks, then appeared to grow wild on its own, as if it was too much to take care of. They were poor women, clearly. As they grew older, Kilkenny knew, they would all become noble mother figures who would strive to keep their husbands sober, their children God-fearing and Catholic, and their homes decent. They were the silent strength of the poor Northern Irish Catholic household. Kilkenny wondered if Sharmon had become like them.

At the third-floor ward, Kilkenny stepped through double swinging doors and looked around. The instant he saw Darlynn Devalain, he knew who she was. She looked nothing at all like Joe, but though he saw only a trace of Sharmon, there was enough so there was no mistaking who she was.

Burnt-blonde hair, eyes a little too close together, lips a little crooked, almost mismatched, there was something distinctly urchin about her. That touch of the gutter, Kilkenny thought. It never entirely leaves us.

She was standing just outside a portable screen that kept the last bed on the ward partitioned from the others. She was staring out at nothing as if in a trance. Kilkenny put his bag by the wall and walked down the ward toward her. When he came into her field of vision, it seemed to break her concentration and she watched him as he walked up to her. Their eyes met and held.

"You're Darlynn," he said. "I'm Royal Kilkenny."

She put out her hand. "Thanks for coming." She bobbed her chin at the bed behind the screen. "Me dad's there. What's left of him."

There were a doctor and two nurses on one side of the bed, the nurses just turning away with covered aluminum trays in their hands, walking past Kilkenny on their way out. When they left, Kilkenny had an unobstructed view of the bed. What he saw did not look like a man at all; it looked like a large pillow under a sheet, with a head placed above it and several rubber tubes running down to it from jars of liquid hung on racks next to the bed. There was an oxygen mask over part of the face. Kilkenny saw no arms or legs under the sheet and felt his mouth go dry.

"Who are you, please?" the doctor asked, noticing Kilkenny.

"A friend. Up from Dublin. His daughter called me." Kilkenny tried to swallow but could not. "Is he still alive?" he asked. The form did not appear to be breathing.

"Yes. Why or how, I don't know. The explosion totally devastated him. Apparently he was right on top of whatever detonated. The flash of the explosion blinded him; the noise destroyed his eardrums so that he's now completely deaf; and the hot gases got into his open mouth and burned up his tongue and vocal cords, making him mute. The force of the blast damaged his lungs and shattered his limbs so badly we had to amputate both arms above the elbow and both legs above the knee. So here he lies, unable to see, hear, or speak, unable to breathe without an oxygen mask, and with no arms or legs. But he's alive." He led Kilkenny out to where Darlynn stood. "I've sedated him for the night," he told the girl. "You go home and rest, young lady. That's an order."

Kilkenny gook Darlynn by the arm and gently led her out of the ward, picking up his bag on the way. There was a snack shop still open on the ground floor and Kilkenny took her there, found a remote table, and ordered tea.

"How's your mother taking it?" he asked.

Darlynn shrugged. "It's not the end of the world for her. She and Dad haven't got on that great the past few years."

Kilkenny decided not to pursue that topic. "What kind of explosion was it? How'd it happen?"

"We don't know. It's supposedly being investigated by the RUC. But you know how that is."

The RUC was the Royal Ulster Constabulary, Northern Ireland's civilian police force. Like all other civil service in Ireland's British-aligned six northern counties, it was controlled by London and more than ninety percent Protestant.

"They're trying to blame it on the IRA," Darlynn added.

"Of course." It would be the natural thing for them to do, Kilkenny thought. But he knew, as most Irishmen did, that for the IRA to be responsible for every crime attributed to it, the outlaw organization would have to be fifty thousand strong instead of the less than a thousand it actually was. "Was your dad still active in the IRA?" he asked.

Darlynn glanced at him and hesitated a beat before answering. Kilkenny expected as much. He was, despite her father's recommendation, still a stranger to her, and to speak of the IRA to strangers could be dangerous. But something about him apparently prompted her trust.

"No, he hadn't been active for about five years. He still supported the organization financially, as much as he could afford, but he no longer took part in raids or anything like that."

"Had he any trouble with the Orangemen?" Kilkenny asked, referring to the pseudo-Masonic order of Protestants that opposed a united Ireland. Their activities were often as violent as the IRA, though never as well publicized.

"Dad had no trouble with them that I know about," Darlynn said. "Except for his IRA donations, he stayed pretty much out of politics. All he cared about these past few years was that shop of his. He was very proud of that shop."

"What sort of shop?" Kilkenny asked. The last he'd heard, Joe Devalain was still trying to work his way up the ladder at the linen factory.

"It was a linen shop. Tablecloths, napkins, handkerchiefs, a few bed-covers, a small line of curtains. If there was one thing Dad knew, it was cloth. He worked in the linen factory for eighteen years and never got a single promotion, but he learned all there was to know about cloth. Finally he decided to pack it in. He drew out all his pension benefits and opened the shop. Mum was furious about it, said those benefits were half hers, for *her* old age as well as his. But Da did it anyway."

"Was that when things started going bad between them?"

"Not really. They'd been at each other off and on for a long time." Darlynn looked down at the tabletop. "Mum's had a boy friend or two."

"Did you tell your mother you were calling me?" Kilkenny asked.

"I told her after."

"What was her reaction."

"She got a funny kind of look on her face, like I haven't seen in a long time. When I was a little girl, she used to look like that whenever Da would bring her a bouquet of posies. When I mentioned your name, it was like I had done something special for her. Were you and my mother close?"

Kilkenny nodded. "Your mum and dad and me were all three close. Your dad and me were best friends, but we were rivals for your mum, too. Your dad won her. He was too much a match for me."

"He wouldn't be much competition now, would he?" she asked. Suddenly tears streaked her cheeks.

Kilkenny calmed her down and got her to finish her tea, then walked the two miles home with her because she didn't feel like riding a bus. It had stopped raining and the bleak, poorly lighted streets smelled wet and the air was heavy. Kilkenny's palm sweated from carrying the suitcase. There was something about the way Darlynn's hair bounced in back that reminded him of Sharmon.

Somewhere along the way, he promised the girl he would look into the matter of the explosion that had destroyed everything about her father except his life.

The Devalains lived as tenants in a little timeworn house that looked like wet newspaper. As Kilkenny and Darlynn got to the door, Sharmon Devalain opened it for them.

"Hello, Roy." she said.

"Hello, Sharmon."

The sight of her reduced him to astonishment. She seemed not to have aged as he had. There were no plump cheeks, no wide hips, nothing even remotely in common with the women he had seen at the lift in the hospital. She didn't look a day over thirty, if that.

"Come in, Roy. I'll make tea."

"We've just had tea, actually. And I've got to go get a room."

"You can stay here. I can sleep with Darlynn. The place isn't much, but it's clean."

"Thanks anyway, but I'd better stay downtown. I told Darlynn I'd try and find out about the explosion."

Sharmon threw her daughter a brief, irritated glance. "She's quick to ask for anything she wants. Even with strangers."

"I don't really feel like a stranger to her. After all, she *is* yours. And Joe's."

"Yes. Well, I'm sure the RUC will appreciate any help you can give them." Her eyes flicked up and down his tall frame. "You're looking well, Roy. Prosperous."

"Hardly that. I make a comfortable living is all. But it's what I want to do."

"Well, you're one of the lucky ones, then. Most people never get what they want out of life. Are you sure about tea? Or staying the night?"

"Yes, thanks. I'll be off. Is there a bus at the corner?"

Sharmon nodded. "Number Five. It'll take you to Great Victoria Street. Will I see you again?"

"Sure," Kilkenny said. "I'll be around."

Only when he was walking down the street did Kilkenny realize that he had not said he was sorry about Joe.

He got a room at the Europa Hotel downtown and spent the night alternating between restless, fitful sleep and sitting on the windowsill, staring out at the night city, remembering.

When the night finally ended and daylight broke over Belfast Lough, when from his hotel window Kilkenny saw smoke rising from the great stacks of Harland and Wolff, the mammoth shipbuilding complex, and when civil servants began hurrying along Howard Street to their jobs in nearby Donegall Square, he showered and shaved and went down for breakfast.

After he ate, he walked over to Oxford Street where the Royal Courts of Justice were located and found that the Royal Ulster Constabulary Headquarters were still situated nearby. After telling his business to a receptionist in the lobby, he was sent up to the first floor and shown to the desk of Sergeant Bill O'Marn of the Bomb Investigation section.

"Well, well," O'Marn said, looking at Kilkenny's identification. "A real flesh-and-blood private eye, just like on the telly." He was a handsome man of forty, with great bushy black eyebrows. One of the "black Irish" that women seemed to find so attractive. He wore a sprig of light green heather on the lapel of his Harris tweed jacket. Dapper, Kilkenny thought. "You realize your detective license is no good up here, don't you?" O'Marn asked.

"Certainly," said Kilkenny. "I'm only making enquiry at the request of Mr. Devalain's daughter."

"Who, I believe, is a minor."

"Yes, I believe she is. As I started to say, though, I haven't been retained or anything like that. The girl just wants to know who detonated her father. As I'm sure you do also."

"We already know," O'Marn said. "It was the IRA."

"I see. May I ask *how* you know?"

"The explosion was caused by gelignite. Nobody but the IRA uses gelignite. Every time we raid an IRA headquarters, we confiscate a foot locker full of the stuff."

Kilkenny nodded. "What reason, I wonder, would the IRA have for blowing up Joe Devalain."

"They don't need reasons for what they do," O'Marn scoffed. "They're madmen, the lot of them."

"Are you saying they simply decided to blow up a shop — any shop — and picked Joe Devalain's place randomly?"

"Looks that way to us."

This time Kilkenny shook his head. "I'm sorry, Sergeant O'Marn, but I can't accept that premise. It's always been my understanding that the IRA was much more precise in its operations than that. I thought it only set off bombs in strategic locations where British Army mustered or patrolled, or where the explosion would produce some subsequent economic impact. I don't see how blowing up a small linen shop is going to do them any good at all."

"Neither do I," O'Marn agreed with an artificial smile. "But then, you and I aren't IRA terrorists, are we?"

"Is this matter still under investigation?" Kilkenny asked, ignoring the sergeant's question.

"Technically, yes."

"But it isn't being worked?"

"I didn't say that, Mr. Kilkenny."

Kilkenny rose. "You didn't have to. I wonder what you'll do about your crime statistics if the IRA ever disbands. Anyway, thanks for your time, Sergeant. Good day."

From the RUC headquarters, Kilkenny rode a bus back out to Unity Flats.

On the way he became aware of some of the graffiti that scarred the city. NO POPE HERE! read one. NO QUEEN HERE! countered another. PROVISIONALS FOR FREEDOM, GOD SAVE OUR POPE! was offset by NO SURRENDER, GOD SAVE THE QUEEN! Some city blocks warned: ARMY KEEP OUT! SOLDIERS ARE BASTARDS! Others proclaimed: ULSTER WILL FIGHT! The most ominous said simply: INFORMERS BEWARE.

Twice along the way, the bus passed moving Saracens, big six-wheeled armored vehicles that carried three soldiers and patrolled the Catholic sections. The great tanks lumbered past children playing on the sidewalk. They didn't even glance at them, never having known streets without such patrols.

At St. Bart's hospital, Kilkenny found Darlynn sitting by her father's bed, gently stroking the stump of one arm above the bandage. She looked scrubbed and fresh, like a schoolgirl. Kilkenny drew a chair round and sat by her.

"When your dad was active in the IRA, did you ever know any of his contacts?" he asked very quietly.

Darlynn shook her head. "The only time the organization was ever mentioned was when he and Mum would fight about it. She claimed it was because he was suspected of being IRA that he never got promoted at the linen factory. According to her, it's been the IRA that's kept us in Unity Flats all these years."

"Did you ever know of any meeting places he went to?"

"I'm not sure. There was a pub out on Falls Road — Bushmill's, it was called. I used to find match boxes from the place when I emptied the pockets of Da's trousers for the wash. I know after he left the IRA I never found them again."

While she was talking, Darlynn had unintentionally stopped stroking her father's mutilated arm. To Kilkenny's surprise, the reduced figure on the bed began emitting from under the oxygen mask a pitiful, begging noise. Darlynn resumed stroking at once, and what was left of Joe Devalain calmed down.

"I don't even know if he's aware it's me," Darlynn said.

"I'm sure he is," Kilkenny told her, though he wasn't sure at all.

"I wish there was some way to communicate with him," the girl said. "Maybe *he'd* know who did this to him."

Yes, Kilkenny thought, he might. But how *did* one communicate with a living soul who could not see, hear, or speak and had no hands with which to write or feel or make signals?

"Would you like to come for supper tonight," Darlynn asked. "Mum's going out, but I'm a better cook, anyway — at least, Dad's always said I was. It wouldn't be anything fancy, you understand."

"I'm sorry, I'll be busy tonight, Darlynn. I want to make contact with the IRA if I can."

She put her free hand on his knee. "Stop by later, then. Just so I'll know you're all right."

He promised he would.

As he left the hospital, Kilkenny imagined that his leg felt warm where she had touched him.

Bushmill's was not unlike a hundred other neighborhood pubs in Belfast. It had a stained-glass window or two, a few secluded nooks, one private booth with frosted glass, and a bar a shiny as a little girl's cheeks on First Holy Communion Day. There was always an accordion player about, and always a stale beer odor in the air. Anyone ordering anything except a pint of stout drawn from the tap got a sidelong glance. All conversation ceased when a stranger entered.

Kilkenny stood in the silence at the end of the bar and ordered his pint. When it came, he paid for it and drank it down in a single, long continuous swallow. Wiping off the foam with the back of his hand, he then spoke to the bartender in a tone that every man on the premise could hear.

"My name is Royal Kilkenny. I'm a detective down in the Free State, but I grew up here in Belfast, over in Ballymurphy. My father was Doyle Kilkenny. My mother was Faye Quinn Kilkenny. My grandfather on my mother's side was Darcy Quinn, who was Padraic Pearse's man in Longford County and served four years in His Majesty's prison at Wormwood Scrubs for the privilege. I'm up here because a friend of mine named Joe Devalain was blown up in his linen shop three days ago. He's still alive, what there is left of him, but that doesn't include eyes, ears, voice, hands, or feet. The RUC tells me the IRA did it. I don't believe that. But I want to hear it from the mouth of a man who knows for sure. I'm at the Europa Hotel, room seven-nineteen. I'll be back there within the hour."

As Kilkenny suspected, it worked. Two men came for him just after dark, escorted him to a panel truck parked near the hotel, put him in the back, and blindfolded him. The truck was driven for about thirty minutes, on rough streets, making many turns. When finally it stopped, Kilkenny was taken out, led into a building and down some stairs, and finally had his blindfold removed in a small, cluttered room in which a white-haired man sat behind a scarred desk.

"My father was in prison with your grandfather," the white-haired man said. "I'm Michael McGuire."

"It's an honor to meet you, sir," Kilkenny said. Iron Mike McGuire was a legend in Northern Ireland. A third-generation Irish freedom fighter, he was the most wanted man in the county. There wasn't a child over six in Belfast who didn't know his name, yet fewer than a dozen people had seen his face in nearly a decade.

"I know about Joe Devalain's misfortune." Iron Mike said. "I was saddened to hear of it. Joe was once a loyal soldier fighting for a united Ireland. He left the cause some years back, for reasons of his own, but I understand he continued to contribute money to us, for which we are grateful. There was no ill will when he left us. There never is. A man does what he can, for as long as he can, and that's all we ask. If Joe had still been one of us, actively, we'd right now be after finding out who bombed him. Since he was not, we choose to stay out of it. I can assure you, however, that the IRA had nothing to do with the incident."

Kilkenny nodded. "I see. Well, I thank you for telling me, sir, and for the trouble of bringing me here."

"It's not been that much trouble. I'd be particular, though, if I were you, where I made that little speech you gave in Bushmill's. There's some pubs you'd not've walked out of. Pubs patronized by the other side."

"I understand," Kilkenny said. "I appreciate the advice. May I ask for a bit more?"

"A man can always ask."

"How would I go about contacting the Orangemen?"

McGuire exchanged a fleeting glance with the two men who had brought Kilkenny. "For what purpose?" he asked.

"The same purpose as my coming here. To see if they were responsible. If it was political, what happened to Joe, then I'll let the matter go. But if the Orangemen also disclaim the act, then I've still got work to do."

Pursing his lips, McGuire silently drummed the thick, stubby fingers of one hand on the scarred desktop. "All right," he said after a moment. "I don't believe the Orangemen were involved, but I could be wrong. At any rate, the only Order of Orange faction that is authorized to take lives is the Black Preceptories. It's an internal terrorist group that specializes in kidnapping, torture, and houseburning. It was them that torched the two hundred Catholic homes in Bogside back in '78. The leader of the bunch is Black Jack Longmuir. He works in the shipyards. You can usually find him through the union office." McGuire smiled as cold a smile as Kilkenny had ever seen. "When y'see him, tell him I'm thinking about him. Day and night. Always thinking about him."

With those words, McGuire nodded and Kilkenny was once again blindfolded and led away.

The union office was open around the clock, because Harland and Wolff Shipbuilding was running three shifts. The office was situated in a little corrugated metal building just outside the shipyard entrance. There was no doubt where the union's sympathy and support lay. Immediately inside the door was an Order of Orange flag and a framed rhyme:

Catholics beware! for your time has come!
Listen to the dread sound of our Protestant drum!
In memory of William, we'll hoist up our flag!
We'll raise the bright orange and burn your green rag!

William was William of Orange, who married the daughter of the last Catholic king of England, James II, then betrayed him, drove him from the throne, and turned Britain into a Protestant country. Five years later the Orange Society was formed in Ireland by the new gentry to whom William had distributed the land. Its purpose, by its own charter, was to maintain the Protestant constitution of the country. Nearly two hundred years later, it was still trying to do that, although it had since met failure in twenty-six of Ireland's thirty-two counties. The organization was strongest in Belfast, where it controlled the trade unions. Nowhere was there a better example of that strength than at Harlan and Wolff, Ulster's greatest single industrial complex. Of ten thousand employees, only one hundred were Catholic.

"Might I be of some service, sor?" a bulldog of a man asked Kilkenny when he entered.

"I was told I night find Jack Longmuir here," Kilkenny said. Several men in the little office glanced at him, then looked away quickly.

"May I ask what your business is, sor?"

"I'm a detective from Dublin. An old mate of mine was seriously injured by a bomb in his shop three days ago. I'd like to ask Mr. Longmuir's advice about how best to go about finding out who did it."

The little bulldog cocked his head. "What makes y'think he'd give you advice on a matter like that?"

"What makes *you* think he wouldn't?" Kilkenny countered. "Or are you authorized to speak for him?"

The little man turned red. "I'll see if he's here."

Several minutes later, a young man in coveralls, with metal shavings and dust on his sleeves, came to fetch Kilkenny. Giving him a visitor's pass, he led Kilkenny past a security gate and into the shipyard. They walked in silence for two hundred yards, then the escort guided him into a welding hangar where at least thirty men were working on sections of steel hull. Pointing, he directed Kilkenny up a metal ladder to a catwalk where a tall man stood with a clipboard in his hand.

Kilkenny climbed the ladder and moved around the metal catwalk until he was near enough to speak. But the man spoke first.

"I'm Longmuir. What do you want?"

"Do you know Joe Devalain?" Kilkenny asked.

Longmuir nodded. He was a cadaverous man with a jaw that was steel blue from a lifetime of using a straight edge razor. His eyes looked like two perfect bullet holes.

"I'd like to find out who did it to him," Kilkenny said. "But only if it was nonpolitical. If it was a political act, I'll leave it be."

"Why come to me?" Longmuir asked. "I'm a law-abiding British subject. I work, take care of my family, and support the Presbyterian Church and my trade union. I know nothing of bombings and such. Who sent you to me?"

"Michael McGuire."

For just an instant Longmuir's face registered surprise, but he quickly contained it. "Iron Mike, eh?" he said, as if the words were a foul taste in his mouth. "You saw him, did you?"

"Yes. He assured me the IRA wasn't involved in what happened to Joe. He said only you could tell me whether the Black Preceptories did it."

"How does Iron Mike look?" Longmuir asked curiously. "I've not seen even a photograph of him in ten years."

Kilkenny thought for a moment, then said: "He looks old. And tired."

Longmuir grunted softly. "Aye. Like me." He squinted at Kilkenny. "Did he say anything about me?"

"Yes. That he thinks about you a lot."

Longmuir smiled a smile as hateful as McGuire's had been. "I hope he's thinking of me when he draws his last breath." The tall man stared out at nothing for a moment, deep in thought. Then he emitted a quiet sigh. "No one associated with the Order of Orange had anything to do with blowing up your friend," he told Kilkenny. "You'll have to look elsewhere for them that's guilty."

Kilkenny thanked him, and Black Jack Longmuir had him escorted out of the shipyard complex.

It wasn't too late, so Kilkenny rode a bus out to the Devalain house to ask how Joe had fared that day and to question Sharmon and Darlynn, now that a political motive had been eliminated, about who else might have had reason to harm Joe. When he got to the house and knocked, no one answered right away. Kilkenny thought they might already have gone to bed. The past few days had to have been very trying for them. Darlynn, especially, looked on the verge of exhaustion. Kilkenny had just turned to leave when Sharmon opened the door, wearing a housecoat.

"Hello, Roy. Darlynn's not here — she's staying at the hospital all night. Joe's mind seems to be going. He's bucking up and down on the bed, making that pathetic sound he makes, raising havoc. The only thing that seems to calm him is to have Darlynn there patting him. The doctor says her touch is all he relates to now, he's been reduced to the primitive level, whatever that means. I'd offer you tea, but I'm just out."

She had not stepped away from the doorway or invited him inside.

"Tea's not necessary," Kilkenny said, "but I would like to ask you a few questions."

"I was just ready for bed, Roy. Can we do it tomorrow?" She must have noticed the curious expression that came over his face, because she amended her reply at once. "I suppose we can do it now. It won't take long, will it?"

"Shouldn't."

She led him to the modest parlor with its threadbare sofa, worn rug, and scratched coffee table. She conducted herself very much like a lady, keeping the housecoat well around her, even holding it closed at the throat. Her reserved demeanor brought back Darlynn's words to him: "Mum's had a boy friend or two." Kilkenny had expected Sharmon to make advances on him first chance she got. Now it appeared she was doing just the opposite.

"I'm sorry Darlynn isn't here," she said. "She'll be so sorry she missed you. She fancies you, y'know."

"Nonsense." Kilkenny scoffed. "She's only a girl."

"Look again, Roy. She's older than I was when we first went under the stairs together."

"That was different. I'm sure she only looks on me as an uncle or something." He sat down. "Now then, to business. I've made contact with the IRA and the Black Preceptories. From both quarters I've been assured that there was no involvement in blowing up Joe's shop."

"And you believe them?" Sharmon asked.

Kilkenny nodded. "No reason not to. If either group had done it, there would have been a purpose — the IRA because Joe had betrayed it in some way, the Black Preceps because he was still providing financial support to the IRA or some other unknown reason. Whatever, the bombing would have been to make an example of him. Not to take credit for it would be defeating the purpose of the act. If either group had done it, they'd have claimed it and said why."

"So, who d'you think did it, then?"

"That's where I go from here. Who do *you* think might have done it?"

"I haven't a notion."

"Did he have any enemies?"

"Joe? Not likely. You have to *do* something to make enemies. Joe never *did* anything. Sure, he joined the IRA, but only because a lot of his mates was doing the same. And he ended up quitting that. The only thing he ever done on his own was leaving the linen factory and opening up that silly shop. That was the only independent decision he ever made in his life, and you see how that turned out."

"Was he gambling, d'you know? Could he have been in debt and you not know it?"

Sharmon grunted scornfully. "He didn't have the guts to gamble."

"Do you think there could have been another woman? A jealous husband or a boy friend?"

She shook her head. "Never."

"Well, *somebody* didn't like him," Kilkenny said. "Can't you think of anybody?"

"Just me," Sharmon answered evenly.

"You?" Kilkenny had known it, but had never expected her to be so candid about it.

"Yes, me." With just a hint of defiance. "And why not? Look around you," she challenged, waving an arm. "This here is what my whole *life* is like. Worn, tattered, musty, colorless. This here is what I gave up my *youth* for, Roy. This here is all I *have*. It's all he's ever given me. Oh yes, I disliked him. And if he'd been poisoned or cut up with a kitchen knife, I'd be your number one suspect. But I wouldn't know how to make a bomb even if I had the proper stuff."

"No, you wouldn't," Kilkenny said. He thought he heard a noise from the rear of the house — a creaking, as if someone had stepped on an unsteady floorboard. "Could that be Darlynn home?"

"No. She always uses the front. It's probably a loose shutter. Listen, can we finish this another time, Roy? I've got a raging headache and really would like to get to bed."

"Sure."

On his way to the front door, Kilkenny noticed an ashtray on one of the tables with something purplish in it. He saw it only for a second, for just as his eyes came to rest on it Sharmon picked it up and emptied it in a wastebasket under the table. "Goodnight then, Roy," she said. "God bless."

"Goodnight, Sharmon."

He did not return her "God bless" because it had just registered in his mind what the purplish thing in the ashtray was.

Irish heather. Green Irish heather. It turned purple when it died.

Kilkenny went to the hospital and found Darlynn asleep on a couch in the waiting room. "She was all wore out," the nun in charge of the ward told him. "When her father finally got calmed, we made her come in here and lie down. She was asleep that quick."

"Is he asleep too?" Kilkenny asked of Joe.

"We never know, do we?" the nun replied quietly. "He doesn't have to close his eyelids to sleep."

Kilkenny went into the ward and stood by Joe's bed. Devalain's form was still, his eyes wide and fixed. "I might know who did this to you, Joe," Kilkenny whispered. "But I must be sure before I do anything."

Stepping to the window at the end of the long room, Kilkenny stared out at the blackness, seeing only his own dim reflection from the nightlight next to Joe's bed. If only I could ask him simple questions he could answer with a nod or a shake of his head, he thought. But how in bloody hell can you communicate with somebody who can't hear or see? If he had fingers, he could use children's wooden alphabet blocks. Joe could feel the letters.

If, sure, Kilkenny thought with frustration. If he had fingers, if he had eyes. If I could work goddamned miracles, I could read his bleeding mind. He turned from the window and looked at Joe again. Sighing, he walked into the hall, wondering if he should wake Darlynn and take her home. Across the hall, above the door to one of the other rooms, a red light was blinking on and off. One of the patients had pressed the call-button to summon a nurse. Kilkenny walked away from it. Then he stopped, turned and stared at it.

Blink-blink Blink—blink.

Dot-dash.

Hurrying back into the ward, Kilkenny drew a chair up to Joe's bed and sat down. It had been a long time, thirty years, perhaps too long. Yet if there was a chance —

Gently, Kilkenny placed the palm of his hand on Joe's sternum, just below the clavicle. Joe stirred. Kilkenny thought back thirty years. Thought back to the blue neckerchiefs and khaki caps, the gold patches then pinned to their shirts with the letters BSI on them. Boy Scouts International. It was the only youth organization that had ever come into the Ballymurphy slum to help the kids there. The first thing they had learned in the Morse Code class, Kilkenny remembered, was how to do their names.

With his index finger, he began to tap lightly on Joe Devalain's sternum. Dot-dash-dash-dash. That was J. Dash-dash-dash. That was O. Dot. That was E.

J-O-E. Joe.

Joe Devalain frowned. Kilkenny began tapping again. He repeated the same letters. J-O-E.

Under the oxygen mask, Joe's lips parted. He began breathing a little faster. He's got it, Kilkenny thought. *He understands it!*

Kilkenny rubbed his hand in a brief circle to indicate he was erasing and starting a new message. He tapped dot-dash-dot for R. Dash-dash-dash for O. Dash-dot-dash-dash for Y. His name. Roy.

Joe's lips parted even more, and he forced a guttural sound from his throat. All it sounded like was a long "Aaaggghhh," but it was beautiful to Kilkenny. It meant he had reached Joe Devalain's mind.

Kilkenny began tapping again, slowly, carefully. Making his message as brief and simple as possible. He tapped: Use eyelids. Dot short blink. Dash long blink. Then he waited.

For a brief, terrible instant, he was afraid Joe wasn't going to be able to do it; his lips remained parted, his sightless eyes unblinking. But then the eyelids closed, remained closed, opened, blinked once, closed again and remained closed for a second, and opened. Dash-dot-dash. That was the letter K. He was doing it!

Kilkenny watched the eyelids as they closed, opened, blinked. The letters they were making etched in his mind. K-I-R-R-G. Then the blinking stopped.

K-I-R-R-G? What the hell did that mean.

Kilkenny took out his pen and tore a sheet of paper from the medical chart hanging on the end of the bed. Turning the paper to its blank side, he wrote down the entire International Code that he and Joe had learned as Boy Scouts. Then he went to work breaking down the blinks Joe had used. The K and the I were all right, he decided. But the two R signals had to be wrong. Unable to quickly decide *how* they were wrong, he moved on to the G. That, in all likelihood, was M-E. One of the most common mistakes in Morse was to misread M, dash-dash, and E, dot, as G, dash-dash-dot. Simply a case of too short a pause between letters, causing the receiver to think it was a single signal.

Kilkenny now had K-I-R-R-M-E. Frowning, he scanned the code symbols he had just written. What was similar to R, dot-dash-dot?

Then it hit him. Dot-dash-dot-*dot*. Two dots at the end instead of one. The letter was L. Joe had signaled K-I-L-L-M-E.

Kill me.

Kilkenny tapped a new message. No.

Devalain blinked back. Please. Pain. Going crazy.

Kilkenny: No.

Why?

Kilkenny tapped: Darlynn.

Joe shook his head furiously and blinked: Burden.

Kilkenny tapped: Sharmon.

The answer came: Finish me. Please.

Who bomb: Kilkenny wanted to know.

Why?

Pay back.

Again the emphatic shake of the head. Hurt Darlynn.

How?

Sharmon.

She bomb?

No.

How hurt Darlynn?

Sharmon.

Involved?

This time Joe nodded as he blinked. Maybe. No matter. Finish me.

No. Who bomb?

Then finish me? Joe asked, blinking a question mark at the end of his signal.

Kilkenny thought about it for several long moments. Then he tapped: Okay.

Joe's next message read: O-M-A-R-N.

Kilkenny nodded to himself. O'Marn. The bomb-investigation sergeant. Neat. He had access to explosives that had been confiscated from the IRA. He knew how to use them. And he was in a position to bury the case without resolving it.

O'Marn. Yes. Kilkenny has suspected as much when he saw the sprig of dying heather in Sharmon's ashtray. The same kind of sprig O'Marn wore on his lapel. He wondered how O'Marn and Sharmon had met. How long they had been lovers. Sharmon, who didn't like policemen, who had picked Joe over him when he told her *he* was going to become a policeman.

He wondered exactly how much Sharmon knew about the bombing. Not that it mattered. If she was still seeing O'Marn after what had happened to Joe, that was enough. And Kilkenny was sure she was still seeing him. That noise he had heard earlier from the back of the Devalain house. Along with Sharmon's eagerness to send him on his way. O'Marn had been there, listening.

Another guttural sound from the bed drew Kilkenny's attention back to Joe. He was blinking rapidly, repeating a message over and over. Do it. You promised. Do it. You prom —

Kilkenny put his hand back on Joe's sternum. He tapped: Later.

Darlynn was still deeply asleep on the couch in the waiting room. One of the nuns had covered her with a blanket. Kilkenny quietly opened her purse and took her door key.

It was very late now, dark and quiet in Unity Flats. He walked the two miles to the Devalain house, passing no one, seeing no one. When he arrived, he let himself in and stood just inside the door. The house was silent. A night light burned dimly in the hall. Kilkenny moved slowly toward the rear of the house, taking care to stay close to the wall where the floorboards were less likely to creak.

At the door to a bedroom, he saw in the faint glow two naked bodies asleep on the bed. On the doorknob hung a Harris tweed sportcoat. Kilkenny moved into the room and over to the single window. It was shut tight and locked.

Slipping back out of the bedroom, he edged along the hall until he found the kitchen. Its window was also shut. Pulling a handkerchief from his pocket, he turned on all the gas jets on the stove.

Before he left, Kilkenny shut the door to Darlynn's small bedroom and the parlor, closing off all the house except the kitchen and the bedroom in which the two lovers slept. Then he let himself back out.

He waited down at the corner, concealed in the dark doorway of a small store, watching the house. No light came on and there was no sign of movement anywhere. Kilkenny gave it an hour. Then he returned to the hospital.

Darlynn was still asleep when he put her door key back in her purse. But Joe was wide awake and responded instantly when Kilkenny tapped his first message: Paid back.

Who? Joe blinked.

Kilkenny signaled: O'Marn. Sharmon.

A great, weary sigh escaped Joe's chest, the first sound Kilkenny had heard from him that sounded human. Then he blinked: Now me.

And Kilkenny answered: Yes.

Kilkenny reached over and pinched the tube that was feeding oxygen to Joe Devalain's lungs. As his breathing started to become labored, Joe blinked: Darlynn.

With his free hand, Kilkenny responded: Yes.

Joe's throat began to constrict, his face contorting as what was left of his body struggled for oxygen. He had time for only one more message.

God bless, he blinked . . .

Kilkenny sat in the waiting room watching the sleeping Darlynn Devalain until daylight came and the buses began running. Then he woke her and they left the hospital together. On the bus downtown, he told her how her parents had died, but not who killed them. Her mother and O'Marn would be considered suicides. Her father simply had not survived his trauma.

When the bus reached Great Victoria Street, they got off.

"Where are we going?" Darlynn asked.

"First to the hotel to get my things."

"And then?"

"The part of Ireland that's free. Dublin."

Darlynn accompanied him with no further questions.

CLARK HOWARD: A CHRONOLOGY, 1956-2000

BOOKS: Fiction

The Arm. Los Angeles: Sherbourne Press, 1967; Paris: Editions Gallimard, 1969; New York: Fawcett Gold Medal, 1970; Tokyo: Kindaiegasha, 1987.

A Movement Toward Eden. Durham, NC: Moore Publishing Co., 1969.

The Doomsday Squad. New York: Weybright & Talley, 1970; London: W. H. Allen, 1971; New York: Pocket Books, 1971; New York: *Stag* Magazine (serialized); Amsterdam: Koninklijke, 1972; London: Corgi Books, 1972.

The Last Contract. New York: Pinnacle Books, 1973.

Siberia 10. New York: Pinnacle Books, 1973.

The Killings. New York: The Dial Press, 1973; London: SouvenirPress, 1974; New York: Warner Books, 1974; Paris: Editions Gallimard, 1975; London: Pan Books, 1977; Tokyo: Hayakawa, 1981.

Summit Kill. New York: Pinnacle Books, 1975.

Mark the Sparrow. New York: The Dial Press, 1975; London: Souvenir Press, 1975; New York: Dell Publishing, 1977; London: Pan Books, 1978; Tokyo: Hayakawa, 1980.

The Hunters. New York: The Dial Press, 1976; Copenhagen: Lademann, 1976; New York: Jove Books, 1978.

The Last Great Death Stunt. New York: Berkley Books, 1977.

Traces of Mercury. New York: Jove Books, 1979.

The Wardens. New York: Richard Marek Publishers, 1979; London: New English Library, 1980; New York: Berkley Books, 1981; London: New English Library, 1981.

Dirt Rich. New York: St. Martin's Press, 1986; London: Bantam Press, 1986; Amsterdam: Weilin & Goos, 1986; Munich: Bastei-Lubbe, 1986; Sao Paulo: Editora, 1986; Malmo: Richters Forlag, 1986; New York: Signet, 1987; London: Corgi Books, 1987; Bayreuth: Hestia Verlag, 1988; Milan: Rizzoli, 1989; Copenhagen: Wangels, 1991.

Quick Silver. New York: E. P. Dutton, 1988; New York: Signet, 1989; Buenos Aires: Emece Editions, 1990.

Hard City. New York: E. P. Dutton, 1990; Sao Paulo: Editora, 1991.

City Blood. New York: Otto Penzler Books, 1994; Tokyo: Masayaki Matsura, 1995.

Horn Man and Other Stories [in Japanese]. Tokyo: Mitsunobu Yamamoto, 1998.

Challenge the Widow-Maker and Others Stories of People in Peril. Norfolk: Crippen & Landru Publishers, 2000. Published in both a trade edition and a signed, numbered edition.

Crowded Lives and Other Stories of Desperation and Danger. Unity, ME: Five Star, 2000.

BOOKS: Non-Fiction

Six Against The Rock. New York: The Dial Press, 1977; London: Granada Publishing, 1978; New York: Jove Books, 1978; Tokyo: Hayakawa, 1979; London: Panther Books, 1979. [Mystery Writers of America Edgar Allan Poe Award nominee]

Zebra. New York: Richard Marek Publishers, 1979; London: New English Library, 1980; New York: Berkley Books, 1980; London: New English Library, 1981; Paris: Flammarion, 1982. [Edgar Allan Poe Award nominee]

American Saturday. New York: Richard Marek Publishers, 1981.

Brothers in Blood. New York: St. Martin's/Marek, 1983; New York: St. Martin's Press, 1983.

Love's Blood. New York: Crown Publishers, 1993; Paris: Editions Jai-lu, 1993; New York: St. Martin's Press, 1994; Munich: Bastei-Lubbe, 1994; Barcelona: Ediciones Grijalbo, 1994.

SHORT STORIES and NOVELETTES: Magazines

[Abbreviations: AHMM = *Alfred Hitchcock's Mystery Magazine;* EQMM = *Ellery Queen's Mystery Magazine;* MSMM = *Mike Shayne Mystery Magazine;* LLWM = *Louis L'Amour Western Magazine*]

"The Last Gunfight," *Stag*, January 1956.
"With This Gun," *Men*, January 1956.
"God Sent a Gunslinger," *Stag*, December 1956.
"Handcuffed," *Crime & Justice*, January 1957.
"Enough Rope For Two," *Manhunt*, February 1957; *Alfred Hitchcock's A Choice of Evils*, ed. Elana Lore, Davis Publications, 1983.
"Spook House," AHMM, June 1961; *Alfred Hitchcock's Tales To Keep You Spellbound*, ed. Eleanor Sullivan, The Dial Press, 1976.; *Alfred Hitchcock's Anthology, Volume 1*, ed. Eleanor Sullivan, Davis Publications, 1977; *The Wickedest Show on Earth*, ed. Marcia Muller & Bill Pronzini, William Morrow, 1985.
"Put Yourself in My Place," AHMM, April 1962.
"Money to Burn," AHMM, September 1962; *Tales to Make You Weak in the Knees*, ed. Eleanor Sullivan, The Dial Press, 1981; *Alfred Hitchcock's Anthology, Volume 10*, ed. Eleanor Sullivan, Davis Publications, 1982; *Portrait of Murder*, (No editor named), Galahad Books, 1988.
"Night Work," AHMM, November 1962.
"The Loners," *Manhunt*, June 1963.
"It Could Be Fatal," AHMM, July 1963.
"The Little Things," AHMM, August 1963.
"Four and Twenty Blackbirds," AHMM, February 1964.
"The Junkie Trap," *Manhunt*, March 1964

"Prisoner," *AHMM*, April 1964.

"A Way to Die," *Mr.*, July 1964.

"That Old Time Religion," *Mr.*, November 1964.

"Recommendation," *AHMM*, November 1964.

"Line of Duty," *AHMM*, December 1964.

"One Way Out," *AHMM*, February 1965; *Historias Que Nunca Esquecerei*, ed. A. B. Pinheiro de Lemos, Rio de Janeiro: Editora Record, 1980; *Alfred Hitchcock's Anthology, Volume 8*, ed. Eleanor Sullivan, Davis Publications, 1981; *Ellery Queen's Media Favorites*, ed. Eleanor Sullivan, Davis Publications, 1988.

"The Target," *AHMM*, March 1965.

"The First of April," *AHMM*, April 1965.

"From the Bard, With Love," *AHMM*, May 1965.

"A Small Dose of Salvation," *AHMM*, June 1965.

"Tramp Song," *Mr.*, June 1965.

"The Peregrine," *AHMM*, July 1965; *Alfred Hitchcock's Fear, Anthology #12*, ed. Cathleen Jordan, Davis Publications, 1982.

"I'll Go My Way," *Mr.*, August 1965.

"The Apprentice," *AHMM*, September 1965.

"Squad's End," *Mr.*, October 1965.

"Keeper of the Crypt," *AHMM*, December 1965.

"The Body of McKay," *Adam*, June 1966.

"The Suspect," *AHMM*, July 1966.

"Attorney of Choice," *AHMM*, August 1966.

"The Sycophant," *AHMM*, September 1966.

"Eyes of the Beholder," *AHMM*, February 1967.

"The Marksman," *AHMM*, March 1967; collected in *Crowded Lives and Other Stories of Desperation and Danger*, Five Star, 2000.

"Time Element," *AHMM*, April 1967.

"Flight Plan," *AHMM*, February 1968.

"Day of the Man," *Pix*, February 1968.

"Goodbye, Mr. Madison," *AHMM*, August 1968.

"Memory of a Murder," *AHMM*, October 1969.

"The Deal," *AHMM*, September 1970.

"We Spy," *AHMM*, October 1970; *Best Detective Stories of the Year - 1971*, ed. Allen J. Hubin, E. P. Dutton, 1971; *Quickie Thrillers*, ed. Arthur Liebman, Pocket Books, 1975.

"The Protectors," *AHMM*, July 1971.

"The Juror," *MSMM*, August 1971.

"The Keeper," *AHMM*, October 1971; *Portrait of Murder*, (No editor named), Galahad Books, 1988.

"The Diver," *AHMM*, December 1971.

"Christmas Plans," *AHMM* January 1972.

"Road Gang," *AHMM*, February 1972.

"A Few Extra Pounds," *AHMM*, March 1972.

"The Escapee," *AHMM*, April 1972.

"The Hostages," *AHMM*, May 197 2.

"Cameron's Kill," *AHMM*, June 1972.

"The Masterpiece," *AHMM*, July 1972.

"The Last Revival," *AHMM*, August 1972; *Alfred Hitchcock's Mortal Errors*, ed. Cathleen Jordan, Davis Publications, 1983.

"The Bitter Pill," *AHMM*, December 1972.

"The Best Hideout," *AHMM*, January 1973.

"The Last Bullet," *AHMM*, April 1973.

"Next in Line," *AHMM*, June 1973.

"Deadly August," *AHMM* August 1973.

"The Inside Man," *MSMM*, September 1973.

"Mother of Pearl, *MSMM*, October 1973.

"The Seven Strangers," *MSMM* , November 1973.

"A Place to Hide," *AHMM*, July 1974.

"Payoff Time," *AHMM*, December 1975; *Alfred Hitchcock's Anthology, Volume 9*, ed. Eleanor Sullivan, Davis Publications, 1981.

"Logan's Cross," *AHMM*, January 1976.

"Horn Man," *EQMM*, June 1980; *Best Detective Stories of the Year, 1981*, ed. Edward D. Hoch, E. P. Dutton, 1981; *The Deadly Arts*, ed. Bill Pronzini & Marcia Muller, Arbor House, 1985; *More Lost Ladies and Men*, ed. Eleanor Sullivan, Davis Publications, 1985; *Black Lizard Anthology of Crime Fiction*, ed. Ed Gorman, Black Lizard Books, 1987; *The New Edgar Winners*, ed. Martin H. Greenberg, Wynwood Press, 1990; *A Modern Treasury of Great Detective and Murder Mysteries*, ed. Ed Gorman, Carroll & Graf, 1994; *The Greatest Mysteries of All Time*, ed. Otto Penzler, Dove audio, 1996; *American Pulp*, Ed Gorman, Bill Pronzini, and Martin H. Greenberg, Carroll & Graf, 1997; *The Crime Library*, Dark Horse Multimedia Internet, October 1999; collected in *Challenge the Widow-Maker and Other Stories of People in Peril*, Crippen & Landru, 2000. [Edgar Allan Poe Award winner]

"A Price On His Life," *EQMM*, October 1980.

"Top Con," *EQMM*, March 1981.

"Hit and Run," *AHMM*, September 1981; *Alfred Hitchcock's Most Wanted*, ed. Cathleen Jordan, Davis Publications, 1988; collected in *Crowded Lives and Other Stories of Desperation and Danger*, Five Star, 2000.

"Mexican Triangle," *EQMM*, October 1981; *The Year's Best Mystery & Suspense Stories, 1982*, ed. Edward D. Hoch, Walker, 1982; collected in *Challenge the Widow-Maker and Other Stories of People in Peril*, Crippen & Landru, 2000.

"The Specialist," *Twilight Zone*, November 1981.

"Second Jeopardy," *EQMM*, December 1981.

"Termination Point," *AHMM*, March 1982.

"The Last Downhill," *AHMM*, May 1982.

"Death Snow," *EQMM*, July 1982.

"Old Soldiers," *EQMM*, September 1982; collected in *Crowded Lives and Other Stories of Desperation and Danger*, Five Star, 2000.

"All the Heroes Are Dead," *EQMM*, December 1982; *The Year's Best Mystery & Suspense Stories, 1983*, ed. Edward D. Hoch, Walker, 1983; *Sunshine Crime*, ed. Frank D. McSherry, Charles G. Waugh, and Martin H. Greenberg, Rutledge Press, 1987; *Death in Dixie*, ed. Billie Sue Mosiman & Martin H. Greenberg, Rutledge Hill Press, 1997; collected in *Challenge the Widow-Maker and Other Stories of People in Peril*, Crippen & Landru, 2000. [Edgar Allan Poe Award Nominee]

"Puerto Rican Blues," *EQMM*, April 1983; *Ellery Queen Presents The Best Short Stories of 1983*, ed. Eleanor Sullivan, Davis Publications, 1984; collected in *Challenge the Widow-Maker and Other Stories of People in Peril*, Crippen & Landru, 2000. [Edgar Allan Poe Award Nominee]

"Custer's Ghost," *EQMM*, May 1983; *The Year's Best Mystery & Suspense Stories 1984*, ed. Edward D. Hoch, Walker, 1984; *Ellery Queen Presents* (audio), Listening for Pleasure, 1986; collected in *Challenge the Widow-Maker and Other Stories of People in Peril*, Crippen & Landru, 2000. [Western Writers of America Spur Award Nominee]

"Run From the Hunter," *EQMM*, July 1983.

"New Orleans Getaway," *EQMM*, August 1983; *Tales From Ellery Queen's Mystery Magazine*, ed. Eleanor Sullivan and Cynthia Manson, Harcourt Brace, 1986; collected in *Crowded Lives and Other Stories of Desperation and Danger*, Five Star, 2000.

"The Pit Vipers," *Chic*, November 1983.

"Return to the O. K. Corral," *EQMM*, November 1983.

"Wild Things," *EQMM*, December 1983; *Blowout in Little Man Flats*, ed. Billie Sue Mosiman & Martin H. Greenberg, Rutledge Hill Press, 1998;

collected in *Crowded Lives and Other Stories of Desperation and Danger*, Five Star, 2000.

"The Last Private Eye," *EQMM*, April 1984.

"The Plateau," *EQMM*, July 1984; *50 Years from the Best of Ellery Queen's Mystery Magazine*, ed. Eleanor Sullivan, Carroll & Graf, 1991; *Beastly Tales*, ed. Sara Paretsky, Dove Audio, 1992; *Mysterious Menagerie*, Cynthia Manson, Berkley Books, 1996; collected in *Challenge the Widow-Maker and Stories of People in Peril*, Crippen & Landru, 2000. [Spur Award Nominee]

"The Dublin Eye," *Ellery Queen's Prime Crimes 2*, ed. Eleanor Sullivan and Karen A. Prince, Davis Publications, 1984; *The Year's Best Mystery & Suspense Stories, 1985*, Edward D. Hoch, Walker, 1985; *Murder Most Irish*, ed. Ed Gorman, Larry Segriff, and Martin H. Greenberg, Barnes & Noble, 1996; collected in *Challenge the Widow-Maker and Other Stories of People in Peril*, Crippen & Landru, 2000.

"In Out of the Cold," *EQMM*, January 1985; *The Crime Library*, Dark Horse Multimedia Internet, October 1999.

"Animals," *EQMM*, June 1985; *The Year's Best Mystery & Suspense Stories 1986*, ed. Edward D. Hoch, Walker, 1986; *Ellery Queen Presents Reader's Choice*, ed. Eleanor Sullivan, Davis Publications, 1990; *More Mystery Cats*, ed. Cynthia Manson, Signet Books, 1993; *Great Cat Mysteries*, Dove Audio, 1996; collected in *Challenge the Widow-Maker and Other Stories of People in Peril*, Crippen & Landru, 2000. [Ellery Queen Readers Award]

"McCulla's Kid," *EQMM*, September 1985; collected in *Crowded Lives and Other Stories of Desperation and Danger*, Five Star, 2000.

"Last Chance in Singapore," *EQMM*, December 1985; *Distant Danger*, ed. Janwillem van de Wetering, Wynwood Press, 1988.

"Breaking Even," *The New Black Mask #3*, ed. Matthew J. Bruccoli & Richard Layman, Harcourt Brace, 1985.

"Harmonic Interlude," *EQMM*, January 1986.

"High Noon at Mach Seven," *EQMM*, March 1986.

"The Last One to Cry," *EQMM*, June 1986.

"Scalplock," *EQMM*, July 1986; *The Year's Best Mystery & Suspense Stories, 1987*, ed. Edward D. Hoch, Walker, 1987; collected in *Challenge the Widow-Maker and Other Stories of People on Peril*, Crippen & Landru, 2000. [Ellery Queen Readers Award]

"The Wide Loop," *EQMM*, October 1986.

"The Color of Death," *EQMM*, June 1988; collected in *Crowded Lives and*

Other Stories of Desperation and Danger, Five Star, 2000.

"The Dakar Run," *EQMM*, August 1988; *The Year's Best Mystery & Suspense Stories, 1989*, ed. Edward D. Hoch, Walker, 1989; *The Best Mystery Stories of the Year 1989*, ed. Josh Pachter & Martin H. Greenberg, Dercum Audio, 1989; *Under the Gun*, ed. Ed Gorman, Bob Randisi, and Martin H. Greenberg, New American Library, 1990; *A Century of Mystery 1980-1989 The Greatest Stories of the Decade*, ed. Marcia Muller and Bill Pronzini, MJF Books, 1996; collected in *Challenge the Widow-Maker and Other Stories of People in Peril*, Crippen & Landru, 2000. [Ellery Queen Readers Award]

"Silhouettes," *EQMM*, October 1988.

"Lie Down with the Lamb," *A Matter of Crime ,Volume 4*, ed. Matthew J. Bruccoli & Richard Layman, Harcourt Brace, 1988.

"Crowded Lives," *EQMM*, November 1989; collected in *Crowded Lives and Other Stories of Desperation and Danger*, Five Star, 2000.

"Hanging It On a Limb," *EQMM*, December 1989; collected in *Crowded Lives and Other Stories of Desperation and Danger*, Five Star, 2000.

"Return to the River Kwai," *EQMM*, April 1990.

"Challenge the Widow-Maker," *EQMM*, August 1990; *The Year's Best Mystery & Suspense Stories, 1991*, ed. Edward D. Hoch, Walker, 1991; *The Year's 25 Finest Crime and Mystery Stories* ed. The Staff of Mystery Scene Magazine, Carroll & Graf, 1992; *The Edgar Award Book*, ed. Martin H. Greenberg, Barnes & Noble, 1996; collected in *Challenge the Widow-Maker and Other Stories of People in Peril*, Crippen & Landru, 2000. [Edgar Allan Poe Award Nominee]

"Deeds of Valor," *EQMM*, October 1990. [Ellery Queen Readers Award]

"While the Rain Forest Burned," *EQMM*, March 1991.

"Dark Conception," *EQMM*, October 1991.

"The Last High Mountain," *EQMM*, February 1992.

"The Long Drop," *EQMM*, February 1993.

"Showdown at Carson City," *LLWM*, July 1994.

"Zapata's Gold," *LLWM*, November 1994.

"Split Decisions," *EQMM*, December 1994; *The Year's Best Mystery & Suspense Stories, 1995*, Edward D. Hoch, Walker, 1995; collected in *Challenge the Widow-Maker and Other Stories of People in Peril*, Crippen & Landru, 2000. [Private Eye Writers Shamus Award Nominee]

"Soft Target," *EQMM*, December 1995.

"The Banzai Pipeline," *EQMM*, November 1996.

"Out of Control," *EQMM*, July 1997.

"Games of Chance," *EQMM*, September 1997.
"The Halfway Woman," *EQMM*, February 1998. [Edgar Allan Poe Nominee]
"The Ice Shelf," *EQMM*, September 1999.
"The Global Man," *EQMM*, December 1999. [Ellery Queen Readers Award]
"Under Suspicion," *EQMM*, March 2000.
"The Spirit Birds," *EQMM*, May 2000.
"The Killing Floor," published as a separate pamphlet to accompany the limited edition of *Challenge the Widow-Maker and Other Stories of People in Peril*, Crippen & Landru, 2000.

ARTICLES

"On the Strip" (Boxing column from Las Vegas, as by Rich Howard), *The Ring Magazine*, 1965-1966.
"The Other Side of the Wilderness" (as by Rich Howard), *Las Vegas Life Magazine*, November 1966.
"The Zebra Murders," *Penthouse Magazine*, November 1979.
"Researching and Writing the Fact Crime Book," *The Writer Magazine*, June 1984.
"Whoppers—The Lies of J. Edgar Hoover," *Murder Ink*, ed. Dilys Winn, Workman Press, 1984.
"Crimes of Passion" (3-part series), *The Globe Newspaper*, April-May 1985.
"Researching and Writing the Crime Book—Fact or Fiction," *Writing Mystery and Crime Fiction*, ed. Sylvia K. Burack, The Writer, Inc., 1985.
"The Reel Doc Holliday," *The Roundup Magazine*, Western Writers of America, January 1986.
"The Edgar Awards—A History," *Real Crime Book Digest*, April 1994.

ELECTRONIC PUBLISHING: Non-fiction

"The True Story of Barbara Graham" (4-Part Series), The Crime Library, Dark Horse Multimedia Internet, November 1999.

CHALLENGE THE WIDOW-MAKER

Challenge the Widow-Maker and Other Stories of People in Peril by Clark Howard is printed on 55-pound Glatfelter Supple Opaque acid-free paper from 11-point Goudy Old Style, a computer-version of a typeface designed in 1915 by the American type designer Frederick W. Goudy. The cover is by Victoria Russell. The first edition comprises approximately one thousand copies in trade softcover, and two hundred twenty-five copies sewn in cloth, signed and numbered by the author. Each of the clothbound copies contains a separately printed pamphlet, *The Killing Floor* by Clark Howard. *Challenge the Widow-Maker* was published in April 2000 by Crippen & Landru Publishers, Norfolk, Virginia.